SLOW BURN

STEPHEN LEATHER

ISIS
LARGE
PRINT

First published in Great Britain 2020
by
Hodder & Stoughton
an Hachette UK company

First Isis Edition
published 2021
by arrangement with
Hachette UK

A catalogue record for this book is available
from the British Library.

ISBN 978–1–78541–920–1

Published by
Ulverscroft Limited
Anstey, Leicestershire

Set by Words & Graphics Ltd.
Anstey, Leicestershire
Printed and bound in Great Britain by
TJ Books Ltd., Padstow, Cornwall

SLOW BURN

There are thousands of jihadi brides in refugee camps in the Middle East. Some of them were once British before they were stripped of their citizenship. Were they brainwashed or simply naive when they set out for Syria as teenagers?

Spider Shepherd is about to be sent on an extraordinary mission to the Syrian border. There he will have to decide which of the women he meets are a threat, and which of them have useful information.

But there is one bride he must take back to the UK whatever her circumstances. She is the wife of a notorious ISIS bombmaker, Salam Jaraf. The bombmaker will only tell MI5 what he knows if his wife and son are brought to him. But it soon becomes obvious that hostile forces are following Spider and Mrs Jaraf across Turkey.

For Jacqueline

The eight helicopters — four twin-rotored Chinooks and four Black Hawks — flew fast and low across the Syrian desert. They were fired on twice by militant groups on the ground, but each time retribution was swift and sure from the MQ-9 Reaper drones that were providing armed support from high overhead.

The flight from a US military base in Erbil, Iraq, to the Syrian village of Barisha took just over seventy minutes. On board the helicopters were elite special forces soldiers from Delta Force and the 75th Ranger Regiment, trained to kill and eager to put that training to good use.

Their target: a walled compound some three hundred metres outside Barisha, just three miles south of the Turkish border.

Their mission: to capture or kill the feared ISIS leader Abu Bakr al-Baghdadi, a man responsible for thousands of deaths in the region. The raid had been codenamed Operation Kayla Mueller, in honour of an American aid worker who was taken captive in Syria and kept as a sex slave by al-Baghdadi before she was finally killed in 2015. Al-Baghdadi was a nasty piece of work and there wasn't a man on the mission who wouldn't have killed him with their bare hands, given the chance.

On the other side of the world, President Donald Trump and his army chiefs had gathered in the Situation Room below the West Wing of the White House to watch events unfold in real time via satellite links.

As the assault force approached the compound, the helicopters came under fire again, this time from two houses occupied by militants. The Black Hawks retaliated, firing air-to-surface missiles that completely destroyed the buildings.

Once the ISIS strongholds had been neutralised, the helicopters landed and the troops piled out, taking with them military robots and specially trained dogs. They were wearing night vision goggles and carrying a range of weapons. Delta Force favoured AR-15 and AR-18 Armalite automatic rifles, and HK416 assault rifles, while the Rangers were equipped with MK 16 and MK 17 carbines.

They gave the occupants of the compound a chance to surrender, shouting instructions in Arabic to lay down their weapons and come out.

The soldiers had intelligence that the main entrance had been booby-trapped, so they used explosives to blow their way in through a side wall. They came under fire and retaliated, killing four men and a woman.

As the American soldiers poured into the compound, Baghdadi fled into a tunnel network under the main building, taking two of his young sons with him. The soldiers gave chase and cornered the ISIS leader in a dead end. When they sent in a dog and a robot, Baghdadi detonated the suicide vest he was wearing, blowing himself and his sons to bits and collapsing the tunnel.

The soldiers dug through the debris to get to Baghdadi's remains so that they had a DNA sample, then they ran back to the helicopters, taking with them two prisoners and any intelligence information they could find, including mobile phones and USB flash drives. Less than two hours after arriving at the compound, the helicopters were in the air on the way back to Iraq.

As the helicopters headed east, F-15 jets blasted the compound with missiles, reducing it to rubble. Back in the White House, a jubilant president was already tweeting about the successful mission.

"Why don't we just fly it into a plane now, Sid? Plenty of British Airways planes coming and going. Let's fucking do it. Strike while the iron's hot."

Siddhartha "Sid" Qasim looked up from the drone in the back of his hatchback. "Mo, bruv, we've got a plan and we stick to that plan."

Mo Harawi threw up his hands. "No offence, bruv. You're the boss."

"Yeah, I'm the fucking boss," said Qasim. "This is just a test run, so that we can store the GPS coordinates in the drone's memory. Then we can program another dozen drones with the same coordinates and that's when we do it for real. You hear me?"

"I hear you, bruv." The two bumped fists.

They had parked the car on Stanwell Moor, two miles to the west of the airport. The drone could be controlled at up to three miles away, so the airport was well within range.

The drone was about two feet across with four rotors and a camera underneath it. Qasim took it out of the car and placed it onto the ground. They couldn't see the airport from where they were standing, but the drone's camera would give them a perfect view once they launched it. Qasim picked up the controller. Like the drone it was gleaming white, with a tablet attached that would show the view from the camera and give him all the drone's flight details, including GPS position, height and speed.

The UK had surprisingly lenient laws when it came to flying drones. Using a drone up to twenty kilograms in weight didn't require a licence, though the drones weren't allowed to fly above four hundred feet, within an airport's flight restriction zone, or be closer than fifty metres to people. The penalties for breaking the rules were an unlimited fine or up to five years in prison, but Qasim had no qualms about breaking the law. If his plan worked, he'd be bringing down a jet and killing hundreds of people, so breaking a few rules wasn't a worry.

He switched on the drone, then put it into automatic launch mode. The rotors whirred and it rose smoothly to thirty metres, where it remained in a perfect hover. Qasim looked at the screen and used a joystick to point the camera towards the airport. It, came into view on

4

the tablet. A United Airlines plane was coming in to land, flaps extended, nose up.

Harawi was right, it would be the easiest thing in the world to fly the drone into one of the plane's engines. But that wasn't going to happen, not that day anyway.

Qasim flicked the joystick with his thumb, sending the drone west. He pulled back on the altitude joystick as well, sending it higher into the air.

Harawi shaded his eyes with his hand as he watched the drone fly away. "That is one mean fucking machine," he said.

Qasim kept the camera angled slightly down so he could see the grass flash by and at the same time see the airport getting close. There was a button on the bottom of the controller and he pressed that with his right index finger, storing the height and location as a waypoint so that it could be revisited at any time in the future.

The drone flashed across a road. The tablet showed its speed as five metres per second. It continued to climb. Qasim planned to have the drone at one hundred metres above the ground when it reached the runway.

Harawi continued to stare up at the drone, though it was now little more than a dot in the sky.

The United Airlines jet landed with puffs of smoke coming from its tyres. Suddenly the picture froze. Qasim frowned at the screen. Then he realised the image hadn't frozen, the drone had stopped moving. He swore under his breath.

"What's wrong?" asked Harawi.

"I don't know. It stopped."

"Stopped? Stopped how?"

"How the fuck would I know, bruv?" He twiddled the joystick but the drone wouldn't move forward. Then he pulled the joystick and the drone backed away from the airport. He moved it forward again, but it stopped after a few feet. "Fuck it, they've blocked it," he said.

"What do you mean?"

"They must be using some sort of jammer," said Qasim.

"So we can't reach the airport?"

Qasim moved the joystick but the drone refused to move any nearer to Heathrow. "That's what it looks like. Bastards." He cursed again.

"Now what?"

Qasim looked around. "If they can jam the drone, there's a chance they can track where it's being controlled from."

"So they know we're here?"

"Maybe, bruv." He tapped on the screen, programming the drone to return to the spot where it had been launched.

"Then we need to get the fuck out of here," said Harawi.

"I know, I know, you get the car started." He peered up at the sky. The drone was on its way back.

Harawi climbed into the car and turned on the engine. The drone was too far away to be heard above the traffic on the road. Then Qasim heard a siren, off in the distance. "Come on, come on," he muttered. The drone reached the first waypoint and hovered where it was. "Come on!" shouted Qasim impatiently, before realising he had to press the button for it to descend. He cursed and touched the screen. The drone dropped and came to a halt again six feet above the ground, just in front of him. Qasim grabbed it, turned it off and put it in the back of the car along with the controller. He slammed the door shut and hurried around to the passenger door. The siren was louder now but there was another — even louder — sound, that of a fast-approaching helicopter. Qasim looked up. It was a police helicopter, heading their way.

He opened the passenger door and as soon as he'd climbed in, Harawi hit the accelerator. They were already moving as Qasim slammed the door, tyres squealing on the tarmac.

They headed south, towards Egham. A police car was barrelling down the road after them, blue lights flashing and siren wailing. Qasim's stomach lurched as he realised it was a BMW X5, the type used by the capital's armed police.

"Faster, bruv!" shouted Qasim. "These bastards have got guns."

Harawi looked nervously in the rear-view mirror.

"Don't fucking look at them, bruv, just get the fuck away from them."

The helicopter swooped overhead in a banking turn.

"We can't outrun a chopper," said Harawi.

"All they can do is follow the car, they can't stop us, bruv," said Qasim. "Drive to Thorpe Park, we can leave the car there and they'll never find us in the park."

"It's too far, we'll never make it," said Harawi.

"Fifteen minutes, max," said Qasim. "Just stay cool." He twisted around in his seat. The BMW was about a hundred metres behind them. As he turned back, he saw that they were about to collide with the back of a black cab. "Bruv!" he screamed. Harawi twisted the wheel to the right to overtake, but as he stamped down on the accelerator he realised that a massive truck was heading towards them. The truck's horn blared and Harawi yanked the wheel to the left, but he was too slow and the truck crashed into the small hatchback, smashing it into pieces. Qasim and Harawi died instantly.

It had been more then twenty-five years since Brendan O'Carroll had visited the Abney Park cemetery in Stoke Newington, north London, but little seemed to have changed. He was wearing a long black overcoat and under the coat he was holding a folding shovel. It was starting to get dark, but there were still people around, mainly dog walkers following their charges with plastic bags, waiting for them to do their business. The cemetery covered a little over thirty-one acres and the grave O'Carroll was looking for was in an out-of-the-way and little-visited section.

Almost two hundred thousand people were buried there, but it was as much a woodland park and nature reserve as a graveyard. There was a towering angel to O'Carroll's left, overgrown with ivy, and next to it a cross that had tilted to the left over the years. The cemetery grounds were well tended by a team of gardeners, but the gravestones were left alone, and in places the cemetery looked as if it had been staged for a horror movie, especially as the sun went down and the shadows lengthened.

The track he was walking along was about six feet wide and the branches of the trees either side were intertwined above, giving it the feel of a tunnel. He looked over his shoulder but there was no one behind him, and he took a narrower trail to his left. The gravestones were smaller now and less impressive. The one O'Carroll was looking for was ten paces from the track. It was a simple block of granite that had been laid on the grass, and the carving on it had been almost unreadable when he had first seen it, weathered over the years and covered with lichen. Now, a decade and a half later, the stone was completely covered with moss and a bush had grown over half of it. O'Carroll was wearing thick leather gloves and he rubbed lichen away until he was able to make out the name of the deceased: MARY O'BRIEN. She had passed away in 1860, aged just twenty-two. O'Carroll had often wondered what her story had been. In his mind he had always pictured her as a rosy-cheeked Irish girl, dark haired with piercing blue eyes, probably pressed into service for a wealthy family in the area and occasionally visited at night by the master of the house. There had been no clue as to what had ended Mary's short life, but in O'Carroll's mind it was probably tuberculosis or pneumonia, some illness that these days would be cured with a quick course of antibiotics.

He took a final look around, then snapped the shovel into place and used it to lift up the gravestone and ease it to the side. It was heavier than he remembered, or maybe he wasn't as strong. There were worms and beetles under the stone and a network of white roots from the bush. He scraped away the roots and then hacked away at the peaty soil. After a few minutes the spade hit the lid of the plastic box and he carefully scraped away the soil until all of the lid was visible. The box was about two feet square; the base was white plastic and the lid was pale blue. He popped off the lid. Inside the box were thirty-two individually wrapped blocks of Semtex explosive, each one weighing half a kilo, and there were half a dozen small Tupperware containers each containing six bubble-wrapped detonators.

The Semtex had arrived in Ireland in 1986, in the last of four arms deliveries paid for by the then Libyan leader Colonel Gaddafi. Gaddafi had been so impressed by the IRA hunger strikes that he decided to help the terrorist group and sent over four shipments of guns, ammunition and Semtex. Included were a thousand Kalashnikov rifles, heavy machine guns, surface-to-air missiles and RPGs, but pride of place went to the six tons of Semtex that arrived in the final shipment. The IRA used the Semtex with a vengeance, killing hundreds with bombs and booby traps, but by the time the terrorist group called it quits in 1997, there were still more than two tons unused, hidden away in arms caches in Ireland and the UK. The detonators in this cache had been stolen from a quarry outside Limerick. They had been designed to work with dynamite but were more than capable of detonating Semtex.

Three men had known about the arms cache in the Stoke Newington cemetery, but Eoin McKee had been shot in the back of the head by a UVF hitman in Belfast just a week before the IRA ceasefire, and Seamus O'Malley had died six weeks previously in St Mary's Hospital in Paddington, after suffering a major heart attack in his Kilburn flat.

O'Malley's body had been flown back to Northern Ireland, and the funeral was in Crossmaglen, close to the border with the Irish republic. O'Carroll had attended the funeral, along with hundreds of others, most of them IRA stalwarts. Despite the Good Friday Agreement and the IRA's declaration that the armed struggle was over, six men in ski masks and paramilitary uniforms fired a salute with AK-47s over the coffin. In the local pub afterwards, O'Carroll had chatted with old friends and colleagues, and he realised that no one was aware of the arms cache in Stoke Newington. It had fallen below the IRA's radar. In effect, it had ceased to exist.

Back in London, O'Carroll had started wondering if there was a way he could make money from the long-forgotten explosives. He was the only person who knew it was there; if anything were to happen to him it would be lost forever. There were sixteen kilos in the cache, and that had to have a value. He tried googling to see how much Semtex sold for, but didn't have much luck. Then he went onto the dark web and saw Semtex being offered for £400 per half-kilo block, with

11

detonators selling for £80. At those prices, the cache was worth more than £15,000. The money would come in useful, no question of that. O'Carroll was in his sixties and hadn't worked for more than a decade. He had a bad back and a wonky knee so his days of labouring on building sites were well over. For a few years he had worked security, standing on the doors of a few Irish pubs and bars in Kilburn, but the council had taken away his licence after he'd thumped a drunken customer who wouldn't take no for an answer. Now he survived on benefits and lived in a council flat, and his only pleasures were cheap cider and roll-up cigarettes. With fifteen grand, he could start living again.

He knew a Russian cocaine dealer in Queen's Park who sold handguns as a sideline, and he'd asked him if there was a market for explosives. O'Carroll only knew him as Ivan, he'd never told him his family name. Ivan had said there was an Asian guy who had bought two Glocks off him who was on the look-out for explosives and detonators. "Fucking jihadists?" O'Carroll had said, and Ivan had laughed and said yeah, probably. O'Carroll thought about it, and then realised that the identity of the buyer didn't really matter — the targets would be the same and when push came to shove, all that mattered was the money.

Ivan said that he didn't know how much the Asian guy would pay, but that he'd ask. Two days later he got back to O'Carroll and said that the guy could come up with ten grand, cash. O'Carroll had figured that the dealer was probably shaving off twenty-five per cent,

12

maybe more, but beggars couldn't be choosers so he'd agreed.

He pulled a Lidl reusable shopping bag from his coat pocket and put the Semtex and detonators in it. There was a handgun wrapped in plastic at the bottom of the box. O'Carroll had forgotten about the gun. He didn't even know if it was loaded. He slipped it into his pocket, figuring that he might be able to sell it to Ivan, then resealed the plastic box and replaced the gravestone. He used his gloved hands to pat the soil down around the gravestone, then stood up and looked around. A woman was calling for her dog off in the distance but there was still nobody in the vicinity. He wiped the soil off his spade, then folded it in half. He took off his gloves and put them in his pocket with the gun, took a final look around and then headed for the exit.

As he walked out of the cemetery, a helicopter flew overhead. O'Carroll's heart started to pound faster even though he knew that the helicopter would have nothing to do with him. Thirty years ago he might have worried about being under police surveillance, but those days had long gone. He walked along the pavement towards Ivan's car, a black Jaguar. Ivan popped the boot as he walked up and O'Carroll put the shovel and the holdall in the back. He opened the passenger door but Ivan put a hand up. "Hey, no, it's okay, I don't need you for the next bit."

"What do you mean?" asked O'Carroll.

"The guy who's buying the stuff, he's not going to want you seeing him."

O'Carroll sat down and slammed the door shut. "Fuck that. Do you think I was born yesterday?"

"You don't trust me?"

"Ivan, you're a drug dealer who sells guns on the side, how the fuck can anyone trust you?"

"My word is my fucking bond," growled Ivan. "If I ripped people off, I wouldn't stay in business."

"Yeah, well that's maybe true, but we're not talking about a twenty quid wrap of coke here. Ten grand's a lot of money and I'm not letting that bag out of my sight until the cash is in my hand."

Ivan glared at him for several seconds, but O'Carroll glared back. He knew that if he let the Russian drive off with the bag, he might well never see him again. And if he did rip him off, it wasn't as if O'Carroll could complain to the cops. Eventually Ivan threw up his hands. "Fine."

"Fine?"

"You can come." He took out his mobile phone and tapped out a message on WhatsApp. A few seconds later he received a reply. He put the phone away and started the Jaguar.

Ivan drove north on the A10 and then headed west towards Harringay. There was a small blue hatchback waiting for them in the station car park. "That's them," said Ivan.

"There's three of them in the car," said O'Carroll, peering through the side window.

"They always travel in threes," said Ivan. "It's their thing. Two in the front, one in the back. And they

14

always drive those little hatchbacks because they can't get insurance for anything else."

"You said one guy. You said there was one buyer."

Ivan laughed. "One buyer, but these Asian cunts always travel in packs. Do you want your fucking money, or not?" He put the car in neutral but left the engine running.

"You want me to take the bag and get the money?" asked O'Carroll.

"No, you stay here. It might spook them if the two of us go over."

"Sure." O'Carroll figured that the Russian didn't want him there when the money was handed over so that he wouldn't see how much he was skimming as his commission. "But are you not worried that there's three of them?"

"I'm not scared of Pakis," sneered Ivan.

"Well, yeah, but you've already sold two Clocks to these Pakis which means they're probably carrying."

"And the guy I deal with paid for the guns in cash. And I've known him for six months, he's always buying weed from me. Big fan of the weed, he is. Most of them are because they can't touch alcohol."

O'Carroll shrugged. "Up to you," he said.

Ivan unzipped his jacket just enough to reveal the butt of a gun in an underarm holster. "This isn't my first rodeo, as the Americans say." He grinned, pressed the button to pop the boot open and climbed out and went to the rear of the car. He took out the Lidl bag and slammed the boot shut, then walked across the car park to the hatchback.

As he drew closer, the hatchback's internal light came on as the two doors opened. Two Asian men climbed out, one from the driver's seat and one from the back. The section of the car park they had parked in was dimly lit but Ivan had left the lights on so the car and the men were easy enough to see. The men were all bearded. The one in the back was the youngest, in his late twenties maybe, while the other two were in their late thirties. All were wearing hoodies with the hoods up, with dark blue jeans and trainers.

The driver held up a hand in greeting. Ivan waved back. When he reached the hatchback, Ivan put the shopping bag on the bonnet. The guy who had been in the back seat was now at the rear of the hatchback. The driver was looking into the shopping bag. He reached in and took out one of the packs of Semtex. He said something to Ivan and Ivan nodded. He put the Semtex back in the bag and took out one of the Tupperware containers. O'Carroll wondered if the man had any idea what he was looking at. Or if he knew how to use a detonator.

The Asian guy put the Tupperware container back into the bag, then patted Ivan on the shoulder.

"Just give him the money, you fucking Paki," O'Carroll muttered — but then he gasped as the man behind Ivan pulled out a carving knife and stuck it into the Russian's back. The attacker moved quickly, stabbing Ivan four times in quick succession, before the guy in front of Ivan, who had also pulled out a knife, slashed it across the Russian's throat. Ivan's legs buckled and he slumped to the ground.

16

The three Asian men were staring at O'Carroll now, or at least looking towards Ivan's car. Could they see him through the windscreen? He had no way of knowing. He looked across at the steering wheel. The key was in the ignition, the engine was running. O'Carroll swung his right leg over the central console. As he moved, two of the Asian men began running towards him — the driver and the guy who had started the stabbing. O'Carroll swore out loud as he hefted himself over to the driving seat.

The younger man was waving his bloodstained knife as he ran to the passenger side and grabbed for the door handle. It wasn't locked, O'Carroll realised. It wasn't fucking locked. He reached over but it was too far and he couldn't get to it.

The other man reached the driver's side. O'Carroll fumbled for the lock and managed to get to it before the man grabbed the door handle. O'Carroll's hands were trembling as he grabbed the steering wheel and stamped on the accelerator. The engine roared but the car didn't move. It wasn't in gear. Shit, shit, shit, it wasn't in gear.

The attacker on the passenger side pulled the door open and leaned in. "Fuck off!" shouted O'Carroll. He reached for the gear stick and pushed it, but it wouldn't move. "Fuck!" he screamed. Then he remembered it was an automatic — he had to put his foot on the brake to change gear. He stamped on the brake pedal but before he could move the gear stick, the man lashed out with the knife and cut O'Carroll's hand. It was a deep cut, severing the tendons, and his fingers flopped uselessly as blood spurted over the console. "You fucker!" he yelled. He ignored the pain in his hand and tried to pull the gearstick into "DRIVE", but it wouldn't move. There was a button that needed to be pressed to move the stick, but his thumb wouldn't work and he screamed in frustration.

The window to his right exploded in a shower of glass and O'Carroll felt as if he'd been punched in the head. Then everything went red, and faded to black, as his blood pooled over the car seat.

Dan Shepherd stared up at the ceiling. He was pretty sure his time was up, but he'd left his watch in the bathroom. The girl was breathing softly and evenly and he couldn't tell if she was asleep or not. She'd said her name was Jasmine, which was almost certainly not true, but as he'd also lied about his name he couldn't really fault her for that. Charlie Warner was the name he'd used. Her hair was jet black and glossy and her soft warm breath fluttered against his side. Her left hand had hardly any weight as it lay on his chest, over his heart. She was barely five feet tall but her high stiletto heels had added four inches to her height. She'd kept them on when she'd walked into the flat and he was almost certain that she'd marked the wooden floor, but it was a rented flat so he didn't care either way.

She must have sensed that he was looking at her because she opened one eye. "Are you sure a massage is all you want?" she whispered.

"I'm sure," he said.

She rolled on top of him, her jet-black hair cascading around her shoulders. "You paid for everything," she said. "Two shots if you want." She was still wearing her black bra and pants. The dress had somehow come off when she was giving him his massage.

He laughed. "Two shots? You sound like an assassin."

She went to kiss him on the lips but he turned his head.

"What?" she said. "Don't you like me?"

"I think you're amazing," he said. "I just . . ." He left the sentence unfinished.

"Because of your wife?"

Shepherd nodded.

"Charlie, it's been almost six months since she died, you said. That's ages."

"I know," said Shepherd. "I just need some time. The massage was great, it was just what I needed. But that's all I need."

"But I want to fuck you," she pouted.

Shepherd laughed and rolled her off him. "Maybe next time," he said. He sat up. "I'm going to shower."

She rolled over onto her back and smiled. "How old are you?" she asked.

"Old enough to know better," he said, and grabbed for his towel which had fallen onto the floor.

She giggled like a schoolgirl. She looked about thirty but she had said she was twenty-two. She'd said she was Japanese but Shepherd was sure she was Chinese. Almost everything she'd said was a lie, but then almost everything he had told her was just as false. "You look good for your age," she said. It was probably the ninth or tenth compliment she'd paid him since she had walked in through the door.

"You don't know how old I am," he laughed. He rolled off the bed and headed for the bathroom. He closed the door but left it ajar just enough so that he could see the foot of the bed. He went over to the shower cubicle, reached inside and turned on the water, then tiptoed back to the door. He saw a flash of olive skin and waist length hair as she slipped off the end of the bed and out of the bedroom. He smiled to himself. He'd give her plenty of time.

He went back to the shower and got in, enjoying the feel of the warm water playing over his skin. He shampooed his hair, soaped himself all over, then stood under the water for about twice as long as usual. Eventually he stepped out of the shower, dried himself and put his watch back on before wrapping a towel around his waist and heading back into the bedroom. She was sprawled across the bed. The bra had joined her dress on the armchair by the window. She reached her arms towards him and smiled lazily. "Come on, baby, let me really relax you."

Shepherd laughed and sat down on the edge of the bed. "I'm knackered," he said. "I just want to sleep. I've got an early start."

She pouted and ran her hands over her perfect breasts. "I'll do all the work," she said.

Shepherd laughed again and tapped his watch. "It's getting late and I've a lot to do tomorrow. There's a rush to get everything done before the Christmas break."

20

"Why don't you book me to be your Christmas present?" she said. "I'll tie a big bow around me and you can unwrap me."

"You're working on Christmas Day?"

"I work every day," she said. "Men without families usually feel lonely at Christmas so there's plenty of work. Why don't you book me now?"

Shepherd laughed. "Maybe," he said.

She sat up and shook her hair so that it shimmered over her breasts. "I like you, Charlie," she said.

"I like you too, Jasmine."

She looked at him seriously. "No, I really like you. You will book me again, won't you?"

"Sure."

She pouted prettily. "I'm serious. I don't want you booking another girl."

Shepherd stood up and put his hand over his heart. "I swear, if I book anybody, it'll be you."

She frowned. "Why do you say 'if'? That means maybe you won't."

"I mean when," he said. "When I book, I'll book you."

She pointed a finger at him, the nail painted blood red. "You better had." She jumped off the bed smiling, stood on tiptoe to kiss him on the lips, then broke away and walked over to the armchair.

She dressed quickly, glancing over her shoulder to check that he was watching her, before sitting down and putting on her high heels. When she stood up she opened her arms for a hug and he walked over and held her, resting his chin on the top of her head. "I'll see you soon," he said.

She nodded. "I hope so."

Her coat was on the sofa. The bottle of wine that he'd opened when she arrived was on the coffee table, as was his iPhone, next to her glass. There was lipstick on the rim. He took her to the front door and opened it. She ran her hand softly down his cheek, gently scraping his flesh with her nails, then she tossed her hair and walked out, her heels clicking on the tiled floor of the corridor.

Shepherd shut the door and went back into the bedroom. He closed the door and padded over to the bedside table. He opened the top drawer, took out a mobile phone and called Amar Singh, one of MI5's top technical experts. Singh answered immediately. He was sitting in a surveillance van around the corner from the flat. "Pretty little thing, isn't she?" said Singh. The flat was wired for sound and vision and Singh had been able to see almost everything that went on in the flat.

"I didn't notice," said Shepherd.

"Yeah, right," said Singh. "You get all the best jobs, Spider, and here I am sitting in a sweaty van watching a naked girl dashing around your flat."

"Semi-naked, to be fair."

Singh laughed. "Okay, semi-naked."

"She did it, yeah? While I was in the shower?"

"She plugged something into your phone for about a minute, so yeah, it looks like she did. You're going to have to assume that it's up and running, so mum's the word. I'll come right around. I'll let myself in."

"I'll have the kettle on," said Shepherd.

He dressed quickly and tidied up the bed, then went through to the kitchen and switched on the kettle. He was just adding milk to two mugs of coffee when he heard a key in the lock of the front door. He went into the sitting room as the door opened. Singh flashed Shepherd an "okay" sign. He was wearing a dark blue Hugo Boss shirt and gleaming black Bally shoes, and carrying a Louis Vuitton briefcase. He grinned at Shepherd and gently closed the door. Shepherd switched on the TV, then sat down on the sofa as Singh dropped down into the armchair and opened the briefcase. There was a small MacBook laptop inside, and Singh put it on his lap and switched it on. Singh looked at Shepherd and mouthed, "Coffee?"

Shepherd grinned and went back to the kitchen. When he returned with the two mugs of coffee, Singh had connected the iPhone to the laptop and was studying the screen. He sipped his coffee as he continued to look at the data on the computer. He tapped softly on the keyboard and nodded his approval as he cast his eyes over whatever was being downloaded. Eventually he unplugged the phone and closed his laptop. He put the computer into his briefcase, then took out a pair of blue latex gloves. He gestured at the wine glasses on the table and Shepherd pointed at the one the girl had used. Singh picked it up, put it into a clear evidence bag and then placed the bag and the gloves into his briefcase. Then he picked up his mug and nodded at the bedroom door. They both went through to the bedroom and Shepherd closed the door behind them. Singh stood by the window and looked out. The surveillance van he'd been using was parked down the road.

"So?" asked Shepherd. "The suspense is killing me."

Singh grinned. "Yeah, she bugged you. And it's state of the art, too. Better than anything that GCHQ has. It's tapped into the GPS and the microphone as well as the phone data. So whoever is monitoring the phone will know exactly where it is and pick up everything that's said in its vicinity. From what I could see, the bug can bypass the phone's on — off switch. That means it's live so long as the battery has power. Switching the phone off won't affect it — the battery either has to be dead or taken out."

"We have similar software, right?"

"Yeah, but this is way more sophisticated. I'll be able to take a closer look when it's in my lab. How do you want to play it?"

"I'll have to follow my legend's regular pattern, so I'll take it with me to Thames House tomorrow. Should be there by nine. I presume if it's in a briefcase or something it's not going to pick up much?"

Singh nodded. "It uses the phone's microphone, and they're not great, so, yeah. But a briefcase won't stop the GPS signal." He sipped his coffee. "So these girls are bugging all their clients?"

"All the ones they think might be useful sources of information," said Shepherd. "This is our second date. The first time I told her I worked for the Home Office. She asked me a couple of questions about my work but I was evasive. When they track the GPS tomorrow they'll know Charlie Warner is based at Thames House, so that should get them very excited."

"How did we get onto this scam?" asked Singh.

"It came through Giles Pritchard. He was in Sydney attending an ASEAN security conference and met a senior cop who told him about a prostitution case he'd worked a few months earlier. The cops busted an internet escort agency that was a front for Chinese prostitutes. Usually when that happens most of the girls immediately claim they were victims of human traffickers and ask for asylum. But none of the two dozen girls they busted would say a word — they let a high-powered lawyer do all the talking and within seventy-two hours they were all deported. The other weird thing was that they all had perfectly valid visas, whereas usually it's illegals who get involved in the sex trade. Then that same evening, Pritchard gets talking to a guy from Taiwan's National Security Bureau, who tells him that they've uncovered a mainland spy ring using an escort agency in Taipei. It was all hushed up because things are always tense between China and Taiwan, but they kicked a dozen girls out."

"So the hookers are spies?"

"Not necessarily trained spies, but certainly capable of bugging phones. Anyway, when Pritchard gets back to the UK, he starts digging and finds three agencies that have been set up over the past two years, all using Chinese girls. Looks like they're running an operation for the Ministry of State Security."

"Pritchard's a smooth operator, isn't he? When you first meet him you assume he's just a desk jockey, but he's bang up to date on the technical side, he never needs anything explaining."

"He's a dark horse, that's true," said Shepherd. "Plays his cards close to his chest. But he knows when to play a hunch, no doubt about that."

Singh finished his coffee. "Okay, I'll be off. I'll see you in my office at nine?"

"Sounds like a plan."

Singh handed Shepherd the mug and let himself out of the bedroom. He tiptoed across the floor and let himself out. Shepherd took the mugs through to the kitchen and washed them. There was still wine in the bottle so he poured some into his glass and dropped down onto the sofa. He picked up the remote and flicked through to Sky Sports. Man City were playing Chelsea. He put his feet up on the coffee table and sipped his wine. The phone sat next to his feet. It was probably already broadcasting to the eavesdroppers. He hoped they liked football, because that was all they would be hearing for the rest of the evening. Shepherd woke at eight, shaved and showered, and changed into a dark blue suit. He used the bugged phone to order an Uber and fifteen minutes later he was in Thames House. Amar Singh was already in his office. He was standing in front of three large screens, tapping away on a keyboard. He looked up as Shepherd walked in and gave him a thumbs up. Shepherd nodded and held up the phone. Singh gave him another thumbs up. He took the phone from Shepherd and plugged it into one of his computers, then waved for Shepherd to follow him out into the corridor. He closed the door. "I'll let it run for an hour or two. The computer I have here has more tricks than my laptop so we'll get to know more about how the program works," said Singh. "Ideally we'll find out how it sends the data. I'm assuming it downloads it to a website somewhere, and if that's the case we might well be able to hack into it."

"Do you think the GPS will tell them what floor the phone is on?"

"No, the phone doesn't have the ability to identify its altitude, just its position."

"I'm heading up to see Pritchard, anything else I can tell him?"

"We've ID'd the girl. Mei-feng Chan. According to Border Force she's here on a student visa issued by the British Embassy in Beijing. They've emailed me her visa application but I'm pretty sure everything on it is false."

He handed Shepherd a four-page printout with the Border Force logo across the top. "What's she studying?" Shepherd asked. The printout contained her photograph, fingerprints, a copy of her passport and a copy of her visa application.

"English. She's registered with a language school in Hampstead."

"Her English is fine."

"She's clearly not a genuine student, in fact that's almost certainly not her real name or date of birth. The only things they can't change are her photograph and fingerprints."

Shepherd folded the printout and slid it into his jacket pocket. He thanked Singh and took the stairs to

Giles Pritchard's office. Pritchard's secretary was at her desk. Amy Miller was in her sixties and rumoured to have once been one of MI6's top officers running agents across East Germany. She had retired to her beekeeping in Surrey, but Pritchard had rehired her a few months ago. She usually had a stern look on her face and Shepherd always felt like a schoolboy visiting the headmistress's office. "Mr Pritchard says you're to go straight in," she said. She waved at his door and half a dozen brightly coloured bracelets rattled on her wrist.

There were two computer screens on Pritchard's desk but he was ignoring them and reading a copy of the *Financial Times* as he sipped a glass of Evian water. "Dan, come in, take a seat," said Pritchard, waving his glass at the sofa by the window. He was about ten years older than Shepherd and several kilos heavier. Shepherd assumed the invitation to sit on the sofa meant his boss was happy to chat — usually visitors were directed to the two wooden chairs facing his desk. It was generally assumed that Pritchard had deliberately chosen uncomfortable chairs to minimise the length of time visitors would stay.

Pritchard walked around his desk and joined Shepherd on the sofa. He was wearing a suit that was slightly darker than Shepherd's and a White's club tie. He looked expectantly over the top of his metal-framed spectacles — he was not a man for small talk and always preferred visitors to get straight to the point.

Shepherd handed him the printout that Singh had given him. "Looks like we've ID'd the girl. We're fairly sure that she works for China's Ministry of State

Security. Though that won't necessarily be easy to prove."

Pritchard wrinkled his nose and ran his hand through his slicked-back hair. "That's not the girl on the website, right?"

"It rarely is with these agencies," said Shepherd. "We think all the photographs are fake. The punters know how it works and they usually don't complain, as long as the girl is a close enough match."

"But it means we can't be sure how many girls there are, right?"

"Fair point," said Shepherd.

"You see what I mean? The agencies are showing what, twenty girls on each site? But they might only have five girls."

Shepherd shook his head. "No, there are twenty-one that we know about. All three agencies are based in a flat in Knightsbridge that we've had under surveillance for the past week. There are three Chinese working there and they are in contact with twenty-one different girls. The calls are answered in the flat and instructions are passed on to the girls by text."

"What do we know about them? The girls?"

"Just the phone numbers," said Shepherd. "All burner phones, obviously."

Pritchard nodded. "We need to work on that. And the Chinese nationals in the Knightsbridge flat?"

"A woman who answers the phone, and two men. We have photographs of all three and have identified them. The woman is British, by marriage, though she divorced her husband six years ago. The two men we haven't been able to match through facial recognition so we're working on getting prints." Shepherd shrugged. "You've got to admire the scale of this operation. Setting up three escort agencies just to trawl for intelligence sources."

"They've got form for this sort of thing," said Pritchard. "The thing about the Chinese is that they take the long-term view. The Russians, they want results straight away and if anything they have a tendency to rush. They have an objective and they throw whatever resources they need at the task to get it done. If you ask me, that's why they fuck things up so often, especially when it comes to liquidating their opponents. There's a whole bull-in-a-china shop thing going on, no pun intended. But the Chinese, they see everything in the context of a history stretching back five thousand years. They're happy to wait to get results. They waited decades to get Hong Kong back and what they're doing in Africa now is laying the foundation for an empire decades ahead. Did you ever hear about the Chinese hardware store in St James's Park?"

Shepherd shook his head.

"This is about eight years ago. At least that was when we found out what was going on — the guy had actually been at it for going on ten years prior to that. He had a hardware store not far from the Tube station. He sold bits and bobs for home improvement, cleaning supplies and electrical stuff, kettles, toasters, coffee makers, all that sort of stuff. See, if a kettle or a coffee maker breaks into an office, the staff get testy, so rather than wait to order a replacement internally, someone will usually raid petty cash and go and buy one. This Chinese guy sold all the latest gear at low prices so he did a roaring trade. What no one knew was that everything he sold had a state-of-the-art chip in it that recorded everything said in its vicinity. And it had a GPS locator so they knew to within a few feet where it was. The chip would store everything it picked up and then release it in a one-second radio burst in the middle of the night. The Chinese Embassy in Marylebone picked up the radio burst and would listen to it. If the kettle ended up in an estate agent or a shop, they'd just disable the chip. But if it was in a government building or the office of a commercially sensitive business, they'd continue to listen. I tell you, they were everywhere, Dan. All the gossip that was exchanged in the tea room, the Chinese got it. It was BP that blew the thing open. They were losing deals to Chinese competitors left, right and centre. They were being overbid, the Chinese were moving in on oil reserves that BP thought they had exclusive knowledge of, and it got so bad the chairman had a word with the PM and asked for MI5's assistance. They thought they might have a mole but the intel the Chinese were getting was coming from right across the organisation, so that could only mean the mole was at the top." He grinned. "Turned out that there was no mole, but they had microchips in two kettles and a coffee maker, each on a different floor. See, that's when people chat and gossip, when they're making themselves a drink. And the Chinese were listening in to it all. Once we knew what they were up to and where the electrical shop was we put a stop to it, but for about ten years the Chinese were picking up all sorts of intel — from the Foreign Office, the Home Office, the Ministry of Defence. There was even a chipped kettle in Buckingham Palace." He leaned forward and lowered his voice. "I was told there was one in the office of the DG's secretary, but I never could get that confirmed." He sat back and stretched out his legs. "Not one of MI5's brightest hours, it has to be said. But they did manage to make a semblance of a silk purse out of a sow's ear. Once they found out what was going on, several of the bugs were used to plant disinformation. The Chinese were so sure that they were pulling a fast one on us that they took all the intel they received as gospel. MI5 had some major coups, and for a while we were running rings around them, diplomatically and economically. They found out eventually, and shut the system down. Burned out all the chips and shut the shop."

"And what about the guy running the shop?"

"Mr Yau, his name was. Freddy Yau. He disappeared."

"Back to China?"

Pritchard shook his head. "There was no evidence of him leaving officially, and it is possible that he was taken out on a diplomatic flight, but the feeling is that his bosses decided to cut their losses and just kill him."

"After all he'd done for them?"

Pritchard shrugged. "He'd served his purpose. And the Chinese are brutal with their own people."

Shepherd forced a smile. "Hopefully MI5 treats its people better," he said.

Pritchard laughed. "The pensions aren't as good as they once were, but at least they'll let you work in the private sector. Or start a career as a bestselling author."

"The world is my oyster?"

"Well not quite, but at least I can promise you that you won't end up under a few feet of earth in the New Forest." He waved the printout. "So, to the matter in hand. This girl bugged your phone?"

Shepherd nodded. "It's a sophisticated program and bloody hard to find even if you're looking for it, but Amar is an expert."

"Voice and text?"

"Everything. FaceTime and WhatsApp, and it's tapped into the microphone so it'll pick up anything said in its vicinity. And it has access to the GPS."

Pritchard leaned back. "We've had a bit of a rethink about our strategy from here on in," he said. "As you know, the original plan was to move in and shut down the agency, and bring them in for questioning. But the thinking now is that we make this an ongoing disinformation operation, pretty much the same as the hardware shop. We can use your phone to pass on information to our advantage. It's as if we have a direct line to China's Ministry of State Security. With everything that China is up to at the moment, it could be a godsend."

"So I have to stay in character twenty-four-seven for the foreseeable future?" Shepherd scowled. Going undercover was all well and good, but with the phone bugged he would have to stick to his legend even when he was on his own. It would also prevent him getting involved in any other cases, and he had several on the go.

Pritchard held up a hand to placate him. "I can see how enthusiastic you are about that," he said. "But logistically it would be a nightmare. If nothing else you would have to be in Thames House for eight hours a day, plus the commute to and from your flat. Remind me again which flat you're using?"

"It's in Pimlico. Not far away."

"Is it nice?"

"It's not bad. Modern."

"And the girl has been there?"

"Twice."

"So here's the plan. We'll get an experienced footie involved, ideally someone who sounds not unlike you. They can then fill the role twenty-four-seven. We can get them a slot here, plug them into your legend's friends network, and start feeding the disinformation through the phone. You'll need to keep the relationship going with the girl, maybe see her once or twice a week."

Shepherd sighed. "Really? She's bugged the phone, isn't that enough?"

"The thinking is that if you seem lovelorn it'll add authenticity to the intel they get. Maybe even make it appear that you want more from the relationship."

Shepherd laughed harshly. "You want to use me as a honey trap?"

Pritchard chuckled. "No, it would just make you appear to be a weaker character. The weaker you seem, the more they'll believe that they're using you, rather than vice versa. It just makes you more believable as an intel source, that's all I'm saying. And we'd like to get details of a few more of the girls to run through Border Force's database."

"I'm not sure I should turn into an escort agency junkie," said Shepherd.

"Perish the thought," said Pritchard, pushing his glasses higher up his nose. "No, the idea is to use a few officers here to book girls, pretty much as you did. But not to offer themselves up as possible sources, just to get pictures and prints."

"Do you have anyone in mind?"

"Colin Bryson has been doing some good undercover work," said Pritchard. "He's single. Then I thought you could pick the other two. Maybe have a chat with Susan Murray, she knows everyone and it will probably be a lot quicker than going through the personnel files looking for men who fit our criteria."

"Criteria?"

"They're going to have to look like the sort of men who would use an escort agency, but you'll have to filter out the married guys, the guys in relationships, the gay guys, the guys with moral issues." He grinned. "Bit of a poisoned chalice," he said. "Which is why I thought you should pick Susan's brains. Once you've put together the team can you brief them and link up with Amar for the necessary equipment?"

"Will do," said Shepherd. "What's the deadline on this?"

"Let's strike while the iron's hot," said Pritchard. "If we could start tonight, that would be perfect."

"And what about the guy you'll use to step into my shoes? He's going to have to be on his toes. Clumpy metaphors notwithstanding."

"They're well used to maintaining legends," said Pritchard. "The fact they have to stay in character around the clock is a wrinkle, but we have someone lined up who will be perfect. His name's Harry Fletcher. He's about to turn sixty and his health isn't great but he fits the bill. You'll need to brief him at some point, obviously. Do you need to go with him to the flat, to show him the lie of the land?"

"I guess so. There's an alarm but I could do with showing him where the cameras are, so at least he can have some privacy."

"Okay, so basically we'll hand the legend over to Harry and you just meet up with the girl when necessary."

"What if they follow him? They'll soon realise he's not me."

"We'll put a counter surveillance team on him when he's outside. In the flat and in Thames House he'll be fine, and we'll keep him inside most of the time. To stay in touch with him, we'll fix up a text-only phone, so it doesn't pick him up talking to the surveillance team. Plus at home he can leave the phone in the bedroom away from prying ears. And from time to time he could let the battery go flat. It's all workable."

"Sounds like a plan," said Shepherd.

"Maybe meet in the canteen at five?"

"I can do that."

"What about the phone that was bugged?"

"Amar has it. I brought it in. It's in his briefcase so it's not picking up anything."

"And can the bug work when the phone's switched off?"

"Yes, it works whether the phone is on or off, Amar's definite about that. The battery has to be dead or removed for the software not to work."

"Okay, so as things stand the Chinese will assume that you came to work as usual?"

"Yeah. After I've briefed Harry I'll give him the phone and we'll be up and running."

"Excellent." Pritchard shifted uncomfortably. "I'm sorry to have to ask this, but how far did you go . . . physically? With the girl?"

"Does that matter?"

Pritchard grimaced. "It sort of does," he said. "The question will be asked and I'll be expected to know the answer. Obviously we don't operate under the same guidelines as police officers when they're undercover, but I don't want any nasty surprises down the line."

Shepherd laughed. "I was in a difficult position." He held up a hand. "No pun intended. But there's no way I could order an escort and not have some sort of physical contact, it would set alarm bells ringing. I told her my wife died not that long ago and that I wasn't ready to make love to anyone else, so all I wanted was a massage. She seemed okay with that."

Pritchard looked at him over the top of his glasses. "You told her about Katra?"

"Not Katra, no. I span her a line, but as you know it's always best to keep your story as close to the truth as you can. And what I said was true enough. I still miss Katra and it was months before I could even think about going with someone else."

"And how's Liam handling it?"

Shepherd's son had been with Shepherd when Katra had been killed, shot by a gangster in Slovenia. "He seems okay, but he's never been one to talk about his feelings. His mum died at a very young age and he doesn't talk about that, either. Like me, he's thrown himself into his work. Keeping yourself busy stops you dwelling on things."

"He's still flying helicopters for the Army?"

Shepherd nodded. "He loves it."

Pritchard looked at his watch, his way of letting Shepherd know that the meeting was over.

Shepherd took the lift down to the second floor and headed for the legends office. He knocked and opened the door but the office was empty. Shepherd cursed under his breath and then jumped as a hand fell on his shoulder. He looked around to see an amused look on the face of Susan Murray. "Sorry, Dan, I didn't mean to startle you."

"You could creep up on the devil himself, Susan."

"I've started wearing slippers in the office," she said. "My feet have been playing up so I dress for comfort these days." She was almost seventy years old but had a memory almost as good as Shepherd's. She had been with MI5 for twenty years and before that had worked for the British Library for another twenty. Her main role was to make sure that the many legends used by MI5 officers working undercover were up to date. In pre-internet days, all an undercover officer needed was a driving licence, a passport and a credit card or two. But social media had changed all that. Everyone had an online footprint, so a lack of one was a major red flag. A network of footies were tasked with maintaining the legends; posting on social media, using loyalty cards, tapping Oyster cards in and out on public transport and keeping mobile phones busy. The footies also maintained safe houses and the homes used by the legends, collecting mail, paying bills and keeping them clean.

Susan also handed out the documents and ID that the officers needed when undercover, which meant that she met them all at some point. She was always Shepherd's first port of call when he started on an undercover operation. "Are you here to return the Charlie Warner documents?"

Shepherd had been issued with a driving licence and credit and debit cards in the name of Charles Warner, just in case any escorts went through his wallet during the operation. "I'm hanging on to them for a while longer," said Shepherd. "I'm actually here to pick your brains," he said, standing to the side to let her into the office. She was wearing a purple wool dress with a string of oversized pearls around her neck. Her purple lipstick and nail varnish matched her dress. He looked down at her slippers and smiled when he saw that they were purple, too. She had clearly gone to a lot of trouble to coordinate her outfit. She walked over to her desk and sat down. There was a pair of reading glasses hanging from a gold chain around her neck, and she wore large chunky rings on most of her fingers. "Pick away, Dan," she said.

There was a chair by the wall and Shepherd sat down. He explained what he needed and she smiled. "My word, that's a strange one," she said. "The officer who springs to mind is Colin Bryson. Middle-aged and single, but definitely has an eye for the ladies."

Shepherd nodded. "Giles suggested him."

"The problem is that most men who use escort agencies are aged thirty or more, probably over fifty, and once our people are that age they are either married . . . or gay. And I suppose a gay officer wouldn't work out?"

"Girls tend to have a fully functioning gaydar, in my experience," said Shepherd. "More so than men."

She smiled. "I can always tell, that's true. Maybe it's the pheromones. Or maybe it's a survival skill that girls pick up and boys don't need." She tapped her lower lip with her index finger. "What about Andrew Peterson? He's with counter subversion at the moment but he's done extensive undercover work in the past."

"I know Andrew, we worked on an operation together five years ago. He's married, though."

"He's divorced, going on three years." She put her glasses on and swivelled around to look at her computer. She tapped on her keyboard, stared at her screen, and then smiled. "Yes, divorced three years ago and no new relationship listed, so he'd be a good choice."

"Agreed," said Shepherd. "So I need just one more."

She took off her glasses and leaned back in her chair, tapping her lip again. "I would have said Jamie Hughes but he got married for the third time two months ago and I have the feeling he wouldn't want to be betraying the new Mrs Hughes, at least not this early in the marriage. There are several who look good on paper but then that gaydar thing kicks in." She frowned, and then smiled. "Jason McKinley. He's been undercover with Extinction Rebellion but we've had to pull him out because he was getting too close to one of the female members."

"Was that a problem?"

"It would have been if her husband had found out. His operation was coming to an end anyway. Do you know him?"

Shepherd shook his head.

"He's a former cop, moved to Five a year or so ago. He's in his late fifties, divorced with a couple of kids. I'm sure he'd work."

"Excellent, can you give me phone numbers for him and for Peterson?"

She turned back to her computer, tapped on the keyboard and wrote down two numbers on a Post-it slip.

Shepherd thanked her.

"What will they be needing in terms of ID?" she asked.

"Probably a passport, driving licence and credit card."

"We've got them on file for all of them," she said.

"I'll check with Giles and get back to you," he said. He went out into the corridor to call Pritchard. MI5 was very hierarchical and he wasn't in a position to recruit officers for operations directly — Pritchard would have to talk to their heads of department first. He gave Pritchard the names and ten minutes later his boss called back to confirm that both men were available and would be in Thames House later that afternoon, along with Colin Bryson.

The three men who would be contacting the escort agencies were gathered in a meeting room on the fourth floor of Thames House. Shepherd arrived with Amar Singh. Amar had brought a cardboard box with him and he placed it on the table. Shepherd shook hands with them all. Andrew Peterson had put on a few pounds since they had worked together and Shepherd had collected a few more grey hairs. Peterson was about Shepherd's age and was wearing a grey suit and an open-necked shirt.

Jason McKinley was tall and lanky, with a full beard and the look of a university lecturer. It was easy to picture him in an Extinction Rebellion demonstration, protesting against climate change. He had a Geordie accent and a friendly smile, with a strong handshake. He was wearing a tweed jacket and cord trousers and Hush Puppies that looked as if they had seen better days.

The third member of the team was Colin Bryson, a small man with receding hair and a neatly trimmed moustache. He was clearly a heavy smoker, with yellow nicotine stains on the fingers of his right hand and greying teeth. He was sucking mints as if he hoped that would improve his breath, but it wasn't working.

Shepherd introduced them to Amar Singh. "One of our top technical whizzes and possibly the snappiest dresser in the building," he said.

"Possibly?" said Singh with a smile. He gestured at his suit. "Show me anyone else here who's wearing Hugo Boss."

"Amar here has the equipment you'll be needing," said Shepherd. "Basically we have three escort agencies that we think are being used by the Chinese to trawl for intelligence sources. We have identified one of the girls being used but we need you guys to get photographs and fingerprints of a few more. You'll be booking into hotels and setting up hidden cameras. You'll book a girl from the websites and get their picture and prints. You'll be working alone so you'll need to set up the equipment yourselves. Amar will show you how to do that."

McKinley raised a hand. "Sorry, I've just got a question," he said. "You're saying they're trawling for intelligence sources. It's a bit hit and miss, isn't it? I mean, when a client calls up, they have no way of knowing who he is or who he works for."

Shepherd nodded. "It's like panning for gold, they've got to go through an awful lot of dross to get a few nuggets."

McKinley frowned. "So they've got agents working as hookers, on the off-chance that they'll come across someone with information the Chinese Government will find useful?"

"That's exactly it," said Shepherd. "For them, it's a numbers game. There are three agencies we know of, with twenty-one girls. We got onto them a few weeks ago but they've been around for just over two years. It's clever in its simplicity. Twenty-one girls, each with just one customer a day, would give them close to seven hundred customers a month. Eight thousand a year. Even if just one in a thousand of those clients works in the Civil Service or government or the Army, that's eight prime intel sources a year. Plus who knows what blackmail material they come up with. They work the airport hotels, too. Lots of foreign businessmen and politicians travelling through, and you'd be surprised how many feel the need for a relaxing massage before their flight. Basically the girl will try to find out what your job is and who you work for. If you seem like a prospect, they will try to get access to your phone to plant a bug. We don't want you to get to that stage. All we need you to do is to book a girl and get her to a hotel room, where you'll set up cameras that Amar here will supply. You won't get any useful intel from them because everything they will tell you is a lie. What we want is their Border Force details, and for that we need a photograph and their prints. You'll be given gloves and evidence bags, all you have to do is to give them a drink and keep the glass. If that doesn't work, just keep an eye out for anything they touch and take prints from that."

Bryson tilted his head on one side and narrowed his eyes. "Dan, just to be clear about this, we're being paid to have sex?" he asked. The other men smiled.

"Not necessarily," said Shepherd. "Plenty of clients only have a massage and the websites say that all the girls are trained masseuses. But as has already been explained to me, MI5 officers aren't bound by the same guidelines as cops, so no one's going to give you any grief if you cross the line. Not that there is a line. It's totally your call to go as far as you think is necessary, so long as you are comfortable with what's happening. You guys were all chosen because you are single and have no declared relationships. The cameras will be supplied by the tech department and you'll be placing them, so you'll be able to keep them away from the bed if you're worried about being filmed."

"What do we do about legends?" asked Peterson.

"You'll be issued with credit cards, driving licences and passports. Susan Murray has them all ready, you just need to pop along to her office and sign for them. Basically all you have to do is check into a hotel using the credit card, then use the landline to call the agency and book a girl. You place the cameras, you get the girl's prints, and after she has left you check out. The following day check into another hotel with another credit card and book another girl. The agencies will keep records of names and hotel details, so make sure you only book each girl once. Now, there is a potential problem. Because the pictures on the websites are all fake, they might send a girl you've already been with, so we have to minimise the chances of that happening. Make your bookings through different agencies, and choose girls who look very different. Choose a short-haired girl and then a long-haired girl, a tall one then a short one, and so on. The girl they send won't be the girl in the picture, but we can assume they will at least try to match the client's requirements. If a client orders a long-haired young girl and gets a short-haired older girl, he might complain. But if she's a close enough match, no one's going to make a fuss. If all goes to plan, within two days we'll have the photographs and prints of six girls. All good?"

The three men nodded. They were all smiling and Shepherd could see they were looking forward to the task.

Singh opened the box he was carrying and took out an electrical adapter that took plugs and USBs. He passed it to Peterson who examined it carefully. Singh gave similar adapters to the other two men. "You plug this into any socket in the room," he said. "It will store high-definition video and sound on an internal memory card and can stream to any phone. The camera is in the light on the front. If the target passes anywhere within ten feet, it will record a clear image." He reached into the box again and took out three small digital clocks, and gave them one each. "These are battery operated and there's a switch on the back that is on, off, or motion-activated. They're fully charged and good for twenty-four hours, so just switch them on when you're ready. The camera is just under the number twelve.

46

Everything it sees and hears is recorded on a memory card, or like the adapter can be streamed to your phone, tablet or computer."

"Right, when you meet the girls, you use the name that you used to make the hotel booking," said Shepherd. "When you first make the call, the agency will take your details and then do a call back to check you are in the room, so the names need to match. These girls are trawling for high-value intel sources, so you need to fly below their radar. You can use any story you want, but stay clear of government or NGO positions; make sure you're seen as a low-level employee in a boring industry. Kitchen designer, maybe. Hotel management. Computer programmer. Jobs that would be of no interest to Chinese intelligence. Once they realise you're of no value to them, they'll lose interest. As soon as the girls have gone, secure their prints and take them and the cameras to Amar. Any questions?"

All three men shook their heads.

"I'll see you in forty-eight hours for a debrief," said Shepherd. He looked at his watch. It was almost five o'clock. Time to meet Harry Fletcher. "I'll leave you with Amar to familiarise yourselves with the equipment."

Shepherd took the lift to the canteen. Harry Fletcher was easy enough to spot. He was wearing a rumpled grey suit with a wrinkled yellow tie at half mast, and was bent over a cup of tea. His hair was thinning and his nails were bitten to the quick. As he picked up a spoon and stirred his coffee, his hand seemed to tremble. He didn't look up as Shepherd walked over — that was a bad sign, because not being aware of what was going around you could be fatal. It wasn't until Shepherd was standing at the table that the man noticed him, squinting up with watery eyes. There were grey bags under them as if he wasn't sleeping well, and his skin had an unhealthy yellowish pallor. He smiled. "You, Dan, yeah?"

Shepherd nodded. "Yeah." He offered his hand and Fletcher shook it. Shepherd gestured at the food service area. "I'm starving, can I get you something?"

"I'm okay," said Fletcher. "Maybe a banana."

Shepherd went over to the counter and ordered fish and chips and baked beans, put a banana on his tray, and made himself a cup of coffee at the machine.

When he sat down opposite Fletcher, the man looked at the fish and chips and licked his lips. Shepherd gave him the banana and Fletcher took it, putting it down next to his tea.

"So how long have you been a footie?" asked Shepherd. He picked up a bottle of tomato sauce, unscrewed the cap, and shook out a decent-sized splodge.

"Best part of eighteen months. I used to be with Six, but I developed a few health problems so they moved me to Five and put me out to grass. These days I spend most of my time online posting racist memes on right-wing websites." He smiled ruefully. "Not that I'm complaining. They could have just kicked me out but

48

they assigned me to the footies so I can keep adding to my pension." He sipped his tea and grimaced.

"Are you okay?"

Fletcher wrinkled his nose. "I'm on calcium blockers to keep my blood pressure down, statins to keep my cholesterol low, I had two of those stent things in to keep my arteries open and my diabetes isn't getting any better either." He shrugged. "It's no fun but better than the alternative, right?" He nodded at the cup in front of him. "I'm on decaf or green tea, I eat mainly vegetables and boiled chicken, and I'm allowed one glass of red wine a day." He forced a smile. "I'm okay."

"Bloody hell, I'm sorry I asked," said Shepherd. He nodded at his plate of fish and chips. "You don't mind, do you? I'm starving."

"Go ahead," said Fletcher, enviously eyeing the food. He grinned as Shepherd speared a chip and slotted it into his mouth. "What's your blood pressure, then?"

"It was fine last time I checked," said Shepherd.

"Mine was fine until I hit fifty," said Fletcher. "I used to be as fit as a butcher's dog." He pointed at his expanding waistline. "Not that you'd know that now. My six pack's more like a barrel these days."

"What happened?"

"Stress," said Fletcher sourly. "I was in Moscow, recruiting and running agents. They just kept increasing my workload. You know how it was, most resources were being targeted at al-Qaeda and ISIS but I was a Russian speaker so I wasn't much use there. As more and more people were pulled into the war against the jihadists, I was working flat out and my stress levels went through the roof. You've run assets, right?"

"Some," said Shepherd.

"So you know what it's like. You start off running them as if they were pawns in a chess game, pieces to be used as part of a bigger picture. But then you start to get attached. You know them, you know their families, you know their troubles, their fears, and then you start to worry about them. You care, you really care, and that takes its toll. And because we were under strength, I was dealing with twice a normal workload."

He was still looking longingly at Shepherd's meal. Shepherd grinned and pushed the plate towards him. "One chip won't hurt."

Fletcher wrinkled his nose, then sighed and grabbed a chip. He bit a small piece as if he was trying to make it last as long as possible. "The rot set in when I lost one of my assets. He was a young lad, still in his twenties, and he worked at the Russian Ministry of Defence. Low-level stuff, but his department was involved in monitoring what was happening in the Ukraine and he was sure something was going to kick off. This was late 2013, so about nine months before the Russians invaded. He could never get me papers or reports, but he had a good memory and was able to tell me the gist of what was said at some quite heavy meetings. Problem was, he had a habit of talking in his sleep. That was his downfall."

"So his wife turned him in?"

Fletcher shook his head. "Anton was gay. And his boyfriend also worked for the Ministry of Defence.

Anton managed to warn me to keep my distance and then a day or two later he called wanting a meeting. I could tell from his voice that he was under duress so I pretended not to know him. I just knew that somebody was listening in, I had some wild hope that if I could convince them I didn't know him that he'd get away with it, but . . ." He shook his head, put the rest of the chip in his mouth and swallowed it without chewing. He was already reaching for a second chip. "It didn't work, of course. I never heard from him again."

"What happened to him?"

"I don't know. Not officially. But I assume he was questioned, tortured and then shot as a spy. I didn't sleep for a week afterwards. I hit the bottle. In a perfect world my bosses would have seen what I was going through and offered to help, but they just increased the pressure. Two years later I had the first of my heart attacks." He shrugged, reached for a third chip but then held himself back. "Anyway, Dan, that's the story of my life. When I was no more use to Six they transferred me to Five and I've been with the footies ever since, basically counting the days until I retire."

Shepherd put down his knife and fork. "Sounds like you had it rough."

"It was my own fault. I let the job get to me. You've got to keep some distance, keep yourself aloof, above it all. At the end of the day, it's just a bloody game anyway, isn't it? Friends become enemies, freedom fighters become terrorists, terrorists enter government. The CIA created monsters like Noriega and Bin Laden, and then they destroyed them. At the end of the day, does anything we do really matter?" He picked up his tea and sipped it. His hand trembled slightly but he didn't spill any.

"Loyalties change, there's no question of that," said Shepherd. "But we save lives on a daily basis, Harry. We're constantly thwarting plots that could result in civilian deaths. Every year we put people away who want to do us harm."

Fletcher nodded. "I know, I know." He forced a smile. "You've just caught me on a bad day."

From the sound of it, every day was a bad day for Fletcher, but Shepherd needed the man to pull himself together. "So, what have you been told about this latest operation?"

"Pritchard said I'm standing in for you and feeding fake intel through a bugged phone," said Fletcher. "Though looking at the two of us I'd say there's been a problem with central casting. There's no way I'm going to pass for you, even on a dark night."

"No one's going to be watching you," said Shepherd. "Or at least, we'll have a counter surveillance team watching you to check that they're not."

"Chinese, right?"

"Yes, but that doesn't mean that Jackie Chan will be on your tail. There's no reason that they should be following you, but even so it's best you stay in the flat when you're not at work."

"You've got Sky, yeah?"

Shepherd thought he was joking, but he was clearly serious. "And Netflix. And the budget will even run to a few Deliveroo orders. Have you got family?"

"Two ex-wives and a son I only hear from when he needs money. Why?"

"The phone will transmit all calls and texts, but it'll also pick up anything it hears within six feet or so. So if you do receive a call on your personal phone you need to make sure you're in another room. Ideally the bathroom with the tap running."

"Or I could just switch your phone off."

"No, the bug works whether the phone is off or on. You can remove the battery but that will be a serious red flag. You could let the battery die and that would look natural, but I don't see the point. If you want privacy you could put it in a drawer or a box, which will cut down its eavesdropping ability — but bear in mind the GPS will still function. Anyway, I've been using the name Charles Warner, I booked the girl as Charlie. Her name's Jasmine. At least that's the name she uses on the website. There's no need for you to have any Charles Warner ID, you're not going to be meeting anyone from the agencies. Basically you're just moving the phone around between the flat and Thames House."

"And how long will this operation be running?"

"It's open-ended," said Shepherd. He finished his meal and looked at his watch. It was just after five-fifteen. "How about we head to the flat," he said. "We should go separately, obviously. I normally walk but you should maybe get an Uber. They'll be able to see the Uber booking and track the GPS. I'll meet you outside. But remember, no conversation when you see me."

"Mum's the word," said Fletcher.

Shepherd reached into his jacket pocket and fished out a set of keys. He put them down in front of Fletcher. "The bigger of the two opens the main door. The flat is on the second floor. The smaller key opens the door to the flat. The burglar alarm console is on the wall to the left. Tap in one-three-nine-seven and you're good to go." He stood up. "You can collect the phone from Amar Singh in the technical department. It's switched off at the moment, but as soon as Amar's briefed you, you can turn it on and order an Uber. I'll follow you with the surveillance team. What number is your mobile?"

Fletcher gave him the number and Shepherd tapped it into his own phone. He winked at Fletcher and headed for the door.

Shepherd walked out of Thames House and along the street to where an Openreach van was parked. Openreach was the company within BT that maintained the company's cable and phone network across the UK and, on the outside at least, the van was identical to the hundreds of others out on the streets. Shepherd put his hand out to knock on the rear door but it opened immediately. A familiar face grinned out at him. It was Janet Rayner, a thirty-something brunette, her hair tied back with a leopard-print scrunchie. Rayner had spent a year with the Metropolitan Police's surveillance team before joining MI5, and was one of the best followers in the country. "Matty's just farted," she said, scowling at the other occupant of the van.

54

Matty Clayton was in his late forties and had spent almost half his life running surveillance operations for MI5. He looked up from his computer keyboard. "What can I say? I had a curry with the lads last night."

"You are disgusting," said Rayner, pulling the door closed and sitting back on her stool. On the inside, the Openreach van was nothing like the real thing. There were half a dozen monitors showing views from the concealed cameras around the vehicle, and a screen showing a GPS plan of the area. There was also a laptop running the Met's automatic number plate recognition software. There were three photographs stuck to the wall of the van — a head-and-shoulders shot of Harry Fletcher, and two pictures of him taken at a distance.

Shepherd pulled over a plastic stool and sat down. Counter surveillance was very different from regular tailing. On a surveillance operation, they would use at least three vehicles, ideally more, often motorcycles. The aim was to follow a target without the target realising what was happening, and for that they needed multiple followers in radio contact, taking it in turns to be closest. But for counter surveillance, the trick was to hang back and look at the bigger picture. On foot, counter surveillance was best done with the cooperation of the target, getting them to double back or move through areas where a tail would stick out. Counter surveillance on a vehicle was easier, especially with ANPR. The cameras around the van could constantly scan the registration plates of vehicles close to the target, identify the owners and spot any that returned.

"Here he comes," said Rayner.

They all looked at the screen showing the front of Thames House. Fletcher was standing on the pavement, looking at his phone. He was wearing a black overcoat and holding a battered brown leather briefcase. "So this guy is supposed to be you, right?" asked Rayner. "Because I'm not seeing the similarity."

"He's just following my routine," said Shepherd. "Or to be more accurate, he's following the routine of the legend I set up."

Fletcher spotted a white Prius parked nearby with its hazard lights flashing. He waved his phone and walked over to it.

"How long will this go on for?" asked Clayton.

"It's open-ended," said Shepherd. "But Fletcher will be in Thames House from nine to five, and the rest of the time he'll be in the flat. If he does leave the flat he'll give us plenty of notice."

"And if we do spot a tail, then what?"

"You let me know straight away. If I'm not around then Pritchard needs to know."

"That's all we do? Just let you or the boss know that Fletcher's being followed?"

"You're insurance," said Shepherd. "There's very little chance that they will tail him because they'll have access to his GPS, so they'll always know where he is. But we need to be watching, just in case."

Fletcher climbed into the back of the Prius. The hazard lights stopped flashing and it pulled away from the kerb. The Openreach van followed.

The ANPR system was working automatically, photographing and recording the numbers of the vehicles around them. Clayton and Rayner watched the screens, looking for anything out of the ordinary. Shepherd's eyes flicked between the monitors. There were a lot of black cabs and Ubers in the area but none stayed close to Fletcher's car for more than a few minutes. If there was a team following him and alternating lead vehicles, the ANPR system would find them and point them out.

It took just over five minutes to reach the apartment building in Pimlico. Fletcher climbed out of the Prius and then walked down the road, away from the building, giving Shepherd a final chance to spot any tail. When it was clear that Fletcher wasn't being followed, the van pulled over and Shepherd climbed out.

Fletcher walked back to the entrance of the building and was opening the door when Shepherd arrived. They walked in together, studiously ignoring each other. Fletcher headed for the stairs and Shepherd followed.

It was only two floors but the effort had Fletcher breathing heavily. Shepherd followed him to the door of the flat. Fletcher unlocked the door and went inside. Shepherd looked over his shoulder to check that the corridor was clear, and then followed him. As he closed the door, Fletcher tapped the four-digit code into the alarm console and it stopped beeping. They walked into the sitting room. Fletcher put the phone down on the coffee table, then picked up the remote and turned on the TV.

Shepherd pointed at the bedroom and led the way. Once they were both inside, he closed the door and nodded at Fletcher. "All good?"

"Sure," said Fletcher. "All I do is hang out here and then head back to Thames House first thing?" He took off his overcoat and dropped it onto a chair.

Shepherd nodded. "You'll need to get clothes and personal effects brought over. You can use your personal phone to organise that." He pointed up at a smoke alarm in the ceiling. "Just so you know, there's a camera in there, but it's pointed at the door so it doesn't see you on the bed. There are no cameras in the bathroom. But the kitchen and the sitting room are comprehensively covered for sound and vision."

"So they'll be watching me?"

"No. But if you enter four nines into the alarm console it will sound an alarm at Thames House and the CCTV will be activated. But there's very little likelihood of there being a problem here." He looked at his watch. "I'll be heading off." He opened the bedroom door and walked across the sitting room to the hallway. He waved goodbye and Fletcher waved back.

Shepherd let himself out of the flat and went downstairs. The Openreach van had already gone. It was a chilly evening but he decided to walk home — his apartment was in Battersea, thirty minutes away across Chelsea Bridge and through Battersea Park. The flat was also a rental, but as soon as he sold his house in

Hereford he planned to make an offer to his landlord. It was convenient for work and the park was a perfect place to exercise. His days of running with a rucksack full of bricks were behind him, but he still enjoyed a decent jog, and there was an outdoor exercise gym that he used regularly.

It was almost dark and the street lights were on. As he walked through the park, a group of middle-aged men and women were practising tai chi, moving their arms and legs through the air in slow motion, following the instructions of an elderly man who must have been in his eighties, his bald scalp spotted with sun damage and his hands forming bony claws. He didn't give any commands or instructions but the class mirrored his every move.

Over at the outdoor gym, a middle-aged woman was shouting encouragement to two teenagers, presumably her sons, as they performed energetic pull-ups. Despite the chill in the air they were bare-chested, their muscles glistening in the overhead lights. Shepherd smiled at their enthusiasm. It had been a few years since he had attempted a pull-up, and while he figured he could probably manage one or two, he wouldn't be able to perform anywhere near as well as the youngsters. Shepherd didn't worry too much about getting older though, and while he occasionally missed the rough and tumble of life in the SAS, he was more than compensated by the intellectual challenges of working for MI5. The woman barked at the boys and they dropped to the ground and began doing press-ups. For a brief moment

Shepherd was tempted to drop and follow their example. He smiled at the way his competitive instinct had kicked in, despite the fact he was wearing a suit and tie.

He left the park, crossed the road, and walked to the modern glass-and-steel apartment block that he'd used as his London base for going on three years. He had been spending less time in Hereford, especially since the death of his girlfriend, Katra. The house was filled with memories of her and that as much as work pressures kept him away. His son Liam rarely visited the Hereford house now that he was flying helicopters for the Army Air Corps, and the previous month Shepherd had put the house on the market with a local estate agency. The flat in Battersea had three bedrooms, so there was plenty of room if and when Liam wanted to stay, though Shepherd had barely spent any time with him since Katra's funeral.

He let himself into the building and took the lift up to his floor. The flat didn't have much character but there was a decent enough view of the park from the sitting room, and he liked the high ceilings and full-length windows. He slotted a pod into his Nespresso coffee machine, but grunted in annoyance when he pulled open the fridge door and realised he'd run out of milk.

He had just dropped down onto the sofa in the living room and taken his first sip of black coffee when his mobile rang. It was Giles Pritchard. "How did it go with Harry?" he asked.

"All good. We followed him back to the flat and he was clear. He's settled in now and he'll take the phone back and forth for as long as needed."

"So you're free and clear?"

"I'm just about to switch on the TV," he said. "But I'm guessing you've got other plans for me."

Pritchard chuckled. "Sorry," he said. "But yes, something's just cropped up and we're short-handed all round at the moment."

"What's happened?"

"We've had an asylum seeker turn up at Heathrow Airport claiming that he's got information on ISIS jihadists in the UK. The local cops called us and we've asked them to take him to a hotel so that someone from Five can debrief him. This could take a few days — you're not planning anything over Christmas, are you?" It was December 22, so Christmas was only three days away.

"No, I'm good. Liam's on a joint NATO exercise so I was going to be on my own anyway. It'll be good to have something to do. Which hotel?"

"I'll text you as soon as I know. Apparently he's asking for asylum for himself and his family."

"Did they fly in with him?"

"No, he came in alone. He's obviously hoping to trade intel for his family, so we need an initial assessment of his value. Can you take a run out and see what's on offer? If he's a chancer than you can pass him back to Border Force. At the moment he's in the custody of the Heathrow police. The officer in charge is a chap called Aspinall."

"I'm on it," said Shepherd.

"Sorry about the late hour," said Pritchard.

"It's not a problem. Like I said, I was only going to watch the TV."

Shepherd ended the call, finished his coffee, then took the lift down to the underground car park where he kept his BMW X3. As he started the engine his phone beeped. It was a text from Pritchard — the name of the hotel at Heathrow and a room number.

Shepherd drove to the Holiday Inn and parked outside. He went straight to the lifts, walking by a towering Christmas tree surrounded by a pile of fake presents. There was a cartoon snowman stuck to the mirrored wall, wishing him a "HAPPY HOLIDAY", and Christmas carols played as the lift headed upwards.

The room where the asylum seeker was being held was at the end of a long corridor, next to the fire exit. Shepherd knocked on the door and it was opened immediately by a man in a Border Force uniform. Immigration officers used to wear suits and ties, but in 2009 they were given uniforms. The latest batch gave them the appearance of SWAT officers, but without the guns. The man stared at Shepherd with pale blue eyes. He had close-cropped hair and a cleft chin, and a slab of gleaming white teeth. "Paul Easton, Home Office, you're expecting me," said Shepherd. MI5 officers rarely, if ever, identified themselves as such, and more often than not didn't use their real names.

The man grunted and Shepherd walked in. It was a standard hotel room, two beds facing a TV on the wall, with a wardrobe to the right and a desk to the left, and at the far end of the room a door that led to the bathroom. On the wall between the beds was a framed painting of a beach scene, white-topped waves crashing onto the sand while seagulls glided overhead. There were two other men there: one a uniformed police officer, the other wearing a dark blue suit. The suited officer took out a warrant card and flashed it. "DS Gerry Aspinall," he said. He was in his thirties with short blond hair and the tired eyes of detectives the world over — as if they had already been faced with a lifetime of lies and disappointments and expected nothing to change in the foreseeable future.

"Paul Easton, Home Office," said Shepherd.

The Border Force officer closed the door. He offered his hand to Shepherd and the formality caught Shepherd by surprise, but he shook. "Ricky Wainer," he said. "I was on the desk when your man came through. He didn't have a passport and he said he wanted to talk to a police officer."

"Where is he now?" asked Shepherd.

"He's in the bathroom," said Wainer, gesturing at the closed door.

"He says his name is Salam Jaraf — not like the animal," said Aspinall. He spelled the name out. "He flew in on an Emirates flight from Dubai. Failed to produce a passport and he said he was former ISIS and wanted asylum in exchange for information. That's when my boss called your boss."

"Okay, thanks," said Shepherd. "I think you, me and Ricky can handle it from here," he said. "Your colleague can call it a night. I'll have a chat and assuming that everything is kosher, I'll take him off your hands."

"Do I need to stay?" asked Wainer. He looked at his watch. "I was hoping I could push off when you turned up. I'm getting to the end of my shift."

"For the moment, I'd like you to stay put," said Shepherd. "It might all be nothing, in which case you can process his asylum application."

Aspinall told the uniformed officer his services were no longer required. The man didn't look happy and Shepherd figured he had been anticipating a healthy overtime payment. As the uniformed officer left, the bathroom door opened. An Asian man stepped out. He was short, not much more than five foot six, with a neatly trimmed beard and thick-lensed round-rimmed spectacles. His skin was the colour of dark mahogany, and his hair was jet black and glistening as if it had been oiled. He was wearing a dark brown knee-length kameez tunic over baggy beige pants, and had plastic sandals on his feet. He looked quizzically at Shepherd, then over at the detective.

"My name is Paul," said Shepherd. "*As-salamu alaykum*."

The man looked back at him in surprise. "*Wa alaykumu s-salam*," he said. "You speak Arabic?"

"Just enough to say hello," said Shepherd. He pulled the chair away from the desk and sat down. "I'm here to assess your suitability for asylum."

"You are from the Home Office?"

Shepherd nodded but didn't answer the question. "Your name is?"

64

"Salam Jaraf." Jaraf went over to the bed nearest the bathroom and sat down with his hands in his lap.

"And your nationality?"

"I am from Palestine."

"You were born there?"

Jaraf nodded.

"So where is your passport?"

"I do not travel on a Palestinian passport. It causes . . . difficulties."

"That's not what I asked."

Jaraf sighed. "I destroyed my passport, on the plane."

"Why?"

"Because I obtained it in Dubai and the man who gave it to me would get into trouble if it was traced back to him."

"By 'obtained' you mean you bought it?"

Jaraf nodded. "Of course."

"So it was fake?"

"It was good enough to get me onto the plane, but it would not have stood up to scrutiny by immigration here. But I had no intention of entering the country illegally. I declared who I was at the first opportunity." He reached into the pocket of his trousers and pulled out a chain of Muslim prayer beads. He started toying with the amber spheres, flicking them between his thumb and first finger. "You do not take notes?" he asked.

Shepherd smiled and tapped the side of his head. "I have a perfect memory."

Jaraf frowned. "You can remember everything you hear?"

"Everything I hear, everything I see, everything I do," said Shepherd.

"That is a gift," said Jaraf.

"It can be," said Shepherd.

"Unless there are things that you wish to forget. Then I would imagine it might be a curse."

He stared at Shepherd with unblinking brown eyes. Shepherd returned his gaze. "What about you?" asked Shepherd. "Are there things that you wish to forget?"

"I saw my father shot dead," said Jaraf. "I will never forget the blood pooling around his head or the way he squeezed my hand as he died." He looked down at the floor.

"When you claimed asylum, you told the officer that you belonged to ISIS."

Jaraf nodded. "That is true."

"Was it because of what happened to your father that you joined them?"

Jaraf looked up and met Shepherd's gaze. "I joined ISIS because I am a Muslim and it is the duty of every Muslim to fight for his faith."

Shepherd continued to stare at Jaraf, allowing the silence to stretch for several seconds. "So what changed?" he asked eventually. "Why did you decide to come to England?"

Jaraf shrugged carelessly. "I am tired of the fighting. Tired of the killing."

"But why come to the United Kingdom?"

"Because only here can I be safe. And only here can my family be safe."

"Where are your family now?"

66

"In a refugee camp in Turkey. My wife and my son. I thought they were dead. I thought I had lost them forever."

"How so?"

"They were in Syria with me. They stayed with friends in a house close to the camp. I thought they would be safe there, but I was wrong. The Americans launched a missile attack at the camp and the house was hit, either by design or by mistake. I thought they had been killed, but my wife and son and others from the village fled across the border into Turkey, where they were met by Turkish forces. After a few months, news reached me that they were in a refugee camp."

"This camp, where is it?" More than six million Syrians had fled their war-torn country and almost four million were living in Turkey, many of them in state-run refugee camps cobbled together out of tents and shipping containers. Displaced Iraqis, Palestinians, Kurds and Somalians were also housed in these camps, with alongside yet more refugees from Yemen and the Sudan. The camps were described as "temporary accommodation centres" and were run with the support of the United Nations and various NGOs. In 2019 the Turks began closing many of the camps near the border and moving people deeper into the country. The flow of refugees had increased when Donald Trump had pulled US forces out of northern Syria, leaving the Kurdish fighters there at the mercy of the Turkish armed forces. It was a bloody mess, and the country's civilians were paying the price.

"The camp is just across the border," answered Jaraf. "They call it the Kilis Öncüpinar Accommodation Facility."

Shepherd nodded. He had heard of the Kilis camp. It had been built from more than two thousand shipping containers and was a more permanent set-up than the tented refugee camps scattered across the country.

"Have you spoken to her?"

Jaraf nodded. "Just once. Well, I didn't actually speak to her. Someone from the camp left a message and said that she was there and that my son was with her."

"And after you learned that they were alive, you decided to come to the UK?"

"It was the only way I could think of that would allow me to be with my family again."

"Where were you? When the camp called you?"

"I was in Iraq. I had friends there."

"So why didn't you go to Turkey and get your family?"

Jaraf hesitated, and Shepherd was pretty sure that meant he was preparing to lie. "I had no money, Mr Easton. I had nothing. What was I to do, move into a refugee camp with my family? No. I had to find a way of getting a better life for them. We had nothing in Palestine. Syria was too dangerous, Iraq is just as bad."

Shepherd nodded thoughtfully. "So this is about your family? Not because you've had a change of heart?"

"I will forever be a Muslim," said Jaraf.

"But you can't expect the British Government to offer you asylum if you're a terrorist."

Jaraf shook his head. "When you are protecting your religion and your people, you are not a terrorist," he said.

"Mr Jaraf, you have to realise that if you continue to talk like this, there's no way you or your family will be allowed to live in England."

Jaraf clasped his hands together and leaned towards him. "Sir, please do not misunderstand me. That part of my life is over. Finished. Done. I just want to live in peace with my wife and son." He forced a smile. "I used to be an electrician. I will be an electrician again. I am told that electricians can earn £100 an hour in England. So that is what I will do. I will help people as an electrician."

Shepherd smiled. "You should think about plumbing," he said. "Plumbers earn even more."

Jaraf nodded enthusiastically. "I can try that, I can try to be a plumber."

Shepherd sat back as he studied the man's face. He seemed genuine enough, but then he had had plenty of time to rehearse his story. "I'm guessing you weren't an electrician for ISIS?"

"No. Of course not."

"So what did you do for them?"

"I made drones. I made drones and I taught others how to make drones."

"What sort of drones?"

Jaraf shrugged. "Many sorts. Big ones, small ones. Whatever was needed."

"So they were weapons?"

"Some were weapons. Some were for surveillance."

"Horses for courses," said Shepherd.

Jaraf frowned, not getting the reference. "I do not understand," he said.

"You made drones for whatever was necessary."

Jaraf nodded. "Yes."

"So the weapons ones, how did they work?"

"We took drones and adapted them. Most of them were made in China. I was able to add explosives and detonators. And poison."

"Poison?" repeated Shepherd.

"Botulism. Anthrax. Ricin." Jaraf shrugged. "Anything we can get."

"You used these in Syria?"

"Often. They were cheap and fighters were not put at risk."

"How did you detonate them?"

"Different ways," said Jaraf. "By radio. By phone. By altitude. By GPS." He smiled. "Horses for courses."

"How much explosive could a drone carry?"

"That would depend on the model. Some of the larger drones could carry as much as a kilo. It affects the running time, obviously, as there is a drain on the battery. Also, you wouldn't just use explosive, you would need shrapnel, so you would wrap metal around it. Nails or barbed wire is good. Obviously poison is a much smaller payload."

"And these were your designs?"

Jaraf nodded again. "I made them, yes."

"And so they would function as hand grenades?"

"Yes. Exactly."

"So why not just adapt a drone to carry a hand grenade?"

"We tried that. The weight is not a problem but we couldn't design a mechanism to pull the pin out. We tried removing the pin and using a mechanism to release the handle but our ideas were clumsy and we had several accidents. Purpose-built IEDs are better."

"And these designs, you taught them to others?"

"Once my superiors saw how effective they were, they had me pass on my knowledge to others, yes."

"Including foreign fighters?"

"I already told your colleague, I have taught fighters from England and Germany and Sweden."

"And these fighters have returned home?"

"Some have, some are still training, some have taken up arms in Syria."

"Okay, Mr Jaraf. Now here's the thing. We are going to need a sign of good faith from you. You need to show us that you are serious about putting your past behind you. And the best way to do that is to give us the details of someone who you trained who is now back in the UK. Then we can check on them and that will confirm your story."

"I understand," said Jaraf.

Shepherd waited for a few seconds, until it was clear that no name was forthcoming. "I need that information now. I need at least one name before we can take this any further."

"I understand," said Jaraf. "You can look for a man called Qasim. Siddhartha Qasim. His friends call him

Sid. He was from London. I trained him last year and he went back to London three months ago."

Shepherd held up his hand. "Let me stop you there, Mr Jaraf," he said. "Siddhartha Qasim is dead. He and one of his friends tried to fly a drone across Heathrow Airport and they died while fleeing from the police."

Jaraf frowned. "Dead?"

Shepherd nodded. "Very much so. Their car hit a truck. He was killed instantly. So was the man he was with."

"But you can see I am telling the truth. I gave you a name."

Shepherd smiled, "Yes, you did. But he's dead. And my boss might well say that the reason you gave me Qasim's name was because you knew he was dead." He shrugged. "I have a very suspicious boss."

"It is not my fault that Qasim died. You asked for a name. I gave you a name."

"Yes, you did. But I need a name that I can check. The name of somebody who is still a threat to our country. I'm sure you can understand that."

Jaraf sighed. "Very well," he said. "There was a man called Ali, he went back to Birmingham." He frowned. "I don't remember his family name. Just Ali."

"Describe this Ali for me."

"He was twenty-five. Twenty-six maybe. He said that his father was a postman. Ali also worked for the Post Office for about a year. He liked cricket. He was always trying to listen to the cricket on the radio even though he knew he would get into trouble."

"What does he look like?"

"His eyes are small and his nose is big. His eyebrows are so wide they almost meet in the middle. The skin on his right hand was scarred. His mother spilled boiling water on him when he was a child."

"Are you sure you don't recall his family name?"

Jaraf bit down on his lower lip as he tried to remember the name, then he smiled. "Karim. Ali Karim. With that name, how could I have forgotten?"

"I don't follow you?"

"Al-Karim is one of the ninety-nine names of Allah. It means 'The Most Generous'. This man's name was Ali Karim."

"And when did Ali return to England?"

"About three months ago."

Shepherd smiled. "Excellent. Thank you."

"So when can you bring my family over?"

"As soon as I've checked out what you told me," said Shepherd.

Jaraf shook his head vigorously. "No, no, my family must be brought to England now. I must see my family."

"You will, Mr Jaraf. I understand your concern. But you have to understand our concern, too. We don't know you, we don't know who you are or if you are who you say you are. We have to check your story —"

"It's not a story," interrupted Jaraf. "It's the truth. I am not making up a story for you."

Shepherd held up his hands to calm him down. "That's not what I meant. I meant we have to check out what you've told us. We have to be sure that you are telling us the truth."

There was a knock at the door. Shepherd looked over at the cop, frowning. "Are we expecting anyone else?"

"It'll be room service," said the Border Force guy. The man gestured at Jaraf. "He was hungry."

Shepherd looked at Jaraf. "I have not eaten for a long time," he said. "They only fed us once on the plane and it wasn't good."

Shepherd nodded and waved for Aspinall to open the door. A pretty brunette was holding a tray. Aspinall took it from her. She had a leather wallet tucked into the waistband of her trousers and she held it out, taking a pen from behind her ear. Aspinall gave the tray to the Border Force officer and looked at Shepherd. "You'll have to sign for this," he said.

"What?" said Shepherd.

"He's your guy now so you'll be picking up the bill, right?" said the detective. "I can't sign for it because I won't be reimbursed."

"Me too," said Wainer, putting the tray down on the coffee table in front of Jaraf. There was a plate covered with a stainless steel dome and a glass of orange juice.

Shepherd sighed and stood up. He took the folder, opened it and signed the bill using the Paul Easton alias. He gave the folder and the pen to the waitress and she flashed him a beaming smile and headed down the corridor.

As Shepherd closed the door and went to sit down, Jaraf lifted the lid on the plate. He frowned when he saw the burger and chips. "What is this?" he asked.

"Chicken," said Wainer. "You said you wanted the chicken."

74

Jaraf picked up the top of the bun and peered at the burger. "This is not chicken."

"It's a chicken burger. It's all they had."

Jaraf looked up. "Is it halal?"

"Is it halal? I guess so."

"Guessing so is not good enough," said Jaraf, replacing the bun. "If it is not halal, I cannot eat it."

"So what do you want me to do about it?" asked Wainer. He folded his arms. "It's a chicken burger. Why does it matter what sort of chicken it is?"

Jaraf opened his mouth to argue but Shepherd cut him short. "Just phone room service and ask if the chicken burger is halal," he said. "If it isn't, we can order something else. I wouldn't mind a coffee, anyway."

Wainer muttered under his breath and went over to the phone. He dialled room service, but after a while it became clear that no one was answering.

"I'm sorry," Shepherd said to Jaraf. "We'll get this sorted."

The detective picked up the room service menu from the bedside table and handed it to Jaraf.

Wainer put down the phone. "They're not answering," he said. He waved at the tray. "If he's not going to eat that, anyone mind if I have it? I haven't eaten since lunch."

"Go ahead," said Shepherd.

Wainer bent down, picked up the tray and took it over to the bed. He sat down with a grunt.

"I can eat the omelette," Jaraf said. "And maybe some fruit."

"I'll arrange that," Shepherd said. He went over to the phone and called room service again. After several rings, no one had answered. Shepherd looked at his watch, wondering if perhaps they'd closed for the night. Wainer picked up the burger with both hands and bit into it, a look of contentment on his face.

Shepherd was just about to hang up when Wainer began to cough. Shepherd turned to look at him. The burger had fallen from his hands and had tumbled over the bed, splattering over the floor. Shepherd replaced the receiver and dashed over to the bed. Wainer was still sitting up but he was in a bad state — bloody froth was oozing from between his lips and his eyes had turned up in his head.

"He's choking!" shouted Aspinall. "You have to do the Heimlich manoeuvre or something."

"No, it's not that," said Shepherd.

Wainer fell back onto the bed and his whole body went into spasm.

"What the fuck's happening?" shouted the detective.

Jaraf had jumped to his feet and was backing away slowly, his mouth wide open.

Shepherd bent over Wainer. His heels were drumming against the bedspread and blood was now running out of his nose. He was breathing in short, sharp gasps and with each movement more bloody foam spewed from between his lips.

"He's been poisoned," Shepherd said. He pointed at the remains of the chicken burger on the floor. "Don't touch that. Wait here and don't let anyone in until I get back."

The detective pointed at the man on the bed, who was still in spasm. "What about him?"

"There's nothing you can do for him," said Shepherd and he hurried over to the door. "Call an ambulance. But no cops. We don't want the place crawling with police." He dashed out into the corridor. The girl had been heading towards the lift but there were emergency stairs to his left. He threw open the door and ran down the concrete steps, his mind racing. Who would want to kill Jaraf? And how had they found him? He'd only been in the country for a few hours.

He reached the ground floor and banged the metal rod to open the door. It opened into the hotel's car park. The reception was to his left and he headed that way. He slowed to pass through the revolving door and he ran over to the desk. There were two receptionists, a middle-aged man and a young woman, wearing matching dark blue blazers, and they were both clearly startled by his appearance. "Did a dark-haired woman come out of the lift?" he asked. "Dressed like she worked for room service. She had black trainers and had a gold watch on her left wrist. Hair about shoulder length. Red nail varnish. Red lipstick."

The two receptionists looked at him blankly and he knew there was no point in throwing more descriptions at them. "A girl," he said. "She probably came out of the lift and went straight outside."

The man nodded. "Yes, maybe, I think so. A minute or so ago. She was in a hurry."

"Was she an employee or a guest?"

"She doesn't work here, I know that much," said the man, but Shepherd had already turned and was running back to the revolving door. He burst outside and looked left and right. There were a young couple walking away but the girl was blonde and wearing high heels. Two businessmen in suits were walking towards the car park, carrying briefcases. He doubted that the girl was working alone or that she'd be using public transport, which meant that she would head either towards the underground car park, or the one outside. He scanned the outdoor car park but other than the two businessmen he didn't see anyone heading towards a vehicle.

He turned towards the entrance to the underground car park, but as he did he heard the squeal of tyres and a black Toyota Camry hurtled out. He only caught a glimpse of the driver — a man in his mid-twenties, dark curly hair, tanned skin — but he got a good look at the dark-haired woman in the front seat as the car roared past him. There were three black cabs lined up outside reception and he ran over and climbed in the back of the first one. "Follow that car, will you?" asked Shepherd. "The black Toyota."

The driver twisted around in his seat. He was in his fifties, his head shaved with a pair of sunglasses pushed back onto his scalp. "We don't do that sort of thing, Guv," he said. "It's not like the movies."

"I'll pay you double the fare," said Shepherd. "Just keep them in sight while I make a call." He took out his phone.

"You a cop?" asked the driver.

78

"No," said Shepherd. He gestured at the Camry, which was turning onto the road, heading east. "Please, just drive."

The driver put the cab in gear and drove towards the road. Shepherd called Pritchard and cupped his hand over his mouth as he explained what had happened.

"And you're in pursuit?"

"I wouldn't call it that, but I can see the car in the distance. Black Toyota Camry." He had only caught a glimpse of the registration plate but it was enough, and he relayed the number to Pritchard.

"Do you think they're armed?" asked Pritchard.

"I've no way of knowing," said Shepherd. The cab turned onto the main road. The Toyota was still in view, just about. He leaned forward and tapped on the window behind the driver's head. "Fast as you can please, mate."

The driver twisted around. "I can't go over the speed limit, there's cameras all over the place."

"Just don't lose them," said Shepherd.

"Guv, I hear what you're saying but I'm not going to lose my licence just because you wanna play at being James Bond."

"Please, just do your best," said Shepherd. He put the phone back to his ear. "I don't think we're going to catch up with them, but I just about have eyeball," he told Pritchard.

"I'm getting the registration number checked as we speak and we're talking to the Met about mobilising Trojan units." The callsign Trojan was given to the Met's armed response vehicles — usually BMW X5s with three armed officers on board, equipped with Glock 17s, Tasers and SIG MCX carbines. There were up to two dozen ARVs prowling the capital's streets, day and night.

The traffic ahead of them was moving slowly and Shepherd cursed under his breath. Even if the taxi driver had wanted to go faster, there was nothing he could do. As if reading his mind, the driver twisted around in his seat. "Sorry, Guv, looks like we're fucked."

Shepherd settled back in his seat. He peered up through the window, hoping to see a helicopter overhead, but other than a British Airways jet descending towards Heathrow, the sky was clear. "What's happening?" asked Pritchard.

"I don't think we're going to be able to catch up with them, the traffic's bad," said Shepherd. "We'll keep after them while we have them in sight, but once they've gone I might as well head back to the hotel."

"Give me a description of the occupants of the car."

Shepherd described them as best as he could.

"Do you think you could recognise them from photographs?" asked Pritchard.

"The girl, definitely. The guy who was driving, maybe."

"Ok. What was the asylum seeker like?"

"Yeah, he seems kosher. He's given me a name I can check but everything he said made sense."

"He obviously can't stay at the hotel," said Pritchard. "I'll get a safe house fixed up."

"You're going to need minders, after this. Whoever it was, they might try again."

"Understood," said Pritchard.

"I can't see them, Guv," said the driver, twisting around in his seat.

Shepherd leaned forward and peered through the windscreen. There was a bend in the road ahead and the traffic was still heavy. "Where's the next turn off?" asked Shepherd.

"A mile or so ahead. But we won't see if they take it or not."

Shepherd sat back in his seat and put the phone to his ear again. "I think we've as good as lost them," he said to Pritchard. "The best we can do is to continue into London, but we won't catch them and we won't see them if they turn off. How are we doing with the ARVs?"

"There have been two stabbings, one north of the river and one south, and reports of shots fired in Brixton, so SCO19 is stretched. But there are patrol cars en route."

"What about a chopper?"

"No can do, I'm afraid," said Pritchard. "It was very short notice and one of their helicopters is down for maintenance."

Shepherd knew there was no point in showing impatience. Pritchard was right. There was no way they could expect the Met to come up with specialist resources at the drop of a hat.

"The car is a rental, I can tell you that much," said Pritchard.

"That's not good news. If they're pros, they won't be traceable."

The driver turned back again. "No sign of them, Guv. This is turning into a fool's errand. I don't want you throwing your money away."

"It's on expenses," said Shepherd. "But yeah, you're right. Take the next turn off and drive me back to the hotel."

The black cab dropped Shepherd outside the hotel. He paid double the fare that was showing, and the driver scribbled out a receipt. There was an ambulance parked on the other side of the entrance, its rear door open.

"Do you want me to wait for you?" asked the driver.

"Nah, I'm good," said Shepherd. He hurried into the reception area and took the lift up to the fifth floor. The room to the door was ajar and he pushed it wide open. A female paramedic was leaning over the body and her male colleague was standing behind her, holding a defibrillator. Aspinall came over to Shepherd as he closed the door. "Any joy?"

"She drove off with an accomplice. I've called it in. Where's Jaraf?"

"I told him to sit in the bathroom until we get this sorted. He's spooked."

"Hardly surprising," said Shepherd. "That burger was meant for him."

"The night manager came up with the paramedics. A Miss Campbell. I showed her my warrant card and said we'd handle everything but she's clearly not happy."

"I've got to talk to her anyway so I'll get her onside," said Shepherd. "I'm pretty sure my boss will talk to your boss and we'll be keeping this under wraps for a while."

"There's a doctor on the way and there'll be a post-mortem."

"Sure, but make sure nothing gets in the papers."

"I'll do my best," said the detective.

Shepherd went over to the paramedics. The one standing over the body straightened up and rubbed the back of her neck. "Never seen anything like this before," she said. She had an Australian accent, possibly New Zealand. "It's not a heart attack or a stroke."

"It was a fast-acting poison," said Shepherd. He pointed at the remains of the burger on the floor. "He took a couple of bites and it was all over." The male paramedic backed away from the burger as if he feared it would attack him. He was in his forties and had a tattoo of a dagger on his forearm, with the words "ROYAL MARINE" above it and "COMMANDO" below it.

"We're going to need the body transported to the coroner's mortuary once the doctor has confirmed death," said Shepherd.

"Not a problem," said the female paramedic.

"When SOCO get here, make sure they bag the food. We'll need to know what the poison was, obviously. But they'll need a lab for that."

"So what's the story?" asked the male paramedic, who had been openly listening to them. "Russians? They use poison, don't they?"

"No way of knowing," said Shepherd.

"The Russians used some radioactive stuff when they poisoned that couple in Salisbury," he said. "Do you think we need to get checked out?"

Shepherd shook his head. "I'd guess that, unless you ate any of the burger, you'll be okay." He gestured at Aspinall. "Gerry and I were here when Ricky bit into the burger and we're both fine. And Ricky died very quickly, so the fact that we're all okay suggests that we haven't come into contact with whatever it was. How do you feel?"

The man shrugged. "I feel okay, I guess."

"Better safe than sorry, obviously. Get yourself checked out as soon as you're back at the hospital."

The paramedic forced a smile but he didn't look convinced. His colleague looked less uneasy. "We haven't come into contact with any body fluids, Dave," she said to him. "And the victim was eating when he died, so it doesn't look as if it's airborne. I think we're good."

Shepherd went over to the bathroom door and knocked. "Mr Jaraf? It's Paul Easton from the Home Office. Could I have a word with you, please?"

The door opened a few inches and Jaraf peered through the gap. "Is everything okay?" he asked nervously.

"Let me in, please, Mr Jaraf. I need to talk to you."

Jaraf moved away from the door and Shepherd pushed it open. As Shepherd closed the door, Jaraf sat on the toilet and put his head in his hands. Shepherd patted him on the shoulder. "Just try to stay calm," he said. "I know how upsetting this must be."

"That was my food," said Jaraf. "That should have been me dead out there."

The bathroom was cramped — in fact there was no bath, just a shower cubicle, a washbasin and the toilet. Shepherd went over to the shower and folded his arms as he stood with his back to it.

Jaraf continued to stare at the tiled floor. "You must get my family out of Turkey now," he said quietly.

"As soon as we've confirmed that your information is good," said Shepherd.

Jaraf lifted his head and looked up at him with tear-filled eyes. "Their lives are in danger. If they tried to kill me they might try to kill my family."

"Who do you think tried to kill you?" asked Shepherd.

"I don't know." Jaraf shrugged. "How could I know?"

"Who knows you came to England? Who did you tell?"

"I didn't tell anyone," said Jaraf. "I got on the plane to Dubai. Then I got on a plane to London."

"You must have told someone," said Shepherd. "Bringing you here wasn't planned. Normally someone like you would be held at the airport and then taken to a police station for processing. But because of what you told the officers, you were brought here. So you must have been followed to the hotel, and that means they must have known you were at the airport."

"Maybe they saw me there."

"Saw you where?"

"In the line at immigration. It was a very long line. There were hundreds of people in front and ahead of me."

"And you think one of them recognised you?" Shepherd wrinkled his nose. It was possible. Anything was possible. But the odds of Jaraf being in the immigration queue with someone who knew who he was were long in the extreme. Whoever had put the poison in the burger were professionals, there was no doubt about that. And professionals tended not to rely on coincidences.

"Perhaps," said Jaraf. "I don't know. But I do know that my family is in danger and I want them here, now. You can do that for me, can't you?"

"Mr Jaraf, if what you have told me about Ali Karim is true, I will personally fly over to Turkey to collect your wife and son."

"Why can't you go now?"

"Because I have a boss breathing down my neck for proof, and until he has that proof he's not going to let me bring your family here. You can see his point of view, right? People will say and do anything to get asylum. We have to check."

"Okay, okay, I understand," he said. "But please, do not waste any time."

"I just have to talk to the manager of the hotel, and then we'll move you to somewhere more secure. Okay?"

Jaraf nodded, but didn't appear convinced.

"Mr Jaraf, it might help things along if you could give me at least one other name of someone you trained with. The more information you give us that can be

86

checked and confirmed, the more I can show how valuable you are, and the sooner we will be able to bring in your family."

Jaraf stared down at the prayer beads. Shepherd couldn't tell if the man was deep in thought or ignoring what he'd said, but he just sat and allowed the silence to continue. Eventually Jaraf looked up. "There were two men I met who kept talking about travelling to England to kill your former prime minister, Tony Blair. They were Iraqis, and they were children when the Americans invaded their country. They blamed Blair for helping the Americans and sending British troops to Iraq, and they wanted revenge. The camp leaders wanted them to return to Baghdad but they kept insisting that they wanted to go to London." Jaraf smiled thinly. "They were crazy. They spoke only broken English and they were Iraqis; there was no way they could get to England. But one night they left the camp." He shrugged. "I think they might have tried to get to England on their own. They were always talking to the British jihadists, asking them about London."

"What are their names?" asked Shepherd.

"Tariq Al-Majid and Naseer Salim. They are young. In their twenties. Full of the fire of youth."

"Do you know the names of all the men you trained?"

Jaraf shook his head. "That's why I had to think when you asked me," he said. "I was an instructor, not their friend. The instructors ate and slept with the imams, the jihadists ate and bunked together. The jihadists were in groups and we taught them in their groups. So I got to know some of their names, but not all."

"How exactly were they grouped?"

"Usually by country. So the British jihadists trained and studied together, as did the Belgians, the Swedes and the Somalians."

"How many British jihadists did you train?"

"In total?"

Shepherd nodded. "In total."

Jaraf fingered his prayer beads and frowned in concentration. "At least thirty," he said. His frown deepened, and then he nodded. "Thirty-two, I think."

"And they were all trained in the use of drones?"

"Drones. Explosives. IEDs. Hand-to-hand combat. Firearms. Grenades. The training they received was very thorough."

"And how many of those thirty-two British jihadists have returned to the UK?" asked Shepherd.

Jaraf shrugged. "Most of them. Maybe all of them by now."

"If I showed you photographs, do you think you could pick them out?"

"Of course. But first you must get my family out of Turkey."

Shepherd patted him on the shoulder. "I'll do what I can. In the meantime, I'm going to arrange to get somewhere safer for you to stay." He looked around the cramped bathroom. "I know this isn't pleasant for you, but do you mind staying in here for a while longer?"

"I am okay here," said Jaraf.

"Good man," said Shepherd. He opened the bathroom door and slipped out. "I've got to see the night manager and make a call," he said to Aspinall. "Don't open the door unless you know who's out there."

"The doctor's on his way."

"Get whoever comes to show you ID before you let them in, and confirm with their surgery or hospital that they are who they say they are."

"You think they'll try again?" asked the detective.

"I don't know, I just want you to be extra vigilant." He nodded encouragingly and Aspinall forced a smile. "You guys okay?" Shepherd asked the paramedics. They both answered in the affirmative but the male paramedic was clearly still worried. "I won't be long," Shepherd said, and let himself out after checking that the corridor was clear.

Shepherd took the lift down to reception and phoned Giles Pritchard. He brought his boss up to speed. "Jaraf has given me three names," said Shepherd. "One is British-born, Ali Karim. According to Jaraf, he returned to the UK three months ago. The other two names are Iraqis, Tariq Al-Majid and Naseer Salim. Jaraf says they talked about coming to England to kill Tony Blair. All three have been trained on drone attacks. He also gave me the name of Siddhartha Qasim, which was interesting."

"Remind me, will you? Not all of us have an eidetic memory."

"Qasim was flying a drone over Heathrow a while back. The drone was tracked and blocked. An ARV and a helicopter were sent out, and Qasim and a guy called Mohammed Harawi made a run for it. Harawi was driving and smashed into a truck. There wasn't much of them left. Their homes were searched and there was lots of ISIS stuff and material that suggested they were planning to adapt drones to carry explosives. But we didn't find their passports and there was no evidence of them having left the country. They'd both been visiting a lot of ISIS tutorial sites, so we figured that's where they'd picked up their knowledge. But Jaraf says Qasim was over in Syria at his training camp."

"But Qasim's name was made public at the time, right?"

Shepherd nodded. "Fair point, yes — Jaraf could have gotten the name from the papers."

"And these Iraqis he talked about, how did they get into the UK?"

"He doesn't know for sure that they're here," said Shepherd. "His bosses wanted them to take the fight back to Baghdad, but they apparently went rogue."

"What about descriptions?"

"Not much on the Iraqis, but he told me a fair bit about Karim. He's twenty-five or twenty-six, from Birmingham and Jaraf says he went back there. His father was a postman and according to Jaraf, Karim also had a job with the Post Office. Physically, small eyes and a large nose, big eyebrows that almost meet, and the skin on his right hand is scarred from a scalding when he was a kid."

"I'll get them checked out," said Pritchard. "How cooperative is he being?"

"He's up for looking at pictures and telling us who he saw at the camp, but as he says there wasn't too much chit-chat going on so he'll be light on details and mainly only knows first names. I think he realises that the more he can give us, the better a deal he'll get. He says that he dealt with more than thirty British jihadists, and most of them are now back in the UK. But it's clear that he doesn't want to give us everything before his family are out. How do you want to play it?"

"We'll have a better idea of where we stand once I've checked the names you've given me," said Pritchard. "But in the meantime, we need to take him under our wing. Unfortunately there's been an issue with our London safe houses and we're in the process of setting up a new network of properties."

"I wouldn't recommend leaving him where he is, and I'm not sure that moving him to another hotel is a good idea. Too many people around, too many transients."

"I hear what you're saying, which is why I have something I'd like to run by you. As I said, there's an issue with our safe houses in London, but we could move him to a property in another city. It occurred to me that your Hereford house isn't being used, right?"

"It's on the market," said Shepherd.

"Exactly. And the market is pretty much stagnant at the moment. Is there any reason that we couldn't keep Jaraf there while we check out his information? It's only a three-hour drive and I'd be much happier getting him out of London anyway. And our friend Major Gannon might be able to supply local manpower, protection-wise."

"The Regiment is stretched at the moment," said Shepherd. "They're short-handed and finding it difficult to get enough bodies through Selection. I'm not sure he'd have anyone spare."

"If that's the case then I'm sure he can draft in former Regiment members who are now in the private sector. I have a budget I can dip into. Four men providing twenty-four-hour cover. What do you think?"

Shepherd wasn't happy at the prospect of using his own home to hide a terrorist — albeit a former one — but it meant that he would be on familiar territory and strangers would stick out. "And that budget would cover rent as well, would it?"

Pritchard chuckled. "I don't see why not," he said.

"A couple of hundred quid a night?"

"You drive a hard bargain," said Pritchard.

"Okay, I'll drive him there once I've had a look at the hotel's CCTV."

"Shall I talk to the Major?"

"Probably best, so you can sort out the financial arrangements. He knows where the house is and he has a spare key."

"Call me after you've checked the CCTV footage," said Pritchard. "Hopefully it'll give us a better idea of who's trying to kill Jaraf. And you're okay driving this time of night? I know you've had a long day."

"I'm good," said Shepherd. He ended the call and walked over to reception. The male receptionist had gone, leaving the young woman to man the desk. She was dealing with a businessman who was claiming not to have watched the porn movie that he'd been charged for. The receptionist patiently explained that there had been no mistake and that the movie had definitely been requested, though apparently the man had only watched the first forty minutes. They argued back and forth for several minutes but the receptionist refused to give way and eventually the man stormed off, threatening to email the chain's chief executive.

The receptionist turned to glare at Shepherd, the adrenaline still coursing through her system, giving her cheeks a healthy glow and probably pushing her pulse rate into three figures. She was quite young, early twenties maybe, with blonde hair that brushed the shoulders of her blazer, and she jutted her chin up as she waited for him to speak, clearly anticipating another argument. He smiled, hoping to put her at ease. "Hi," he said. "Can I speak to the night manager? Miss Campbell?"

Her chin jutted up even more. "Can I tell her what it's about?"

"I think she's expecting me. My name is Paul Easton. It's about what happened on the fifth floor."

The woman's smile tightened a little, and she picked up the phone and called the manager. In less than two minutes a tall brunette in a black suit opened a door to his right and strode over to him, her high heels clicking on the marble floor. Her title was on a badge on the breast pocket of her jacket, along with her name: "LYDIA". Shepherd offered his hand and introduced himself. He said that he was with the police, which was almost the truth. She shook his hand and flashed him a professional smile. "Do you have any idea when the room will be ready?" she asked.

"It shouldn't be too long," he said. Two men in matching dark blue suits walked past them, heading for the reception desk. "Perhaps we could have a chat in your office," he said. "And at some point I'd like a look at your CCTV."

"We can kill two birds with one stone," she said. She gestured at the door she'd appeared through and took him over. It led to a long narrow room, with a desk close to the door and a bank of CCTV screens at the far end. She closed the door and went over to the screens. There were two high-backed black leather executive chairs facing them, and she dropped down onto the one on the left. Shepherd took the other chair.

"To answer your question, a doctor has been called, and once he's confirmed the death we'll have the body removed and you can have the room back," said Shepherd. "I know it's late at night but they tend to come out pretty quickly in these cases."

"What about SOCO? SOCO always come out when there's an unexpected death, don't they?" She smiled when she saw the look of surprise on his face. "We have several deaths a year here. Most hotels do."

"Night-time calls can be a problem, but they will come and they won't be here long," said Shepherd.

"So it was a suicide?" She sighed. "It's always either suicide, heart attack or stroke."

"No, it wasn't suicide, but all SOCO will do is remove the room service meal that we believe caused the death."

Miss Campbell's eyes widened. "He was poisoned? Is that what happened?"

"I'm afraid so, yes."

"By hotel food?" She grimaced. "Well that's it then, we'll have to close the kitchen and there'll be a health and safety inspection. I am so screwed."

Shepherd held up his hands. "Don't get ahead of yourself, Miss Campbell," he said. "I'm pretty certain that whatever it was that killed him was added to the food after it left the kitchen and before it got to the room. Which is why I want to look at the CCTV, starting with the corridor outside the room."

The phone on the manager's desk rang. "I'll have to get that," she said, and hurried over. Shepherd looked at the bank of screens. There were twelve in all, showing views of various corridors and the insides of the three lifts. Above the twelve small screens was a much larger one showing a view of the reception desk. A man in a raincoat was checking in, a briefcase at his feet. In front of the screens was a console with numbered keys and next to it was a laminated list of numbers and locations. There were forty-eight numbers, which Shepherd assumed corresponded to individual cameras. The manager ended the call and Shepherd turned to look at her. She was frowning and massaging the back of her neck. "Guests are complaining that no one is answering the room service phone," she said. She dialled a number and held the receiver to her ear. "Hotel policy is to answer within six rings," she said. Her frown deepened and she replaced the receiver. "That's not good," she said.

Shepherd was already on his feet. "Can you show me the kitchen?"

She nodded and opened the door. Shepherd followed her out. She took him through reception and then turned right to the hotel's restaurant-cum-coffee shop. There was a sign stating that the restaurant was closed and that it would reopen at 7 a.m.

"You're normally shut at this time?" asked Shepherd.

The manager nodded. "We stop taking orders at nine-thirty, but room service is available until midnight."

She pushed open a pair of double doors and they walked into a small kitchen. There was a gas oven with four burners next to a stainless steel table to the right, a large metal table in the middle of the room, and a walk-in fridge to the left. There was a frying pan on one of the burners and a bag of burger buns on the table, along with a breadboard and a large stainless steel bowl of salad.

"Who should be on duty?" asked Shepherd.

"The night cook. He handles room service orders."

"Who takes them up to the room?"

"There's a housekeeper on duty throughout the night and she'll usually take the orders up." She went over to the walk-in fridge and pulled it open. She gasped and took a step back. Shepherd hurried over. There were two bodies on the floor of the fridge, bound and gagged and lying face down. One was a man wearing chef whites, the other was a girl who had been stripped down to her underwear. He felt for a pulse in the girl's neck, but when he touched her she flinched, so he pulled back his hand and touched the man's neck. He too shifted on the floor. "It's okay," he said. "They're alive."

"Thank God for that," said the manager.

"Can you pass me a knife?"

The manager hurried over to the metal counter and pulled a knife from a wooden block. Shepherd used it to cut the duct tape that had been wound around the girl's mouth, and she began to cough and splutter. "Take it easy," he said. "Just lie still while I cut you loose." He cut the duct tape that was binding her wrists, and then freed her feet. He helped her up and she staggered out and fell into the arms of the manager.

Shepherd cut the gag away from the chef's face and then freed his arms and legs. "Fucking bastards jumped me," said the chef as he got up. "Who the fuck robs a kitchen?" He was Scottish, short and stocky with a crew cut. He put his hand up to his head and it came away glistening with blood.

"You should get a scan, check that there's no internal damage," said Shepherd.

"I've got a thick skull," growled the chef.

"He's right, Ronnie," said the manager, still holding the girl. "I'll get someone to run you to the hospital." She looked at the girl. "What about you, Lisa, did they hurt you?"

The girl shook her head. "They just grabbed me and tied me up."

"How many of them were there?" asked Shepherd.

"I didn't see them," said the girl. "They grabbed me from behind."

"They hit me from behind, too," said the chef, touching his scalp again. "Bastards."

"And neither of you got a look at them?"

"It all happened so quickly," said the girl.

The chef took a jacket from a hook on the wall and wrapped it around the girl.

"You were wearing your uniform — black skirt and a white shirt?" asked Shepherd.

The girl nodded. The girl who had delivered the burger to the room must have taken her uniform. And either she or one of her accomplices had cooked the burger.

"How do we handle this?" asked the manager.

"They can go home," said Shepherd. "The police can talk to them later." He looked at the chef. "You should go to hospital and get checked out."

"What about the paramedics?" asked the manager. "Couldn't they take him in the ambulance?"

"They have to transport the body to the mortuary," said Shepherd.

"What body?" asked the chef.

"It doesn't matter," said Shepherd. "What matters is that you get to hospital for a scan."

"I can drive myself," said the chef.

"Are you sure?" asked the manager.

"I'm fine. I can drive." He nodded at the girl. "I can drop Lisa home on the way."

98

The manager frowned. "I'd be happier if someone drove you. Come with me and I'll fix something up."

"What happened?" asked Lisa. "Why did they take my uniform?"

"I'll explain everything tomorrow," said the manager. "At the moment I have to help the police. But the important thing is that you and Ronnie are okay." She hugged Lisa.

"You can wait in the office for me," the manager said to Shepherd. "It won't take long."

"Of course," said Shepherd. They left the kitchen and while the manager took the two employees to reception, Shepherd walked back to her office and sat down in front of the monitors. He wasn't familiar with the system but it was similar to others that he'd used so it didn't take him long to work out how to view historical footage. By the time the manager returned, he had the view of the corridor outside Jaraf's room on the main screen and was watching the woman carrying the tray with the poisoned burger. The camera was at the far end of the corridor, near to where the lifts were, and all he saw was her back as she walked to the room. She kept her back to the camera as she knocked on the door and handed the tray to Aspinall, and didn't move until Shepherd handed her the folder with the signed bill. As the door closed she turned away and walked back towards the elevators, keeping her head down so that her hair hung over her face. She was deliberately avoiding the camera.

The door opened and the manager joined him. "So that's the girl who took Lisa's uniform?" she said as she saw what he was looking at.

Shepherd nodded. "She's clearly aware of the cameras."

"Do you have any in the lifts?" he asked.

"Sure," she said, and reached across for the mouse, before scrolling through the timeline until she found the woman in the lift. She had her back to the camera.

"She knows what she's doing, all right," said Shepherd. "Is there a camera in the kitchen?"

"No," she said. "That was considered too Big Brother-ish. The cameras are confined to the public areas. But she would have walked through reception to get to the lifts." She clicked the mouse again and went back through the timeline so that they could watch the woman walk through reception carrying the tray. Again she kept her face away from the camera. The manager clicked through to another camera but the view from that was no better. And she kept her face away from the camera covering the area in front of the lifts.

"That's the best I can do," said the manager.

"What about later, after she went back downstairs? Can you show me the footage of her getting into the lift, going through reception and into the car park?"

"Of course," she said. She played the footage on the main screen. In the lift and in reception, the woman hid her face. And she did the same as she walked through the car park and climbed into the passenger seat of the Toyota Camry. The driver and the woman kept their heads down as they drove out of the car park.

"What about of them arriving?" asked Shepherd.

She clicked on the footage from the camera at the entrance to the car park and played it in reverse at fast speed until she found the Toyota. Then she played it at regular speed. Again both the driver and the passenger had their heads turned away.

"That's not a coincidence, is it?" asked the manager.

"They're professionals," said Shepherd.

The manager clicked to stop the footage but he asked her to keep it running. He watched the next two dozen vehicles drive into the car park, then told her she could stop. He sat back in his chair and clasped his hands behind his neck as he stared at the screen. The time and date was at the bottom. The Toyota had arrived at just after eight-thirty. That must have been close to the time that Jaraf had been brought to the hotel, which suggested that they had followed him from the airport. The couple had avoided the CCTV cameras but he had got a good look at the girl when he'd handed her the bill and she definitely wasn't Asian. He was fairly sure that the guy driving the Toyota Camry wasn't Asian, either, and that didn't make sense if it was ISIS who was behind the attempt on Jaraf's life.

A figure appeared on the screen showing the live view from the camera covering the corridor outside Jaraf's room. It was a woman carrying a medical bag. She stopped outside the door and knocked, and a few seconds later disappeared inside. "Looks like the doc's here," said Shepherd. "I'll go up and talk to her."

Shepherd knocked on the door and stood back so that Aspinall could check him out through the security viewer. The door opened and Aspinall stood to the side to allow him in. The two paramedics were standing close to the bathroom door. The doctor was standing by the bed, scribbling on a pad. "This is Doctor Kawczynski," he said.

The doctor nodded at Shepherd. "Paul Easton, I'm with the Home Office," he said. "I'm sorry about the late hour. The coroner's office has already been informed and the paramedics here will take the body to Westminster Public Mortuary."

"Most of my work happens at night," said the doctor, "so no need to apologise for the late call. To be honest, peak time for me is between three and five. Anyway a post-mortem is definitely called for. I've no problem with issuing the death certificate, obviously. But I've never seen a poison act like this before. It'll be down to the coroner to identify it." She tore off a sheet of paper and held it out. Aspinall took it. "Were you here when it happened?" she asked Shepherd.

Shepherd nodded. "He took a bite from the burger and he was dead within seconds."

"Well it clearly wasn't common-or-garden food poisoning," said the doctor. She put her pad in her bag and nodded curtly. "I'll be off," she said.

Aspinall thanked her and let her out.

Shepherd nodded at the paramedics. "Right, you guys are free to take the body now," he said.

"I'll go and get the gurney," said the female paramedic. Her colleague began unrolling a black body bag. "What time did you guys get here?" Shepherd asked Aspinall as the paramedic headed out.

"About half past eight," said the detective.

"And you drove straight from the airport?"

Aspinall nodded. "Sure."

"Stupid question I know, but you didn't think you were being followed at any point?"

The detective shrugged. "It didn't even occur to me," he said. "You think that's what happened?"

"Yeah, they got here just after you. Whose idea was it to order food from room service?"

Aspinall frowned. "What do you mean?"

"Jaraf wanted a chicken burger, right?"

"Sure. He said he was hungry."

"So you called room service?"

The detective ran a hand through his hair. "Ah, wait, no. They called us. They said the restaurant was closing and asked us if we wanted to order something. I asked Jaraf and he said he wanted chicken. What's the problem?"

"Just checking," said Shepherd. "They locked the cook and the waitress in a fridge. They must have known what room you were in. I'm guessing that if you'd turned down the offer of food they'd have found some other reason to get into the room."

"Who were they?" asked Aspinall.

"No idea," said Shepherd. "But whoever they are, they're well organised." He gestured at the bathroom door. "I'm going to take Jaraf with me. Can you stay here until SOCO have collected the burger? Tell them to dust the tray and cutlery for prints and swab for DNA but there's no need to do the room. I doubt they'll find anything, she was wearing gloves."

"I didn't notice that."

"I did but didn't think anything of it at the time," said Shepherd. He looked at his watch. It was almost eleven o'clock.

The paramedic had finished laying the body bag on the bed next to the corpse. He looked over at Shepherd. "Could one of you guys give me a hand?"

Shepherd went over to the bed. Together they rolled the body into the bag and the paramedic zipped it closed. "Thanks," he said.

"What happens regarding the investigation now?" asked the detective.

"My boss will talk to your boss," Shepherd said. "I'm sure they'll work something out." He went over to the bathroom and knocked gently on the door. "It's Paul, Mr Jaraf," he said. The door opened and Jaraf peered out. "I'm going to take you somewhere safer," said Shepherd.

"Where?"

"Somewhere safer, that's all you need to worry about. Did you have a bag with you?"

"The Border Force officer had it," said Jaraf.

Shepherd looked around the room. There was a small holdall under the dressing table and he bent down and pulled it out. Jaraf reached for it but Shepherd moved it away. "Do you mind if I take a look?" he asked.

104

"Why?"

"The people who tried to hurt you must have been following you."

"And you think they put something in my bag?" Jaraf shook his head. "That's not possible. It was with me all the time."

"You didn't check it in?"

"I took it on the plane with me." He reached for the bag again but Shepherd put it down on the bed and unzipped it.

"Better safe than sorry," he said. He took out two shirts and two pairs of baggy underwear, a washbag, and a dog-eared copy of the Koran. "No phone?" he asked.

"I left my phone in Dubai," said Jaraf.

"Why?"

"I wasn't sure what would happen here. I didn't want to put my friends at risk."

"What about the SIM card?"

Jaraf frowned. "What do you mean?"

"What did you do with the SIM card?"

Jaraf frowned as if he didn't understand the question.

"Did you destroy it?"

"It was in the phone."

"And what did you do with the phone?"

"I threw it in a bin. At the airport."

Shepherd sensed that the man was lying, but if he had brought the SIM card with him and hidden it, it would be difficult to find without doing a fingertip search of all his possessions and a strip search of the man himself. "Okay, that's not a problem," he said. He picked up the Koran, flicked through the pages and examined the spine. He was about to put it back in the bag, but Jaraf held out his hand and Shepherd gave it to him. He unzipped the washbag and rifled through it. A toothbrush, toothpaste, lip salve and a tube of Zovirax cold sore cream. He zipped the bag closed, then checked the clothing before putting everything back in the holdall.

"Right, let's go," Shepherd said. He took Jaraf to his car and opened the passenger door for him. When Jaraf was seated, he closed the door and phoned Pritchard. "Where do we stand with protection?" Shepherd asked. "I'm getting ready to leave now."

"I've spoken to Major Gannon and he's arranging to have two men at your house later tonight. As you said, he's got a key so they'll be there waiting for you."

Yusuf Butt's phone buzzed to let him know that he'd received a WhatsApp message. He opened the app. The message was brief and to the point: "*Kebab shop, now*".

Butt grabbed his puffer jacket and left his flat. He hurried down the three flights of stairs and out into the street. The kebab shop was a two-minute walk from Butt's home. It was Anwar Rafiq's favourite meeting place, not because of the quality of the kebabs — which in Butt's opinion weren't great — but because Rafiq knew the owners, and strangers could be easily spotted.

He walked by two Asian men wearing heavy overcoats, who were clearly watching him. He nodded and smiled and said "Evening to you, brothers," but they just stared at him coldly. "Suit yourselves," he muttered as he walked towards the entrance of the kebab house. There was a blue Mazda 3 parked across the road with two Asian men in it; one in the driver's seat and one sitting behind. They were always with Rafiq though Butt had never been introduced to them.

He walked into the kebab shop. A big man with a shaved head and a sweat-stained t-shirt was carving glistening meat off one of two rotisseries. There were two young girls with black hijabs standing at the counter, and two old men in thawbs and skullcaps were wolfing down kebabs at a table by the window.

To the right was a line of small booths. Rafiq was sitting at the far end, closest to the toilets. "What's up, bruv?" asked Butt as he slid into the booth opposite Rafiq.

"All good, bruv." Rafiq kicked a holdall under the table towards Butt. He leaned forward and lowered his voice. "So, there's four kilos of Semtex in that bag, and two packs of detonators. Two kilos are for you, I need you to take the other two kilos up north. And split the detonators fifty-fifty. Okay?"

"Okay, sure."

"There's a burner phone in the bag and one number in the memory. The guy on that number will message you with a location, you take the stuff to him. When the job's done, you destroy the phone and the SIM card."

"Not a problem," said Butt.

Rafiq scowled at him. "I know it's not a problem, bruv. I'm just telling you what needs to be done."

"Yeah, I hear you. I'm on it."

Rafiq forced a smile. "I know you are. You're a good lad, Butty. And *inshallah* you'll get your reward in heaven for this."

"It's going to be big, right?"

"The whole world will talk about it, and they'll never forget," said Rafiq.

"How many brothers are involved?"

Rafiq raised a warning finger. "You cannot ask questions like that, brother. Each cell has its job, and together we will create something wondrous. But for security reasons, no one cell can know what another cell is doing."

"I'm sorry, yes, I know that."

"Trust me brother, this will be big."

The bald-headed man came over with a kebab and salad that he placed before Rafiq. Rafiq smiled and thanked him. As he walked away, Rafiq winked at Butt. "On your way, bruv," he said. "*Hafidaka Allah*." May Allah protect you.

"And you, bruv," said Butt. He picked up the holdall and headed out.

"I need the bathroom," said Jaraf. He was in the passenger seat of Shepherd's white BMW SUV, heading west on the M40. He had his bag on his lap and was holding the handles with both hands as if he feared it would be taken off him at any moment.

"Can't you wait?" asked Shepherd. They were about ten miles from Oxford and had only been driving for about forty-five minutes.

108

"How long until we get to where we are going?" asked Jaraf.

"Just over two hours."

Jaraf hugged his holdall to his chest. "Then I cannot wait."

Shepherd felt like pointing out that the man had spent several hours sitting in the bathroom in the hotel, so he'd had plenty of opportunity to go before they left. But there was a Welcome Break service station up ahead, and he felt like he could do with a coffee anyway, so he sighed and moved over to the inside lane. He checked his rear-view mirror and didn't see anyone copy his manoeuvre, but just to be on the safe side he moved back into the middle lane and accelerated. He overtook half a dozen vehicles before moving back into the inside lane. Jaraf looked at him quizzically but didn't say anything. Shepherd turned off the motorway and drove to the service station, still checking his rear-view mirror. He was sure they weren't being followed.

He parked as close to the main building as he could get and switched off the engine. "Right, stay close to me at all times, don't go wandering off."

"I am not a child, Paul."

"I know, but after what happened at the hotel I don't want you out of my sight for one second."

"That might be awkward in the bathroom."

"Be that as it may, I'll be right with you every step of the way." He gestured at the holdall. "Do you need that?"

"I thought I would clean my teeth."

"Then just take the washbag. Leave the holdall here."

Jaraf took the washbag out of the holdall and they both climbed out of the car. It was close to midnight but there was still plenty of traffic on the motorway and the service station was busy. Shepherd scanned the cars around them, then headed to the main entrance. Jaraf walked alongside him. "Can you tell me yet where we're going?" he asked.

"To the bathroom," said Shepherd.

"No, I mean . . ." He hesitated and then laughed. "Oh, you are joking."

"English humour," said Shepherd. "You'll need to get used to it if you're going to live here."

They went inside the building and headed for the toilets. Shepherd was checking left and right, looking for any signs that they were being followed, but nothing appeared untoward. Jaraf went into the toilets and Shepherd followed. There were two men using the urinals: a man in blue overalls and an older man with a walking stick. Shepherd motioned for Jaraf to use one of the cubicles and then went to the far end of the row of urinals and unzipped his fly. The door opened and he glanced over his shoulder. It was a man in his twenties with a young boy, four or five years old. Shepherd couldn't help but smile at the memory of when he'd had to take his son, Liam, into public bathrooms, reminding him to put the seat up, to flush, and to wash his hands. The father guided his son into the cubicle next to the one that Jaraf was using, then closed the door and stood with his back to it, his arms folded, like a bouncer outside a nightclub.

Shepherd stared at the wall and began to pee. The door opened again. He took a quick look over his shoulder. It was the man in overalls, heading out. As the door started to close a hand pushed it open and an Asian man walked in; tall, thin with a bushy beard and a white Muslim skullcap. He was wearing a puffer jacket and tight jeans and holding a WHSmith carrier bag. Shepherd tensed. He zipped himself up but stayed facing the wall, watching to see what the newcomer did.

He heard a toilet flush but couldn't tell if it was Jaraf or the small boy. The father had turned his back on Shepherd and was saying something to his son through the door. The Asian man walked over to the row of sinks and put his carrier bag by a washbasin, then began splashing water on his face. Shepherd was too far away to see what was in the bag. The door to Jaraf's cubicle opened. Shepherd stepped away from the urinal.

Jaraf walked out of the cubicle. He saw Shepherd and nodded. Shepherd gestured with his chin at the man by the washbasins but Jaraf was already looking away and walking over to the sinks. He reached the washbasin next to the bearded man and turned on the tap. The other man continued to splash water onto his face. Jaraf began to wash his hands. There was a third washbasin and Shepherd went over to it. As he turned on the tap he looked across at the WHSmith bag. There were two paperback books inside. He relaxed a little and washed his hands.

Jaraf finished first and pulled a sheet of paper towel from the dispenser on the wall. Shepherd did the same.

Once he had dried his hands, Jaraf took a toothbrush and a tube of toothpaste from his washbag and cleaned his teeth. The other man dried his hands and face, and left.

His teeth cleaned, Jaraf left the toilet with Shepherd. "I need a coffee," said Shepherd. "Do you want anything?"

"Just a water," said Jaraf.

"Do you want a sandwich? I don't have any food in my house."

"Your house? We're going to your house?"

Shepherd nodded. "It's safe, and there are people there who can protect you," he said. He nodded at the Costa shop where half a dozen customers were queuing up for coffee. "Come and see what they have."

Shepherd joined the queue. There were three staff behind the counter and in less than four minutes a Polish girl with bleached blonde hair was taking his order. Jaraf asked for a cheese sandwich. Shepherd wanted an egg and bacon sandwich but he didn't want to risk offending Jaraf's Muslim sensitivities, so he had a cheese sandwich too, plus a couple of chocolate muffins. He paid the bill and they collected their coffees. Jaraf headed for a table but Shepherd shook his head. "Let's eat in the car," he said.

They walked out of the building. A teenage couple were smoking and as they walked by, Shepherd caught the sweet smell of cannabis. A horn sounded and Shepherd looked over his shoulder. A van was reversing into the path of a hatchback and the hatchback driver was trying to get him to stop. Behind the hatchback was a trail bike with two figures on it, both wearing full-face helmets. Shepherd frowned. He'd seen the bike before, on the CCTV footage that the hotel manager had shown him. The bike had driven into the hotel car park a few minutes after the Toyota Camry. There had only been one man on the bike then, wearing a black leather jacket and a white helmet with a tinted visor. It was the same man driving the bike now, but this time he had a passenger. The passenger could have been a small man or a large woman, there was no way of telling.

"Get back inside," said Shepherd, stepping in between Jaraf and the bike.

"What?" said Jaraf, confused.

"Just do it," hissed Shepherd.

The passenger reached inside their jacket and pulled out a large gun. It was an Uzi, Shepherd realised. An Uzi with a bulbous silencer.

Shepherd dropped the bag containing his sandwich and muffins. Jaraf was still hesitating, he hadn't seen the bike or the gun. The bike had slowed to just over walking pace and was about twenty feet away. The barrel of the gun was still pointing at the ground but was moving up. It wasn't a standard Uzi, Shepherd realised. It was a Mini Uzi, just fourteen inches long with the stock folded and weighing only six pounds.

Everything had slowed and Shepherd was aware of the smallest details. The passenger was wearing black gloves. The finger was on the trigger. The driver was looking straight ahead, concentrating on the road and

113

letting the passenger worry about the shooting. The passenger's visor was impenetrable. There was a manufacturer's sticker on the helmet above the visor: HJC. The passenger was wearing black Nikes.

Shepherd reached around with his left hand and pushed Jaraf away. "Get back!" he shouted.

The two teenagers turned to look at Shepherd. The girl had a roll-up in her mouth. She was blonde, wearing a denim jacket and had a thin gold chain around her neck. She was squinting, as if she was having trouble seeing him.

The bike was still moving. Ahead of it, a car was reversing out of a parking space. The driver started to turn to the right. The barrel of the Uzi was up now. The passenger's finger was tightening on the trigger. There was no cover, nowhere to hide, and the Uzi was capable of spewing out nine hundred and fifty rounds a minute, emptying its twenty-round magazine in just over a second.

Jaraf had seen the bike now and was backing away, dropping his coffee and sandwich and washbag and putting his hands up over his face in a vain attempt to protect himself.

Shepherd drew back his right hand and threw his coffee at the gun-toting passenger, then started to run forward. The coffee cup span through the air and smashed into the passenger's helmet. The Uzi fired, a burst of three shots that went low and to the left, the bullets ricocheting off the tarmac. Coffee was dripping down the visor as the cup tumbled to the floor. The driver of the bike had been hit by some of the coffee

114

and the bike wobbled as the driver looked over at Shepherd. The passenger fired again but the bike was wobbling so much that the burst went high.

The girl smoking cannabis was screaming. Her boyfriend had dropped down into a crouch, his mouth open in shock.

Shepherd was moving at full speed now, determined to reach the Uzi before it fired again. There had been two short bursts but the shots were so close together that there was no way of knowing how many rounds were still in the magazine.

The gun was swinging around to aim at Shepherd but he was close enough to push it to the side with his left hand as his momentum sent him crashing into the bike. The driver accelerated and the passenger tumbled off the back of the bike, still holding the gun.

The bike roared away, then the driver pulled it into a tight turn, spinning around the front wheel with rubber smoking on the road surface.

The passenger hit the ground hard. Shepherd lashed out with his foot, trying to kick the gun away, but the passenger was already rolling over. Shepherd kicked out again but missed, then the Uzi was firing again and he ducked and threw himself to the side as bullets headed skywards.

There were screams from behind him but Shepherd ignored them as he got to his feet. The passenger was up on one knee, swinging the Uzi towards Jaraf, who was still backing away with his hands over his face.

Shepherd threw himself at the passenger just as the Uzi kicked into life. He knocked the weapon to the side

115

as a single shot thudded into the wall behind Jaraf. The passenger got up and smacked the gun against the side of Shepherd's head, stunning him. He staggered back, fighting to stay conscious.

Off to his left, the bike roared as the driver twisted the throttle. It leaped forward, heading straight for Shepherd. He took a step back and just managed to avoid it, though the wing mirror clipped his arm. The bike came to a halt and then span around the front wheel again. The passenger pointed the Uzi at Shepherd's chest. Shepherd saw his own reflection in the full-face visor and realised that it was the last thing he would ever see. The gloved finger pulled the trigger and there was a metallic click. Shepherd gasped. The magazine was empty.

He moved forward, pulling back his fist, but the bike sped towards him and he had to step back. It drove between him and the passenger and then screeched to a halt. The passenger leaped on the back, holding the gun high, and the bike sped off. It swerved to avoid a car, then accelerated towards the motorway.

Shepherd watched it go, gasping for breath. More than a dozen people came out of the main building to see what all the commotion was about. Shepherd's mind raced as he considered his options. Two men who had witnessed the attack were already on their phones, presumably calling the police. No one appeared to be filming Shepherd and Jaraf, and it had all happened so quickly that no one had videoed the attack. The police wouldn't send out a regular patrol car, not with firearms reported, which meant they would have to wait

116

for an armed response vehicle. That would take ten, maybe fifteen minutes.

"We're going to have to go," he said to Jaraf.

"They were trying to k-k-kill me," stammered the man.

"Take deep breaths, you'll be fine," said Shepherd. He put his mouth close to Jaraf's ear. "We have to go now. If the police pull us in, it'll take forever to sort it out."

Jaraf nodded. Shepherd patted him on the back. He knelt down, picked up the washbag and thrust it into his hands. "Walk, don't run," he said.

He put his arm around Jaraf's shoulder and walked with him towards the car. There had been so much confusion during the shooting that no one seemed to have realised that Jaraf had been the intended target. A few people were pointing at Shepherd — presumably they had seen him struggling with the pillion passenger. But no one tried to stop him and thankfully no one pointed their phone in his direction. He kept his head down as he walked, keeping his arm around Jaraf. By the time they reached the car, there were sirens off in the distance. They climbed in. Shepherd started the engine, drove slowly around the car park to the filling station, and then slipped back onto the M40. He drove in the inside lane at just below the speed limit.

"What if they are on the road, waiting for us?" asked Jaraf, looking around anxiously. He had picked up his holdall and was holding it against his chest, as if to have some protection if he was shot at again.

"Unlikely," said Shepherd. "But keep your eyes open." He used his phone on hands-free and called the Major. He told him what had happened and where they were.

"So you're about two hours away," said the Major. "How about we split the difference and meet you outside Gloucester? We can run counter surveillance on you and escort you into Hereford."

"That would be great," said Shepherd.

"We're on our way," said the Major.

Shepherd's phone rang as they approached Gloucester. It was the Major. "Okay, I'm coming up behind you now," said Gannon. "Black Range Rover. Some way behind me are two of our guys in another Range Rover. You know one of them. Burt Reynolds."

"I thought he was on attachment with the Navy Seals?" Kevin "Burt" Reynolds had joined the SAS about eight years after Shepherd had left, but they had met several times at Stirling Lines.

"Got back last week but still hasn't rejoined the Regiment, so he's perfect for a spot of personal protection," said Gannon. "He's with a newbie, Sean Hook. They call him 'Captain'. He's just back from Iraq so is due some time off. So look, from where you are, there are three routes to Hereford: the A438, the A49 or the B4224. Do you have any preferences?"

"I usually take the A49," said Shepherd.

"The A49 it is. I'm going to overtake and check out the traffic ahead of you. You keep at five miles per hour below the speed limit. Burt and Captain will stay behind you. Keep on the A49."

"Roger that," said Shepherd and ended the call.

"What's happening?" asked Jaraf, still looking around nervously.

"Some friends of mine are going to check that we're not being followed," said Shepherd. He looked in his rear-view mirror in time to see a vehicle pull out and accelerate. The glare from the headlights meant he couldn't identify it, but a few seconds later it roared past and he could see it was a black Range Rover. The windows were tinted, so he only got a glimpse of the figure at the wheel.

"Is that them?" asked Jaraf.

Shepherd nodded.

"Are they police?"

"No," said Shepherd. "But they sometimes work with the police."

"SAS?"

"Let's just say they're friends and leave it at that, shall we?"

The Range Rover continued to pull away. Shepherd glanced at his speedometer. He'd been accelerating without realising it and he eased on the brake just enough to get below the speed limit.

"Mr Jaraf, tell me, when you were in Syria, was your life threatened like this?"

Jaraf turned to look at him, frowning. "What do you mean?"

"I mean were people trying to kill you before you came to England?"

"You mean apart from the American Army and Turkish troops and your own SAS?" He smiled thinly and shook his head. "Everyone out there wanted me dead. The last camp I was in was destroyed by American missiles fired from a drone. Not the sort of drones I specialise in, I mean the big ones. Reapers. Do you know about the Reapers?"

Shepherd nodded. Yes, he knew.

"And you know about Hellfire missiles?"

Shepherd nodded again. The Hellfire air-to-surface missile was the weapon of choice for the Reaper drone, capable of taking out targets with pinpoint accuracy while the operator sat in an air-conditioned box thousands of miles away. The name "Hellfire" was a shortened version of the weapon's name when it was first developed: "heliborne laser fire-and-forget missile".

"The Americans fired four at the camp. I assume from the same drone, but there is no way of knowing because they fly so high they are almost invisible. I was lucky. But many were killed. As I said before, I was sure my wife and son had been caught up in the attack. They were lucky too. *Alhamdulillah.*"

Alhamdulillah. All the praises and thanks be to Allah. It was a phrase that Muslims used a lot, but Shepherd could never understand how someone who truly believed in a god — any god — could carry out the sort of atrocities committed by ISIS, al-Qaeda and the like.

"But the question you asked, about me being attacked in Syria: no, not like we were attacked today. This is the work of ISIS. They know that I have offered to help you and are doing whatever they can to stop me."

"And what about Dubai? Did you have problems there before you boarded the plane to London?"

Before Jaraf could reply, Shepherd's phone rang again. It was the Major. "Right, all looks good so far. I'm about a mile ahead of you. The lads have you in sight but they are quite a way back."

Shepherd's eyes flicked to his rear-view mirror. All he could see were headlights.

"You need to increase your speed to about ten miles an hour above the speed limit," said the Major. "Keep going until you almost reach me, then match my speed. The guys will be watching to see if there's any action behind you."

"Will do, boss." He accelerated smoothly and moved out to the right to overtake the truck in front of him. He levelled his speed off and moved back into the left lane. He checked his rear-view mirror. More cars were overtaking the truck.

"Do you have eyes on me?" asked the Major.

"Not yet," said Shepherd.

"I've dropped down to fifty and I'm in the inside lane," said the Major. "I'm getting some filthy looks."

"Shouldn't be long now," said Shepherd.

He checked his rear-view mirror. A large vehicle was a few cars behind him now. Probably the second Range Rover.

"Right, let me call Burt for a sitrep." The Major ended the call.

Three cars whizzed by — a black BMW, a red Audi and a white BMW, clearly racing and all driven by young men. Then he was overtaken by a white van, then an SUV towing a horsebox. Shepherd looked in his rear-view mirror. The large vehicle was directly behind him now.

His phone rang. "We're all good," said the Major. "Do you have eyes yet?"

The Major's black Range Rover was about a hundred metres ahead of Shepherd. "I see you," he said.

"Burt and Captain have checked all the vehicles that kept pace with you and there's nothing untoward," said Gannon. "Let's run one final check. You overtake me and take the lead for a few minutes, then Burt will overtake us both and lead us back to the house. I'll keep a watch on your rear all the way."

"Roger that, boss," said Shepherd.

The Major ended the call. Shepherd checked his mirror, indicated, and accelerated. He went by the Major's Range Rover and then went back into the inside lane. Three minutes later the second black Range Rover went by.

"We are okay?" asked Jaraf.

"It looks like it," said Shepherd.

Jaraf sat back and folded his arms as he stared out of the windscreen. He clearly didn't want to talk, which suited Shepherd because he had a lot to think about.

It was just after two o'clock in the morning when they reached Shepherd's house in Hereford, with its "FOR

SALE" sign in the front garden. The first Range Rover pulled up at the side of the road so that Shepherd could park his SUV in the driveway. As he and Jaraf got out, Major Gannon arrived and parked behind the first Range Rover. The Major climbed out and walked towards Shepherd, grinning. He was wearing a brown leather jacket and black jeans and his skin was tanned, presumably from a spell somewhere sunny with a lot of sand. The Major was a big man, broad-shouldered with a nose that had been broken several times, and he looked fitter and trimmer than the last time they'd met. "Good to see you, Spider," said Gannon, shaking hands vigorously. He nodded at the men standing on the pavement. "Burt you know, and his wingman there is Sean Hook."

"Sean," said Shepherd, shaking the man's hand. He was typical SAS stock: medium height, medium build, wiry rather than muscle-bound. His hair was long and had been bleached by the sun, and his tan was darker than the Major's.

Shepherd released his grip on Hook's hand and turned to Reynolds. "Good to see you again, Burt." The two men shook hands, then hugged. Reynolds was slightly taller than Hook and about ten years older, but they could have been brothers. Both were wearing black bomber jackets. Reynolds had unzipped his, and when they shook hands Shepherd caught a glimpse of a Glock in an underarm holster.

"This is Mr Jaraf, the principal," said Shepherd.

All three men looked at Jaraf. He clasped his bag to his chest and smiled nervously at them. "We'll be taking care of you from now on, Mr Jaraf," said Major Gannon. "Please don't worry, you're in good hands." He waved at the house. "Let's go inside, I could murder a brew."

"A brew?" repeated Jaraf, frowning.

"He means tea," explained Shepherd. "And by murder, he means drink."

Shepherd took Jaraf to the front door. Reynolds and Hook stayed on the pavement. There was no one else around and the road was empty, but their eyes scanned the area relentlessly. The Major followed Shepherd to the front door and covered them as Shepherd unlocked it.

"Let me go in first," said the Major, drawing a Glock from inside his jacket. He disappeared inside. There was almost no sound as Gannon moved through the ground floor and then headed upstairs. He returned a minute or so later and opened the door for them. "All clear," he said.

Reynolds and Hook stayed where they were until Shepherd and Jaraf were inside, then they jogged down the drive and followed them in. Reynolds closed the door.

"I'll show you to your room," Shepherd said. "It's late and you should sleep."

"Will you be here tomorrow?" asked Jaraf.

"I have to go back to London."

"I don't want you to leave me," pleaded Jaraf.

"I have to check the information you gave us, and there are arrangements to be made so that we can bring your family over." He gestured at the Major and his

124

men. "They will look after you, I promise. You'll be safe here."

"How long will you be gone?"

"A few days." Shepherd smiled as encouragingly as he could. "You'll be fine. Come on, follow me." He led Jaraf up the stairs and along the landing to the spare room. There was a double bed and a small television on a chest of drawers. "You can sleep here, and the bathroom is next door. If you need towels, there are spare ones hanging above the radiator. We drink the tap water in England, it's perfectly safe, and there are glasses above the sink."

Jaraf looked around the room and managed a smile. "Thank you," he said.

"If you want anything, ask the guys downstairs. They'll get you any food you want, and any stuff you need. I wouldn't suggest that you leave the house, but if you really need to get out, the back garden isn't overlooked and you could get some fresh air."

"Do you know which way Mecca is?"

Shepherd pointed at the window. "I know that way is due north," he said. "I'm sure you'll be able to work it out."

"This is your house?"

Shepherd nodded. "Yes."

"And your family?"

"Just my son, and he's away."

Shepherd left the room, closed the door, and went downstairs. Hook was in the front room, flicking through the channels of the TV with the sound down. The Major was in the kitchen with Reynolds. They had

125

both taken off their jackets to reveal Glocks in nylon holsters. "Is he okay?" asked the Major.

"He's in shock, hardly surprising after what he's been through." Shepherd explained what had happened in the Heathrow hotel, and about the attack at the service station.

"So who wants him dead?" asked the Major.

"He says ISIS, and that makes sense because the intel he could give us could shut down a lot of their operations. But the poisoning attempt didn't feel like ISIS and the motorcycle drive-by wasn't their style at all."

"Professional?" said the Major.

Shepherd nodded. "Yeah. It's possible that ISIS have paid professionals to do their dirty work. But that's not normally how they do things. And the poisoning was straight out of the Russian textbook." He shrugged. "I'm not sure what to think."

"At the end of the day it doesn't matter who it is," said Gannon. "All that matters is that we stop them from succeeding."

"Exactly. And you should be okay here," said Shepherd. "We weren't followed and this place isn't on any official lists."

"It's a nice place," said Hook. "Not too far from Stirling Lines, but far enough so that you're away from the madness."

"Make me an offer," said Shepherd.

"Spider spends most of his time in London these days," said the Major. He stood up and went over to the fridge. It was empty except for a couple of bottles of

126

champagne. He turned and grinned at Shepherd. "Looks like you've got the essentials."

"Katra always insisted on keeping a couple of bottles, for birthdays and celebrations." He pointed to the freezer section. "The real essentials are in there," he said.

The Major opened the freezer door and took out a frozen loaf of bread, bacon, black pudding and sausage. He put them on the work top to thaw. "That's breakfast sorted."

Shepherd laughed. "Yeah, just don't give Jaraf a bacon sarnie," he said.

"He'll be fine with tea and toast," said the Major.

Shepherd went over to one of the overhead cupboards and opened it. He took out a jar of strawberry jam and a jar of marmalade. He put them next to the defrosting bread.

"There's always Deliveroo," said the Major.

"Yeah, well just remember what happened last time he ordered food," said Shepherd.

"No problem, we'll get Burt to take a bite first."

"Thanks, boss," said Reynolds.

Shepherd looked at his watch. It was half past two. He had two options — to drive back to London and snatch a couple of hours' sleep in his Battersea flat, or to grab some sleep in Hereford and then drive to work. He was dog-tired and didn't really want to drive through the night, but he couldn't risk being late and he had no idea what the traffic would be like later that day. "I'm going to head back," he said.

"I'll walk you out," said the Major.

Shepherd said goodbye to Reynolds and headed out of the kitchen door into the garden with the Major. "I told Jaraf he could get some exercise in the garden, but obviously it's your call," he said.

"I'm not going to be here all the time, but Burt and Captain are on twenty-four-seven," said Gannon. "I'm looking for two more bodies as we speak. I'll be at Stirling Lines so I'm not far away. How long do you think this will take?" They walked around the side of the house, towards the street.

"I've got to go to Turkey to pick up his wife and son," said Shepherd. "So two days, maybe three, depending on the flights."

"Do you need company? I can round up a few more guys."

"It should be okay. It's not as if they're in Syria, Turkey is pretty safe these days. And probably better to keep it low profile."

"If you change your mind, let me know," said the Major. "Plenty of guys who'd be happy for a bit of extra money. Plus the ones without families are always looking for something to do over Christmas and New Year. The barracks can get a bit lonely. What about you? Is this screwing up your Christmas?"

"Nah, Liam's on manoeuvres and I had nothing planned." He grinned. "I'll be in Turkey, so I guess that's seasonal."

They reached Shepherd's BMW. The Major hugged him and patted him on the back. "Good to see you again. I'd say 'don't be a stranger' but that ship has sailed."

Shepherd untangled himself from the Major's hug. "Yeah, too many memories. And Liam's never here these days. But I'll still be coming back. You'll just have to find me a billet at Stirling Lines."

"Any time you want, Spider."

Shepherd climbed back into his car, waved goodbye to the Major, and drove away from the house.

Shepherd got back to Battersea at just before six o'clock in the morning. He parked and went up to the flat. Like soldiers the world over he had developed the knack of grabbing sleep — and food — whenever it was available. He found a microwaveable lasagne in his fridge that was only a couple of days past its sell-by date, heated it up and devoured it with a mug of coffee. Then, he stripped off his clothes, set the alarm on his phone for eight-thirty and dived into bed. He was asleep within minutes and slept dreamlessly until the alarm went off.

He felt tired when he got up, but a cold shower freshened him up and he changed into a clean suit and shirt. At nine-fifteen he caught a cab to Westminster Public Mortuary on Horseferry Road, not far from Lambeth Bridge. It was by far the biggest mortuary in the country and could handle up to a hundred bodies at a time. Shepherd had called ahead to arrange a meeting with the pathologist who had carried out the post-mortem on Ricky Wainer, the Border Force officer who had died in Jaraf's hotel room. Her name was Lucy Wakeham and she came out to meet him in the mortuary's reception area. "Mr Easton?" She had a

Geordie accent and a firm grip as they shook hands. Her dyed blonde hair was cut short and she was wearing a white lab coat over pale blue scrubs. "It's a bit unusual to have the Home Office asking for details of a post-mortem," she said.

"It's a very unusual situation," said Shepherd. "The victim was a Border Force officer, but we think the intended victim was an asylum seeker who had just arrived in the country."

"But it's not a police matter yet?"

"At the moment we are trying to establish what happened."

"Well, he was poisoned, there's no question of that," said Wakeham. "We ran it through a mass spectrometer and it's actually a nerve agent rather than a poison. It's called VX. Less than half a milligram is fatal."

"VX? What does that stand for?"

"It doesn't stand for anything. It's just the name the manufacturers gave it. It's a very potent nerve agent, not something we'd expect to see civilians exposed to."

"How easy is it to obtain?" asked Shepherd.

"For the man in the street? Impossible. This is the sort of agent that only governments have. Kim Jong Un used it to kill his half-brother in Kuala Lumpur airport a few years ago, and Saddam Hussein used it to kill five thousand Kurds back in 1988."

"What is it, Russian?"

The pathologist shook her head. "It was actually developed by ICI in the 1950s as a pesticide, but it was far too deadly to use in food production. During the Cold War the Americans began producing it as a nerve

130

agent and the Russians had their own version, but it's now been banned under the 1997 Chemical Weapons Convention."

"But they would still have stocks of it."

"I assume so. I've no doubt that we have our own stocks at Porton Down, for research purposes."

The Ministry of Defence's Science and Technology Laboratory — one of the country's most secret germ warfare labs — was based in Porton Down, near Salisbury.

"The nerve agent was in the chicken burger, but I suppose you had already assumed that," said the pathologist.

Shepherd nodded. "I was there when the victim ingested it," he said. "It was over very quickly."

"It's fast-acting and deadly. Once ingested or sprayed — or even painted — onto the skin, there's really no time to do anything."

"And it would have had to come from a government lab?"

"Initially, yes. But these days who knows what's available on the black market. The world has become a scary place."

"Tell me about it," said Shepherd.

The pathologist looked at her watch. "I'm going to have to dash," she said. "I'm giving evidence at an inquest in half an hour."

Shepherd thanked her and headed out to the street. He walked back to Thames House, deep in thought. The obvious candidate for wanting Jaraf dead was ISIS, but there had been no indication in the past that ISIS had access to nerve agents. If they did, there was nothing to stop them using them as a weapon of terror. There had been cases of ISIS-inspired terrorists trying to obtain poisons like ricin and anthrax, but this VX seemed to be a whole different ballgame. If ISIS had access to it, what was stopping them using it to attack, say, the transport system, or a shopping centre? Back in 1995, Japanese terrorists had attacked commuters on the Tokyo subway system with sarin nerve gas, killing thirteen people and injuring another fifty. It remained Japan's deadliest terrorist incident and had been studied by police forces around the world. The fear was that another terrorist group would use the technique, but so far the world had been lucky. Maybe that was about to change.

It was a five-minute walk from the mortuary to Thames House and Shepherd arrived at Pritchard's office at just before ten. Pritchard was tied up in a meeting elsewhere in the building, but there was no apology when he eventually arrived, just a curt nod and a tight smile. Shepherd followed him into the office. Pritchard walked around his desk and sat down — clearly a sofa chat was not on the agenda. "So how is Jaraf?" asked Pritchard, pushing his glasses further up his nose.

"Jumpy, obviously. Not happy that I've left him, but the guys looking after him are professionals, they'll keep him safe."

"Does he have any idea who wants him dead?"

"He says ISIS, but it didn't feel like an ISIS attack to me. It feels too professional."

"Guys on a bike with guns? That's simple enough."

"But they had an Uzi. If it was ISIS-inspired you'd expect them to have a machete or at best a handgun. An Uzi is a specialist gun."

"There are plenty of gangbangers with Uzis," said Pritchard.

"Sure," said Shepherd. "But two up on a bike with an Uzi suggests a degree of professionalism that our home-grown jihadists generally lack. Plus there's the business at the hotel. They must have had a full team to follow Jaraf from the airport, and taking over the kitchen took balls. And according to the pathologist, the poison was a nerve agent. VX."

"VX?" repeated Pritchard. "Now that's not good news."

"You've heard of it?"

Pritchard nodded. "We've had several briefings on it over the years, along with other nerve agents. It can only be made in a lab, and a government lab at that, but the worry was that Gaddafi might use it for terrorism purposes. Al-Qaeda were trying to buy it just before 9-11, but luckily their attempts never got anywhere."

"So it's usually used for mass attacks?"

"Not necessarily. But that was always the fear. Well, it still is, actually." He looked over the top of his glasses. "One of the many nightmare scenarios we face is terrorists getting hold of something like VX." He grimaced. "To date there's no evidence that ISIS have got their hands on it. But the Syrians have stocks of VX. And they would certainly want Jaraf dead."

"That's possible," said Shepherd. "And the Russians have XV and they hate ISIS — maybe that's where we should be looking."

"Agreed," said Pritchard. "But why would the Russians kill him when he's planning to give us information that will help us hit back at ISIS? The same goes for the Turks. If anything they'd want him alive and well, and giving us all the intel he has. We need to keep an open mind. The most obvious culprits are ISIS — Jaraf is promising to give us intel on their fighters, it would make sense for them to take him out."

"If that's true, then we've bigger things to worry about than Jaraf," said Shepherd. "If they link drone technology with a nerve agent like VX, they'll be able to kill thousands. Think what would happen if they flew VX-loaded drones into a football stadium."

"Exactly," said Pritchard, sitting back in his chair and running his hands through his hair. "Did Jaraf say anything about using VX?"

"He didn't. Mostly he talked about using drones to deliver explosives. IEDs. He did mention poisons but only anthrax, botulism and ricin."

Pritchard sighed. "Well let's hope it isn't ISIS who tried to kill him, then," he said. "Because if ISIS has stocks of VX, it's a game changer." He dropped his hands onto the desk and sat forward in his chair again. "Okay, the three names that Jaraf gave you. Two are a dead end, literally: the Iraqis, Tariq Al-Majid and Naseer Salim. They did indeed try to get into the UK, but they ended up dead in the back of a refrigerated lorry in Portsmouth, along with another fifteen immigrants — most of them from Afghanistan and Iraq."

Shepherd shook his head sadly. "I can't believe that anyone would be stupid enough to allow themselves to be locked into a refrigerated container," he said.

"They believe what they're told," said Pritchard. "And I'm assuming that by that stage they'd already paid the traffickers, so if they say no they'd just be told to get lost. Anyway, of the fifteen men in the back of the lorry, seven died, including the two Iraqis. Their bodies were never claimed. But we've had more luck with the British-born jihadist, Ali Karim. He flew in from Turkey three months ago and has just started working for the Post Office in Birmingham. He's due to work an afternoon-evening shift today. I have a surveillance team outside his home as we speak, and I'm sending an entry team up to check out his personal effects. I'd like you to go with them."

"And if we get evidence that he's planning something?"

"Then we give Jaraf a gold star and you can go get his family." He looked at his watch. "Amar will be going with you to handle the tech side. If you come up with anything, let me know straight away."

"Will do," said Shepherd.

Amar Singh's Audi still had its new car smell. Shepherd glanced at the milometer. There were just over eight hundred miles on the clock. "Bloody hell, Amar, did you win the lottery?"

Singh grinned. "I don't have many vices, Dan," he said. "Just clothes and cars."

"And kids."

Singh's grin widened. "We're in the catchment area of a great State school and my kids are low maintenance," he said. "Seriously though, I don't gamble, I don't drink, I don't smoke, my wife is the best cook in the world so we don't eat out much, my running costs are low. Mind you, Christmas is a killer. My youngest wants a PlayStation and has given Santa a list of games that comes to more than two hundred quid."

"You're lucky, you've only had the one wife," said the man sitting directly behind Shepherd. His name was Rob Miller and he was one of MI5's top locks and alarms specialists. Miller prided himself on being able to open any lock in less than a minute, and most of the time it took him less than twenty seconds. He had spent a decade as a burglar alarms technician and the rumour was that he had been recruited after he had installed a security system at the house of a former MI5 director general. "I'm got two divorces behind me, there's no way I could afford a motor like this."

"You make your own choices," said Singh.

They were on the motorway, heading north to Birmingham. The traffic was light and Singh was adding ten miles an hour to the speed limit, which meant it would take less than two and a half hours to get to their destination.

"To be fair, now, it was my ex-wives who made the choices," said Miller. "The first one decided after three years of being married to me that she was actually a lesbian. And wife number two chose to go onto Tinder six months after we got married and chose to screw at least five men she met on there before I found out."

"Bloody hell, how unlucky can you get?" asked Shepherd.

"Is it luck, though, or is it you making bad choices?" asked Singh.

"Mate, I never saw it coming, both times," said Miller. "And you know what, they both took me to the cleaners. I never put a foot wrong in either marriage, but I'm paying maintenance to them both."

"Which is why I'm never getting married," said the fourth member of the group, John Weston. Weston was in his fifties and overweight, with a comb-over that did little to conceal his baldness. He was a search expert, one of the best, and Shepherd had worked with him several times. Searching a room was mainly a matter of technique and logic, and MI5 officers were all trained to do it. But while Weston knew all the procedures that had to be followed, he also had an intuition that few others possessed. There was no rational explanation, but time and time again Weston had found things when everyone else had drawn a blank.

"Oh, *that's* the reason you're not married?" laughed Singh.

"What do you mean?" asked Weston.

"Putting it as diplomatically as I can, you're no catch, are you?"

"Fuck you, Amar," said Weston.

Singh grinned as he looked at Weston in the rear-view mirror. "See, right there is part of the problem. No sense of humour."

"Yeah, well I bet my dick is twice the size of yours," snapped Weston.

"Guys, guys, will someone open a window and let out the testosterone in here," said Shepherd.

"Yeah," laughed Miller, "can we get back to the matter in hand? Who is this guy we're turning over?"

"Home-grown jihadist," said Shepherd. "He's at work and we've got surveillance on him there, so we won't be getting any unpleasant surprises. Lives alone in a bedsit and the team say there's no evidence of a burglar alarm."

"Easy peasy, then," said Miller.

"We've been told that he was at an ISIS training camp in Syria, so we're looking for any intel he might have picked up while he was there, plus any contacts he has here or abroad, any inkling of what he's up to. Part of his training involved drones, so receipts for anything like that. Plus all the usual stuff — manuals, videos, literature."

"Drones?" said Miller. "Those things that kids fly?"

"The small ones, yeah. ISIS are working on ways that they can be adapted to carry weapons. Explosive charges and the like. And they could be used to deliver nerve agents and poisons."

"They really are fucking evil," said Weston. "They must literally just sit around trying to think up nasty ways of killing people."

138

"That's just about how it works," said Shepherd. "It means we have to constantly play catch-up."

"And this guy, he was in a training camp in Syria and he just waltzed back into the UK?" asked Weston.

"He wasn't on a watch list so there's no record of him leaving the UK," said Shepherd.

Miller folded his arms. "It's a bloody nonsense. Time and time again we have these home-grown jihadists committing mayhem here, and then afterwards the papers find out that they were abroad, either fighting for ISIS or al-Qaeda or being trained by them. We have no problems picking up crims when they fly in from the Costa del Crime, how hard can it be to do the same with jihadists?"

"Sounds like you should ask for a transfer to Border Force," said Singh.

"Border Farce, more like," said Miller.

They arrived outside Ali Karim's bedsit just before one o'clock in the afternoon. Shepherd phoned the surveillance team who were watching Karim and confirmed that he was still inside the sorting office. He ended the call. "Right, his shift ends at eight o'clock this evening so we've plenty of time."

Singh looked up and down the road. "I'm not sure I want to be leaving my car on the street."

"You're insured, right?" asked Weston.

"That's not the point," said Singh. "I don't want to come out and find that my wheels are missing."

"Pull up in front of the shops over there," said Shepherd, pointing ahead.

Singh nodded and put the car into gear, but he clearly wasn't happy.

"You should have brought a pool car if you're that worried," said Miller.

"He wanted the mileage, right Amar?" said Weston.

Singh ignored the jibe and parked in front of a supermarket. The four men climbed out. Singh popped the boot and Miller took out his case, a black box with a plastic handle, the type used by airline pilots. Weston had a small Arsenal holdall and Singh had his Louis Vuitton briefcase.

Miller headed towards the bedsit while Shepherd and Singh looked in the window of the supermarket. Weston crossed over the road and walked parallel to Miller. All were on the alert for surveillance, scanning the faces of pedestrians and noting any vehicles that passed by.

Karim's bedsit was in a semi-detached house with half a dozen doorbells and a row of steel letterboxes. The front garden had been paved over and there was an old Toyota parked there, along with two mopeds with Deliveroo carriers on the back. Miller looked around as he walked up to the front door, but the nearest pedestrian was fifty metres away. He took a pick gun from his coat pocket as he walked past the two mopeds. He smiled when he saw that the lock was a bog-standard Yale. It was the sort of lock he had practised on when he first started picking, and it took him less than ten seconds to open it. He stepped inside. Weston hurried across the road and joined him. Shepherd and Singh stayed where they were, chatting

140

about nothing in particular as they scanned the area for possible surveillance.

Karim's bedsit was on the first floor. The lock was equally easy to pick, a cheap Chinese Yale knock-off. Either Karim or the landlord had added a padlock for extra security, but that too was a joke. Miller took out a Wi-Fi jammer from his coat pocket and switched it on. There were no signs of a burglar alarm, but these days Wi-Fi security cameras were common. If there was one in the bedsit, the jammer would render it useless.

It took Miller just ten seconds to pick the padlock and a few seconds longer to open the main door lock. As he opened the door and slipped inside, Weston went downstairs and opened the front door. Shepherd and Singh were already outside and the three men headed upstairs.

The bedsit was a twelve-foot-by-twelve-foot box with a single window overlooking the back garden. There was a shower room to the right and the men wrinkled their noses at the foul stench coming up from the drains.

"How the other half lives," said Singh scornfully.

There was a single bed against one wall, and a small desk at the foot of it on which there was a cheap Dell computer, a well-thumbed copy of the Koran and an Arabic — English dictionary. There were more books on a shelf above the desk.

Next to the window was a Formica table with a double hotplate and a stainless steel kettle, and below it was a small fridge that was humming quietly. "Rob, this is all a bit cramped, maybe you should wait outside."

Singh took his car keys and tossed them to Miller. "You can mind the Audi," he said.

"No problem," said Miller. "You're okay if I smoke in the car, right?"

"No bloody way," snapped Singh, then he grinned when he realised that Miller was only winding him up. "Bastard."

"Love you too, Amar," said Miller, and let himself out.

Weston took out his iPhone and recorded a three hundred and sixty-degree video of the room, then took individual shots of the bed, the desk, the floor and the bathroom, holding his breath as he snapped away through the doorway. "All done," he said eventually, and put the phone away.

Singh took out a portable hard disk drive from his pocket and connected it to the laptop before switching it on. The drive would bypass the laptop's password and copy everything that was stored on its hard drive.

"Shall I do the bathroom?" Shepherd asked Weston.

"I'd be grateful," said Weston. "The smell is making me gag." He opened his briefcase and took out a portable scanner, the size and shape of a table tennis bat. He switched it on and started passing it over the bed.

Shepherd went into the bathroom. The smell was disgusting but he knew that within a minute or so he'd get used to it. There was a shower in one corner covered with a mould-spotted plastic curtain. The shower cubicle itself was grey with grime and there were wads of hair blocking the drain. The plastic toilet

142

seat was yellowed with age and there were brown stains running down the bowl. There was black mould on the ceiling and a damp patch close to the window.

The floor tiles were cracked and didn't look as if they had been cleaned in years. There was a small window with frosted glass. Set into it was a plastic ventilation fan, but it wasn't moving and was encrusted with dirt.

Shepherd reached into his jacket pocket and took out a pair of blue latex gloves. He put them on and gingerly lifted the lid off the toilet cistern. He smiled when he saw the plastic bottle in a sealed Ziploc bag. He put the lid down and retrieved the bag, twisting the lid off the bottle. He peered inside and then sniffed. Cannabis. He replaced the lid, resealed the bag, and dropped it back into the water.

He put the lid back on the cistern. There was a wooden cupboard under the sink and Shepherd kneeled down and opened it. Three small cockroaches scuttled away from the light. There was a blue plastic bucket with two mouldy sponges and two bottles of toilet cleaner. He took the caps off the bottles, but there was only liquid inside. He carefully unscrewed the plastic U-bend and smiled when he saw the rolled-up Ziploc bag. He fished it out and unrolled it to reveal a thumb drive.

He took the thumb drive back into the main room and showed it to Singh. "Excellent," he said. "Give me a minute or two until I've copied the hard drive."

"Where was it?" asked Weston.

"Sink U-bend," said Shepherd.

Weston nodded his approval, then pointed at a stack of pamphlets and brochures. "ISIS propaganda, under the mattress. I've taken pictures."

Shepherd picked up one of the brochures. It was in English and Arabic and detailed various terrorist acts, including driving into crowds, poisoning products on supermarket shelves, and attacking uniformed service-men with knives and acid. Possession of such material was enough to guarantee a prison sentence for Karim, but as with the cannabis, they had bigger fish to fry.

Weston walked around the perimeter of the room, running the scanner along the skirting board, then checked the walls.

Singh finished copying the laptop's hard drive and he unplugged his portable drive. He took his MacBook from his briefcase, booted it up and then inserted the thumb drive into the USB slot. There were dozens of files on the drive, including a file of photographs of the Bullring shopping centre, one of the largest in the country, and another file of pictures taken around Birmingham Airport.

"Possible targets?" said Singh.

"The obvious ones," said Shepherd.

Singh flicked through the files. There were screenshots of Google Maps and satellite photographs, mainly of government buildings and public areas. One of the files was named "BANKS" and Singh clicked on it. Inside were details of three bank accounts.

"Nice," said Shepherd.

"I'm copying it all as we speak," said Singh, tapping on his keyboard. "Including all the porn, and there's a lot of it. There's enough kiddie porn on his computer to put him away for a long time, never mind the terrorism files."

Shepherd picked up the copy of the Koran and flicked through it. Towards the end there were several phone numbers written in the margin. He took out his phone and photographed the numbers, then picked up the dictionary. There were no notes in it, though dozens of words and phrases had been underlined, presumably ones that Karim had difficulty with.

Weston finished checking the walls. He stood in the middle of the room, the scanner at his side, and looked around. There was a faded carpet on the floor speckled with crumbs and stray hairs. It didn't look as if it had been cleaned in years, if ever.

The curtains were just as grubby as the carpet, stained from years of being pulled open and closed by unwashed hands. Weston went over to the curtains and ran his hands down them. He smiled when he felt something at the bottom in the hem. "Naughty, naughty," he said. He gently pried out two keys attached to a fob and held them up. "Keys to a storage locker," he said — the name of the storage company was written on the fob.

"Bingo," said Shepherd.

Weston placed the keys down on the bed and took several photographs of them.

Shepherd took out his phone and called Miller, and five minutes later he went down to the front door and let him in. When the locksmith saw the key, he grinned.

"You can copy it?" asked Shepherd.

"Of course," said Miller. He put down his case, opened it and took out a small metal box, about the size of a tobacco tin. As Miller put the tin down on the desk, Shepherd realised it actually *was* a tobacco tin, one that had once contained Old Holborn tobacco. "My grandad's," said Miller. "I found a dozen in his shed after he died. They're the perfect size." The tin had been filled with wax and Miller pressed both keys in twice, making an impression of both sides before wiping them clean and giving them back to Weston. "I'll need a couple of hours because I'll have to do them by hand."

"We'll book you into a hotel," said Shepherd. He looked at his watch. "I'd like to check out the storage locker before Karim finishes work."

"There's a Holiday Inn down the road, I could check in and get started," said Miller, closing the lid on the tin and putting it into his bag.

Weston put the keys back where he'd found them. Miller let himself out. Singh took out the thumb drive and gave it to Shepherd. "All done," he said.

Shepherd put the thumb drive into the Ziploc bag, rolled it up, then put it back where he'd found it.

When he got back to the bedroom, Singh had plugged the portable hard drive into his own laptop and was checking Karim's browsing history. In the past week the jihadist had visited dozens of ISIS websites and chat rooms, and an equal number of porn sites, where his preference appeared to be very young girls who had been tied up and gagged.

"He's one sick puppy," said Singh. He clicked through to a Yahoo email account. There were several emails in the draft folder, a common way for jihadists to communicate. Emails sent between different accounts in the normal way could be tracked and read by intelligence agencies such as GCHQ and the NSA, but emails that stayed in draft folders were invisible to prying eyes. Other members of the cell could simply log in to the account and read any new messages in the folder. Singh flicked through the emails. He was talking to jihadists around the UK, offering them advice and encouragement. The emails were low on details but it was clear that there were several attacks being planned. The subject of many of the emails was an Arabic phrase: حرق بطيء

"What's that?" asked Shepherd. "What does it mean?"

Singh copied and pasted the phrase into an online Arabic dictionary. "Slow burn," he said. "Looks like this has been a long time in the planning."

"We'll go through these back at Thames House," said Shepherd. He looked around the room. "I think we're done now, don't you?" he asked Weston.

Weston nodded. "I'm pretty sure we've found all there is to find," he said.

"What about a bug, Amar?" asked Shepherd.

"Your wish is my command, oh master." He opened his briefcase and put his MacBook away. He took out a screwdriver and looked around. There was a fuse box above the door and he stood on a chair to switch off the electricity before unscrewing a power socket under the

147

desk. He stood up and compared the socket with half a dozen he had in his briefcase. One was a close match and he held it up. "My lucky day," he said. "Sound and vision." He went down under the desk again and wired the socket into the circuit, then screwed it into the wall. When he'd finished he took out his iPhone and showed Shepherd the view from the concealed camera. "State of the art," he said.

Shepherd grinned. The picture was crystal clear and covered most of the bedsit. "Nice one," he said.

Singh put the phone away. "So, are we good to go?"

"Yeah, you go first and wait for us by the car. We'll check that everything is back where it should be and we'll go check with Rob."

As Singh let himself out, Weston took out his phone and compared the room with the photographs he had taken earlier, to make sure that nothing had been moved. Then he did the same with the video. "All good," he said eventually.

They left and Shepherd pulled the door closed and refitted the padlock. They both removed their latex gloves as they walked down the stairs and headed out.

The Ford Fiesta was in the inside lane of the M1, heading north. The car was trapped between two large trucks and Yusuf Butt would have been happier getting into the middle lane, but the traffic was heavy and there were no gaps. Plus the hatchback was underpowered, and with three on board it was only just managing to keep pace with the trucks. Mohammed Desai was driving and Nazam Miah, as usual, was sitting in the back. He was the youngest so that was where he always sat.

They had left London two hours earlier and were about forty minutes from their destination according to the satnav. "I don't see why we're the ones driving to see them," said Desai.

"You think the mountain should come to Mohammed, do you?" laughed Miah. "Fuck me, get over yourself, bruv."

"I'm just saying, they should come to us."

"It's what I agreed," said Butt. "And we're not going the whole way, we're meeting them at Trowell Services."

"Mate, we could have met them at London Gateway, which is a lot closer to us," said Desai.

"Neutral territory," said Butt.

"Milton Keynes then. This is shit, I hate driving outside London."

"It's a motorway, bruv," said Butt. "It's no hardship."

"You're not the one driving," said Desai. He took a quick look in his wing mirror, indicated, and pulled out into the middle lane. He pressed hard on the accelerator but the hatchback only managed to crawl past the truck.

"Who is this guy we're going to see, anyway?" asked Miah.

"I wasn't told his name," said Butt. He held up the cheap Samsung phone he was holding. "I don't know him, but we've been in touch on WhatsApp."

"You don't know him but we're acting as his delivery boys? Fuck that!"

"Bruv, you don't know what you're talking about," said Butt. "Anwar asked me to do this, and you don't say no to Anwar." There were two kilos of the Semtex plastic explosive and six detonators in a Tesco carrier bag between Butt's feet. He hadn't told them that they were delivering explosives because they were jittery enough already.

They arrived at the service station ten minutes before the appointed time. They parked at the edge of the car park and Butt sent a message on WhatsApp: "*We're early*".

The reply came almost immediately: "*So are we*". The headlights on a black Honda Jazz parked about fifty feet away flashed twice.

"Right, keep the engine running," said Butt. He climbed out of the car and walked over to the Honda, holding the carrier bag at his side, trying not to swing it too much even though he knew that the explosive was perfectly stable.

As he got closer he could see that there were three Asian men in the car, all with beards. The driver was wearing dark glasses and the front passenger had a baseball cap pulled down low over his eyes. The passenger side window wound down. Butt passed through the carrier bag and the man took it without a word. Then the driver leaned over. "Hey, bruv, do I know you?" he asked.

Butt bent down and peered through the open window. "I don't think so."

"It's Butty, right?" The driver took off his dark glasses and leaned across his passenger. "Yeah, I thought it was you."

150

He opened his door and climbed out. As he walked around the front of the car, Butt recognised him. "Noodles!" he said. "Fuck me, bruv. Long time no see." The two men embraced. It had been more than a year since he had seen Abdullah Rahman. As he had arrived at the training camp in Syria, Rahman had been about to leave. Rahman had been Butt's guide for a week, explaining the basics of life in the ISIS camp and carrying out basic weapons training with him. Noodles was the nickname that had been given to Rahman at school by his classmates when one of them had discovered that his favourite dish was ramen.

"So you're involved in this thing?" said Butt.

"Hell, yeah. We've been practising like fuck for the last three months." He patted Butt on the back. "Good to see you, bruv." He jabbed a finger at Butt's stomach. "Putting on weight like me," he laughed.

"The food over there was crap," said Butt. "I was skin and bone when I got back."

"But fit as fuck, right?" said Rahman. "They put us through our paces, that's for sure. So you're in the Big Smoke, yeah?"

"Yeah. Where are you guys based?"

"Leeds, but we're heading down to London next week." He punched Butt on the shoulder. "We should get together after this is over," he said. "Talk about the old times."

"That'd be good, bruv."

"Keep a hold of the burner phone. We can message each other."

"They said I'm to chuck the phone after this."

"Yeah, they told me the same but they're untraceable. I'll keep hold of mine and that way we can always stay in touch."

Butt nodded. "Yeah, okay."

"*Barakallahu fiikum*," said Rahman. May Allah bless you.

"Right back at you, bruv," said Butt. He returned to the Fiesta.

"Who was that?" asked Mohammed as Butt sat down and slammed the door.

"No one," said Butt. He waved at the car park exit. "Come on, let's go home."

Weston and Singh waited in the coffee shop of the Holiday Inn while Shepherd went up to Miller's room. The locksmith had finished one key and was working on the second. He had attached a vice to the dressing table and was using an electric grinder, peering through protective goggles. After a few seconds he compared the key with the wax impression in the tobacco tin, wrinkled his nose, and went back to work on it. "All good?" asked Shepherd.

"Piece of cake," said Miller. "It's a standard blank. I'll be done soon."

Shepherd sat on the bed and phoned Pritchard to update him on their progress. "So it looks as if Jaraf is on the level," said Pritchard, once Shepherd had filled him in. "That's good news."

"We'll have a better idea once we've checked out his storage locker," said Shepherd.

"And you'll be back in London tonight?"

152

"That's the plan."

"Excellent. Drop by my office as soon as you're back and we'll talk about where we go from here."

Pritchard ended the call and Shepherd put the phone away.

Miller held up the second key. "All done," he said. He gave the two keys to Shepherd, then put his equipment away. They headed downstairs. Weston and Singh paid for their coffees and they walked outside to the Audi.

The storage company was on an industrial estate to the south of Birmingham. There were signs that announced the facility was open twenty-four hours a day and subject to full CCTV coverage. There was an office close to the entrance but there was no need for them to check in and one of the keys opened the main gate to the premises. The number of the storage locker had been on the key fob, and there were signs pointing the way to the various areas. Karim's locker was to the left, close to the end of a concrete-floored corridor. It was a walk-in locker with a shutter. Miller used the key he'd made and pushed the shutter up. There were a dozen cardboard boxes inside, along with a bicycle and two suitcases.

There was a light switch on the wall and Shepherd flicked it on. They walked in and Weston pulled down the shutter. Shepherd checked his phone. The surveillance team were outside Karim's place of work and they would text him if the target left the building. There was nothing from the team. "We're good to go," he said.

Weston took out his iPhone and took a video of the storage locker, then took individual photographs of all the items. By the looks of the packaging, the boxes all contained drones of various sizes and styles. When Weston had finished taking his photographs, Shepherd pulled on his latex gloves and opened one of the boxes. Inside was a Chinese-made drone, still in its polythene wrapping. It was about two feet across with six horizontal propellers. The control unit was also still in its bag, with the batteries separate. Karim clearly hadn't got around to testing it. The other eleven drones were also still in their original wrapping. There were three identical to the one in the box that Shepherd had opened, but the others were larger, the biggest almost three feet across with eight rotors. "Amar, do you think you can put GPS trackers in them all?" asked Shepherd.

Singh nodded. "The big ones, sure. I might have to get a bit creative with the smaller ones." He peered over Shepherd's shoulder. "That's a beauty. It's sold as an agricultural sprayer. Farmers use them to spray crops."

"What sort of payload will it carry?"

"Twenty pounds or so," said Singh.

"With a flight time of . . .?"

Singh shrugged. "Half an hour or thereabouts. Depends on the payload, altitude, speed, lots of variables."

"Can you imagine the damage you could do with a twenty-pound IED on board?" asked Weston.

"Unfortunately, I can," said Shepherd. "You can just buy these off the shelf?"

154

"You can buy them on Amazon in the States," said Singh. "I've not seen them on sale in the UK, but you can order them from China for ten thousand dollars or so. You don't even need a licence to fly them, though that's going to change in the near future." He placed his briefcase on top of one of the boxes and clicked the locks open.

"Put a GPS on the bike, too," he said. "Just to be on the safe side." He looked around the locker. The walls were featureless and white and there were no power sockets. "Some sort of video surveillance would be nice."

Singh looked up from his briefcase. "I've a camera that can slot into the end of one of the fluorescent light units," he said, nodding up at the ceiling. There were three fluorescent lamps running parallel to each other.

"Good man," said Shepherd.

Miller had knelt down in front of the two suitcases and was working on the lock of the top one. He opened it and unzipped the case. It was full of packs of dried beans. Miller picked up one of the packs. "Castor beans," he said, repeating the words on the packaging. "What are they, some sort of Asian snack?"

Shepherd chuckled. "Check the second case," he said. "Pound to a penny you'll find drain cleaner. And nail varnish remover."

"What are you now, psychic?" said Miller. He dropped the pack back in the case and closed the lid. He opened the lock on the second case, then sat back on his heels and opened it. It was full of plastic bottles of sodium hydroxide drain cleaner.

Singh laughed at the look of amazement on the locksmith's face. "Have you never seen *Breaking Bad?*" Singh said.

Miller's frown deepened. "What's *Breaking Bad?*"

"The TV show."

"I don't watch TV," said Miller. "I've got a life."

"It's about a high school teacher who starts making meth," said Singh. "And in one episode he makes ricin. It's one of the most potent poisons there is and you make it from castor beans. You let the beans soak in sodium hydroxide then you put them in a blender with acetone — that's the nail varnish remover — dry it out and you end up with ricin powder. A few milligrams will kill you stone dead."

"Are you serious?" asked Miller.

Shepherd nodded. "Inhaled, injected or ingested. You could just throw it into a shopping centre and kill dozens of people. Use a drone delivery system and you could kill hundreds."

"It's that easy to make?" asked Miller.

"You need to get the ratios right, but yeah, it's pretty straightforward," said Singh. "There's no power socket here so they'll be doing it somewhere else." He looked over at Shepherd. "This alone is enough to put him away for a long time. Throw in the kiddie porn and he'll be an old man before he gets out."

Shepherd nodded. "That's not our call, though," he said. "Let's take the pictures and set up the video bug, and we'll let Giles Pritchard decide what to do next."

Weston took photographs of the contents of the cases, and of the individual drones. Singh placed a

156

small white plastic unit on the end of one of the fluorescent lights and then checked the signal on his iPhone.

Miller helped Singh install GPS transmitters in the drones. That was a time-consuming process as each drone had to be carefully unwrapped and opened, the transmitter placed where it wouldn't be found, and then the drone rewrapped. They still had three drones to go when Shepherd's phone rang. It was the leader of the surveillance team. "Tango One has just left the sorting office," he said. "He's mobile, on a scooter, and heading home."

"Let me know if he changes direction," said Shepherd. "We're in a storage facility about six miles away from his house."

"Will do."

Shepherd ended the call. "Karim's on the way home," he said. "Even though he's not heading here, let's not take any risks — it's time to pack up and go."

Singh finished bugging the drone he was working on while Miller and Shepherd closed the boxes of the others. Weston used the video and photographs on his phone to check that everything was put back in its original position before they left.

Half an hour later they were back in Singh's Audi, heading for London. Shepherd used Singh's iPhone to get the feed from the camera they'd placed in his bedsit. Karim was sitting at his desk, doing something on his laptop. "We can see what he's doing on the laptop, right?" Shepherd asked Singh.

"Every word he types, every website he visits," said Singh. "There's now a keylogger on his hard drive that'll tell us everything."

Karim had picked up a pen and was writing something in a notebook. Shepherd wondered what was going through the man's mind. He was living in one of the best countries in the world. Every year tens of thousands of people risked their lives to get to the UK in the hope of starting a new life here. The country offered asylum and security to legal (and illegal) immigrants; it gave them homes, hospital treatment, schools; it took care of them in a way that their own countries never would. And yet Karim and fellow jihadists wanted to bring death and destruction to the UK? For what? What did they hope to achieve with the callous murder of innocent civilians? To turn Britain into an Islamic republic? To replace the country's legal system with Sharia law? No matter what they did, any such objectives were totally unachievable. All their terrorist attacks did was to turn the population further against them, and while the backlash might result in a handful of British Muslims embracing fundamentalism and jihad, there was still no way that they would ever succeed in their ambitions. Ali Karim clearly didn't realise that as he sat in his bedsit and planned to murder innocent civilians. In his mind, killing non-believers would strengthen his religion, but to anyone whose mind wasn't clouded by fundamentalism and hatred, the faults in his logic were inescapable.

"I never understood what these guys think they're going to achieve," said Shepherd, voicing his thoughts.

158

"If they want the UK to become an Islamic republic, well that's not going to happen, is it? Troops out of the Middle East?" He shrugged. "Most of them are out already."

"It's not about achieving objectives," said Singh. "It's about the adrenaline rush."

Shepherd turned to look at him. "You believe that?"

Singh gestured at Karim on the screen of the iPhone. "You think he's a religious scholar doing this because God has spoken to him? He's doing it because it gives his boring life some meaning. It makes him feel special. What is he? A postal worker in Birmingham. Do you think he ever gets laid? Dead-end job, no prospects, in a society where he can only speak to a girl if there's a chaperone around. There's only two ways a saddo like that can get some excitement in his life — join a child-grooming ring or get involved with jihad. Sex or guns, either way they get the adrenaline rush."

"That's harsh, Amar."

"Harsh but true," said Singh. "It annoys the hell out of me. I'm not even Muslim, but have you any idea the looks I get when I get on the Tube with my gym gear? Or walk into a pub or a restaurant? People like me with brown skin — we all get tarred with the same brush. And for what? Because pricks like that can't get laid."

"So what's the answer?" asked Shepherd. "Because putting these guys in prison doesn't work. They spend six or seven years in Belmarsh and they come out even more fundamentalist than they went in. And better trained."

Singh shrugged. "It's not my call, is it? I'm just a small cog in a very big machine."

"But if you had the power, what would you do?"

Singh grinned. "Me, I'd make all eighteen-year-old boys do two years national service. It's a testosterone problem. I'd put all the eighteen-year-olds together, mix them up, feed them the same food and put them through the same training. A lot of these lads who get radicalised get told by the people who groom them that everyone who isn't a Muslim is a kafir, less than a dog. But if they were put in a barracks with dozens of guys from other backgrounds, they'd soon learn that people are people. And being trained to shoot and fight and all that good stuff will get the aggression out of their system."

"Or make them better-trained terrorists?"

Singh shook his head. "The only reason they become terrorists is because they're led to believe they're superior to everyone else. But two years being forced to train and live with people from other backgrounds and religions will make them realise that everyone's the same, right? Black, brown, white, whatever. You've got an Army background, haven't you? Paras and SAS. You know what I'm talking about?"

"Sure," said Shepherd. He knew exactly what Singh meant. Basic training stressed the importance of teamwork, and while soldiers in the SAS tended to have more freedom, the principle was the same — you lived and died with your comrades. And when the bullets were flying, no one cared about the colour, religion or sexual preference of the man next to them. Warriors

160

were warriors. "There is a flaw in your argument, though, Amar."

"I'm listening."

"The Army hates amateurs. They don't want conscripts, they want professionals."

"They wouldn't have to be sent to fight," said Singh. "Just trained."

"It's never going to happen."

"I think you're right," said Singh. "Which means that it's only going to get worse."

Shepherd continued to watch Karim working on his laptop. "At least this one will get nipped in the bud," he said.

Singh dropped Shepherd outside Thames House and then drove off to park his Audi. Shepherd went inside and straight up to Pritchard's office. He told Pritchard everything they'd done in Birmingham, and showed him the live feed from the hidden camera. Karim was still on his laptop.

"We're monitoring his computer use?" said Pritchard.

Shepherd nodded. "And Amar has copied everything on his hard disc and will be working on that today. But Karim is a jihadist, one thousand per cent. And the fact that he has the raw materials for ricin production in his lock-up is a worry."

"He hadn't made any actual ricin?" asked Pritchard.

"Not that we found. Just the raw materials."

Pritchard shifted uncomfortably in his chair. "What I'm wondering is if he'd called a halt to ricin production because he'd been offered something more potent."

"You think Karim might have got his hands on VX?"

"I think it's a possibility we're going to have to consider." He drummed his fingers on his desktop. "Jaraf's obviously the real deal," he said eventually. "Ali Karim wasn't on our radar at all."

"Which raises the question of what the hell Border Force is doing," said Shepherd. "How could this guy fly to Syria for terrorist training and then come back to start planning a major terrorist outrage without anyone knowing?"

"You're preaching to the converted," said Pritchard. "The government has been told time and time again that we need to be checking the passports of people who leave the country."

"Most other countries stamp passports in and out," said Shepherd. "I don't see why it would be so hard for the UK to do the same. Then when a guy like Karim flies back, someone can look at how long he's been out of the country and ask him where he's been. And if he doesn't have a decent explanation he can be red-flagged and we can put him under the microscope. If Jaraf hadn't given us Karim's name he could have mounted a ricin attack and killed dozens, maybe hundreds, of people."

"But he did give us Karim's name, so we're good."

"He gave us Karim, but Karim's not the only one. Who knows how many others are out there?"

"Well the sooner we get Jaraf's family over, the sooner we'll know," said Pritchard. "I'd like you to fly over to Turkey to bring them over."

"Not a problem," said Shepherd. "Are you arranging a plane?"

Pritchard chuckled. "Chance'd be a fine thing," he said. "There's no way we can budget for a private jet. You'll have to bring them on a commercial flight."

"The airline is going to want to see passports and visas before they'll let them on."

Pritchard rubbed his chin. "Good point," he said. "Did you ask Jaraf what their passport situation is?"

"He said he had a Palestinian passport, but he destroyed it on the flight in."

"So his wife and children probably have the same," said Pritchard.

"They're in a refugee camp," said Shepherd. "Who knows what paperwork they have on them. And even if they have their passports, they won't be allowed on a commercial flight without a valid visa."

"How about this: you take them to the British Embassy in Ankara. If they have their passports they can be issued with visas. If they don't have their passports, MI6's man in Ankara can arrange for them to be given British passports. It's not ideal but at least it'll get them into the country." MI6, the Secret Intelligence Service, had officers at most of the UK's embassies collecting and analysing human intelligence, often by running foreign agents.

"Fortuitously, there is something else you can do for me while you are out there," said Pritchard. "We keep getting requests from our embassy to interview three jihadist brides who are in the camp."

"British?"

Pritchard nodded. "Two are British-born, their parents immigrants who had fled their own countries. One is Swedish — Somalian, but she lived in London with her family. All three girls left for Syria when they were sixteen or seventeen. They all married jihadists and two of them had children with them. The Home Secretary stripped two of them of their citizenship last year and is refusing to allow any of them back to the UK."

"So they're stateless?"

"No. They all have dual nationality. One has Dutch citizenship through her father, one has a Pakistani passport, and another has Bangladeshi citizenship. But they all want to come back here."

"How did they end up in Turkey?"

"Two of them were in the Ain Issa camp in Raqqa. There were ten thousand refugees there but the camp was shelled by the Turks when they crossed the border in October 2019 to attack the Kurds. A lot of the refugees fled into Turkey, including two of the girls. The Turks moved them to Kilis and they've been there ever since. The third girl arrived in the camp last month. She claims she was in an ISIS camp that was attacked and made her way across the border with a group of Syrian refugees. A woman who works for the British Embassy in Ankara has visited the girls several times and has been fighting their corner — with very little success, it has to be said. Now she's saying that the girls

164

have information that we might find useful and wants us to interview them."

"What about the MI6 staff at the embassy?"

"The feeling at Six is that the girls will say absolutely anything to get back to the UK."

"And you think differently?"

"The woman is being quite vociferous. I think that as you're going to be at the camp to collect Jaraf's family, it wouldn't do any harm to visit the three girls and see what they have to say." He looked at his watch, a not-too-subtle hint that the meeting was over.

Ali Karim walked out of Euston station and looked around. He saw Anwar Rafiq sitting on a bench in the small strip of park between the station and Euston Road. Karim's instructions had been clear and he followed them, turning right and walking alongside the park to give Rafiq the chance to see if he was being followed. Karim turned left towards the road, walked a dozen or so steps and then turned around and walked back to the station. He looked over at Rafiq and Rafiq nodded. He wasn't being followed.

Karim walked over to the bench and sat down next to Rafiq. There was a Nike backpack on the floor by his feet, black with a white swoosh. "*As-salamu alaykum,*" said Rafiq.

Karim nodded. "*Wa alaykumu s-salam wa rahmatullah.*"

Rafiq pushed the bag towards Karim with his foot. "There is Semtex inside, and detonators. All you will need."

"I don't understand the change of plan," said Karim. "I have everything we need to make the ricin. What happened?"

"Before we didn't have a decent explosive, and now we do," said Rafiq. "We will kill more with the explosive than with the poison."

"How so?" asked Karim.

Rafiq leaned towards Karim. "Remember the funeral of Qassem Soleimani, after that bastard Trump blew him away with missiles? They buried what was left of him in his home town, Kerman."

"Of course." The Iranian general was killed in a US drone strike in the first few days of 2020, in an attack personally ordered by US president DonaldTrump. There were demonstrations decrying the assassination around the world, but like most Sunni Muslims, Karim had welcomed the man's death. Soleimani was a Shia Muslim who hated al-Qaeda and ISIS with a vengeance and who regarded Sunni Muslims as animals who deserved to be exterminated along with all kafirs.

Rafiq held up his hand as if he knew exactly what Karim was thinking. "I know, no one cheered louder than me when his death was announced. But there are lessons to be learned from what happened at the old bastard's funeral. Remember? There was a stampede. Fifty brothers were trampled to death and hundreds were injured. And there were no explosions there, no one was attacking them." He gestured at the bag. "There will be three million people crowded together by the river. Imagine the panic when drones start

166

exploding above their heads. The kafirs will panic and trample each other. Hundreds will die. Thousands maybe. This could be bigger than 9-11, bruv."

Karim nodded. "I understand, bruv."

"Your guys are ready to go?"

"We've practised with the drones and everyone's up to speed. We were just about to start making the ricin, but we can switch to IEDs. We'll use phones to detonate, or will timers be okay?"

"Use phones," said Rafiq. "And your guys aren't to use waypoints, fly by sight, okay?"

"Sure."

Rafiq stood up. "You're going back to Birmingham now, right?"

Karim nodded. "I'll take the bag to the storage locker, and I'll get the guys started on the IEDs in a couple of days."

"The sooner the better," said Rafiq.

"I understand. Two of the guys are down in London, getting the lie of the land. As soon as they're back we can get started."

Rafiq nodded. "*Hafidaka Allah*," he said. He walked away before Karim could reply.

Shepherd flew into Ankara at just before five-thirty in the afternoon on a Turkish Airlines flight from Gatwick via Istanbul. It was Christmas Eve and the plane was half empty. He cleared immigration in Istanbul with no problems using his Paul Easton passport. He only had hand luggage, so twenty minutes after the plane touched down he was in the arrivals area and looking for the taxi rank. "Dan Shepherd?" said a voice to his left, and Shepherd turned to see a man in his late forties or early fifties, longish hair starting to grey, wearing a rumpled brown suit and well-polished black shoes.

Shepherd frowned, wondering how the man knew his name. He was sure he'd never met him before.

"I'm from the embassy," said the man. His teeth were almost beige, his first and second fingers on his right hand were yellowed from nicotine, and even from three feet away Shepherd could smell stale tobacco.

Shepherd frowned. "Really? I wasn't aware that the embassy knew I was coming."

The man leaned forward and lowered his voice. "I said I'm from the embassy, not working for the embassy. I'm with Six." He stuck out his hand. "Michael Warren-Madden."

Shepherd sighed. Pritchard had told him who the MI6 contact was, but hadn't said that he'd be meeting him at the airport. He shook the man's hand.

"All good?" asked Warren-Madden. He grinned, showing even more stained teeth and a sprinkling of amalgam fillings.

"Who told you I'd be on that flight?"

Warren-Madden grinned. "I'd be remiss in my job if I didn't know that a representative of Box was on my turf, wouldn't I?" Box was how most insiders referred to MI5 — based on its old wartime address of Box 500.

"And they sent you a picture?"

168

"You were described to me, and you fit the description to a tee." He smiled, but his eyes were hard.

Shepherd stared at Warren-Madden, trying to get the measure of the man, but his smile didn't falter. Had Pritchard told Warren-Madden that he was on the flight? If so, why hadn't he mentioned it to him?

"The thing is, Michael, I don't know you and I don't know what your profile is here in Turkey," Shepherd said eventually. "For all I know there might be half a dozen members of the MIT watching us as we speak." Millî İstihbarat Teçskilati was Turkey's state intelligence agency, and while most of its duties were carried out in Turkey, there was strong evidence that MIT agents had committed assassinations around the world — including the murder of Kurdish nationalist Mehmet Kaygisiz, who was shot in a café in London's Newington Green.

Warren-Madden's smile tightened. "First of all, I've no reason to think that I'm on MIT's radar," he said. "And second of all, give me some credit. I carried out a full range of anti-surveillance techniques before I came and if I'd had the slightest hint that I was being followed, I'd have aborted the meeting."

"There's CCTV everywhere, they could be watching through that."

Warren-Madden shrugged. "I'm just here to meet and greet," he said, "no ulterior motive. I'm just going to drive you to your hotel and we can chat along the way."

Shepherd nodded. "Okay. Where's your car?"

"Outside," said Warren-Madden.

He held out his hand for Shepherd's holdall but Shepherd shook his head. "That's okay, I can carry my own bag."

Warren-Madden shrugged and took Shepherd outside. Shepherd was wearing a black jacket over a polo shirt. He'd been expecting hot weather but while the sky was a cloudless blue, the temperature was below twenty. "Does it get hotter than this?" he asked Warren-Madden.

"This is warm for December," said the MI6 officer. "And it gets quite cold at night. Summer's a different matter." He took Shepherd towards a multi-storey car park. On the way he took out a pack of Benson & Hedges and lit one with a disposable lighter. He offered the pack to Shepherd but he shook his head. "I know, disgusting habit," said Warren-Madden. "But I figure I'm allowed one vice." His white Nissan Qashqai was on the third floor. Shepherd kept a close eye out for followers but he didn't see anyone tailing them. He tossed his bag onto the back seat and climbed in next to Warren-Madden. Warren-Madden started the car and drove slowly out of the block. Shepherd wound down the window to let the smoke out.

"So you've got nothing better to do over Christmas than come to Turkey?" asked Warren-Madden.

"Just following orders," said Shepherd. "Do they even celebrate Christmas here?"

"They're Muslims, so technically no," said Warren-Madden. "But perversely Santa Claus was born in Turkey. They call him Noel Baba here and he brings gifts to children on New Year's Eve. You'll see

170

Christmas decorations in the shops and restaurants, it's as commercial here as anywhere else."

Shepherd couldn't contain his surprise. "Santa Claus was born in Turkey?"

"Oh yes. Saint Nicholas was born about AD 270 in Patara."

"Well you live and learn," said Shepherd.

"Yes you do," said Warren-Madden. "Hopefully."

The roads were fairly clear so it was easy to see that they weren't being followed. Warren-Madden smiled when he saw Shepherd checking the side mirror but didn't say anything.

"What's the plan re the visas, assuming they have passports?" asked Shepherd eventually.

"Assuming their passports are in order we'll take them to the embassy and we can get visas issued for the UK," said Warren-Madden. He finished his cigarette and dropped the butt into a polystyrene cup in the central console.

"I was told that if they didn't have passports you could issue British passports through the embassy."

"Sure. That's easily done."

"And if they don't have Turkish visas?" asked Shepherd. "If they crossed the border on foot they probably didn't enter the country legally."

"It won't be an issue," he said. "We've got good contacts in the immigration department and we regularly fly out refugees who have been accepted into Britain. And none of the refugees who cross over from Syria into Turkey have their passports stamped."

"Have you spoken to the wife?"

"No. They said that it was an MI5 operation and I was just to offer you every service."

"And you don't envisage any problems?"

"It seems pretty straightforward to me. I could have brought them over myself, to be honest."

"As you said, it's an MI5 operation," said Shepherd.

"Exactly." Warren-Madden flashed him a tight smile.

They drove in silence for a while. Shepherd had been booked into the Mövenpick Hotel, which was a seventeen-mile drive from the airport. They passed several other hotels and Warren-Madden still hadn't asked where he was staying, so he obviously knew already. Shepherd had the feeling that the MI6 officer was waiting for Shepherd to mention it, but he didn't. If Warren-Madden was playing some sort of game, then Shepherd was determined not to get involved. He figured Warren-Madden wanted to show how clever he was and that sort of behaviour just annoyed Shepherd. It seemed the more his career had progressed, the more his colleagues and bosses had played games. As a soldier, a paratrooper, there had never been any game-playing. The officers told you what to do and you did it to the best of your abilities. There was no choice — for a military unit to function efficiently people had to do exactly as they were told. That changed somewhat when he joined the SAS. With the confidence of being a member of the best special forces group in the world came a modicum of arrogance, but game-players tended not to last long in the close-knit group. The exception to the rule was in the way the troopers treated their officers, the Ruperts, because whereas the troopers were generally in the regiment for the long haul, the Ruperts came and went. Playing mind games with officers, especially the less-than-capable ones, was accepted practice, so long as it didn't interfere with the job in hand.

It was when Shepherd moved from the SAS to police work that he began to be confronted with colleagues trying to score political points. Getting promoted in the Army was almost always down to merit, but in the police it was more a matter of ticking the right boxes. Officers had to demonstrate a commitment to diversity and community, to attend the right courses and promote politically correct dogma. Solving crimes and putting away criminals was a low priority so far as promotion was concerned, and appearances mattered more than results. The higher up the ranks, the more game-playing went on, and over the years senior officers had started to have more in common with politicians than the average bobby on the beat.

Shepherd had been lucky in that most of his police career had been spent in an elite undercover unit, and his bosses had shielded him from much of the point-scoring and turf wars. But when he transferred to SOCA, the ill-fated Serious Organised Crime Agency, game-playing had moved up a notch. SOCA had been formed by forcing together police, HM Revenue and Customs investigators and immigration officials, on the assumption that they would cooperate and work as a single agency, similar to the FBI in the United States. In fact very little investigative work was done and the senior officers spent most of their time jockeying for position and defending what they saw as their own empires. The agency was eventually reorganised and rebranded as the National Crime Agency, but so far as Shepherd could see things hadn't much improved.

MI5 officers tended to be better educated and better connected than their police counterparts, so it was only to be expected that they were more adept at game-playing and point-scoring. There was also the matter of trust. MI5's history was littered with double agents and traitors, so it was hardly surprising that much of what went on within the agency was on a need-to-know basis. Turf was guarded jealously and there was always a rush to claim credit when things went right — and a tendency to blame others when operations went wrong. Giles Pritchard, Shepherd's current boss, was the best of a bad bunch, and at least Shepherd trusted the man to watch his back. But Pritchard had started his intelligence career working for MI6, so it might well be that he was the one who had briefed Warren-Madden.

"So what's your plan for tomorrow?" asked Warren-Madden eventually.

"I'm due to take a run out to the refugee camp at nine," said Shepherd. "One of the embassy officials is going to drive me."

"Margie Barker?"

Shepherd didn't react, but Warren-Madden was really starting to get on his nerves. If he knew Margie Barker was involved then he must have known that she was taking him to the camp, so why had he asked what

Shepherd's plan was? "Yeah," said Shepherd. "What's she like?"

"She's well intentioned," said the MI6 officer.

"That's damning with faint praise."

"She wants to help the less fortunate, and that's great, it's just that security-wise we obviously have to be careful who we help, right?"

Shepherd ignored Warren-Madden's attempt to get him to agree. "That's her job, presumably. She works for the embassy."

"No, she works for an NGO. The embassy doesn't pay her wages. These three jihadist brides she's trying to help, that's just a disaster waiting to happen."

"How far away is the camp from here?"

"Eight or nine hours by car," said Warren-Madden. "You might want to think about setting off early. As you can see, it gets dark about five-thirty this time of year."

They drove in silence for a while longer, before Warren-Madden suddenly spoke. "Cards on the table, I think you should steer well clear of the jihadist brides," he said.

"Because?"

"Because they're nothing but trouble. I told Margie but she won't listen. It's like some bloody crusade for her." He grinned. "Though crusade is probably not the thing to say, right."

Shepherd was starting to think that Warren-Madden had an ulterior motive for meeting him at the airport. He had barely mentioned Jaraf and his wife and son; all he seemed to be concerned about were the jihadist brides. He folded his arms and said nothing, waiting for the MI6 man to fill the silence.

"She's one of the 'oh they were only children they didn't know what they were doing' brigade, but that's bollocks. They were all eighteen and over, and two of them had babies while they were in Syria."

"I was told they were sixteen and seventeen."

Warren-Madden waved his hand dismissively. "Well that's as maybe, but they're all over eighteen now."

"I haven't seen anything about them in the media," said Shepherd.

"Margie's worried about the backlash that happened when Shamima Begum went public," said Warren-Madden. "They took away her citizenship and every time she puts her head above the parapet these days she gets shot at. Figuratively speaking." He groped for his pack of cigarettes and shook one out. He slipped it between his lips and pushed in the cigarette lighter on the dashboard.

Shepherd nodded. He knew about the Begum case, as did practically everybody in the UK. She had left east London when she was fifteen and travelled to Syria, where ISIS paired her with a Dutch fighter. She had had three children with him, all of whom had died. When Begum was eventually captured by Syrian forces, she had begged to be allowed back to the UK, but her appeals had been ignored. Her parents were from Bangladesh, so the UK Government washed their hands of her and suggested that she be repatriated to Bangladesh.

"Begum has tainted the whole idea that jihadist brides should be allowed back in the UK, so Margie is trying to get these three dealt with under the table. She tried the Foreign Office and the Home Office, but both times she went behind the back of the ambassador so he wasn't best pleased. Now she's obviously trying to get the security service involved."

"That's not how it was put to me," said Shepherd.

"Really?" said Warren-Madden, looking over at him.

Shepherd sighed. He really didn't like giving any information to the MI6 officer, not after the mind games he'd been playing. But he needed the man's cooperation, for the passports if nothing else, and there was nothing to be gained by antagonising him. "I don't think the interest is coming from our side," he said. "It was just put to me that I was at the camp anyway so I might as well drop by and talk to them."

"Just talk?"

"I was told that this Margie Barker had been requesting that the girls be repatriated. I didn't realise she'd done that without the ambassador's approval."

"He's spitting feathers," said Warren-Madden.

"Can't he have her moved?"

"She's treated as a member of staff and has an office at the embassy, but at the end of the day the UN pays her salary."

"And they pay her to deal with refugees? So she's doing her job, right?"

The cigarette lighter popped out and Warren-Madden used it to light his cigarette with his left hand. He had the feeling that Warren-Madden's smoking was a displacement activity, something he did when he was under stress. He blew smoke before answering. "I can't fault your logic, but her responsibility should be to her country, not to the fanatics who deliberately left our country to breed junior jihadists. These girls didn't have to do what they did, they made deliberate choices. They could have stayed in the UK, gone to university, got good jobs, become valued members of society. Or they could fly to Syria to fuck men who throw gays off rooftops and burn Christians alive. They made their beds, and now they have to lie in them." He flicked ash into the cup. "Can I be honest with you?"

Shepherd resisted the urge to laugh. "Sure." The Mövenpick was ahead of them to the right, and Warren-Madden slapped the indicator. Shepherd checked the wing mirror, not caring whether or not Warren-Madden thought he was being over-cautious. The car immediately behind them was also leaving the main road, but it was a small Fiat being driven by an old woman in a black headscarf. The three vehicles after her all continued down the main road. Then a truck laden with wooden pallets followed them. Shepherd relaxed.

"Okay, here's the scoop as I see it," said Warren-Madden. "It'd be better for all concerned if you just concentrate on collecting your people and taking them back to the UK," said the MI6 officer. "Leave the jihadist wives to rot in the camp until they get sent elsewhere. Then they'll be someone else's problem."

178

"That's not my call," said Shepherd. "My instructions are to talk to them."

"I suppose so," said Warren-Madden. "I just think you'll be wasting your time, that's all."

Shepherd shrugged. "My time's paid for," he said.

"I hear you." Warren-Madden flicked ash again. The hotel was directly ahead of them and Warren-Madden headed for the car park. "The thing is though, I'll be the one arranging the passports for your people, so it makes sense for me to drive you to the camp. Then I can take you all to the embassy and then to the airport."

"That's okay, Margie's met with Mrs Jaraf and she's familiar with the girls and the camp, so it makes sense to go with her."

"Why are they so important, the woman and the boy you're taking back?" Warren-Madden stuck the cigarette between his lips and kept both hands on the wheel as he drove into the car park and brought the SUV to a halt.

Shepherd didn't answer until Warren-Madden had switched off the engine. He was a difficult man to read. He smiled a lot, but his pale blue eyes were cold and emotionless. Shepherd figured he'd benefited from a public school education and three years at Oxford or Cambridge. His accent was Estuary English, but it wasn't quite right, as if he'd acquired it from practice rather than birth. If he was lying about how much he knew about the Jaraf case, Shepherd couldn't tell. "I was just told to bring them back," said Shepherd. "I'm the proverbial mushroom on this one." He looked at

Warren-Madden and smiled, and he smiled back. Shepherd had spent years lying, as an undercover cop and as an MI5 officer, and he knew he was good at it. What he didn't know was how good Warren-Madden was at spotting it.

"Bit of a mystery then," said Warren-Madden. He stubbed his cigarette butt out on the side of the cup, then dropped it in. The two men climbed out of the car. Shepherd opened the rear passenger door and took out his holdall. "I'll be okay checking in myself," said Shepherd.

"No problem." Warren-Madden looked at his watch. "You're sure you don't want me to drive you out to the camp tomorrow? I'm free all day."

Again Shepherd had to force himself not to grin at the MI6 man's transparent attempt to cut Margie Barker out of the loop. "I'd rather stick with the existing arrangement," he said.

"Sure, no problem," said Warren-Madden. "I'll give you my number and you can call me when you're ready for the passports."

"Sure, go ahead," said Shepherd.

Warren-Madden gave him the digits. "You're not going to write it down or put it in your phone?"

Shepherd shook his head. "My memory's pretty good." He waved goodbye and headed into the hotel.

In another hotel room, this one two miles to the east of the Mövenpick Hotel, a group of five men and one woman stared down at a line of surveillance photographs on a table. The group had taken two

180

rooms in the hotel, with a connecting door. The woman was in her late twenties and had only recently left the Israeli Army. Her name was Dinah Klein and she was as hard as nails, though she had the killer cheekbones and pouting lips of a fashion model. The man standing next to her was the youngest of the team, Nathan Segal, just twenty-four years old, with tanned skin and black curly hair. Next to him was Adam Sharon, a short and stocky man with a thick gold chain around his neck. Sharon had prepared the burger in the kitchen that they had tried to poison their target with. The girl who had delivered the burger, and the man who had driven her away from the hotel, had stayed in London.

Klein, Segal and Sharon had flown to Ankara the previous day, along with the leader of the group, a man in his late fifties, his head shaved and his right cheek a mass of scar tissue from a grenade that had exploded just feet away from him twenty years earlier. The only reason Gil Stern hadn't been killed in the blast was that most of the shrapnel had ripped through a mother and two young children before it had reached him. Gil spoke slowly and clearly, with authority.

"This man is using the name Paul Easton, a representative of the Home Office, and he has booked into the Mövenpick Hotel using that name." He tapped one of the surveillance photographs — it showed "Easton" in the arrivals area of the airport. The pictures had been taken by the remaining two men in the team using cameras hidden in backpacks. Micha Abramov and Ben Elon had been on the plane with their target, sitting a few rows behind him in economy. They were surveillance experts and often posed as a gay couple, though both were married and the older of the two — Micha — was a father to three girls. They had sat together but had boarded separately, one before the target and one after. Micha had passed through immigration first and had waited in the departures area, embracing his colleague while their hidden cameras recorded their target.

"He was met by the British Embassy's MI6 representative, Michael Warren-Madden," said Gil, indicating Warren-Madden on the photograph. "He drove him to the hotel, which is where he is now. We have two men outside the hotel to make sure that Easton doesn't leave." He gestured at a tablet that showed a Google Earth map of the area. "There's a GPS tracker on Warren-Madden's car so we know where he is."

"How come an MI6 officer doesn't know his car is bugged?" asked Dinah.

"It's very sophisticated, it only works when the car is in motion," said Gil. "So it's impossible to find if the car's stationary. It's off now because he's at home and the car is parked." He opened a large map and spread it across the table as Klein moved the photographs out of the way. "Tomorrow, Easton will probably head out to the refugee camp. We don't know yet if Warren-Madden will take him. If it isn't Warren-Madden who drives him — if he rents a car or uses a driver — we need to be geared up to follow him, but at a distance. We know where he'll be headed, so we'll have one car half a mile ahead and another half a mile behind. There's no need to get close, not while he's on the way to the camp."

Gil tapped the location of the camp on the map. "We're not sure what will happen next. He might take them to his hotel, to the British Embassy, or straight to the airport, so once he has picked them up we need to be on full alert, there can be no mistakes. We know that they are all booked on the 7.15p.m. Turkish Airlines flight to Gatwick the day after tomorrow. So, it looks as if he will take them back with him to England on his own. Unless he had minders booked elsewhere on the flight."

"What about Warren-Madden?" asked Dinah.

"He would already be booked on the flight if he was going," said Gil. "We have contacts at the airline so I'll be monitoring to see what names, if any, match the flight from London. But my gut feeling is that this Easton assumes he isn't in any danger and hasn't bothered with security. The fact that he was openly met by an MI6 agent also suggests he's not being surreptitious about what he's doing. So: Easton will at some point visit the camp, and at some point will take the woman and the boy to the airport. I have already booked six seats on the plane and I will have another team waiting at Gatwick: two cars and two motorbikes. Assuming they all get on the plane, we board, too. Obviously the crucial time will be when we're in London. We don't want to follow them all the way to the UK only to lose them there."

His team nodded.

"Now, any questions?"

He was faced with shaking heads.

"Excellent." He smiled. "I don't see any reason why it won't go smoothly." He looked at his watch, a chunky diving model. "I'm going to stay up, but if any of you want to grab some sleep, now's the time to do it."

Margie Barker was waiting in reception when Shepherd came down to check out. She was in her thirties, with shoulder-length curly brown hair and a sprinkling of freckles across her pert nose. She was wearing a quilted jacket, cargo pants with lots of pockets, and Ugg boots, and had a battered leather bag over her right shoulder. They shook hands and said their hellos and then she waited while he paid his bill. Shepherd was wearing a long-sleeved white linen shirt under his jacket and had put on a blue tie in keeping with his Home Office legend.

"Merry Christmas," she said.

"Oh, wow, yes, I'd forgotten what day it is." He grinned. "Merry Christmas."

Once he had paid his bill, she took him outside to her car, a white Land Cruiser with mud-splattered tyres. "Just toss your bag on the back seat," she said as she climbed in.

Shepherd fastened his seat belt as she started the engine and edged slowly out of the car park. "How long will it take to get to the camp?" he asked.

"It usually takes me just under eight hours," she said. "I'm happy to share the driving with you."

She grinned across at him. "I might take you up on that," she said. "I've been there and back a lot over the past few weeks."

"When was the last time?"

"Two days ago, once I got the message about Mrs Jaraf and her son."

"You've spoken to them?"

"Sure. That's why I went, to start things rolling."

"Did you see their passports?"

"Yes, of course. I needed confirmation that they are who they say they are, obviously."

"Palestinian passports?"

"Yes."

"Still valid? And valid for at least six months?"

Margie frowned. "Yes, I think so. Is there a problem?"

"No, not at all. It's just that if they have valid passports, all we need to do is issue them with visas at the embassy. It makes my life easier." He looked at his watch. "So we're not going to be able to get back to Ankara tonight, are we?"

"We should be there by four. The admin paperwork shouldn't take more than an hour, so in theory we could be back here by 1 a.m. or so. But better to book into a hotel in Adana maybe? That's a six-hour drive from here. So we could have dinner, catch a few hours' sleep, and still be back by noon if we make an early start."

"Sounds like a plan," said Shepherd.

"How much do you know about the Kilis Öncüpinar Accommodation Facility?" asked Margie.

185

"Just that it's big."

She laughed. "It's big all right. More than 15,000 refugees are there at the moment. It's actually not that bad, and certainly much better than what passes for a camp in Syria. Kilis has schools and medical facilities and shops where refugees are able to buy their own food using a card system. If they have money they can even pay for satellite TV."

"A home from home, it sounds like."

"For many of the people there it's their only home," she said. "There's nothing for them in Syria, even if they were able to go back. With the US and Europe cutting back on the number of refugees they're taking, most of them are stuck in limbo. The camp's starting to look like a permanent feature. You'll understand when you see it."

She joined a motorway, heading south, and accelerated.

"So, tell me about the three girls you've been helping," said Shepherd.

Margie nodded eagerly. "Yes, Jamila, Lulu and Nadia. None of them should be in the camp, they should all be back in the UK. What the British Government is doing is reprehensible. You can't take away someone's citizenship. People have rights. We all have rights."

"Yes, but we didn't all leave our country to join a terrorist organisation, did we?"

"They were children, Paul. Kids. They didn't know what they were doing."

"They knew enough to travel from the UK to Syria and join ISIS."

Margie sighed. "I hope you'll listen to what they have to say," she said. "I think they've had a rough deal."

"Tell me about them," said Shepherd.

"You weren't briefed?"

"My primary mission is to deal with Mrs Jaraf and her son," said Shepherd. "But while I'm here I'm to check up on the three girls. So what can you tell me about them?"

"They were all kids when they came out," said Margie. "Jamila had just turned sixteen, Lulu was seventeen and so was Nadia. They all have the same story, just about. They're not from the best of backgrounds, to be honest, and as daughters in working-class Muslim families, they were always second best compared with their male siblings. All the money and effort goes into raising the boys and the girls are an afterthought. They were all seduced into believing that they'd find true love with a jihadist." She laughed when she saw the look of surprise on Shepherd's face. "I know, it sounds ridiculous to us, but you have to look at it from their point of view. Boring lives, poor housing, under-funded schools, subservient to all the men in their culture, then they see videos of muscular young men firing guns and proclaiming that they're prepared to die defending their religion. They're told they can go out and join the fight, and some of them do."

"Do you think they're brainwashed?"

"I think that they're easily led," she said. "They get talked into it, either online or down at the local

187

mosque. There are recruiters all over the country looking for local Muslims who can be signed up for jihad, but there are recruiters out looking for girls, too. Jamila was approached online. In a Facebook group, initially, I think. She says she talked about going to Syria for more than a year before she actually went. That was almost three years ago. She married a Syrian jihadist and had a child, but the child died before its first birthday. She ended up in a refugee camp over the border for about six months and then she moved to Kilis just over a year ago. That was when the British Government first became aware of her and they revoked her citizenship."

"So she's stateless?"

Margie shook her head. "Strictly speaking no. Her parents are from Bangladesh, so she's entitled to citizenship through them. But Jamila was born in London. She's as British as you and I."

"And the second girl?"

"Her name's Lulu Abati and her case is more complicated. Her family moved to Sweden from Somalia about fifteen years ago. Her parents and three children. She was the youngest. The father was a businessman and paid people traffickers to get his family to Sweden. As soon as they got Swedish passports, the father moved the family to west London. So Lulu has spent most of her life in the UK, but she doesn't have British citizenship. Her family is still there and they want her back, obviously. The Home Office has made it clear that she'll be refused entry."

"Couldn't she go and live in Sweden?"

"She knows nothing about Sweden."

"No, but her family could move there."

"The family's on benefits, Paul. They're not going anywhere. They live in a council house in Ealing, her father has health issues, the mother speaks very little English and even less Swedish."

Shepherd shook his head. "I see what you mean about it being complicated. But it sounds as if she has no claim at all to returning to the UK."

"Especially after Brexit," said Margie. "But Lulu was raised in England, and went to school in England. She was also recruited online and she was introduced to Jamila. They became friends in London and came to Turkey together. Lulu had twins to a Syrian jihadist but they died. Her life is an absolute mess, she needs to be back with her parents."

"And how did she end up in the camp?"

"She was in the same Syrian refugee camp as Jamila, across the border. Ain Issa, it's called. It's a hellhole, by all accounts. Nothing more than a prison, really. Remember when Trump announced he was pulling American troops out of Syria? The Turks started attacking the Kurds in the area, and either by accident or design they shelled Ain Issa. In the confusion almost a thousand people broke out, half of them children. A lot of them crossed the border and the Turks rounded most of them up and brought them here."

"And the third girl?" asked Shepherd.

"Nadia. Born in Pakistan, moved to Birmingham with her family when she was two years old. Her father is an electrician, mother works in a school canteen, family name of Shah. The government has revoked her British passport. She's never held a Pakistani one and she has no desire to go to Pakistan, even if they would take her."

"Does she know the other two? Lulu and Jamila?"

"No. She wasn't in Ain Issa. She was in an ISIS camp, but she managed to escape and she made it across the border."

"And how did she end up in Syria in the first place?"

"She went out with two teenage girls from Birmingham. They thought it was an adventure." She shook her head sadly. "Nadia was groomed. It's clear from talking to her. She was cajoled and conned and talked into it. And now she realises that she made a mistake and wants to go home."

"Did she get pregnant?"

"No, thank God. The ISIS camps are used as baby farms. They don't allow condoms or any form of birth control. The idea is to produce as many children as possible, especially boys, so that they can grow up to be jihadist warriors. Apparently she met up with a guy she knew in Birmingham and he took care of her."

Margie accelerated to overtake a truck packed with sheep.

"I really hope you can help them, Paul."

"I'll see what I can do," said Shepherd.

The three men walked across Jubilee Gardens towards the river. It was 4a.m. on Christmas Day, so the park was a lot less busy than usual. Yusuf Butt, Mohammed Desai and Nazam Miah were all wearing black puffer

190

jackets with the hoods up and baggy cargo pants. There was a chill in the air that had their breath feathering around their hoods. Each man carried a sports bag — Butt's was Adidas and the other two had Nike swooshes on the side. Off to their left was the London Eye, the one hundred and thirty five-metre observation wheel that dominated the south bank of the river. On the far side of the river were the Houses of Parliament. The tower that housed Big Ben was covered in scaffolding as part of a major refurbishment. "You know, why don't we do the London Eye?" asked Desai.

"Because we've been told what our target is," said Butt. "There's a plan and we're going to follow that plan."

"I hear you, bruv, but I'm just saying, three drones with IEDs and bang, they'd knock the shit out of that wheel."

"Nah, bruv, it's strong as fuck, and the glass in those pods, it's reinforced," said Butt. "They've looked at it from top to bottom and the only way to do any real damage would be to drive a truck load of explosive up to it, but the approaches are all blocked. Stay focused, bruv, we don't want to be making any mistakes here."

They reached the edge of the park, placed their holdalls on the pavement and unzipped them. Each contained a large drone along with its control unit. Attached to each control unit was a tablet. Each man switched on his drone and tablet then they stood together, looking out across The Queen's Walk to the Thames. Directly opposite them was the dark blue hull of the Tattershall Castle, the floating pub and restaurant that had once been a ferry running across the Humber estuary. Butt pointed at the eight-storey concrete building on the far side of the river, illuminated by floodlights even though there was little of architectural interest in the neo-classical façade. "That's the target," he said. "The terrace is on the top floor. See it?"

The two men peered over the river and nodded. "Got it, bruv," said Miah.

"Right. We take them up to a hundred metres and establish the first waypoint. Then fly across the river at three metres per second. You establish waypoints every hundred metres or so, which means between thirty and thirty-five seconds. It doesn't have to be exact. Once we've crossed the river we drop to eighty metres and then slow to two metres a second as we approach the building. Then we slow again as we approach the terrace. Get as close to the terrace as you can and set the final waypoint. Then we store the mission and recall the drones."

"What if the cops see them?" asked Desai.

"At this time of the morning, they won't," said Butt. "But even if they do, they'll only be hovering for thirty seconds or so. Then they'll be back over the river. Even if they were to try to get a car to chase them we'll be long gone before they've even reached the bridge." He looked at the two men in turn, checking that they were ready. "Okay, let's do it," he said.

All three men used their controls to activate their drones. The rotors whirred and then one by one they rose into the air. Each drone had a camera underneath it and they could see the view from the cameras on their tablets, along with the GPS location, height and speed. Once they reached a hundred metres, they put the drones into hover, and then tapped on the tablet to call up waypoint details. There were two buttons on the backs of the controls and by pressing them, the GPS position and height could be stored as a waypoint. All three men stored the location. "Okay, over we go," said Butt. "Remember, every thirty seconds or so, store the waypoint."

The three drones moved across the river. Any sound was soon lost in the wind.

The river was about two hundred and fifty metres wide, so at three metres a second it took about a minute and a half for the drones to cross the water, and for the men to store three more waypoints.

Once over the river the men twiddled the joysticks to take the drones down to eighty metres, stored another waypoint, then moved towards the building at two metres a second, crossing Victoria Embankment between Westminster Millennium Pier and the monument to the RAF, a stone pylon topped with a globe and a gilded eagle.

They slowed even further until all three tablets showed clear views of the terrace at the top of the building, complete with tables, chairs and ornamental lights.

"Right, final waypoint," said Butt. The men all pressed the buttons to fix the final position. "Store the mission," said Butt. The men tapped on the screens. The waypoints were then stored in the drone's memory and at the push of a button they could be made to follow the precise route, in either direction.

"And bring them back," said Butt.

The three men tapped on the screens. The drones moved away from the building, rose to a hundred metres, and zoomed back across the river. Ninety seconds later they were back at the first waypoint, above their heads. The men brought the drones down manually, switched them off, and put them back in the holdalls with the controllers.

"Nice work, everybody," said Butt. He headed across the park and the other two hurried to keep up with him.

Margie and Shepherd arrived at the Kilis Öncüpinar Accommodation Facility at just after four o'clock in the afternoon. Shepherd had done some of the driving but Margie was behind the wheel when they drove up to the camp. It was surrounded by two parallel twelve-feet-high grey concrete walls, topped with razor wire. There was a sweeping arced sign over the entrance with the Turkish flag, the name of the camp in Turkish, and a logo with the letters "AFAD" in it.

"What's AFAD?" he asked.

"It's the organisation that runs the camp," she said. "The Disaster and Emergency Management Presidency, when you translate it into English. Most refugee camps in the world are run by the UN through the United Nations High Commissioner for Refugees, but the Turks wanted to do it themselves. They asked the

194

UNHCR for advice and took a lot of it on board, but they run the show."

Soldiers were guarding the main entrance. One of them checked Margie's credentials and the registration number of her vehicle before raising a barrier and waving her through.

"It's more of a prison than a camp," said Shepherd as they drove to the main administration building, a brick-built two-storey office block with a red tiled roof.

"It looks pretty intimidating on the outside, but the people inside are generally happy to be here," she said. "The walls are as much to stop people breaking in as breaking out. The refugees are free to move around, there are schools and playgrounds, mosques and clinics. It's like a self-contained town, though obviously all the food has to be brought in."

As she drove away from the entrance, Shepherd could see what she meant. There were wide brick pathways criss-crossing the camp, and trees had been planted on open ground. There were children playing tag, kicking footballs around and riding bikes. Women were walking with children or sitting on benches. In the distance he could see lines of identical white containers that housed the refugees.

There was a line of white SUVs parked behind the block and Margie joined them. They climbed out and looked towards the nearest cluster of metal containers. Most had blankets and bedding hanging from their windows, drying in the last of the day's sunlight.

"They look like shipping containers and that's how the media describes them," said Margie. She took a dark blue scarf from her pocket and wrapped it around her head. "But they have windows and the newer ones have small kitchens and shower rooms, and they all have heaters for the cold nights. I've been in worse student halls of residence." She slung her bag on her shoulder and looked at her watch. "Let me just go and have a word with the camp administrator," she said. "He's expecting us."

"I'd like to talk to them now before we collect Mrs Jaraf and her son," said Shepherd. "And I'd like to speak to the girls separately."

"Are you sure? It'll save time if we see them in a group. That's how I usually do it."

"I get that, but in my experience I get more out of interviews when people are on their own."

"No problem," said Margie. "Just let me tell the office I'm here and we'll go and see them."

Margie disappeared inside the building. Shepherd looked around. In the middle of the camp was a huge flagpole, at least a hundred feet high, with a massive Turkish flag waving in the wind, a white crescent and star on a red background. To the left, right, and straight ahead were ranks of the white containers. Many had satellite dishes on the roofs. There were men on the roofs, too, all around the camp. Sometimes they were in pairs, but usually there was just one man, mostly standing but several were sitting on plastic chairs. A lot of the men were smoking and most had a plastic bottle of water with them. They were carrying out surveillance, Shepherd realised. From their vantage

196

points the men could see every inch of the camp, and note who came and went.

Children were playing on colourful plastic slides and swings in a playground directly in front of him, as their mothers watched from nearby benches. All the women had their heads covered and many were wearing full length burqas. The men in the camp wore a mixture of traditional Islamic clothing and Western wear, with jeans, leather jackets and trainers appearing most prevalent.

From where he was standing, Shepherd could see two mosques, each with a single blue-and-white minaret. Off to his left was a massive warehouse where boxes of food supplies were being unloaded by forklift trucks and carried inside. He saw a glint of light from one of the container roofs and realised that a man there was observing him. He turned his back on the watcher.

An old man in a grey-and-white-striped thawb, who was fingering a set of prayer beads in his right hand, passed by, followed by two women in full burqas carrying bags of food, talking loudly in Arabic.

Margie came out of the building. "Right, we're good to go," she said. "The girls are in the same part of the camp but they're in different units."

She pointed to the collection of containers to their left, beyond one of the mosques. "Over there," she said. They walked along the brick pathway, around the mosque and across a patch of dirt. There were streetlights dotted around but sunset was still more than an hour away.

Groups of men watched them walk by, turning to stare and mutter in Arabic. Shepherd could feel the hostility pouring off them. He knew that ISIS were rife in the refugee camps in the region. The terrorists tended to fight until the last moment and then throw away their weapons and disappear among the genuine refugees, biding their time until they could fight again.

"How's your Arabic?" he asked Margie.

"Fairly good. Speaking anyway. It's a difficult language to read. And my Turkish is getting better."

"Some of the men here, they look more like fighters than refugees."

Margie took her cigarettes out of her bag and lit one. "It's an ongoing problem," she said. "Some of them are with their wives and kids, but there's a lot of single men of military age in here. The Turks don't question them and neither do the NGOs. We tend to take the refugees at their word."

"Do they take their fingerprints and DNA?"

"Everyone here is fingerprinted and they get a card that allows them to come and go. When they enter the camp they use the card and put their hands on a scanner."

"Do they pass on the fingerprints to the authorities overseas?"

She frowned. "What do you mean?"

"To check against the Interpol or Europol most wanted lists, for instance," he said.

"I don't think that happens, unless they apply for asylum overseas."

"What about the others? The ones that don't apply. What do they want to do?"

"A lot of them are hoping that Turkey will take them in permanently," she said. "But there are more than four million refugees in the country, ninety per cent of them from Syria, so it's unlikely that they can all be assimilated. The rest of the world needs to help but they're not. Now Turkey is talking about setting up protected areas on the border with Syria and making the refugees live there."

They reached the containers. They were white with a door in the middle and a window either side. Most had blinds that could be pulled over the windows to keep out the glare of the sun.

Shepherd heard shouts of "Bang! Bang! Bang!" off to his right and he turned to see a group of children having a mock gunfight with wooden weapons. One of the boys fell to the ground and rolled over and the others cheered.

"This way," said Margie, and Shepherd followed her between two containers to another path. She went left, looking at the numbers on the doors until she found the one she was looking for. "Are you sure you don't want me with you when you talk to her?" she asked.

"I'd prefer a one-on-one," he said.

"No problem," she said, and knocked on the door. It was opened by a woman in a black burqa, covering her whole body and face. "Margie, hey, how are you?" she asked in a London accent.

"I'm good, Jamila." She nodded at Shepherd. "This is Paul Easton from the Home Office, the man I told you about. He'd like a few words with you."

"Sure, yes, come in," said the woman, opening the door wider. Shepherd stepped inside. The container had been split into three sections. To the left was a door leading to a shower room, to the right was another door that opened into a small bedroom containing bunk beds. In the main room there was a kitchen area with a hotplate, a kettle and a small sink, and there was a sitting area with a small plastic sofa and a white plastic chair. There was an electric heater by the bedroom door and two shirts hanging on a wooden rack. It was cramped, but functional. There was enough room for two people but it wouldn't be pleasant for a family of four or more.

"You can have the sofa," said Jamila, sitting down on the plastic chair and gathering her robe around her.

Shepherd sat down. He was about to wish her Merry Christmas, but then realised as a Muslim she maybe didn't celebrate the holiday, so he held his tongue.

"So Margie says you can take me home," said Jamila.

"I can make recommendations," said Shepherd. "Any decision will be made in London." He leaned forward. "Look, do you mind removing the veil? I really need to be able to see who I'm talking to."

"It's my religion," she said. "The Koran says I must cover myself when there are men around."

"I understand that. But I also understand that the Koran doesn't say that women have to cover their faces. Or their heads for that matter. But this isn't about religion or about interpreting what the Koran says. This is about me being able to look at the face of the person I'm talking to. If I don't see your face, you could be anybody. If it was up to me, fine, but when I get back to London, what do I say if my boss asks me if I'm sure you're the girl who left the UK three years ago? If I tell him I didn't actually see your face, what's he going to say?"

Jamila sighed. "Fine," she said, and removed her veil. There was a bruise on her chin and there was dried blood on her lip.

"What happened?"

She shrugged. "Nothing."

Shepherd leaned forward to get a better look. She'd been slapped or punched; either way the blow had split her lip. She moved back and turned her face away from him. "Someone hit you?"

"There's no use crying over spilled milk, or split lips," she said. She fumbled with the veil, trying to cover her face.

"Who hit you?"

"Some Syrian guy. It happens all the time. They hate us, because we're British. They think we get special treatment in the camp and that we're going to be fast-tracked to the UK."

"Did you tell anyone?"

She snorted contemptuously. "Tell who? ISIS runs this camp and if you cross them you end up dead." She gestured at her mouth. "This is nothing. There are girls getting gang raped and worse in here. That's why you need to get me home, Mr Easton. I need to get out of here." She had the veil back in place and she turned to look at him.

"How long have you been here?" he asked.

"Since mid-October."

"And before that you were in a camp on the other side of the border?"

She nodded. "Yeah, and it was a shithole. Worse than this and that's saying something. Then for some reason the Turkish Army attacked the camp. They knew it wasn't a terrorist camp, they knew it was full of refugees. The Turks didn't care that there were women and children in the camp. I saw a whole family get blown to bits. A husband and wife and three kids. One moment they were huddled behind a wall, the next they were just . . ." She shuddered. "You've never seen bodies blown apart. You've no idea what it looks like."

Shepherd didn't say anything. Actually he'd seen more than his share of dead bodies, but he was Paul Easton of the Home Office, not Dan "Spider" Shepherd, former paratrooper and SAS warrior.

"During the shelling, most of the guards ran away and hundreds of us fled," she said. "Grabbed what we could and ran for our lives. We got to the border and no one stopped us crossing into Turkey. Then we were rounded up by troops and brought here. I said I was British and that I wanted to go back to England. They said I had to stay here. I don't get that. Turkey's in Europe, right? I've got freedom of movement. They can't keep me here."

"Turkey isn't in the EU," said Shepherd. "And freedom of movement doesn't apply to terrorists."

202

Her face was hidden but he was sure she was sneering at him. "How can you say that? I'm not a terrorist. I've never killed anyone."

"So why did you go to Syria?" asked Shepherd.

"I was brainwashed," said Jamila. "I was in a Facebook group talking about what was happening in Syria, and I spoke to a girl who was recruiting girls to go and meet up with the fighters there. She talked me into it. Before that, I never thought of leaving the UK. She put the idea into my head."

"And you went to an ISIS camp in Syria? You went to join the jihadists?"

"I was stupid. I know. I did a dumb thing and I'm sorry."

"But you made the decision to go, right? Nobody forced you."

She threw up her hands. "You don't understand."

"Then explain it to me."

She leaned forward, her eyes burning with a fierce intensity. "I'm the victim here," she said. "I'm the one whose life is in danger, whose rights have been taken away. I lost my baby. My baby died. Now they've taken away my citizenship. I'm stateless. I'm nothing. How does anyone have the right to do that?"

"You have Bangladeshi citizenship. The UK Government thinks you should go back to Bangladesh."

"Bangladesh? Do you know what a shithole Bangladesh is? That's why my parents left. I'm not Bangladeshi. I'm British. I belong in Britain."

"But you have a Bangladeshi passport, right?"

"Only because my parents took me on holiday to see relatives when I was a kid. It was just easier if I had a Bangladeshi passport so they applied for one for me. Look, I was born in London. I went to school in London. All my friends are there. I don't understand why the government is so scared of me. What do they think? They think I'm going to go back and blow myself up in a shopping centre?"

"You have to understand, Jamila — you were in an ISIS training camp, you were married to an ISIS fighter, who knows what you're capable of." He saw that she was about to snap at him so he raised his hands to placate her. "I'm just playing devil's advocate," he said.

She folded her arms and glared at him. "You're all the same."

"What do you mean?"

"The other embassy guy that was here. He looked at me the same way that you're looking at me. Like you hate me."

"Jamila, I don't hate you. I was told to come here to see if I can help, but so far . . ." He shrugged.

"That's what he said."

"This other man, what was his name?"

"He didn't say. He just said he was from the embassy."

"What did he look like?"

She shrugged. "A bit older than you. His hair was longer and going grey. He kept smoking. Cigarette after cigarette. The smell stayed in here for ages."

Shepherd nodded. Michael Warren-Madden. "What help did he want?"

"Information on jihadists I'd met, especially those who were from England."

"And what did you say?"

"How could I help him? I was never a jihadist. I didn't train with them, and the women were kept separate from the men. The only man I spoke to was my husband."

"Your husband, who was he?"

"He was a Syrian. Idris. Like Idris Elba. He looked a bit like him, too. Big guy. Well over six feet. He was jealous, too. Wouldn't let me even look at another man. As soon as the embassy guy heard that, he lost interest." She sneered at Shepherd. "I'm guessing you're going to be the same, right?"

"You're in a difficult position, Jamila."

"No shit, Sherlock."

"Revoking your citizenship is a done deal, and without a British passport you won't be allowed into the UK. The other visitor was offering you a way out. If you could provide evidence that would be useful to the UK Government, they might treat you as an informer."

"But I don't know anything. I came to Syria, I was introduced to Idris, I lived in a small hut in the camp. I didn't train as a terrorist."

"And you didn't get to meet any of the other fighters?"

She shook her head. "I told you, Idris was very jealous. He hardly let me leave our hut. He brought me food and we had sex. Three or four times a day. He

205

never loved me, I know that, I was just there to be his sex slave. Even when I got pregnant he still fucked me every day, right up until the baby was born. It was a girl, and he lost interest. He wanted a son and it was like he thought I'd failed him."

"What happened to the baby?" asked Shepherd.

"I fed her as best as I could but she hardly gained weight at all. And there was no baby formula or anything there to help her. Then she got sick. There was a doctor there but he didn't give a fuck. She died. Six months old. She never stood a chance." She shuddered. "Not long after she died, Idris gave me the clap. They kept captured women in a large block and any of the fighters who wanted sex could go there whenever they wanted. He used to go there to fuck when I was on my period. When I told him he'd given me the clap he just beat me. He still fucked me, mind, but I knew then that he'd never loved me." Tears were welling up in her eyes.

"Where is Idris now?"

"Dead." She shuddered again. "He died in front of me, trying to get out of the hut. Three men with Kalashnikovs mowed him down. Kurdish fighters. They stormed the camp at night while everyone was sleeping. I thought they were going to kill me but when they saw I was a woman they stopped firing. They killed most of the men and took the women and children to the Ain Issa camp." She dabbed at her eyes with her sleeve. "I've suffered enough, Mr Easton. You need to tell the government that I'm a victim, I need compassion and I need help." She sniffed. "What about my human rights? I have rights, don't I?"

206

Shepherd had half a mind to tell her that she'd given up any rights she had when she left her country of birth to join a terrorist group on the other side of the world. But he realised that Jamila was a few years younger than his own son, and Liam had made his fair share of bad decisions over the years. All teenagers did, it was part of growing up. Jamila's mistake had been a bad one, but was it fair to penalise her for the rest of her life by removing her citizenship? Even murderers could serve their sentence and then start afresh. There would be no starting afresh for Jamila. "I'll see what I can do," he said, though even as the words left his mouth he knew that he was offering her false hope. Someone like Salam Jaraf could fly into the UK and demand citizenship in exchange for what he knew, but Jamila didn't have that sort of information. She was right, of course, she was a victim. She hadn't been when she'd left the UK, but that had all changed when she'd reached Syria. But the Great British public wouldn't see it that way. They saw a traitor, someone who hated their way of life so much that she was prepared to help terrorists kill and maim them, and they wouldn't ever forgive her for that.

She reached for him, grabbing his hands with hers. They were small, the nails bitten to the quick, dirt engrained in the flesh. "Thank you," she whispered. "From the bottom of my heart, thank you."

Shepherd opened the door of Jamila's container and stepped outside. Margie Barker was waiting for him, finishing a cigarette. She dropped it onto the brick pathway and ground it out with her foot. "Everything okay?" she asked Jamila, who was standing in the doorway.

Jamila nodded, hurried across the pathway and hugged her. "Thank you."

Margie patted her on the back. "Don't worry, I'll see you again this weekend."

"I need Tampax," said Jamila. "I'm out and, you know . . ."

"You need them now?"

"I'm sorry."

Margie opened her bag, took out a Tampax and gave it to her. "That's my emergency supply," she said. "Don't you have any money on your card?"

"I spent this month's allowance."

"On what?"

"Just stuff," she said tearfully.

Margie reached into her bag again, took out a purse and gave the girl some money. Jamila hugged her again, thanked Shepherd, then walked back inside.

"How did it go?" Margie asked as soon as Jamila had closed the door.

"I'm not sure what I can tell her," said Shepherd. "I don't want to raise her hopes."

"She's remorseful, right? She's sorry for what she did?" She started to walk down the pathway and Shepherd kept pace with her.

"She's sorry for the position she's in," said Shepherd. "I didn't hear much regret about her actions."

"Paul, she was practically a sex slave," said Barker. "You could say she was trafficked."

"You could, but it wouldn't be true," said Shepherd. "Nobody forced her."

"She was a young, impressionable girl in a culture where women tend to do what they're told."

"You're saying this is a Muslim thing?"

"Oh come on, Paul, don't try to make me out an Islamophobe here. I don't see Christian girls or Jewish girls queuing up to lie down with jihadists. Of course it's a Muslim thing. She's a kid, an impressionable kid. If someone tells her to jump she'll ask how high. Especially if it's a man asking."

"She says she was recruited on Facebook by a girl in the UK."

Margie nodded. "Tooba Gondal. The ISIS matchmaker, they called her. She was in the Ain Issa camp, too."

"Where is she now?"

"No one knows," said Margie. "But if anyone is the villain in this, it's her. She was doing the recruiting, she was bringing the girls out." She grimaced. "I get so bloody frustrated."

Shepherd grinned. "I can see that."

Her cheeks reddened. "It's not funny."

"I know, I didn't mean to suggest it was. I admire your enthusiasm, honestly I do, but sometimes you have to keep some distance between yourself and the people you're trying to help."

"You've seen her, she's just a kid who got out of her depth. She didn't kill anyone, she wouldn't hurt a fly."

"I hear you," said Shepherd. "It's not me you have to convince."

209

"Actually it is. If you go back and tell your bosses at the Home Office that these girls are victims and not terrorists, then maybe you can get them to change their minds."

"I'll do my best," said Shepherd.

"Really?"

She had the same earnest look that he'd seen on Jamila's face. He wasn't lying, he would tell Pritchard that the woman clearly wasn't a threat to national security, but he doubted that anything would change. She had no useful intel so there was no point in MI5 pressing to bring her back.

"She said she'd spoken to someone else from the embassy. I'm assuming Michael Warren-Madden."

She nodded. "He came out a few weeks ago."

"With you?"

"No, he said he wanted to talk to them alone. Same as you."

"And what was his verdict?"

Her face tightened. "I can't remember his exact words, but the gist was that they were of no use to him so they could rot in hell for all he cared." She forced a smile. "He's not a great one for social skills."

"I got that impression."

"You've met him?" she asked, and Shepherd realised that she didn't know that Warren-Madden had picked him up at the airport.

"Just the once," he said. "Look, there's something you should know. Jamila was beaten. Or at least punched or slapped."

"What? When?"

210

"Recently. I had her take off her veil and her mouth is a bit of a mess. That might be why she has no money."

Margie cursed under her breath. "The card system is supposed to stop theft and robbery. It's not all that common, but it still happens."

"She says there's resentment against the British girls."

"The high-profile ones, yes. But Jamila has kept her head down. They all have."

"Well, someone has noticed her. Is there anything you can do?"

Margie grimaced. "It's not easy. You can see how open the place is. Anyone can go anywhere. There are police on the gate and they can be called in, but as I said, theft and robbery aren't common because there's so little of value in the camp."

"What about rapes and assaults?"

"I'm sure it happens, but not much."

Shepherd didn't say anything. He knew from experience that when there was violence in prisons it often didn't get reported to the guards. "Snitches get stitches" was the saying, and it probably applied as much to refugee camps as it did to high-security prisons.

"Do you think I should mention it to the camp administrator?" asked Margie.

"Do you think there's anything they can do?" said Shepherd. "If you bring it to their attention, it might make it worse for Jamila."

"There'd be no point in moving her to a different part of the camp. I suppose we could try and get her moved to a different camp, but facilities-wise Kilis is head and shoulders above the rest. It could well be out of the frying pan and into the fire."

"What about moving more girls into her unit?" asked Shepherd. "Safety in numbers. Or moving her to a unit closer to the administration block."

"I'll see what can be done," said Margie.

An old woman had put out a dozen pairs of used jeans in the pathway and was calling out in Arabic, clearly offering them for sale. Further along the path, half a dozen bicycles were lined up in front of one of the containers, while a man with a bushy beard and a white skullcap was squatting next to a washing up bowl as he checked an inner tube for a leak.

They passed a group of men, all bearded and wearing what looked like brand new trainers. One of them spat on the ground and muttered something in Arabic. Margie's cheeks reddened.

"What did he say?" asked Shepherd.

"Nothing," said Margie.

"It didn't sound like nothing," said Shepherd.

"There's a lot of frustration in here," said Margie. "Some of them have been here for five years or more. They can't work, there's nothing for them to do, and for many of them there's no light at the end of the tunnel. They can't go home and no other country will take them, so they're stuck in limbo."

"That doesn't give them the right to abuse you."

"He's a man from a male-dominated culture, but here he's powerless. It annoys him to see a woman driving around in an SUV and coming and going as she pleases."

"He should be grateful that someone is trying to help him." Shepherd looked over his shoulder. The man was glaring at them with undisguised hatred. Shepherd had seen similar looks on the faces of men in Afghanistan and Iraq, but usually they were fighters with AK-47s or RPGs, and Shepherd was able to show his contempt with a burst of fire from whatever weapon he was carrying at the time. Part of him wanted to go back and confront the man, and to point out the error of his ways. But he was Paul Easton, Home Office civil servant, so he just flashed the man a sarcastic smile and turned back to Margie. "I admire your tolerance," he said.

They went by the mosque to another container area. Men standing on the containers nearby monitored their progress. Several teenagers rode by on bicycles, ringing their bells. One of them waved at Margie and she waved back. "It's the children I feel most sorry for," she said. "But at least here they get schooling and we can deal with any health issues."

She led him between two containers. Arab music was blaring from one of them, and an old man sat smoking a hookah pipe in the doorway of the other.

"Why isn't Lulu staying with Jamila?" he asked. "They're friends, right?"

"They were. They went to Syria together but they fell out, either when they were in the ISIS camp or afterwards, when they were in the refugee camp in Syria. Something happened but neither of them will tell me what it was. I think that maybe Lulu blames Jamila for what happened." She shrugged. "Like I said, they don't talk about it. But they both made it clear they didn't want to stay together."

She took Shepherd down a line of containers, and stopped outside one. There was a pair of jeans and a Chelsea football shirt hanging from the window. Margie knocked on the door. It was opened by a short, dark-skinned girl in a white hijab. Margie asked to speak to Lulu and the girl disappeared. A few seconds later a much taller, thinner black girl appeared wearing a black hijab over another Chelsea shirt. The girl beamed when she saw Margie and hugged her. She was a good three inches taller than Margie and she stooped a little as they hugged.

Margie introduced Shepherd, and she shook hands with him. She had a firm grip and looked him in the eyes as they shook. She smiled, showing a row of brilliantly white teeth. "Thank you for coming to see me," she said, her accent pure London. "I know you're a long way from home. We both are." Her smile looked genuine but Shepherd could see the fear and uncertainty in her eyes.

"Mr Easton would like a chat with you in private," said Margie. "Do you think the other girls would give you some privacy?"

"Sure, yes, I'll ask them." Lulu went back inside the container and after a minute or so the girl who had opened the door came out, followed by two other girls in full burqas. They all said hello to Margie and then walked down the path to the main building. Lulu appeared in the doorway and waved for Shepherd and Margie to come inside.

"I'll leave you two alone," said Margie.

Lulu looked suddenly apprehensive and she grabbed Margie by the arm. "Can't you stay?"

"You need to talk to Mr Easton on your own," said Margie. "I'll be right outside." She gently pried the girl's fingers from her arm, smiling encouragement. "Don't worry, Mr Easton is here to help."

Lulu nodded. "Okay," she said quietly.

She stood back so that Shepherd could get into the container. The layout was identical to the one Jamila was living in, but this one had two mattresses on the floor and a small television set on a cheap chipboard cabinet. There were two white plastic chairs by the bathroom door. Lulu waved for him to sit. "Do you want a water?" she asked.

"A water would be great," said Shepherd. She bent down, opened the door to a small fridge and took out two bottles of water.

She gave one to Shepherd and unscrewed the cap of the one she was holding. She stood by the bedroom door and leaned against the wall. "Why can't Margie be with us?"

"I just wanted a personal chat," said Shepherd. "One to one."

"I just feel safer when Margie is around," said Lulu, and she took a long drink from her bottle.

"I understand," said Shepherd. "The situation you're in must be incredibly stressful."

"Tell me about it." Her eyes were brimming with tears. "I just want to go home. I want to be with my family." She walked over and sat down on the other chair.

"I understand that," he said. "The problem is that you're not British. You're Somali-Swedish. You have the right to live in those countries, but not in the UK."

She shook her head fiercely. "No, you don't understand. I only lived in Sweden for a couple of years, then we moved to London. We didn't have any problems moving there. We had the right to live in the UK because it's part of Europe. I went to school there. My family lives there. All my friends are there. I don't have anyone in Sweden. And Somalia? Have you ever been to Somalia?"

Actually, Shepherd had. And he could understand why she wouldn't want to live there. "No," he said.

"I have family there, sure, but I don't know them and they sure as hell wouldn't want me staying with them. Mr Easton, London is my home. It's where I belong. I made a big mistake, a huge mistake, and I'm sorry and I'll say or do whatever the government wants me to say or do to make it right. If it means sending me to prison, that's fine. I'll do my time, and I'll do it gladly." The words had come tumbling out so quickly that she found herself short of breath and she sat back, gasping, her hand on her chest.

"Relax, Lulu," he said. "Don't get upset."

She took a deep breath, and then nodded. "I'm really, really scared, Mr Easton," she said. "You've no idea what I've been through. The camp in Syria, it was hell. The food wasn't enough to keep an animal alive. The healthcare was non-existent. My babies died. They died and no one gave a shit."

"How did you come to get pregnant?"

She frowned as if she hadn't understood the question, then realisation dawned. "You mean who was the father?" She shrugged carelessly. "His name was Saad, which means noble, but there was nothing noble about him. I was paired off with him as soon as I arrived. No choice, no nothing, just pushed towards him and told that I was his wife. He spoke almost no English, he didn't give a shit about me. I told him, "No way am I sleeping with you," and he beat me black and blue while all his friends laughed."

"He was a jihadist, right?"

Her eyes opened wide. "You do ask some dumb questions," she said. She closed her eyes and took a deep breath. "I'm sorry," she whispered, and she opened her eyes again. "Yes, he was a jihadist. Look, I'm not stupid, Mr Easton. I knew what I was doing. At least I thought I did. They told me I'd be joining the jihad and that I'd be married to a fighter. But they said I'd have a choice. Like speed dating, you know? I'd get to meet the guys and choose." She shook her head. "But it wasn't like that. There was no choice. It was rape. I was raped. And I was raped for months." She paused, haunted by the memory. "I got pregnant and my sons were born a year ago. Twins. They got sick and the doctors in the camp weren't really doctors. More like bloody witch doctors. When the Kurds attacked the ISIS camp I managed to get away to a refugee camp in Syria and that's where they died."

"I'm sorry," said Shepherd.

She brushed away his apology. "I'm not telling you that because I want your sympathy. I'm telling you because you need to know that I could die here. The women here, the Syrian women, they hate us. In fact all the Syrians hate us. The Turks too. They see British people as the enemy. They steal food from us, they spit at us. They treat us like dogs."

"Did your husband get out of the camp?"

She shook her head. "The Kurds killed all the men, the ones that stayed and didn't run away. My husband was hit by an RPG. Blew him to bits. One moment he was there, the next he was just a hole in the ground."

She forced a smile. "I don't know why I keep calling him my husband. We were never married. He never treated me like a wife. He was a rapist more than a husband."

Shepherd took a sip from his water bottle. "I don't understand why you would leave your life in London to travel to a war zone."

She smiled. "You and me both."

"But no one put a gun to your head, did they?"

"Looking back, I can see how stupid I was. But at the time . . ." She shrugged. "It was that bitch Jamila who persuaded me. She made all sorts of promises about what life would be like in Syria and it was all bullshit."

218

"What did your parents say when you told them what you planned to do?"

"I didn't tell them, obviously."

"How old were you?"

"Seventeen. Just turned."

"Seventeen is young to be flying around the world on your own."

"I wasn't alone. I came with Jamila."

"You were friends in London?"

"We were at the same mosque, in Ealing. We were in Koran school together. She's the one that got me into the jihad website thing and introduced me to Tooba."

"Tooba? Who's Tooba?"

"Tooba Gondal. I never actually met her in person, but we FaceTimed and talked online. She said girls like me were what jihad needed. We could support our men and raise their children and make the world a better place." She saw the look of confusion on Shepherd's face and she shrugged. "I know, it sounds ridiculous now, but at the time it made sense and I wanted to do it. So did Jamila. Tooba helped us arrange the flights and told us what to do."

"Where did you fly to?"

"We got cheap flights to Turkey and then a minibus picked us up at the airport and drove us across the border. There were half a dozen other girls with us, from all over. We were all excited, it was like some crazy school trip. When we crossed the border they took our phones off us, they said that the Americans could track phones wherever you were and they promised we'd get them back but we never did. Everything changed once

219

they'd taken our phones. They stopped answering our questions, they wouldn't speak to us in English. We got to the camp and dozens of men crowded around the van, pawing at us and trying to grab us. They had AK-47s and they were waving them around. Saad grabbed me and said I was his and that was it." She shook her head. "I was a fucking idiot." She sat back in her chair and folded her arms.

"How long were you at the ISIS camp before it was attacked?"

"Eighteen months. Maybe a bit longer. We lost track of time because we didn't have our phones and there was no TV or internet or nothing. The only thing they let us read was the Koran. The Kurds attacked at night with mortars and missiles and I don't know what else. I hid in my hut but it got hit and I ran out, and a couple of foreign girls grabbed me and took me through a hole in the perimeter wire. I don't know how but one of them knew which way it was to the refugee camp in Ain Issa and we all followed her. She saved our lives, that girl."

"Is she in this camp, too?"

Lulu shook her head and wiped her eyes. "She was killed when Ain Issa was attacked. The bastard Turks shot her. They could see she was a girl and they didn't give a fuck."

"How did you escape that time?"

"We just ran. I don't know how we got across the border but we did, and the Turkish troops captured us and brought us here. Jamila got out, too, but I made it clear I wanted nothing to do with the bitch. It's her

220

fault I'm here." She leaned forward. "You have to help me get back to my family," she said. "I meant what I said, I'll die here."

"Are your parents doing anything back in the UK?"

"They've spoken to their MP but he's no help. They don't want to go to the press because they know that the British people hate us. They don't want us back. Look, I'll do whatever is asked of me, Mr Easton. I can go public saying what bastards ISIS are, how they only care about their own people and don't care if Muslims like me live or die. I could talk to schools, I can warn kids of the dangers of the sort of websites I used to visit. I could stop girls making the same mistakes I made."

"I hear what you're saying, Lulu. I do."

"So you'll help me?"

"I'll talk to my bosses in London. But you know what the problem is. Public opinion is against you. MPs are scared of looking weak in front of the voters, and that includes the PM. The girls who have had their citizenship taken away might be able to mount a legal challenge, but you're not British."

"I lived in Britain for most of my life. Listen to me, do I sound Swedish?"

"No. You don't. Look, I'll tell you what I told Jamila. Your best chance of being taken back to the UK would be if you were able to help the security services. If you had information that could help them in the fight against terror I'm sure they'd be more helpful."

"But I'm not a terrorist."

"No, but you spent time in an ISIS training camp. You were married to an ISIS fighter. Did you see or hear anything, anything that might be useful?"

"We were locked up most of the time. And the only time Saad spoke to me was to tell me what he wanted me to do to him."

"Did you recognise anyone in the ISIS camp? Anyone you knew from London? From your mosque?"

Lulu shook her head. "I wasn't allowed to look at the faces of any men who came near us."

"And in the van that picked you up from the airport, were there any men on it?"

"Just the driver and the guy in the front passenger seat. And they said almost nothing to us. Mr Easton, I don't have any information to trade because I'm not a terrorist. I was held prisoner and raped. Do you understand that?"

"I do, yes."

Her voice hardened. "I don't think you do. Because if you did you'd realise that I'm a victim here and I need to be helped, not punished."

"And I'll do what I can, Lulu," said Shepherd.

She gritted her teeth together and shook her head. "No you won't," she said. "I can hear it in your voice. You're like all the rest of them, you don't give a fuck about me. It's because I'm black, right? If I was a blonde-haired blue-eyed little Christian girl you'd have me out of here like a shot." Flecks of spittle sprayed across the table and her eyes burned with hatred. "You hate me, don't you? Just fucking admit it."

Shepherd shook his head. "I don't hate you, Lulu," he said quietly. "I'm here to help."

She stood up so quickly that her chair fell back and hit the floor with the sound of a pistol shot. She leaned towards him, her lip curled back in a snarl. "Nah, mate, you don't want to fucking help me, you want me to rot here. Out of sight, out of fucking mind. You'd send every black and Asian person in England out here if you could, just admit it."

Shepherd held up his hands. "Lulu, you've got me all wrong, really."

She grabbed her water bottle and threw it at him, as hard as she could. It smashed into his chest, the top flew off and water went all over him. "Fuck you, fuck the lot of you!" she screamed.

Lulu stormed out of the container and Shepherd followed her. She pushed Margie to the side and stamped along the brick pathway, then she turned and pointed an accusing finger at Shepherd. "You deserve what's coming, all of you!" she screamed. "The brothers will wreak vengeance on your country and no one will shed any tears for you!" She whirled around and headed down the path.

"What happened?" asked Margie, her hand over her mouth.

"I think she's started to realise the hopelessness of her position," said Shepherd.

She stared at his soaking wet shirt and jacket. "Did she do that?"

"She threw her bottle at me." He smiled. "It was plastic. No harm done."

"I've never seen her like that before."

"I guess you've always offered her hope. A way out."

"And you didn't?"

Shepherd shrugged. "She's not British, Margie. She needs to be trying to get the Swedes to take her."

"But her family's in London."

"Then they should go with her, if they want to take care of her. But let's face it, she was strong enough to go to Syria on her own, would it be that much of a hardship to go to Sweden?"

"So you won't help her?"

He pointed down the path. Lulu was walking quickly, stamping her feet hard on the pathway. "You saw the way she was just now. 'The brothers will wreak vengeance on your country'. Did that sound like someone who has learned the error of her ways? There's a lot of anger there, and who knows how she might express that anger if she got back to London." He looked at his watch. "Look, I'll talk to the third girl and then I really need to collect Mr Jaraf's wife and daughter."

"Nadia has decided she doesn't want to talk to you."

Shepherd frowned. "Did she say why?"

"She said there was no point."

"That doesn't make sense. You said she wanted to speak to me. Why the change of heart?"

"She just said it was a waste of time."

"Yesterday she was okay, though? She knew I was coming?"

"Sure."

224

"So something must have changed." He looked at his watch. He had time. "Can you take me to see her?"

"She was adamant that she didn't want to talk to you."

"Maybe I can get her to change her mind."

Margie looked as if she was about to argue, but then she shrugged. "Why not?"

They reached the door to a container in the middle of a line of about twenty. "This is where Nadia lives," said Margie. She knocked on the door and called out "Nadia, it's me."

There was a scuffling sound and a young woman appeared in the doorway. She was wearing a blue long-sleeved shirt and jeans, and had a black scarf wrapped around her head. She smiled when she saw Margie but her face fell when she caught sight of Shepherd. She stepped back into the gloom of the container. "I said I didn't want to see him," she said, in a strong Birmingham accent. She was holding a broom.

"Mr Easton just wants to say hello," she said.

"We just need to know what physical condition you're in," said Shepherd.

"I'm fine, please go away," she said.

"I just need a few words with you, Nadia," said Shepherd. He stepped forward but Margie put a hand on his shoulder and shook her head. Shepherd moved back and motioned for her to go ahead. She stepped over the threshold and began talking to Nadia in hushed tones. Shepherd folded his arms and waited. Eventually Margie stepped out. "Okay, she'll see you, but only as a courtesy because you've come so far. But she's not happy."

Shepherd thanked her and stepped through the doorway and into the container. It was almost identical to Jamila's unit, with a black sofa and a single plastic chair, and bunk beds in the bedroom. Items of clothing were hanging on hooks that had been fixed to the walls. Nadia was standing at the far end of the room, by the bedroom door, her hands clasped together on the handle of the broom. There was a dustpan at her feet. She was short, not much over five feet tall. It was hard to tell her age; her face was lined, there were dark patches under her eyes and her cheeks were sunken. "I won't take up too much of your time, Nadia," he said. "I just wanted to check how you are."

"I'm fine. Please just go." Her fingers tightened on the broom handle as if she was desperate to keep hold of it.

"I will. But perhaps I can be of some help."

She shook her head. "You can't."

"You seem very sure of that," he said.

"Look, you can see I'm okay, but I really don't want to talk to you. Just go."

Shepherd held up a hand. "Okay, don't say anything, but just listen to what I have to say. It won't take more than a few minutes."

"And then you'll go?"

Shepherd put his hand over his heart. "I swear."

She waved at him to continue as she glared at him sullenly.

"Okay, Margie tells me you've had a change of heart about talking to me. That's fine. No one's going to force you to do anything. But I can tell you that unless you do something, you won't be leaving here. Or at least you won't be going back to the UK. That door has been closed to you, and I'll be honest, the chances of you re-opening that door are slim at best." She opened her mouth to speak but he held up his hand to silence her. "Let me finish," he said. "Just hear me out. The reason I'm here is to take back a woman who is in the camp with her son. Tomorrow I'll be taking her to the airport and flying with them to London. So it is possible. It's not easy, but it's possible. Now, before today you were desperate to get out of here, Margie tells me. You want to get back to the UK, and I understand that. I know what it's like here, and I know what you're going through. But something has clearly changed. Something has happened, something that has made you not want to talk to me." He stopped talking, watching her closely for any reaction, but she stared back at him, her face a blank mask.

"I think someone has said something to you, Nadia. Someone has told you not to talk to me. And I'm guessing that someone has told you that if you do speak to me, you'll be in trouble. Maybe it will kill off any chance you have of getting back to the UK."

Nadia's jaw tightened and Shepherd knew that he had guessed right. Someone had spoken to her, and he was pretty sure it was Michael Warren-Madden. Warren-Madden had made it clear he wasn't happy with Shepherd talking to the three jihad brides, but now it was starting to look as if it was just the one that he was concerned about. She looked down at her dustpan and then began sweeping again, even though the floor looked perfectly clean.

"There's only you and me here, Nadia. And you can trust me. Believe me. And I might be the one person who really can help you."

He could see the indecision in her eyes, but then she shook her head. "Just go," he said. She bit down on her lower lip as she concentrated on sweeping under one of the bunk beds.

"Mr Warren-Madden doesn't want you talking to me, but I don't know why."

Her eyes widened and Shepherd knew for sure that he was right about Warren-Madden.

"So what you've got to ask yourself is, can you trust him? Can you really trust him, Nadia? Because your life depends on it. Do you trust him with your life?"

Nadia made a wailing sound like an animal in pain, then she threw the broom away, slumped down on one of the bunk beds and put her head in her hands. She began to sob. Shepherd didn't move. He wasn't proud that he'd made the young girl cry but it was the only way to get her to open up to him. He picked up the discarded broom and propped it against the wall.

Margie appeared at the doorway, concern written over her face, but Shepherd waved her away. "Everything's okay," he said.

He stood watching Nadia sob, knowing that it was up to her now. He'd said everything he could say.

228

Eventually she wiped her eyes and turned to look at him. "Just go," she whispered. "Leave me alone."

Margie was standing in the shadow of the container, pulling on a cigarette. She dropped it and stamped it out as Shepherd walked over. "What happened?" she asked.

"Like you said, she doesn't want to talk to me."

"Why?"

Shepherd shrugged. "She didn't say. When was the last time you spoke to her? Before today."

"Two days ago. I said the Home Office was sending someone out and she got very excited. I had to tell her not to get her hopes up. I don't understand what happened."

Shepherd didn't say anything, but he had a pretty good idea what had happened. Michael Warren-Madden. "I gave it my best shot," he said. "Okay, let's go and collect Mrs Jaraf."

"They should be in the main admin block," said Margie. "I started the process rolling yesterday, but you'll have to sign off on it. And you've got the paperwork from London."

Shepherd nodded and patted his chest. "All present and correct."

Margie started walking along the brick pathway and Shepherd followed her.

"Mr Easton?"

Shepherd turned. Nadia was standing in the doorway of her container, her cheeks glistening with tears. She motioned for him to go back. "Give me a minute, Margie," he said.

Nadia disappeared back into the container. When Shepherd joined her she was sitting on the sofa, her arms folded. "How do I know I can trust you?" she asked quietly.

"Because I don't have an axe to grind," he said. "I'm just here to help. No ulterior motive."

"What if I said that I was told that if I said anything to you, I'd never be allowed home?"

"I'd say that I don't think anyone can make a threat like that. If you have the right to go home, you will do, an individual can't stop due process. That's not how our system works. There are appeals you can make, procedures you can follow. No one person can derail that process." He sat down on the plastic chair and leaned towards her.

She flashed him a pained smile. "It depends who they work for," she said.

"Tell me what happened, Nadia."

She sighed and closed her eyes. "You have no idea how fucked I am," she said.

"Then tell me."

She opened her eyes again. "If you let me down, I . . ." She left the sentence unfinished, and sighed again.

"I won't let you down," said Shepherd. "That much I promise you. Just tell me what happened and then I can tell you what your best course of action is." He pulled the door closed. "No one else will know," he said.

She looked at him with narrowed eyes and eventually nodded slowly. "It's about my boyfriend. His name's Hasan. It means handsome in Arabic and he is, he's a good-looking boy. He's the brother of a friend of mine, I met him in the mosque."

"In Birmingham?"

She nodded. "He liked me, I knew that, but he was a good boy and he was always polite and respectful. Took him ages to ask me out and even then he made sure his sister came along with us the first few times. But even when we went out on our own, he never tried anything on. He was a good Muslim boy, honoured his parents, didn't drink or do drugs, prayed when he should. Then one day he just went."

"Went where?"

"At the time I didn't know. Nor did his sister, not for sure anyway. There were rumours that he'd gone to Syria to join ISIS, but that didn't make sense because he wasn't the type. He never talked about jihad or anything like that. Music and football and video games were what he was interested in. And movies. All sorts of movies. Horror, sci-fi, comedies. Bollywood, he'd see anything. We lived near the Everyman cinema, you know, you sit on sofas and you can eat burgers and pizza. He loved it. He had this membership that meant he could have two seats for every performance for a year. He'd see some movies three or four times. Remember *La La Land*? He saw that seven times."

"So he was romantic?"

"In his way, yeah. He wasn't pushy with me. He was a real gentleman."

"What was his family name?"

"Mahmoud. Hasan Mahmoud."

"And who was it who said that he'd gone to Syria?"

"Friends of his. They said he'd gone for training and that he'd maybe be back in six months or so, but it was all rumour. No one knew for sure and his family didn't know where he was."

Shepherd wanted her to get to the point, but he knew it was best not to push her. She was talking, which was a sharp contrast to her reaction a few minutes earlier.

"I never forgot about him, but I accepted the fact that he'd moved on. I started spending more time at the mosque, and joined one of the Koran study groups. The imam was an old guy, in his seventies, and he was as sharp as a whip. Opened my eyes to what the Koran was about and what it meant to be a Muslim. Looking back, I realise that he was grooming me, almost brainwashing me, and after a few months he introduced me to one of the women at the mosque. Her name was Rida. The imam said she could teach me more about the role of a young woman in Islam and how I could best serve my faith. It started off with studying the passages in the Koran that refer to a woman's place in the religion. It was crap, a lot of it, just words written fifteen hundred years ago when things were different. There were six of us in the class, all teenagers. After a while Rida started showing us websites about women who had gone out to join ISIS and how fulfilled they were and how much better they felt about themselves now that they were involved in jihad." She held up her hands. "I know, I know, I know how ridiculous that sounds, but at the time, when she was talking, it all seemed to make perfect sense." Her voice had started to get raspy and she unscrewed the top off a bottle of water and drank some before continuing.

"When was this?"

"Two years ago, I suppose."

"So you were what then, sixteen?"

She nodded. "Gradually she got us all to agree that we wanted to go out to Syria and join the fight. After a while it was all we talked about, all we could think about. And then eventually, that's what we did. We all flew to Turkey with Rida and she introduced us to the man she said would be looking after us. He was a young guy, name of Ahmed, always laughing and joking, it was like we were on a hen night or something. They took us to this cheap hotel and they brought more girls from somewhere else. Eventually there were about twenty of us. Most didn't speak English, I think they were from Africa, maybe. And there were two white girls there, from Germany. They were really young. Thirteen or fourteen, I think. Ahmed kept asking them if they were virgins, but I don't think they understood. He was a bit creepy with them. Anyway, they took us over the border at night, in an old coach. Before we crossed he made us all give him our phones, our passports, driving licences, even our credit cards. He said it was because that way we wouldn't have any trouble if we were stopped, but it was bollocks, we never saw our things again. He took us to this camp somewhere in Syria and it was nothing like it was in the videos. It was dirty and there was rubbish everywhere and the men hadn't washed in months by the smell of them. Ahmed took us to this big tent and told us to wait there. He wasn't joking by then, it was all serious. We were all shitting ourselves, wondering what we'd gotten into. Then men started coming to the tent and taking girls away. No conversation, no chat, they'd just grab a girl by the arm and pull her away. If a girl resisted, she'd get slapped or punched. Eventually there was just three of us left. This old guy came in, he must have been sixty, with a long straggly beard with food in it and yellow teeth and he smelled so bad. He pointed at me and gestured for me to go with him. I said no, no fucking way. He had a Kalashnikov on his back and he swung it around and I swear I thought he was going to shoot me but then he tried to hit me with it and I screamed." She forced a smile. "And then Hasan appeared, from nowhere." Her smile widened. "Like a knight in shining armour. Except he was wearing a thawb, a grey one, and instead of a lance he was carrying a Kalashnikov. I don't know who was more surprised, him or me. He had no idea I was there. Anyway he stepped in and told the other guy to back off. They argued back and forth and then the old guy gave up and grabbed another girl."

Shepherd smiled and nodded, encouraging her to continue.

"Hasan took me to his quarters. He was in a room with three other men but he shooed them away and got me some tea and some bread and goat's cheese, and we sat on the floor and just talked about Birmingham and everybody we knew. We talked and talked like we'd never been apart."

"So you were seventeen. How old was he?"

"I'm not sure. Twenty-three. Twenty-four maybe."

"You didn't ask, back when you were going out?"

She shook her head. Tears were welling up in her eyes and she wiped them away. "It didn't seem important. I mean, I knew he was older than me, but how old didn't matter." She drank some more water before continuing. "He wasn't happy about me being in Syria, he said I was crazy. I said we were both crazy and he said no, it was different, and then he started asking me all sorts of questions about who at the mosque had helped me and what route I'd taken and who I'd spoken to. So many questions. I should have realised then what was going on but I was so tired. Eventually he let me sleep. The next day he got us a room together. More like a cell, it was. Bars on the window, a door with a big bolt on it, just a bed that creaked and a mattress that stank of stale piss. You've no idea how bad the place was. I told Hasan I wanted to go home but he said no one could leave. He could make sure that none of the other men touched me, but I couldn't go home. I kept asking him why he'd joined ISIS, but he always said I wouldn't understand. He said it was complicated. But I knew he was hiding something from me."

She was getting close to telling him everything, Shepherd was sure of that, so he just kept quiet and nodded encouragingly. Confessions usually went one of two ways. Sometimes the person telling the story went slowly as if they were running everything through a filter, choosing their words with care. The closer they got to the end, the slower they went, as if they wanted to postpone the conclusion as long as possible. Other times the story came out at full speed, as if rushing the facts out made them less painful. Fast or slow was no indication of truthfulness; it was more about making the confession as painless as possible. The key to getting the full story in both cases was not to interrupt and to just listen, to do nothing to stem the flow. Questions could come later.

"Every day Hasan would leave me at first light and spend the day training. One of the Syrian women would come and get me and set me to work. I couldn't cook so I was no use in the kitchen, so they had me doing laundry and cleaning. I had breakfast with the women, just bread and fruit and tea, and I wouldn't see Hasan again until night had fallen. He'd bring food to our hut and we'd eat and he'd tell me everything he'd done that day. He'd tell me who he'd been training with and where they were from. He started bad-mouthing ISIS, too. Small things at first, about the way they were organised and the stupid things they did. I agreed with him, I could see that everything I'd been told about them had been a lie. It was never about Islam, not about the true religion, the religion that my parents had taught me. What ISIS believed in was a travesty of Islam, a way of grabbing power and subjugating women. He told me how stupid some of the British jihadists were, how they were mainly just violent kids with psychological problems, kids who just wanted to lash out at anything to make up for the fact

236

that their lives were so meaningless. And the girls, they were just as stupid, they didn't know what they were letting themselves in for."

She took a deep breath, sighed, then gulped down some more water. Shepherd could see that she was on the final stretch.

"He was testing me, I realise that now, looking back," she said as she screwed the top back on the water bottle. "He was trying to see how committed I was to ISIS. And when he was eventually convinced that I hated them with a vengeance because of what they'd done to me and the other girls from England, that's when he told me the truth."

She took a deep breath as if she was steadying herself. "He was working for MI5. They had sent him to Syria to get information on what ISIS had been doing there."

Shepherd's jaw dropped. It was the last thing he had expected to hear.

"You don't believe me?" said Nadia.

"It's not that I don't believe you, it's . . . it's just so unlikely."

"Why don't you just call me a liar like the other guy did?"

"Nadia, I'm not saying you're lying. I'm just saying that, one, it's unlikely that MI5 would have an agent working for ISIS in Syria, and two, if Hasan really was an agent, he wouldn't tell anyone. That's the first rule of being a spy. You tell no one. Not your friends, not your family, and certainly not someone who has just arrived in the enemy's camp."

"Like I said, he tested me first. He sounded out how I really felt about ISIS, and after what had happened, I obviously wasn't a fan." She drank some more water but her hand was shaking so much that some dribbled down her chin. She wiped her mouth with the back of her hand. "He said it was doing his head in, not being able to tell anybody."

Shepherd understood exactly. One of the hardest things about working undercover was that usually you had no one to share the experience with. Occasionally an operation might involve two operatives being undercover, but usually it was a solitary occupation. And Hasan would have been under unimaginable stress as he was so far from home, surrounded by fanatics who would torture and kill him if they even suspected that he was betraying them. "Did he tell you how he came to be working for MI5?" he asked.

"He said he applied to join West Midlands Police, and that he was asked to go to a meeting in an office somewhere in the city centre. It wasn't a police station and the man he spoke to wasn't a police officer. The man told him that he would be more valuable working for MI5 than walking a beat, and that they wanted him to try to infiltrate fundamentalists in Birmingham and to try to get them to take him out to Syria."

"This man who told Hasan all this. What was his name?"

"Hasan said his name was Roger. No surname. Just Roger."

"And this Roger definitely said MI5?"

"Hasan kept calling him a spook. But I'm pretty sure at one point he said MI5."

"Not MI6?"

She shook her head. "No. MI5. Why?"

Shepherd sat back. It wouldn't have made sense for MI5 to be recruiting an agent to send him overseas. MI5's brief was to combat terrorism in the UK — actions overseas were the responsibility of MI6.

"I just want to be sure," said Shepherd. "So this Roger encouraged Hasan to get involved with extremists, was that the plan?"

"That's what he said. Hasan was working as a Deliveroo driver and he knew a guy who he worked with who'd been to Afghanistan a few years ago. This guy was always talking about turning Britain into a Muslim country. Hasan got close to him and he introduced him to other guys, and within a few months Hasan was offered training over in Syria. Roger said he was to go."

"Was Roger Hasan's only point of contact?"

She nodded. "Hasan said it had to be that way because you couldn't trust anybody."

"But how did Roger keep in touch? Did he go to Syria, too?"

"No, I don't think so. He gave Hasan a special watch that he said MI5 could use to track him. And Hasan could use it to send messages."

"What sort of watch was it?"

"It looked like a regular Casio, but if you pressed a button you could leave a message and it got sent I don't know where."

"And he used the watch to send messages to this Roger?"

"That's what Hasan said. At first I didn't believe him. It was like something James Bond might use, right?"

Shepherd frowned. It sounded possible but it wasn't the sort of equipment he'd come across during his time with MI5. "And Hasan was reporting back regularly?"

"Only when he had something important to pass on. Communication was one way so he never knew if they were getting his information or not. But Roger had told him to stay in Syria as long as he could."

"And where is he now? Hasan?"

"I don't know. He told me he'd be away for a few weeks but that he'd be back. That was about four months ago and I never saw him again. Then one of the Syrian women said that I was getting a new husband. She said Hasan wouldn't be coming back but that one of the old ISIS imams had his eye on me. That's when I got out."

"How?"

"I hid in a truck they used to bring in supplies. It was driving to a nearby village and I jumped out. A farmer took care of me for a day or two and then he got his brother to drive me to an area controlled by the Turks. There were hundreds of refugees there, thousands maybe. The Turks let us walk across the border and I ended up here."

"When was that?"

"About a month ago. Please, Mr Easton. I just want to go home. I'll help you in whatever way I can. I made

240

a mistake, a huge mistake, and I'll do whatever I can to put it right."

Shepherd studied her with unblinking eyes. He was sure she was telling the truth — or at least what she believed to be the truth. He was sure that she'd been in an ISIS camp in Syria, and equally sure that she had escaped and made her way across the border, but it didn't make any sense that MI5 would be behind such a dangerous — almost foolhardy — mission. But what would Hasan Mahmoud have had to gain by lying to her?

Nadia leaned forward and looked at him imploringly. "So what do you think, Mr Easton? Can you help me? Or is Warren-Madden right, you're going to leave me here to rot?"

Shepherd stepped out of the unit and closed the door behind him. Margie was outside, smoking yet another cigarette. Shepherd wasn't sure if she was smoking because of the stress she was under that day or if it was her regular intake, but she'd barely stopped since they had arrived at the camp. "Is everything all right?" she asked anxiously.

"I need to make a call," said Shepherd, taking out his mobile phone. "Can you look after her?"

"Is she okay?"

"She's fine."

Margie opened the door and went inside. Shepherd walked away from the unit and called Pritchard on his mobile. He ran through everything Nadia had told him: that Hasan Mahmoud had claimed to have been working as an MI5 agent, initially passing on information about extremist activity at his mosque in Birmingham. "Mahmoud said his handler was called Roger and it was Roger who had encouraged him to go to Syria for further training," said Shepherd. "Mahmoud was apparently on a very long leash, where he had some sort of watch gizmo that could send messages to his handler. Nadia says he used to tell her all sorts of details about what was going on there, including names, and I think he was doing that as a way of reinforcing his memory. It looks to me as if the idea was to debrief him at some point when he got back to England."

"Where is he now?" asked Pritchard.

"She doesn't know," said Shepherd. "The last time she saw him was about four months ago. He just left. And she escaped after that and made her own way to Turkey. The Turks picked her up and put her in the Kilis camp."

"How reliable is this girl?" asked Pritchard.

"She believes what she's telling me, I'm convinced of that," said Shepherd. "The problem is, there's no way of knowing whether or not he was telling her the truth. But I can't see why he'd lie. He was putting his life on the line by telling her that he was there as a spy."

"Spell this guy's name," said Pritchard when he'd finished. Shepherd did and Pritchard told him to wait. After a couple of minutes Pritchard came back on the line. "Okay, so there's nothing on the PNC or on any of our databases for Hasan Mahmoud, at least not from Birmingham or connected to the mosque that Nadia attended. There is a Hasan Mahmoud in Bristol but he's in his sixties, and a Hasan Mahmoud in Bradford, but he's been in prison on drugs charges for the past nine months. I've put in a request with Six to see if they have anyone of that name on the books as an agent."

"Nadia says that she told this story to Warren-Madden and that he accused her of lying, and said that she shouldn't tell anyone else what she'd told him."

"It could be that Six are running him from London without telling Warren-Madden," said Pritchard. "Need to know, and all that."

"Yeah, well Nadia tells me that Warren-Madden was out at the camp and that he told her not to talk to me."

"Did he now?"

"She says he told her that if she said anything to me, she'd stay in the camp forever."

"Didn't she realise that he doesn't have the authority to make a threat like that?"

"She's a young girl, scared out of her wits. She doesn't know who to believe. But I explained things to her."

"It could be that he just doesn't believe her and doesn't want her causing problems on what he sees as his patch," said Pritchard. "One would assume that he would have checked with London. But as I said, need to know. Let's see how they react to my request. Look Daniel, you're the man on the spot. How do you want to play this?"

"I think she'll be useful. She knows a few names of jihadists who have returned to the UK, but she says she saw the faces of a lot more of them. She wasn't supposed to speak with any of the men except for Mahmoud, but she saw them all the time. I think we could run photographs by her and she'd have no trouble recognising faces. That in itself could be a goldmine, irrespective of what Mahmoud was doing."

"What about the other two girls?"

"No useful intel that I can see. One of them, Lulu Abati, is still a positive danger, I'd say. She tries to come across as a victim who didn't know what she was doing, but under pressure she shows her true colours. Nadia is a different kettle of fish entirely. I think she genuinely wants to help and there's good intel to be had. And she could definitely spot this Hasan Mahmoud if he's in our database. I think I should bring her back."

"Then do it."

"Michael Warren-Madden won't be happy. As I said, he did all he could to stop me from talking to her."

"It's not his call. They had their chance; if they don't want to use her, that's their loss."

"What about the mechanics of getting her back to the UK? Can we get her on the same flight?"

"I should think so," said Pritchard. "I'll get that sorted at this end. We can get the embassy to issue her with a passport in her own name."

"Even though she's had her citizenship revoked?"

"All that happens is that any current passport is cancelled. And if she applies in the UK for a passport, the passport office won't issue one. But if we issue her a passport overseas, it'll work just fine when she enters the UK. There's no actual database of people who have had their citizenship revoked."

"Just so you know, I'm expecting resistance from Warren-Madden when I get to Ankara."

"I'll be going above his head, so don't worry about that. What about Jaraf's wife and daughter?"

"I'm on the way to collect them. I wanted to run Nadia by you first."

"Let me know when you've got the passports," said Pritchard, and ended the call.

Shepherd put his phone away and knocked on the door to Nadia's container. Margie came out, closed the door behind her and looked at him anxiously. "Okay, so we're good to go with Nadia," said Shepherd. "The embassy will issue her with a new passport and I'll take her back to London with me."

Her eyes brightened. "That's great news," she said. "Really great news. What about Lulu and Jamila?"

"I'm sorry. There's nothing I can do for them."

Margie's face fell. "That's not fair," she said.

"Life's not fair," said Shepherd. "If it was, children wouldn't end up in a place like this. But you have to realise that those three girls are here because of the choices they made. A lot of the people here never made a choice, their lives were turned upside down. Those girls had perfectly good lives in one of the best countries in the world and no one forced them to come here."

"I know," she said. "I just . . ."

"You just have to accept the fact that sometimes you can only do so much," said Shepherd. "I think all you can do is to persuade Jamila and Lulu to accept that they won't be going back to the UK. They have other options."

"Jamila couldn't survive in Bangladesh."

"Millions of people do. And Lulu can probably go straight to Sweden." He saw her about to argue and he held up a hand. "I know what you're going to say, but Sweden has to be better than here. I've done all I can, Margie. And so have you."

"I could go to the press."

"You could, but that hasn't worked for the other jihadist brides that went public. And if you do cause a fuss over Lulu and Jamila, you might queer the pitch for Nadia. As I said, I should be able to fly out with Nadia tomorrow. That's a victory and that's down to you. You should be proud of yourself on that score. The other two girls have options. If Lulu's family love their daughter, they can join her in Sweden. I get that Jamila's situation is a bit more awkward, but it looks to me as if you've done all you can."

"So why can you help Nadia and not the other two?" asked Margie. She narrowed her eyes and watched him closely.

"Truth be told, she has information that could be very useful," said Shepherd. "That information could save lives."

"What sort of information?"

"That I can't tell you."

"But Lulu and Jamila don't have any information?"

Shepherd shook his head. "Nothing useful, no."

246

Her eyes narrowed further. "You're not really with the Home Office, are you?"

Shepherd ignored the question, figuring it was almost certainly rhetorical. He looked at his watch. He'd spent longer than he planned talking to Nadia. "Let's go and collect Jaraf's wife and son. Then we can pick up Nadia."

Shepherd could see that Margie wasn't happy, but there was nothing he could say that would make her feel any better. She led him down the path towards the centre of the camp. "You're not embassy staff, right?" He wanted to keep her talking so that she didn't dwell on the bad news he'd given her.

"No, but I'm based there and I know my way around the camp better than any of the staffers. They tend to keep their distance. To be honest, I think most of them are scared to set foot in here. There are a lot of desperate people in the camp, and they can get aggressive. It really is only the strong who survive."

"Survival of the fittest?"

"It's a crock of shit that the meek will inherit the earth. Out here the meek get trodden into the dust."

"And Mrs Jaraf and the boy? How are they?"

"They're in good spirits, considering what they've been through. Delighted that Mr Jaraf is alive. They'd given him up for dead."

"What were they planning to do, before we contacted them?"

"What could they do? They're here in limbo like thousands of others."

"They're Palestinians, right?"

Margie nodded. "Yes. And unusually they still have their passports with them."

"So why haven't they gone back?"

They reached another brick path and Margie headed to the west, towards one of the mosques. "They have no money and apparently no family there. They left everything behind when they went to Syria with Mr Jaraf. They thought that he was dead and they were penniless, so they had been hoping to be accepted by a European country. But there's a huge backlog of applications, obviously." She groped in her bag for her cigarettes and lit one.

"Where did they want to go?"

"The UK, like most of them. The UK is the Holy Grail. If not the UK then maybe Sweden or Australia. Germany, maybe. Canada, though they always complain about the cold."

"The US?"

Margie shook her head. "Not while Trump's running the show. He's slashed refugee intakes to the bone, especially from this part of the world. If you don't mind me asking, why are the Jarafs being fast-tracked into the country?"

"That decision was taken at well above my pay grade," said Shepherd.

"They didn't tell you?"

Shepherd shrugged but didn't answer. He didn't want to lie to her unless he had to. "Do you know why they ended up here in the camp?" he asked.

"She was vague on the details but it's not unusual for the men and women here to have memory problems.

248

They go through such horrors that they tend to blot out the worst bits." They reached another crossroads and she took him to the left. "They were in an ISIS camp in Syria, with her husband. She didn't — or wouldn't — say what he was doing there but I'm assuming he was involved in some way — they weren't prisoners or anything like that. Which is why I'm so surprised that the UK Government is so keen to allow them in."

Margie had a number written on a piece of paper. She walked along the line of containers checking it against those painted on the sides until she found the right one. She pointed at the door and Shepherd knocked. There was no answer and he knocked again. This time the door was opened by a woman in a black headscarf with a black niqab covering her face below her eyes. She was in her late forties going by the crow's feet around her eyes and she squinted through round glasses as she looked at him quizzically. "Mrs Jaraf? I'm Paul Easton from the Home Office. I'm here to take you to the UK to join your husband." She frowned and blinked several times, and for a moment Shepherd wondered if she spoke English or not.

"Paul Easton?" she repeated eventually.

Shepherd smiled. "From the Home Office. Is your son with you?"

The woman opened the door wider. There were four camp beds in the container, along with a chipboard chest of drawers with a small television on top. There was a wire running up the wall from the TV, presumably to a satellite dish on the roof. An Arab news report was on the screen. All four beds were clearly in use but there was only one other person in the container: an olive-skinned teenager with dark, curly hair. He was wearing faded jeans and an AC Milan football shirt, and had a cheap black plastic watch on his left wrist. The boy was lying on the bed in the far corner, his bare feet pointing towards Shepherd, reading a football magazine. There was a pair of Adidas trainers on the floor. Mrs Jaraf saw Margie and she smiled. "Hello Mrs Barker," she said.

"Hello Aisha, nice to see you again. Mr Easton is here to make arrangements to take you to England."

Mrs Jaraf spoke to her son in Arabic and he sighed and sat up, tossing the magazine onto the bed. "My son has no manners," she said to Shepherd.

"That's OK, I have a son myself."

"How old is he?"

"He's a man now, but I remember the teenage years well."

"Malik, say hello to Mr Easton. He will be taking us to London."

"Hello Mr Easton," said Malik, his eyes on the magazine he'd thrown away.

"So, Mrs Jaraf, can I have a look at your passport? And Malik's?"

Mrs Jaraf reached into her backpack and took out two black passports, with "THE PALESTINIAN AUTHORITY" written across the top. She gave them to him. They had been issued three years earlier. Malik shared his date of birth with Shepherd's son, though the Palestinian teenager was six years younger.

"I'm sorry to have to ask, Mrs Jaraf, but would you mind removing your niqab?"

Mrs Jaraf looked at Margie. "Do I have to?"

"It's just for identification purposes," said Shepherd.

She stared at him for several seconds, then nodded and removed the veil from her face. Shepherd looked at the photograph in her passport. It was definitely her. She had thin lips and a distinctive mole on her chin. "Okay, thank you," he said. She replaced the veil. "Do you mind if I keep these?" Shepherd asked, holding up the passports. "We'll issue you with visas for the UK at the British Embassy in Ankara."

"When do we leave?"

"We'll head to the embassy now and the plan is to fly to London tomorrow."

Her eyes brightened. "Is that where Salam is? London?"

"No, he's in a safe house somewhere else." He grinned. "Actually he's in my house. When was the last time you talked to him?" He tucked the passports into his back pocket.

"Not since we were together in Syria. The camp was attacked and Malik and I fled. We thought that Salam was dead. And I suppose he thought the same of us. He had a phone but it stopped working."

"What about when you found out he was alive?"

"He called the camp and they got a message to me, but it took three days before I got it. He'd left a number but when I called it, it didn't work either. Then Mrs Barker came to see me and told me that he was alive." She smiled. "I was so happy. I still can't believe we're going to be together again." She sat down on the camp bed and put her arm around her son.

Shepherd looked at his watch. "We need to be getting a move on. How much do you need to bring with you?"

"We don't have much," she said, and forced a smile. "We only brought what we could carry and we were robbed shortly after we got here."

"Robbed?"

"There are thieves everywhere and the guards can do nothing. ISIS runs the camp. They decide who has what and who gets punished."

"You say they're guards, but they're not guards, are they?" said Shepherd.

"How else would you describe them?" asked Mrs Jaraf.

"Nobody stops you from leaving, do they? You're not prisoners here, are you?"

"Where else would we go?" she asked. She shrugged. "Anyway, the question you asked was what we needed to take with us, and we have only these two bags." She pointed at a large black holdall with bulging side pockets, and a wheeled suitcase that had been fastened shut with a length of cord.

"What about your son?" asked Shepherd.

"Just the backpack." She pointed at a black bag at the end of one of the beds.

Shepherd gestured at some clothing hanging on a line at the back of the container. "Are those yours?"

She turned to look. "They are but they're wet and I'll leave them here." She nodded at a small radio and a

252

copy of the Koran. "I'll leave these too." She smiled at her son and spoke to him in Arabic and the boy nodded. Mrs Jaraf turned to Shepherd. "I was asking him if he was happy to leave his football here so that the other boys could play and he said yes."

"Sure, easy enough to get a new ball in England," he said. He smiled at the boy. He looked older than his sixteen years, but then he'd been through a lot. He wanted to ask the woman why she and Jaraf had taken the boy to Syria. Palestine wasn't exactly a safe place but it was surely far safer than war-torn Syria, and he couldn't understand why they would put their child at risk. Jaraf had made it sound as if he had been training ISIS jihadists for at least two years, which meant Malik couldn't have been much more than fourteen when they'd arrived in the country. Shepherd couldn't imagine putting his own son in harm's way. But then Shepherd wasn't ideologically driven in the way that Jaraf was. Religion could override parental love, and in Afghanistan he had even seen Taliban fighters use their own children as suicide bombers. "Are you excited to go to England?" Shepherd asked the boy.

The boy nodded eagerly.

"Okay then, let's get your new passports sorted," said Shepherd.

"Where will we stay tonight?" asked Mrs Jaraf.

"We'll arrange a hotel."

"A hotel?" Her face brightened. "Will there be a bath? A real bath? I can't remember when I last had a real bath."

Shepherd couldn't help but smile at her enthusiasm. "I'll do my best to get you a room with a bath," he said. He picked up the holdall and grunted when he realised just how heavy it was. The boy slung his backpack over his shoulder and grabbed the handle of the wheeled suitcase.

Shepherd and Margie went outside and held the door open while Mrs Jaraf and her son joined them. They walked together along the brick pathway to the main administration block. "I'll leave you here to go through the paperwork while I go to get Nadia," Shepherd said to Margie.

"Are you sure you can find your way back?" she asked. "This place is huge and all the units look the same."

"I've got a pretty good memory," he said. He flashed Mrs Jaraf a reassuring smile. "I won't be long," he said. "We'll be taking another passenger with us." Mrs Jaraf nodded but didn't say anything. Her eyes looked nervous but that was to be expected considering what she had been through. "There's no need to worry, everything is going to be okay."

He headed towards Nadia's container. The girl's change of heart had been an eye-opener, but Shepherd knew it was going to cause friction with Warren-Madden. The MI6 agent had either made a huge error of judgement or had been playing some sort of game. He either knew that Nadia was a good intel source and was trying to bury her, or he didn't believe her. But if it was a matter of not trusting the girl's veracity,

254

Warren-Madden should have explained that to Shepherd and not sent him in blind.

A young boy cried out a warning and as Shepherd flinched, a large metal circle whizzed by his ear. At first he thought he'd been attacked but then he saw a group of children looking anxiously in his direction and he realised they were playing a makeshift game of frisbee. He jogged over and picked up the lid. There was white paint around the edge and there were marks where a screwdriver had been used to lever it off a can. Shepherd threw the lid over their heads and they laughed and gave chase. The oldest couldn't have been more than ten and they were all barefoot.

Shepherd reached a crossroads and he walked in the direction of Nadia's container. It was about ten containers away. There were three men ahead of him, walking purposefully. They didn't appear to be talking to each other. The man in the middle was wearing a grey thawb and had a black-and-white-checked keffiyeh headscarf. The two on the outside were in jeans and long jackets. All were wearing flip-flops.

The area ahead of them had gone quiet. When Shepherd had left Nadia's container there had been groups of teenagers standing around smoking cigarettes and chatting; there had been children playing and women hanging out washing to dry. But now there was no one around.

Shepherd looked over his shoulder. A bearded old man was ushering the children towards one of the containers. A woman was standing in the doorway of her container, and when she saw him look in her direction she disappeared inside and closed the door.

The three men reached Nadia's container and stopped. Shepherd's heart began to race. One of the men grabbed the handle of the door and opened it. The taller of the three men reached inside his jacket and Shepherd caught the flash of sunlight on something metal. The two men in jeans went inside and the man in the thawb stood with his back to the door, his arms folded.

Shepherd broke into a run, his shoes slapping on the brick path, and the man turned to look at him. His mouth opened and he banged on the door with the flat of his hand, but then Shepherd reached him and grabbed him by the throat. The man tried to throw a punch but he was too slow and Shepherd hit him in the solar plexus with three rapid punches. The strength went from his legs and he slumped to the ground, his mouth working soundlessly. Shepherd pushed the door but it wouldn't open. He took a step back and kicked it, hard, just below the handle. The door buckled a bit but didn't give way. He took a step back and kicked again, this time putting all of his weight into it. The door flew open and Shepherd rushed in.

Nadia was crouched in the bedroom, squeezed into the gap between the bunk bed furthest from the door and the wall. One of the men stood over her, holding a machete. The other man turned towards Shepherd, a curved knife in his hand, blocking the bedroom doorway with his body. Shepherd lashed out with his foot, catching him just below the right knee. As his leg gave way, Shepherd grabbed for the man's wrist and twisted it so hard that he heard bones crack. The man yelped and the knife clattered on the floor. Shepherd kept the pressure on his arm, then twisted it back and around, forcing his head down. He pulled him out of the bedroom and brought up his knee, slamming it into his chest. The man roared in pain. Shepherd released his grip on his wrist, kicked his legs out from underneath him and as he slumped to the floor he kicked him twice in the chest. He was still moving and as he tried to get up, Shepherd kicked him in the head. The man went still, blood trickling from between his lips and down his beard.

The other attacker had turned to face Shepherd, the machete held high. He was in his twenties, bearded with a manic stare. He stepped out of the bedroom and Shepherd moved back, his hands up, fingers curled, staring at the man's face, breathing slowly and evenly even though his heart was pounding. The fact that the man had a weapon gave him an advantage, but it also limited his options. He wouldn't be punching with his left hand and he probably wouldn't kick — he had the weapon and he'd want to use it. He had the machete high, which meant he'd be slashing down with it rather than stabbing, so Shepherd would have a chance of blocking the blow if he moved quickly enough. He faked an attack and Shepherd started to move forward, his left arm rising to block the arm, but the man jumped back, swung the machete down and then lunged forward. The move caught Shepherd by surprise and even though he managed to twist to the side, the machete caught him on the left arm, slicing through his jacket sleeve and biting into the flesh just above his elbow. There was hardly any pain — the adrenaline coursing through his system took care of that — but he felt the blood flow.

The man roared in triumph and raised the machete again. Shepherd backed away. The cut hadn't gone deep enough to do any real damage so he could still use his arm. His breathing was coming faster now, but he stayed calm, waiting for the man's next move. The man faked another attack but Shepherd was ready. He jumped back and the machete missed him by inches.

He tried to grab the machete but the man moved it away. Shepherd picked up the plastic chair but realised immediately that it was too light to do any damage, so he threw it at his attacker's head to distract him. As the man ducked. Shepherd took the opportunity to grab the broom that was leaning against the wall. He held it brush outward. It wouldn't do any damage, but moving it in front of the man's face would help keep him at bay. The man on the ground started to groan and his legs twitched. Shepherd thrust the brush at the face of the man with the machete, then kicked the man on the floor in the head again. He went still.

The other attacker roared with anger and began slashing at the broom. Shepherd let him do it, knowing that every blow was sapping his assailant's strength. Eventually he ran out of steam and Shepherd lowered the broom, stuck it under his chin and pushed, hard. He fell back and Shepherd kept up the pressure, shoving with all his might. The attacker lost his balance and staggered back until he crashed into one of the bunks. Shepherd stepped to the side, reversed his grip on the broom handle and slammed the stick against his knee. He screamed in pain, cursed in Arabic and raised the machete. Shepherd dropped into a crouch and thrust the end of the broom handle into his groin. He bent double as the breath exploded from his lungs in a bellow of agony. Shepherd took another step back and walloped him on the side of the head with the handle. He fell to the side and slammed face down onto the floor with such force that the whole unit vibrated.

Shepherd stood over him with the brush raised high but he was out for the count. Nadia was sobbing on the floor. Shepherd dropped the brush and went over to her. He crouched down. She had buried her head in her hands and her whole body was wracked with sobs. "Nadia?" he said softly. She continued to cry. Shepherd reached out to touch her on the shoulder, but when he did she flinched as if he'd burned her. "It's okay, Nadia," he said. "We can go now."

She took her trembling hands away from her face. "They were going to kill me," she whispered.

"I'm sorry, I shouldn't have left you alone," he said. "But it's over. They can't hurt you." He stood up and held out his hand. "Come on."

She reached for his hand, grabbed it, and pulled herself to her feet, then gasped as she saw the two men on the floor.

"Don't look at them, Nadia," he said. "Look at me."

She did as she was told and then gasped again when she saw his blood-soaked jacket sleeve. "They stabbed you," she said.

"It's okay," he said. "Just get your things and we'll go." She continued to stare at the bloody sleeve. He put a hand on her shoulder and looked into her fearful eyes. "I know you're in shock, but you have to focus on what we have to do. The camp isn't safe for you now and the longer you stay here the more danger you'll be in. We have to go. Okay?"

She nodded fearfully. "Okay," she said.

"Where is your bag?"

"I've got two," she said. She pointed at the wall by the door. There was a bulging backpack and a hard-shell wheeled suitcase, and next to it a black plastic rubbish bag. "I've got some clothes in the plastic bag but I can leave those behind," she said.

"We'll try to take it all," he said. "I'm sure we can fix you up with a suitcase at the embassy." He put his head closer to hers and she averted her eyes. "It's going to be all right, Nadia. I promise."

She bit down on her lower lip and nodded.

"Good girl," he said. He let go of her shoulder and she walked around the bodies on the floor to the bags. "I'll take the suitcase and the backpack, you bring the black bag."

She picked up the garbage bag. He shouldered the backpack and grabbed the handle of the suitcase. His arm hurt when he lifted the case, but the pain wasn't too bad and he ignored it. Nadia opened the door and they stumbled out. The first man that Shepherd had hit was still unconscious. Off to their right a group of five men were huddled together, looking in their direction. They were all wearing baggy tunics and trousers with skullcaps on their heads. One of them pointed at Shepherd and said something to the others. "Come on, Nadia," said Shepherd. "Quick as you can." He didn't like the odds, not when he had an injured arm, though he doubted they would try anything in full view of the camp. There were now refugees in most of the doorways, all of them looking towards Shepherd and Nadia as they carried the bags towards the administration building.

Nadia kept her head down and her eyes on the path, but Shepherd was constantly scanning his surroundings, meeting any intimidating gazes with undisguised contempt. His adrenaline levels were still high and he was more than prepared to dish out any violence that was necessary.

Two of the children who had been playing with the paint lid appeared at the doorway of their container and called out to him in Arabic, but they were chased inside by an old man waving a walking stick.

They kept walking quickly until they reached the admin block. Margie was outside the main entrance, smoking yet another cigarette. Her eyes widened when she saw the blood on Shepherd's jacket. "What happened?"

"Nothing," said Shepherd, ushering Nadia inside.

Margie tossed her cigarette away and reached for the suitcase. Shepherd shook his head. "I'm okay," he said.

"You're clearly not okay," she said. "Give me that." She took the suitcase from him and pulled it into the building.

Shepherd followed her inside. "How's everything with Mrs Jaraf?" he asked.

"All the paperwork's done, they're good to go," said Margie. "We need to process Nadia but it'll be easy enough."

"Even though her citizenship was cancelled?"

"They don't care about that here. That's only an issue when she tries to enter the UK, but you'll be arranging a new passport for her, right?"

"Michael Warren-Madden will be handling that," he said. "I doubt that he'll be happy about it, but it's not his call." He put Nadia's backpack on the floor and winced as he felt a stab of pain in his shoulder.

Nadia was watching him anxiously. "You need to see a doctor," she said.

"It's okay, it didn't go deep," said Shepherd.

"It's still bleeding," she said. She looked at Margie. "They were trying to kill me. Mr Easton saved my life."

"What the hell happened?" Margie asked Shepherd.

"It was nothing. Someone must have realised that Nadia was talking to us about things they didn't want talked about."

"And they attacked you?"

"We can talk about this later, Margie. The important thing now is that we get Nadia and the Jarafs out of here."

She took hold of his arm and looked at the blood-soaked sleeve. "No, the important thing is that we get this sorted before you bleed to death." She gestured at a row of plastic chairs. "Sit down while I get Nadia's paperwork started, then I'll take you to the clinic."

Shepherd opened his mouth to argue, but he realised she was right — the wound wasn't going to heal by itself and he had a long way to travel. "Okay," he said, and sat down.

Margie grabbed the suitcase handle and Nadia picked up the backpack. They walked away down the corridor leaving Shepherd looking at a poster detailing the rules of the camp. Rule number five was "NO WEAPONS", which made him smile ruefully.

Margie returned after a few minutes. "Right, I found someone to keep an eye on Nadia," she said. "You need to come with me now." She took him out of the main building and along a brick pathway to a concrete block with a red crescent painted on the wall. It had a sign saying "CLINIC" in English, and several lines of other script, including Arabic. She pushed open the door. There were two dozen people sitting on plastic chairs, mostly women with children, though there was a man in his twenties with his left leg missing, crutches leaning against the chair next to him. All the women wore long black robes and most of them had their faces covered. One of the children, who looked to be about eight years old, was holding a white-painted handmade wooden Kalashnikov, complete with a carved sniper scope. The boy pointed the gun at Shepherd and pretended to pull the trigger. His mother saw what he was doing and scolded him in Arabic, but the boy shook his head, said something, and pretended to fire again.

"Have a seat while I talk to the receptionist," said Margie. She went over to a hatch where a woman in pale blue scrubs and a matching headscarf was looking at a clipboard.

Shepherd lowered himself onto a seat by the door and winced. His arm was starting to throb as his adrenaline levels began to return to normal. The boy was continuing to stare at Shepherd. Shepherd smiled and winked. The boy grinned and winked back. Shepherd mimed forming a gun with his right hand and pretended to fire two shots at the lad. "Bang, bang," he said. The boy clasped his hand to his chest, moaned, and slumped to the floor. Shepherd couldn't help but laugh. The boy's mother bent down and prodded him in the stomach, chiding him in Arabic again. Then she looked up at Shepherd. Even with her face covered, he could see from her eyes that she was smiling. "I'm sorry," she said in heavily accented English. "My son likes to play war games."

"That's okay," said Shepherd. "I have a son, too. When he was young, he liked to play cowboys and Indians."

"What is cowboys and Indians?" she asked.

Shepherd mimed a gun with his hand. "Shooting," he said.

"I tell him shooting is not a game." She shrugged. "But what can you do? Children will be children."

Shepherd thought it best not to mention that if she wanted him to lay off the shooting games she should take the wooden AK-47 off her son, but Liam had plenty of toy guns when he was a kid, and Shepherd had taken him to the SAS's camp in Hereford and let him use the real thing from an early age. Kids liked to play with guns, that was the way of the world. It was how they used them as adults that was important.

Margie finished talking to the woman in the hatch and hurried back to Shepherd. "Okay, a nurse will take a look at you now," she said.

"I can wait, I'm not one for queue-jumping," said Shepherd.

"You're the only one in here who's bleeding to death," said Margie. "They'll see you now."

She took hold of his right arm and helped him to his feet. His head swam and he realised that he had lost a lot of blood already, so he allowed her to lead him down a corridor to a small room where a young nurse in a headscarf was waiting. He sat down on a metal examination table and the nurse helped him take his jacket off. The wound was just below his shoulder. The shirt had soaked up a fair amount of blood. She placed the jacket in a plastic bag and put it on a table.

"We should take the shirt off, too," said the nurse. "Actually cutting it would be better." She smiled. "It's already ruined."

She took off his tie and then cut away the shirt with a large pair of scissors, putting the pieces in a hazardous waste bin. She went back to him and ran her finger along the old scar on the back of his shoulder. "That must have hurt," she said.

"Actually it didn't, not at the time. It felt as if I'd been thumped hard. Though it hurt like hell afterwards."

"You were a soldier?"

Shepherd didn't like talking about his past, certainly not when he was supposed to be a civil servant. "It was a long time ago," he said.

Shepherd looked at the wound on his arm and wrinkled his nose. The cut wasn't deep but it was almost three inches long and was definitely going to need stitches. "I'll give you something for the pain," said the nurse.

"I'm okay," said Shepherd. "I've had stitches before without anaesthetic."

"It's just a local," said the nurse, preparing a syringe. "It'll stop you flinching and spoiling my needlework."

Shepherd laughed. "Your English is very good."

"I lived in America for more than ten years," she said. "Baltimore. My parents took me there. I became a citizen but I wanted to come back and help." She gave him three injections along the length of the wound, then dropped the syringe into the bin. "What's happening in Syria is a scandal," she said. "Our government won't help, but they can't stop me from trying to make a difference."

Shepherd looked over at Margie, who by the look of it was eager to have another cigarette. She was shifting her weight from foot to foot and tapping the bag where she kept her cigarettes and lighter. "Hey Margie, can you do me a favour and get me a shirt from my bag?" he said. "Probably best if I don't turn up shirtless."

"No problem," she said. She headed out, reaching for her cigarettes almost before she was in the corridor.

The nurse was finishing the last stitch when Margie returned, holding a blue denim shirt that she'd taken from his holdall and a heavy black reefer jacket. "I found the jacket in a consignment of charity clothes and it looks as if it hasn't been worn."

"I can't take a refugee's coat," he said.

"There's plenty, more than plenty," she said. "And you're going to need something warm, it gets cold at night."

"Are you sure?"

"Trust me, there's no shortage of clothing at this camp," she said. "Hope is in short supply, but there's an abundance of clothing."

The nurse put a dressing over the wound and Shepherd gingerly put on the shirt.

"Keep the wound clean and dry, and the stitches can come out in a week or so," she said. "I'd suggest you go to a clinic but I get the feeling you're the type who'll just pull them out with his teeth."

Shepherd buttoned up his shirt and slid off the table. "Thanks," he said.

"Pleasure," said the nurse, taking off her latex gloves and disposing of them. "I wish all my patients were as stoic."

Margie helped Shepherd on with the coat. "Nadia's almost done, I'll take you along to the office."

They went back through the waiting room where an old man in a threadbare thawb was shouting and gesticulating at the receptionist. "What was his problem?" asked Shepherd as they walked along the path to the admin block.

"My Arabic is pretty basic, but it sounded like he was demanding to be seen ahead of the women and children."

"Nice," said Shepherd.

"Old habits die hard," said Margie. "In their culture, men come first. He doesn't see anything wrong with asserting what he sees as his rights."

"I'd like to see him try that in a GP's surgery in London," said Shepherd. "They'd soon send him packing. But now you're making me feel bad for queue-jumping."

She patted him on the shoulder. "You were bleeding heavily. He's just a crotchety old man with a bad knee. No comparison."

They reached the administration block and Shepherd followed her down a corridor to a large office where half a dozen men and women were working at computer screens. Mrs Jaraf and her son were sitting to the side of the room, their belongings in front of them. Nadia was sitting at one of the desks.

"Let's not tell Mrs Jaraf what happened," Shepherd whispered to Margie. He nodded at Nadia. "Can you tell Nadia that mum's the word? I don't want Mrs Jaraf to worry, she's got enough on her plate as it is."

"Not a problem," said Margie. She went over to Nadia and began talking to her.

Shepherd waved at Mrs Jaraf and she waved back. She seemed less nervous than she had been when he had first met her, though it was hard to tell with half her face covered. The boy also appeared more comfortable. Shepherd walked over to them. "It won't be long now," said Shepherd.

"Who is that girl?" asked Mrs Jaraf, gesturing at Nadia.

"She's British and I'm taking her home," said Shepherd.

"Why is she in Turkey?"

"It's a long story." Shepherd looked at his watch. "The plan is to drive back to Ankara and we'll stop at a hotel on the way. We're booked onto a flight to London tomorrow evening."

"And will Salam be there to meet us?"

"No, he's in a house outside London."

"So I'll see him the day after tomorrow?"

"That's the plan," said Shepherd.

Nadia and Margie stood up and the girl who had been helping them handed Margie a sheet of paper. Nadia went over to her bags and picked up her backpack. Margie walked over to Shepherd and waved the sheet of paper. "All done," she said.

"Great." He gestured at Nadia's garbage bag. "Is there any way we can get a proper suitcase or holdall here, or at the embassy? I can't see the airline letting us check in a rubbish bag."

Margie nodded. "Give me a couple of minutes." She hurried out and Shepherd went over to Nadia.

"So it's okay, I can go back to England?" she asked him, her eyes wide.

"Yes, we're booked onto a flight tomorrow. But you have to realise that you staying in the UK depends on you cooperating with us. You have to tell us everything you know."

"I will," she said. "I promise." She stepped forward and hugged him, then rested her head against his shoulder. "Thank you so much." He patted her on the back.

Margie came back with a small wheeled suitcase that had been knocked around but was still serviceable. She helped Nadia transfer the clothing from the rubbish bag. There was plenty of room. "We could probably put the backpack in, too," said Margie. "It'll make it easier to carry."

Nadia made room for the backpack and closed the case. "Perfect," she said.

"Right," said Margie. "Let's hit the road."

Between them they carried the bags out into the car park and loaded up the Land Cruiser. Then Shepherd got into the front with Margie as Mrs Jaraf, her son and Nadia got into the back. Shepherd fastened his seat belt and twisted around to smile encouragement at the three passengers. "Everybody okay?" he asked.

Nadia grinned and nodded enthusiastically. Mrs Jaraf and the boy seemed less happy but Shepherd figured that was to be expected. They had been through a lot and were leaving for a new life in a country they knew little about. "It'll be okay," he said to Mrs Jaraf. "You'll be with your husband soon."

"You're a good man," she said.

"I do my best," said Shepherd. He turned back in his seat as Margie started the car and put it in gear. She looked even less happy than Mrs Jaraf. "Are you okay?" he asked quietly.

She nodded. "I just feel awful at leaving Lulu and Jamila," she said. She looked across at him and he saw that her eyes were brimming with tears. "It's not fair that they have to stay behind."

Shepherd smiled sympathetically, but there was nothing he could say that would make her feel better. And he doubted that she wanted to hear him tell her that life wasn't fair and sometimes you just had to live with that fact.

Gil Stern was drinking coffee with Micha Abramov and Ben Elon when his phone rang. It was Dinah Klein. "They've just left the camp," she said. "Five people in a Land Cruiser. Paul Easton is in the front passenger seat, the woman and the kid are in the back, with another woman."

"Who?" asked Gil. "Who is this other woman?"

"I don't know. An Asian woman in a hijab."

"Where are you now?"

"I'm a few miles behind them. Adam is about five miles ahead of them."

"No need to get too close," said Stern. "I had the number checked and the vehicle is owned by an NGO. The registered driver is Margie Barker, she's employed by the NGO but because most of her work involves British citizens they've given her a desk at the British Embassy. They'll be going to the embassy first and they'll be at the airport tomorrow, so we can keep them on a long leash. There's a good chance they'll stop off at a hotel on the way, so be aware of that. It's absolutely vital that they don't spot us tailing them. If they do stop, it'll give you the chance to install a tracker on the car. It's not the end of the world if you can't, because we already have a tracker with the passengers." He ended the call and grinned at Abramov and Elon. "So far so good," he said.

It had been dark for almost three hours when the Land Cruiser arrived at Adana, a city that consisted mainly of ugly concrete high rises and elaborate mosques. Margie took them to a hotel she had used before, the Park Royal. As they drove up, Shepherd could see that there was no public parking. "Where do you normally leave the car?" he asked.

"There's parking a few blocks away," she said. "There are always free places."

Shepherd shook his head. "I'd feel happier if the car was on site," he said.

"Then that rules out the Park Royal. Are you worried about something?"

Shepherd didn't want to run through his concerns while the three passengers were in the back so he just shrugged. "Humour me," he said.

"Okay, well the Sheraton Grand isn't far away, and that's got secure parking."

"Perfect," said Shepherd.

Margie drove away from the hotel and headed east, across the Seyhan River, which bisected the city on its way to the Mediterranean. Five minutes later they were in the Sheraton's car park. "Better?" said Margie.

272

"Much," said Shepherd. They took their bags and carried them through to the reception. Mrs Jaraf, her son and Nadia sat on overstuffed sofas while Shepherd went with Margie to the reception desk. He gave his Paul Easton Mastercard to a man with a sweeping black moustache and thick eyebrows that almost met over his nose. He asked for four rooms together, ideally with connecting doors. The receptionist frowned as he tapped on his computer keyboard, then he smiled apologetically before explaining that the best he could do was one pair of adjoining rooms, a double bed in one and two singles in the other, and another double room on a different floor. "We are very busy, I am afraid," said the receptionist.

"Does one of the adjoining rooms have a bath?" asked Shepherd.

"They all have baths," said the receptionist with a smile. He booked them in and gave Shepherd keycards for two rooms on the seventh floor and one room on the ninth.

"Is it a problem?" Margie asked as they walked back to the others.

"I'd just be happier if we were all together," he said.

"Same as you're happier when the car is close by?"

"I'm just being careful," said Shepherd.

"Because of what happened in the camp? Surely you don't think Nadia is still at risk?"

"Better safe than sorry," said Shepherd. He handed her the keycard for the room on the ninth floor. "Are you okay to stay with Nadia tonight?"

"Sure."

"Come with us and check out our rooms and then you can take Nadia upstairs."

They carried their bags to the lift and went up to the seventh floor. Shepherd opened one of the rooms and ushered everyone inside. It was a decent enough room with a double bed and a city view that included a huge blue-domed mosque with six needle-thin minarets on the other side of the Seyhan River.

"That's Sabanci Central Mosque," said Margie. "The second largest in the country."

"There's a bath!" said Mrs Jaraf, who was standing at the bathroom door. "A bath and a shower."

"This will be my room," said Shepherd. "Next door should have two single beds." He opened the connecting door and Mrs Jaraf walked into the second room, heading straight for the bathroom. It was identical to the first room but with two smaller beds. Mrs Jaraf popped her head around the bathroom door.

"It's got a bath?" asked Shepherd.

She nodded excitedly. It was the happiest Shepherd had seen her since they'd first met. Her son picked up the TV remote, flopped onto the bed nearest the window and began flicking through the channels.

Shepherd flashed her a thumbs up. "Okay, so you and Malik stay in this room all night. If you need anything, you ask me."

She nodded. "Okay."

"Can we order room service?" asked the boy.

Images of what had happened in the hotel at Heathrow flashed through Shepherd's mind. Could the same thing happen in Turkey? He was confident that they hadn't been tailed from the refugee camp, and there was no reason that Mrs Jaraf or the boy would be targets. And if they were, they could easily have been attacked in the camp. "That's fine," he said to Malik. "But if you want anything, tell me and I'll order it to my room." He nodded at their main door. "Keep that locked at all times and don't open it for anyone. If anyone knocks, tell me and I'll deal with it."

"I want a burger," said the boy, his eyes on the TV screen. "With fries. And a Coke."

"Abu!" said Mrs Jaraf, wagging a warning finger at her son.

"He said I could have whatever I wanted."

"It's okay," laughed Shepherd. "You can have whatever you want."

"I'll have a look at the menu and let you know," she said. She walked to the window and looked over at the mosque. "How long are we staying here?"

"Not long," said Shepherd. "We need to get to the British Embassy in Ankara before noon, which means leaving here about six. But there's time for a meal, a bath and a nap." He turned to Margie who was standing by the connecting door. "Okay, you can take Nadia up to your room now. Order anything you want and charge it to me. I think we shouldn't bother with breakfast."

"They probably won't be serving at that time of the morning anyway," she said. She seized the handle of Nadia's suitcase. "Good night, then, see you all tomorrow." She headed into the corridor and Nadia followed her with the second suitcase.

Shepherd closed the door. Malik had found a movie channel and Mrs Jaraf was still staring out of the window. "I'll leave you both to it," said Shepherd. He gestured at the connecting door. "Leave that open, please. It doesn't have to be wide open, but don't shut it. And as I said, if you need anything, ask me. Please don't leave the room." Mrs Jaraf nodded but didn't say anything, and the boy was too engrossed in the movie to acknowledge Shepherd.

Shepherd took his holdall through to his room and put it on the desk there. He wasn't tired but he felt sticky and dirty from his hours in the camp. He stripped and showered, taking care not to get water on his dressing. He dried himself and put his clothes back on.

He sat in an armchair by the window and called Pritchard. He answered on the third ring. "I'm in the car on hands-free," said Pritchard. "If you hear me swear it's because the bus driver in front of me is being an absolute arsehole. I managed to get the extra seat on the flight tomorrow, how is everything your end?"

"We're in a hotel about five hours' drive from Ankara," said Shepherd. "Everything's going well. Did you have any joy with Hasan Mahmoud?"

"Nothing back from Six so far. If they continue to drag their feet I might have to have a word with the DG and get him to make the approach."

"And what about Nadia's passport?"

"There was some reluctance and I was told it would be discussed and they'd get back to me. They haven't so I'll get on the case first thing in the morning."

276

"That'll be cutting it close, we're three hours ahead of you."

"I hear you, and I'll get it done, even if I have to ruin the DG's breakfast. So no problems today?"

"A small one," said Shepherd, lowering his voice. The television was on in the other room but he didn't want to risk being overheard. "A couple of guys tried to attack Nadia. She's okay but one of them nicked me."

"Nicked?"

"A few stitches, it's no biggie. I think word must have got out that she was talking about Mahmoud or that she was cooperating with the authorities — at least I hope that's all it was. I'm obviously a bit on edge at the moment, especially after what happened with Jaraf."

"You're okay?"

"I'm fine. Look, I thought I might call Major Gannon and get him to send a couple of his lads to ride shotgun with me to Hereford."

"That sounds like a good idea."

"They can meet me at the airport. I'll hand over Nadia to you and they can take me and Mrs Jaraf and her son to my house."

"It won't be me personally at the airport, but yes, that works."

"What will you do with Nadia?"

"We'll take her straight to Thames House and start debriefing her. As you said, we can run our surveillance footage by her and see if she can recognise any faces. We'll probably keep her here for a few days, the safe house situation is still in a state of flux." Pritchard suddenly swore and Shepherd heard the car's horn blare. "Sorry about that," said Pritchard. "Bloody bus drivers. Do they actually have licences or do they just take people off the street?"

Shepherd assumed the question was rhetorical, and ended the call. Then he rang Major Gannon, but the call went through to voicemail. Shepherd left a short message and the Major called back within thirty seconds. "Sorry about that, Spider, I'm with a group of VIPs in the Sergeant's Mess."

"Just checking that all's well with our guy."

"He's been as good as gold, apparently. There's always at least two men with him, usually three. He's been sleeping most of the time."

"I'm heading back tomorrow night, landing at Gatwick at twenty to nine," said Shepherd. "Is there any way you could fix me up with an escort?"

"Not a problem," said Gannon. "Two guys and a car?"

"That should do it," said Shepherd.

"Consider it done," said Gannon. "Now forgive me if I rush off, I need to keep these VIPs on the straight and narrow."

The Major ended the call and Shepherd leaned over and put his mobile on the coffee table at the side of his chair. As he straightened up, he realised that Mrs Jaraf was standing in the doorway. She waved a copy of the room service menu. "They have a mezze platter that looks good. And a hot appetiser plate. Maybe we could share it?"

278

"Sure," said Shepherd, wondering how much of the phone conversation she'd heard.

"And Malik wants his burger and fries."

"And Coke. I'll order it now."

"Thank you." She tapped the menu against her veil and frowned. "Is my husband all right?"

"He's fine. I'm told he's sleeping a lot, but there are no problems. I would have let you speak with him but the man I was speaking to isn't with him at the moment."

"But there are people looking after him?"

Shepherd nodded. "Good people, there's no need to worry."

Her face brightened. "I'm not worried," she said. "I know you're a good man and that he's in safe hands." She averted her eyes shyly. "Thank you for everything you are doing for us."

"It's my job, Mrs Jaraf."

"Then thank you for doing your job so efficiently," she said. "I'll get my bath now."

She went back into her room. Shepherd stared at the connecting door thoughtfully. Mrs Jaraf hadn't mentioned her husband during the drive from the refugee camp. He had expected more questions from her about where he was and what he was doing. Shepherd was actually quite relieved that she didn't seem curious about his situation because he was loath to tell her why he was in protective custody. He assumed that Jaraf would tell her once they were together, but learning that her husband had been the subject of an assassination attempt while she was still thousands of miles away would only increase her stress levels. He picked up the hotel phone and placed Mrs Jaraf's order, adding a pot of coffee for himself. He wasn't planning on getting into bed that night — at best he'd cat-nap.

Dinah Klein settled back in her seat and called Gil Stern. It was a cold night and Nathan Segal had the engine running to keep the heater on. Stern answered with a gruff, "Yeah?"

"They're booked into the Sheraton Grand," said Klein. "I haven't got the room number yet but it won't be difficult."

"Don't bother," said Stern. "They're on a tight schedule if they're going to make their flight so they won't be there long."

"One thing was strange: they went to the Park Royal, parked outside and then went to the Sheraton. Do you think they were running counter surveillance?"

Stern chuckled. "Parking," he said.

"Parking?"

"The Park Royal has off-site parking, they wanted to keep the car close by. This Paul Easton, I don't think he's regular Home Office. So where is the car now?"

"In the hotel car park."

"Can you get a tracker on it?"

"Sure. But I thought there was already one — in a watch, right?"

"Yes, but we should probably have a fallback just in case the watch fails," said Stern. "We can't afford to lose them at this point in the game. Where's Adam?"

280

"Close by."

"Take it in turns to grab some sleep once you've attached the tracker."

Stern ended the call and Klein put her phone away. She opened the glove compartment and took out a small black box. Segal twisted around and retrieved a tablet from the back seat.

There was a small on — off sliding switch on one side of the black box and Klein slid it to the "on" position. Segal turned the tablet on and launched the tracker app. Within a few seconds a small green blinking dot showed the box's position on Google Earth. Klein nodded. "Perfect," she said.

The drive up to Ankara was uneventful. Shepherd had checked them out of the hotel at five-fifteen and Margie had made good time. Shepherd had been regularly watching via the side mirror and there had been no sign of a tail.

The British Embassy was a nondescript white-walled three-storey building, with a red roof and rectangular chimneys, surrounded by a high stone wall topped with railings. There were concrete bollards outside a white metal gate that was overlooked by a concrete sentry box with a large bulletproof window. A uniformed guard checked Margie's credentials and then a black-and-yellow metal barrier slid into the ground and the gate rattled back. Margie drove around to the car park behind the embassy, and took them all through a rear entrance to a row of offices.

281

Michael Warren-Madden came out of one of the offices, and he smiled when he saw Shepherd. "I see you got back in one piece," he said, then his face hardened when he saw Nadia. He gestured at his office. "We need to talk," he snapped, and gestured for Shepherd to go inside. Warren-Madden followed him and slammed the door shut. The office was spacious with two windows overlooking the gardens at the rear of the embassy. Warren-Madden's desk was dominated by two large monitors and on the wall behind it was a large map of Turkey and the surrounding countries.

"What the fuck is she doing here?" snapped Warren-Madden, folding his arms.

"I think Nadia might have information that could be useful."

"I told you already, they're fucking chancers trying to con their way back into the UK. You had no right to bring her here."

"I spoke to my boss in Thames House. He's happy for me to take her back for a debriefing."

"Debriefing? What the fuck are you talking about? I already spoke to the bitch and she's a fucking fantasist. How the fuck did you let her pull the wool over your eyes?" He glared at Shepherd.

Shepherd glared back. "You need to moderate your tone and your language when you talk to me, Michael," he said quietly. "I'll only tell you once."

Warren-Madden went over to the window and looked out over the garden. "I'm sorry," he said eventually. He turned to look at Shepherd. "I apologise. But you've put me in a very difficult position."

"This is nothing to do with you. She has information about terrorists planning operations in the UK, this is MI5 business."

"You can't be serious," said Warren-Madden. "Do you think I'm fucking stupid?" He saw the look of contempt flash across Shepherd's face and he raised his left hand to cut him short. "I'm sorry. But I already checked out her story. It's complete and utter bollocks." He walked back to his desk and stood with his back to Shepherd as he lit a cigarette.

"Checked it out, how?" asked Shepherd.

"How do you think?" snapped Warren-Madden. "She says that her boyfriend is an MI6 agent, feeding information on jihadists being trained in Syria. That he gave her names and details of home-grown terrorists, some of whom are already back in the UK. Don't you think I would know about it if we had an agent like that in place in Syria?"

"She said MI5, not MI6."

"Which is another example of how fucked up she is. MI5 don't run agents overseas. That's our remit. And I checked and we do not have an agent in place who comes anywhere near close to the one she describes."

"Sometimes they keep the man on the ground in the dark," said Shepherd. "They keep it on a need-to-know basis."

"How would I not need to know?" asked Warren-Madden, flicking ash into an ashtray on his desk.

"Maybe a matter of trust," said Shepherd.

"Now you're just being offensive," said Warren-Madden, turning around to face him.

"He might have been run out of London and they didn't want any local interference," said Shepherd.

"Sure, but if that was the case then once I'd raised it, they'd tell me to back off. Or bring me on board. But all I got was a flat denial. There is no Hasan Mahmoud working for MI6. And it's been at least five years since we had anyone in the mosque that she went to. And we have no one active in any of the camps in Syria. We just don't have that sort of human intelligence at the moment. Truth be told, we'd probably kill for an asset like Hasan Mahmoud, but he doesn't exist."

"She said Mahmoud's handler used the name Roger."

Warren-Madden shrugged. "That's no help. Officers almost never use their real names with agents, you know that."

"So he was lying to her, is that what you're saying?"

Warren-Madden walked over to a sofa by the window and dropped down onto it. He swung his feet up onto a pine coffee table. "I think it's more that she's the one who's lying. Look at it from her point of view. The government has branded her persona non grata. So she either stays in the camp or she seeks sanctuary in Pakistan, and of course neither option appeals to her. So she creates this story about having information that would be useful for us, and we say 'all is forgiven' and welcome her back with open arms. Like I said, I checked out what she said and it's complete and utter bollocks. I was told to just ignore her."

"You didn't tell Margie any of this?"

Warren-Madden shook his head. "Of course not. You realise you've put her life in danger by doing this?"

"Margie?"

"The girl. Nadia. Turkey is full of ISIS sympathisers. If it gets out that she's informing on ISIS, she won't last ten minutes. Any one of them would slit her throat as soon as look at her, whether or not she's telling the truth."

"Which is another reason for getting her out."

Warren-Madden sneered scornfully. "Don't you get it? She's banned from the UK. The government has said she can't go back."

"Strictly speaking that's not what's happened. Her citizenship has been revoked, yes. That means she can't use the passport she had before, but she can enter on a new one, one that you can issue her with."

"You're playing fast and loose with the rules."

"That's what we do, Michael. We operate in the grey areas. The two I'm taking back — the woman and her son — don't have the right of residence in the UK, but we're still letting them in because they serve the greater good. In my opinion Nadia falls into the same category."

"What proof has she given you?"

Shepherd didn't answer for several seconds. "I take your point," he said eventually. "There's no hard evidence, I agree with you on that. But I believe her. I think she's telling the truth."

"All that would mean is that she believed what this Mahmoud told her," said Warren-Madden. "But I don't

285

think he even exists. I think she made him up." He stood up, walked over to his desk and stubbed out the remains of his cigarette in an ashtray. "But let's give her the benefit of the doubt and say that he does exist. He might have been lying. ISIS is on the run out here, he maybe told her all that stuff as an insurance policy down the line."

"He gave her names and details, I can get those checked out."

"Sure, but that'll take time. You could well get her back to the UK and discover that everything she's told you is a crock of shit."

"We can cross that bridge when we get to it."

"What, can you send her back if it turns out she's lying? That'll never happen."

"I don't think she is lying."

"Yeah, you said. So what are you, some sort of infallible lie detector?"

"I'm not infallible, but I'm a pretty good judge of people."

"You and me both. And *I* think she's lying."

Shepherd shrugged. "So we agree to disagree."

"Except that by disagreeing, you're making me out to be an arsehole."

Shepherd shook his head. "There's no need to take this personally."

"How can I not?" snapped Warren-Madden. "I go to my boss and tell him that it's all a crock of shit and he agrees with me. Now you're telling all and sundry that she's a valuable asset that needs to be fast-tracked into the UK. How does that not reflect on me personally?"

"Did you check out the names she gave you?"

"She gave me the one name. Mahmoud. And like I said, we drew a blank."

"She's a bit more forthcoming now. I suppose because she realises she wasn't getting anywhere with you and Margie."

"Which makes it more likely that she's lying now to save her skin."

Shepherd sighed and pointedly looked at his watch. "We're going around in circles now, and the clock is ticking."

"I don't have the authority to issue her a passport," said Warren-Madden. He shook his head. "No can do."

"I told my boss that might be the case," he said. "He said he'd talk to your boss."

"Yeah, well good luck with that." At that moment, his office phone rang. He walked around his desk, sat down and picked up the receiver. He kept his head down as he took the call. Shepherd heard him say "yes" a few times, and then "I understand". He put the receiver down and gritted his teeth as he sat back in his chair. "It appears I am to offer you every assistance," said the MI6 officer.

"Good to know," said Shepherd.

Abdullah Rahman parked the black Honda hatchback and switched off the engine. The main road back to Leeds was six miles away and it had been ten minutes since they had seen any other traffic. Rahman had driven out the previous week, looking for a suitable place, and had found a farm in the Yorkshire Dales

National Park, less than an hour's drive from where he lived. There was a field on the edge of a farm and the farmhouse was on the other side of a valley, shielded by a copse of beech trees. There was a hill to the right and no other buildings close by — no one to see or hear what they were doing.

"Let's do it," said the man in the front passenger seat. His name was Muktar Kamel and he had been friends with Rahman since they had attended primary school together in the Hyde Park area of Leeds.

They climbed out of the car and Kamel pulled the front seat forward so that the passenger in the rear could get out. His name was Waheed Choudary and he was five years younger than Kamel and Rahman. Choudary had been introduced to them by the imam at their local mosque. It was the imam who had arranged for Kamel and Rahman to go to Syria for specialist jihad training, and on their return he had suggested that Choudary might come in useful. The imam had been right — Choudary was addicted to video games and had turned out to be a natural when it came to flying drones.

Kamel opened the rear of the hatchback. The drone was surrounded by bubble wrap and he carefully removed it. The drone was just over two feet wide with six rotors. Choudary reached in and grabbed the controller. "Steady, bruv," said Kamel. "Slowly but surely."

There was a small plastic box underneath the drone. Inside were two hundred grams of Semtex, to which had been taped several dozen screws and bolts. A detonator had been inserted into the explosive and there was a nine-volt battery and the workings of an Apple Watch attached. The watch could be used as a timer to detonate the bomb, but it had been wired so that calling the watch's number set it off. Wiring the watch into the circuit wasn't an easy thing to do but Kamel had been well taught.

Rahman closed the door and the three men walked over to a five-barred metal gate set into a stone wall. Choudary opened the gate and they filed into the field. Kamel looked over at the beech trees in the distance. The leaves were barely moving. The drone could cope with a light wind, but the stiller the air, the better.

Choudary closed the gate.

"You're sure it's all good?" asked Rahman.

"I did exactly like Salam told us," said Kamel.

"Who's Salam?" asked Choudary.

"Salam's the guy who taught us, out in Syria," said Rahman. "He's a fucking wizard, a real Harry fucking Potter. He can turn any drone into a weapon." He placed the drone on the ground and looked around the field. A small flock of sheep was grazing at the far end, about two hundred metres away. He looked over at Rahman. "You got the phone?"

Rahman patted his pockets and groaned. "Fuck, bruv, I left it at home." His face broke into a grin when he saw the look of contempt flash across Kamel's face. "I'm joking, bruv, I'm pulling your fucking chain." He took a Samsung phone from his pocket and held it out. "See?"

"This isn't a fucking joke, Noodles," snarled Kamel. "This is deadly fucking serious."

"Man, I was only trying to lighten the moment."

"The moment doesn't need lightening," said Kamel. He gestured at the phone. "It's switched on, yeah?"

"Yeah, bruv. And I've got the watch's number on speed dial."

"Just be careful," said Kamel.

"I know what I'm doing, bruv."

Kamel nodded, still far from happy at Rahman's play-acting. He gestured at Choudary, who now had both hands on the black controller. "You ready, Waheed?"

"Fuck, yeah," said Choudary, nodding enthusiastically.

"So here's the plan. Take it up to a hundred feet or so, and fly it around the field. Get the feel for how it handles with the IED on board. Nothing fancy, smooth and easy. Then take it up and down, check that you can get altitude if we need it." He pointed at the far end of the field, away from the grazing sheep. "When I'm happy with the way it's handling, take it over there and bring it down to about twenty feet above the ground and put it on a hover. That's when Noodles will detonate it. Okay?"

"Let's do it, bruv," said Choudary.

Kamel patted him on the shoulder. "I know you're mustard keen, bruv, and that's great, but you need to keep a calm head on your shoulders. Here we're out in the open but on the day we're going to be in London and there'll be thousands of people around. You need to stay calm and centred. This is just a trial run, a chance for us to work out any kinks. But you need to treat it as the real thing. We don't want any bad habits to set in. Feel me?"

Choudary nodded again. "I won't let you down," he said.

"I know you won't," said Kamel, and patted him on the shoulder. He looked over at Rahman. "Okay?"

Rahman held up the phone. "Okay."

Kamel kneeled down and switched the drone on. Then he stood up and took a couple of steps back. "Okay, Waheed, take it up."

Choudary was biting down on his lower lip as he concentrated. He twiddled his thumbs and the six rotors began to spin, making a high-pitched whine. There were two joysticks on the controller — the one on the left controlled the throttle, which determined the height the drone flew at, and the one on the right controlled the drone's direction. Kamel was capable of flying the drone himself, but he knew his limitations and accepted that Choudary was by far the better pilot.

Choudary used the left stick to increase the throttle and the drone lifted off the grass. It moved smoothly up through the air, and when it got to a hundred feet he reduced the power and the drone stayed where it was. Kamel nodded his approval. Choudary used the right joystick to move the drone across the field. When it was about two hundred feet away he put the drone in a series of sweeping turns, then took it up another hundred feet and did more manoeuvres. Kamel and

Rahman shielded their eyes with their hands as they watched the drone perform.

One of the sheep separated from the flock and began to wander across the field.

"Let's do the sheep," said Rahman.

"What?" said Kamel.

"The sheep. Let's see what the IED does."

"We can't kill a fucking sheep," said Kamel.

"Why not?" said Rahman. "We're going to be taking out people, aren't we? Why worry about a fucking sheep?"

"This is supposed to be a test, just a test."

"So let's test it against the sheep. Then we can see how much damage that amount of explosive will do."

"This is supposed to be low profile," said Kamel.

"We're in the middle of nowhere," said Rahman. "We can dump the body in a ditch. The foxes will take care of it."

"Foxes? What are you now, a fucking farmer?"

"It'll get eaten by something," said Rahman. "Come on, bruv, you can't tell me you don't want to see what it'll do. We won't get another chance. When we do this for real we'll be getting the hell out as soon as it goes off." He looked over at Choudary. "You want to see what it'll do, don't you?"

"Fuck yeah," said Choudary.

"So that's two against one," said Rahman.

"Except this isn't a fucking democracy," said Kamel. "I'm running this show."

"I thought we were both doing this, bruv."

292

"We are. But I'm the one handling the communications and the bank accounts, and that's because they've put me in charge."

"Are you serious, man?"

Kamel sighed. "Look bruv, this isn't worth fighting about."

"I'm not fighting, I'm just saying that I want to see what the IED will do. I don't see what's wrong with that."

"Fuck it bruv, if we kill the fucking sheep will you get off my back?"

Rahman grinned. "Yeah."

Kamel shook his head. "Okay. What the fuck." He nodded at Choudary. "Kill the sheep."

Choudary grinned. "Message received and understood." His thumbs toyed with the joysticks. The drone descended smoothly until it was about twenty feet above the grass and then moved slowly across the field towards the sheep, which was now grazing contentedly. When the drone reached the sheep, Choudary put it into a hover. The sheep continued to eat, oblivious to what was going on above its head.

Kamel nodded at Rahman. "Do it."

Rahman raised the phone, his thumb poised. "Ten, nine, eight . . ."

"What the fuck are you doing, bruv?" asked Kamel.

"Counting down," said Rahman.

"Just press the fucking button."

"Whatever you say, bruv," said Rahman. He pressed the button and they all looked over at the drone.

"Nothing's . . ." began Choudary, but then the drone exploded before he could finish. There was a flash and a cloud of black smoke, and then they heard the bang. The sheep turned red and collapsed. The other sheep looked over at the dissipating cloud of black smoke and then went back to eating.

"Wow," said Choudary, lowering the controller. "Did you see that?"

"Yeah, we saw it," said Kamel.

"I thought it would make more noise," said Rahman.

"Sound disperses when it's outside," said Kamel. He started walking towards the dead sheep. Rahman and Choudary followed him.

The shrapnel had torn through the animal from nose to tail, ripping through its fleece which now glistened with blood. Entrails oozed out through slashes in its side and one of its eyes was hanging down its cheek. "Look at the fucking state of that," said Rahman. "You'd have thought its fur would have protected it."

"Fleece," said Kamel. "Sheep don't have fur. It's wool. Fleece."

"Whatever it is, the shrapnel went straight through it. If there had been a dozen sheep here it would have killed them all. And that was only two hundred grams of explosive. We can double that, easily." He high-fived Choudary. "We are really going to shake things up, bruv." He turned to Kamel and high-fived him, too. "When do we do it for real, bruv? When do we show these kafirs what we can do?"

Kamel continued to stare at the mutilated sheep. "Soon, bruv," he said. "Soon."

294

Shepherd gave Warren-Madden the two Palestinian passports and the MI6 officer flicked through them. Mrs Jaraf was sitting with her son on the sofa while Margie stood by the window looking out over the gardens. A young man in a grey suit brought in two chairs and Nadia took one and sat down. The man offered the other chair to Shepherd and he took it and put it next to Warren-Madden's desk. There was an overflowing ashtray on the desk and the office stank of stale smoke, even though Shepherd was fairly sure that smoking wasn't permitted in the embassy, or in any Turkish place of work for that matter. They had taken all the luggage from Margie's Land Cruiser and it was piled underneath the window.

Warren-Madden looked over at Shepherd and waved the passports. "These will be fine, we can put in regular UK visas and they're good to go." He looked at Nadia. "Do you have your passport?"

She shook her head. "They took it off me when I arrived in Turkey," she said. "I haven't seen it since."

"They probably sold it on the black market," said the MI6 officer. "Not to worry, it's been cancelled anyway. Okay, so we need to get a photograph taken. Come with me." Warren-Madden took Nadia out of the office.

"So we don't need British passports to get into the country?" Mrs Jaraf asked Shepherd.

"A visa with your Palestinian passport will get you in. And we can review the situation once we've reunited you with your husband."

"We will all be British?"

"That's the plan," said Shepherd. "But a lot depends on how cooperative your husband is."

"You need information from him, is that it?"

"He needs to help us, yes. And if he does that, he'll get the right to live in the UK, with you."

She nodded, clearly worried. Shepherd could understand her fears; everything was out of her hands. Life in the refugee camp couldn't have been easy, but now she and her son were being asked to take a leap of faith.

"How long have you been married?" he asked.

"Seventeen years," she said. "We married a year before Malik was born."

"I don't understand why your husband took you and the boy to Syria," said Shepherd. "I know Palestine has its problems, but it's not a war zone like Syria."

"My husband believed in what he was doing," said Mrs Jaraf.

"And what about you? Did you believe in it?"

The woman's eyes narrowed. "Are you asking if I am a good Muslim, because that is an insulting question."

Shepherd held up his hands. "I'm sorry," he said quickly. "I didn't mean to be offensive. It's just such a big step, to take a child into a war zone."

"I followed my husband," she said. "Why is that so hard to understand?"

"No, I understand. But life must have been hard for you."

She shrugged. "Life is hard for most Muslims," she said. "And if we do not fight back, it will get harder." She looked away, clearly uncomfortable with the

296

conversation, and Shepherd realised he had made a mistake by mentioning it. He resisted the urge to apologise again. Instead he went to the window and stood with Margie, looking out over the embassy's gardens until Warren-Madden returned with Nadia.

"Right, picture taken, it shouldn't take longer than an hour to produce the passport, and the two visas for Mrs Jaraf and Malik are in hand. Does anyone want a tea or a coffee while we're waiting?"

"Can I have a Coke?" asked Malik. "And a burger?"

"No burgers, but I can get the kitchen to make you a sandwich," said Warren-Madden.

They were interrupted by Margie's phone ringing. She fished the phone out of her bag and went out into the corridor.

"I'd like tea, please," said Mrs Jaraf.

"Me too," said Nadia.

"Any food?" asked Warren-Madden. The two women shook their heads.

Margie appeared in the doorway, her face ashen. "Can I have a word?" she said. Shepherd and Warren-Madden followed her out into the corridor and Margie closed the door. "I have to go back to Kilis," she said. "Jamila has been attacked."

Shepherd's stomach lurched. "What happened?"

"Two men broke into her unit and stabbed her," she said. "They took her to the clinic but her injuries were too severe for them to deal with, so she's in an ambulance now heading for hospital."

"I'm so sorry," said Shepherd.

"You should be," snapped Margie. "It wouldn't have happened if you'd brought her here."

"Margie, come on . . ."

Her eyes flashed fire. "No," she said, pointing a finger at him. "You went in there and raised her hopes and then you abandoned her." She glared contemptuously at Warren-Madden. "The two of you are as bad as each other," she said. "You use people, that's what you do. And because Jamila wasn't any use to you, you abandoned her. And now she might die."

"That's not fair," said Warren-Madden. "You have no right to blame us for her being in the situation she's in. She chose to leave her country and to side with terrorists. No one forced her."

"She was a child!" shouted Margie. Several people popped their heads out of their offices to see what was happening. Warren-Madden waved to let them know everything was okay. Margie realised how loudly she had shouted and she took a deep breath in an attempt to calm herself down.

Shepherd took the opportunity to speak. "Margie, you need to go to her now."

"It might be too late. Life-threatening injuries, they said." She shook her head. "We should have brought her with us."

"That wasn't an option," said Shepherd. "I am so sorry for what's happened, but our hands were tied."

"Because she was of no use to you," said Margie, her voice loaded with bitterness. She opened her mouth to say more, but then changed her mind. "Fuck it," she said, and pulled her cigarettes out of her bag. She lit

298

one as she strode towards the exit, her shoes slapping on the tiled floor.

The two men watched her go. "Wrong time of the month?" said Warren-Madden dismissively.

"She's invested a lot of time and effort into those girls," said Shepherd.

"She has to learn that you can't take it personally," said Warren-Madden. "What you said was bang on; no one put a gun to Jamila's head. She flew to Syria of her own free will."

"I get that, but by going to the camp, we put the spotlight on them. That's why they were attacked."

"They?"

"Nadia was attacked too, while I was there. I'm guessing they weren't happy about her talking to outsiders."

Warren-Madden tilted his head on one side. "You didn't tell me that."

Shepherd shrugged. "I didn't think it worth mentioning. She wasn't hurt."

"Who do you think it was? ISIS?"

"Fundamentalist, for sure. I don't know if they were ISIS or not. We were watched all the time we were there, I guess they resented the girls talking to Westerners." He looked at his watch. "Do you mind driving us to the airport later?"

"As you know, I've been told to offer you every assistance — so I don't mind, no."

It took just over an hour to produce the passport for Nadia and the two visas for Mrs Jaraf and her son. They were delivered to Warren-Madden's office by the young man who had brought in the chairs. Warren-Madden checked them, nodded his approval, and passed them to Shepherd. Shepherd flicked through the Palestinian passports and checked the names and dates on the visas. Then he opened Nadia's passport and checked the photograph and details. She was wearing her hijab in the picture but her face was clearly visible. He smiled and gave it to Nadia. She grabbed it eagerly and smiled as she opened it. "It's real?" she asked Shepherd.

"It's real in the sense that it'll get you into the UK," said Shepherd. "But it can be rescinded at any time."

She frowned up at him. "What do you mean?"

Shepherd gestured at the passport. "I mean you have that as a gift, not as a right. And it can be taken away from you at any time. Whether or not you keep it depends on the quality of the information you give us."

"I'll tell you everything Hasan told me." She looked at him earnestly. "Look, Mr Easton, I'm not the same person I was two years ago. I understand now that ISIS doesn't care about Muslims, about our faith; it's about wanting power, that's all. I made a mistake and I swear that I'll do everything I can to make up for what I did."

"Well, we'll see how it goes when we're back in the UK."

"And you'll look for Hasan?"

"We'll do what we can," said Shepherd. "Can you take us to the airport now?" he asked Warren-Madden. "I'd rather be early than late." He put the Jaraf passports in his inside coat pocket and held out his hand for Nadia's passport.

She clasped it to her chest. "I don't want to let it go."

Shepherd laughed. "Don't worry, I'll take good care of it for you." She handed it over reluctantly and he added it to the other two. "Right, let's get the luggage in the car, shall we?"

They all grabbed their luggage and followed Warren-Madden outside to his SUV, where he started packing everything into the boot. Mrs Jaraf and Nadia sat in the back either side of the boy, and Shepherd got into the front passenger seat.

Warren-Madden started the engine and drove slowly to the main gate, where a uniformed security guard waved and lowered the metal barrier into the ground. The gate opened and they drove out onto the street. Shepherd looked left and right but the street was clear, though he kept checking the side mirror as they picked up speed. Warren-Madden's eyes flicked between his side mirror and the rear-view mirror, and after a couple of minutes he turned into a filling station and drove slowly by the pumps before turning back into the road.

The airport was only a thirty-minute drive from the embassy and Shepherd was sure that they weren't tailed. Warren-Madden pulled up in front of the terminal building. Dozens of taxis and private cars were unloading passengers and their luggage. Warren-Madden looked over at Shepherd. "I guess this is it," he said.

"Thanks for all your help," said Shepherd. He offered his hand and Warren-Madden shook it.

"It was a pleasure," said Warren-Madden. He grinned. "You know I'm only saying that, right?"

Shepherd laughed. "Yeah, I know."

The two men climbed out of the SUV and unloaded the luggage. The boy went to retrieve a trolley and they loaded the bags onto it.

"Well, good luck to you," said Warren-Madden. He looked at Mrs Jaraf and Nadia. "To you all," he said. He got back into the car and drove away. Shepherd pushed the trolley towards the terminal. Nadia walked next to him and Mrs Jaraf and her son followed behind.

They walked through sliding glass doors and Shepherd looked up at an electronic signboard to see where they needed to go to check in. He found the desk he needed and started pushing his trolley. As he picked up speed, he was scanning faces in the vicinity. Families, couples, businessmen, mothers with babies, students — his eyes took them all in, running the faces through his infallible memory. It was something he did without thinking, as much a part of his life as breathing or blinking. From time to time he got eye contact but his glance would flick away. Left, right, left, right, sweeping the surrounding area in segments. He was about fifty feet away from the check-in desks when he saw them. Two men, one in his thirties, one a bit younger, both dark haired with tanned skin. Both with wheeled hand luggage, dressed smart-casual. Jackets, chinos, loafers. They were paying Shepherd absolutely zero attention but they had been on his flight from Gatwick and he had seen them again in the arrivals area when he arrived at Ankara Airport. He stopped and Nadia looked across at him. "What's wrong?" she asked.

"Just give me a second," he said. He was looking straight ahead but had enough peripheral vision to see the two men off to his right.

"Is something wrong?" asked Mrs Jaraf.

"I'm not sure," said Shepherd. "Just stand here for a second or two. Don't look around, just keep looking at me." He took his phone out and pressed it to his left ear. He was still looking straight ahead but all his attention was focused on the two men. He ticked off the seconds in his head. If they had him under surveillance then at some point they would realise he had stopped moving. He continued to count. Four. Five. Six. He was just starting to think that it was a coincidence, that the two men were flying out at the same time as he was, but as he got to seven they both turned to look in his direction. They stared at him for a couple of seconds, then turned to look at each other. The older one said something to the younger one, and the younger one looked over at Shepherd again.

Shepherd took the phone away from his ear and turned his back on the two men. "What's happening?" asked Mrs Jaraf.

"There's been a change of plan," said Shepherd. He called Warren-Madden and the MI6 officer answered almost immediately. "I need you back here now," he said. He took a few steps away from the trolley and kept his voice down as he spoke into the phone. "There's surveillance here."

"You're sure?"

"I'm sure."

"Give me a second and I'll put you on hands-free." Shepherd heard the squeal of tyres and horns blaring and then Warren-Madden came back on the line. "Fucking Turkish drivers," he said. "Okay, I'm on my way back to you now. I'll be there in five minutes, maybe six. Are you in danger?"

"I don't think so, surveillance only so far as I can see."

"We weren't followed from the embassy, I'm sure of that."

"They were already in place. Two men, waiting for us."

"How did you ID them?" asked Warren-Madden. "I mean, I know you're good, but . . ."

"They were on the flight I came in on, from Gatwick," said Shepherd. "They were near the front of the plane and they were travelling together, but they boarded separately, one in front of me and one at the last moment. I didn't think anything of it at the time. They got off the plane before me and I saw them together in the arrivals area."

"Couldn't it just be a coincidence?"

"No. I faked a phone call and they both turned to look at me. Rookie mistake. Then they talked and one looked back at me."

"Okay," said Warren-Madden. "And we both know that for every one you spot, there's another half-dozen you don't. Like cockroaches."

"Call me as soon as you're outside," said Shepherd. "We'll come straight out and then just get away from the airport. With any luck they won't have mobile surveillance, but if they do we're going to have to lose them."

Warren-Madden laughed. "And when you say 'we', you mean me, I suppose." He ended the call and Shepherd lowered his phone.

"What's wrong?" asked Mrs Jaraf.

"Change of plan," said Shepherd, trying to sound more relaxed than he felt. "There was a problem with our tickets."

"So what are we going to do?"

"Michael's going to pick us up."

"We're not going home?" asked Nadia.

"No, we're definitely going home," said Shepherd. "We're just going to have to make alternative arrangements, that's all."

"This doesn't make any sense," said Mrs Jaraf. "We're here, we have tickets, let's just go."

"I'm afraid we can't," said Shepherd.

"You say we can't, you say we have to make alternative arrangements, but you won't tell us what's happened." He could hear the frustration in her voice.

"Everything's up in the air at the moment," said Shepherd. "As soon as I know what we're doing, I'll tell you."

Mrs Jaraf folded her arms and glared at him. "This is unacceptable," she said.

Shepherd resisted the urge to snap at her. He understood her frustration but he didn't want to tell her that he was sure they were being watched by the people who had twice tried to kill her husband. "I'm not sure what I can tell you," he said. "I'm as unhappy as you."

"We have the tickets, we have the passports and visas." She waved at the desk. "All we have to do is to check in and we can go to England." She folded her arms again. "Why is that so difficult?"

"I'm sorry, but our flights were all booked last minute and I was told that although we were on standby, we'd be able to get onto the plane." It was a lie, but he preferred to lie to her than tell her the truth. "That's now changed and there are no seats for us."

"So we tell them it's an emergency," she said. "You're with the Home Office, tell them we need to get home."

Shepherd smiled thinly. "Mrs Jaraf, the airline is Turkish, not British. If it was British Airways then maybe my word might carry some weight, but the Turks really aren't going to care what I say. Please, trust me, we will get to the UK, just not on this flight."

"I don't want to stay here," said Nadia, who was close to tears. "You said I could go home."

"And you are going home," insisted Shepherd. "I promise."

He was about to say more when his phone rang. It was Warren-Madden. He took the call and put the phone to his ear. "Okay, I'm driving into the airport now," said the MI6 officer. "There isn't much traffic so I'll be with you in a minute or two."

"I'm on my way," said Shepherd. He ended the call and put his phone away. He smiled reassuringly at Mrs

Jaraf and Nadia. "Right, Michael will pick us up outside."

"Why aren't we rebooking our flight here?" said Mrs Jaraf. "That would make more sense, wouldn't it?"

Shepherd said nothing. He gritted his teeth, grabbed the handle of the trolley and started pushing it towards the exit. Nadia walked with him. After several steps he looked over his shoulder. Mrs Jaraf was still glaring at him, and her son was looking at her, clearly confused. And behind them, in the distance, the two men were watching everything.

Shepherd continued to push the trolley to the exit. He took another look over his shoulder. Mrs Jaraf and the boy were following, albeit reluctantly.

As they walked out of the terminal, Warren-Madden drove up. He stopped, climbed out of the SUV and had the back open by the time Shepherd walked up. Together they quickly loaded the luggage and ushered Mrs Jaraf, the boy and Nadia into the back seats. Shepherd pushed the trolley away and climbed into the front seat. The moment his door closed, Warren-Madden had his foot on the accelerator.

Gil Stern walked over to Micha Abramov and Ben Elon, frowning. "What happened?" he asked.

"We don't know," said Elon. "They were heading towards the check-in desk and then Easton took a call on his cellphone and they turned around and went outside."

"Did they see you?"

"They can't have done," said Abramov. "We were all the way over here and we weren't looking at him. Not directly. We were standing right here, talking. There isn't anything that could have made us stand out."

Stern's phone rang and he took it out. It was Dinah Klein. "Warren-Madden came back and picked them up," said Klein. "They seemed in a rush."

"Where are you?"

"Parked up."

"Wait for me, I'm coming right out," he said. "What about Adam?"

"He's parking his car."

"Tell him he'll be coming with us." Stern ended the call. His mind was racing as he considered his options. There had clearly been a sudden change of plan because they were all booked onto the Turkish Airlines flight to Gatwick. He scratched his chin. They had to go to the UK at some point, that had been the whole point of Paul Easton flying over. The stop-off at the embassy was obviously to collect the necessary travel documents. They wouldn't have gone to the airport if the flights and passports weren't in order, so what could have brought about the change of heart? "So, this phone call. It was Easton on the phone, right?"

The two men nodded.

"So had he already stopped when he used the phone? Or did the phone ring and then he stopped?"

Both men frowned. "I wasn't looking directly at him," said Abramov. "I just saw the group stop and then he had his phone up."

"What do you remember?" Stern asked Elon.

Elon shrugged. "I think he took the phone out and then he stopped. But I wouldn't want to stake my life on it."

"It won't come to that," said Stern sarcastically. "Is there any way they had counter surveillance here and you didn't see it? Maybe you were spotted and they called him to warn him off?"

"I didn't see anyone but then I wasn't looking," said Elon.

Stern's eyes narrowed. "You should always be looking for counter surveillance," he said. "Always."

Elon looked down but didn't say anything.

"Anyway, water under the bridge," said Stern. "I'm going to tell Dinah and the others to continue tracking their car. You two should take the flight to Gatwick and link up with the team there. I'll let Leah know you're coming. At some point they're going to have to fly to the UK and if there's any chance at all that he spotted you two, then better you're over there than over here." He looked over at the exit. "Right, I've got to go. I'll see you both back in the UK."

Warren-Madden pulled up outside a restaurant, down a side street close to Kizilay Square. "I've been to this place before," he said to Shepherd. "It's out of the way, it's a good place to meet people if you don't want to be noticed."

"Mr Easton, will you please tell us what's happening?" asked Mrs Jaraf from the back seat. It was the third time she'd asked.

"It didn't feel safe, Mrs Jaraf. I'm sorry, but there isn't much else I can tell you."

"That doesn't make any sense at all. What do you mean it wasn't safe?"

Shepherd sighed. "Please, can we talk about this later?"

"I think we need to talk about it now," she said, and crossed her arms. "You shouldn't treat us like this. We're not animals."

"I know that. But please, let's go inside and we can get something to eat. We'll all feel a lot better with some food inside us, I'm sure."

Mrs Jaraf continued to complain but Shepherd ignored her and climbed out of the car. Warren-Madden joined him. "I'll take them inside and then come back for a chat," said Shepherd.

Warren-Madden nodded and took out his cigarettes. "There's plenty to talk about, that's for sure," he said.

Shepherd took Mrs Jaraf, her son, and Nadia over to the entrance of the restaurant. It took up the ground floor of a three-storey building, with what looked like apartments above it. There were conifers in concrete tubs either side of a double door with glass windows. There was a sign in the left-hand window that said "*Açcik*", which Shepherd knew meant "open". He opened the door and Mrs Jaraf and her son walked inside, deliberately avoiding looking at him. A man in a black suit with a thick moustache and his hair tied back in a ponytail flashed them a smile that showed a gold tooth at the front of his mouth. "Table for five, please," said Shepherd.

"My pleasure," said the man, waving at the almost empty interior. "Sit anywhere." There was a Christmas tree festooned with tinsel and baubles next to a roaring log fire.

Shepherd looked over at the SUV where Warren-Madden was lighting a cigarette. He smiled at Nadia. "Order what you want, I'll keep Michael company while he gets his nicotine hit."

"Okay," said Nadia. She went over to the table where Mrs Jaraf and her son had seated themselves.

Shepherd waited until Nadia had sat down before going out to Warren-Madden, who was halfway through his cigarette.

"There's been no one by since we pulled up," said Warren-Madden.

"And there was no one on our tail when we left the airport," said Shepherd. "This place is out of the way, I think we're good. The question is, what do we do now? We can't fly out of Ankara, clearly."

"Why not? Just book yourself onto another flight."

"I'm pretty sure they didn't follow us to the airport," said Shepherd. "They were waiting for us. That might have been random — they might have people there round the clock — but it's more likely that they have access to flight manifests out of Ankara. Either way, next time I might not spot the tail. They might try something on the plane. Or they'll have a reception committee waiting for us in London. So we need to try something else."

"Sounds like you have a plan." Warren-Madden blew smoke up at the sky.

311

"They won't be expecting us to fly out of Sofia. We can drive into Bulgaria, right?"

"It takes about eleven hours to get to Sofia," said the MI6 officer. "The border is computerised and usually only takes a few minutes. The only problem might be the Jarafs, because they have Palestinian passports. But if we show the UK visas, we should be okay."

He took several long pulls on his cigarette while Shepherd used his phone to check for direct flights between Sofia and London. "Plenty of choices," he said eventually. "Ryanair, British Airways, EasyJet and Wizz Air fly direct. Just under three and a half hours."

"Are you going to book in advance?" said Warren-Madden, flicking away what was left of his cigarette. It hit the ground in a shower of sparks.

"No, I think we'll just turn up and book onto the next available flight. I don't know how good these guys are, they might well be able to check airline bookings."

"When do you want to drive?"

"The first flight is at six in the morning. It's into Luton but that's not a problem. But there's three flights leaving around midday, so that will probably work better. It'll give us plenty of time to fix up a new car and guns."

"Guns?" Warren-Madden shook his head. "I don't have the necessary authorisation for weapons. And even if I did we don't have them in the embassy."

"Last time I came across these guys, they sprayed me with an Uzi," said Shepherd. "And that was in the UK. I'm assuming they'll have even less trouble shooting at me in Turkey. This time I want to be able to fire back. And they'll be shooting at you, too."

"What bit of 'we don't have guns at the embassy' don't you understand?"

"I don't care whether the guns are on the books or not, I just want something in my hand that goes bang."

Warren-Madden lit another cigarette and blew smoke. "Look, I don't know what your situation is, but for me to even think about picking up a gun I need written authorisation from my boss, and she'll need it from hers. You know how it works."

"I hear what you're saying, but while we're arguing the toss about authorisation, the bad guys are probably armed to the teeth and planning God knows what. If this is the same team that was operating in the UK, they won't think twice about shooting. You must know someone."

"I can't be caught buying guns on the black market. You can see how that might backfire — no pun intended."

"I've got cash. I'll do it."

Warren-Madden narrowed his eyes. "You've got authorisation to do that?"

"I've got a boss who generally trusts my judgement. My task is to get Mrs Jaraf and her son to the UK in one piece, and if buying a couple of guns helps me achieve that objective, nobody's going to complain."

"And if you kill somebody and the Turkish police haul you in, what then?"

"Let's cross that bridge if and when we come to it."

"And you said guns, plural. I'm assuming you're not planning on giving one to Mrs Jaraf."

"Michael, if you like I'll put the gun in the car and if nothing happens you don't have to even touch it. But if we get attacked, at least you'll be able to protect yourself."

Warren-Madden took a long pull on his cigarette and flicked ash onto the ground. "Why can't you call in armed support?"

"Because we don't have armed support here, and I wouldn't feel safe with armed Turkish police around us. We need to go below the radar, which means you and me in an unmarked car. Speaking of which, we need to change vehicles."

"That I can do easily enough, there are pool cars at the embassy."

Shepherd shook his head. "These people are pros, there's every chance they'd know what cars the embassy has at its disposal."

"How would they know that?"

"Come on, Michael, don't be naïve. You just sit a kid in the road outside the embassy with a notepad and a pen. If he sits there long enough he'll get the number of every pool car. You need to fix up a rental, and ideally pay in cash."

Warren-Madden sighed. "Okay, yes, I can do that."

"First things first. The guns?"

Warren-Madden sighed. "Fine. There's a guy called Metin who sells guns out of a bar in Ulus. He also deals drugs and traffics women, he's a jack of all trades."

"Trustworthy?"

"In so far as you can ever trust a people-trafficking drug-dealing arms seller, sure. But he'll try to rip you off if he can."

"What's the bar called?"

"Angelique's. It's on Google Maps." He looked at his watch. "He's usually there this time of the evening. He plays guitar."

"And you know him?"

"Sure. He's a good source of intel, but you have to pay."

"He knows you're Six?"

"I don't think he cares. I told him I was with Europol and he said that he'd sell anything to anyone." His eyes narrowed. "If you're thinking of sending me to buy the guns, forget it."

"I just want to check what I'm getting myself into. Can I use your name?"

"He knows me as Andy Dunham. No reason you can't say you know me, but like I said, he'll sell to anyone with money."

"Okay, and assuming I get guns, what's the position when we cross the border?"

"Checks are rudimentary. They might run a drugs dog by the car but they don't pat down passengers and I've never seen them do a physical check of a car. Trucks are a different matter, but they're looking for people traffickers and drugs."

"And you'll stay here until I'm back?"

"Sure."

"And can you do me a favour and not check in with your bosses until we're on the plane?"

"You don't trust me?"

"If I didn't trust you, I wouldn't be here with you now. I would just be happier with as few people in the loop as possible." He nodded at the table where the two women and the boy were ordering from the menu as the man in the black suit scribbled in a notepad. "Don't let them go anywhere," he said. He held out his hand.

Warren-Madden frowned. "What?"

"Keys."

Warren-Madden grinned. "You don't need to drive, and to be honest I wouldn't want you leaving my car in the street in that area. Let me have your phone and I'll set up a route on Google Maps for you."

The Ulus district was in the heart of Ankara, about a mile from the restaurant. Shepherd followed the route on Google Maps, albeit with several counter surveillance detours along the way. He reached Ulus Square, with its four bronze statues — a soldier on horseback, two soldiers at the front, and a woman carrying a cannonball — which together formed the Victory Monument that celebrated the end of the Turkish War of Independence in 1923. He headed down a side road towards Angelique's, which was in the basement of a nondescript office block. There were two big men standing by black railings at the top of the stairs leading down to the club, and the bigger one moved to block Shepherd's way. He was wearing the traditional doorman's get-up of black bomber jacket, black jeans and black lace-up boots. His head was shaved and he had a spider's-web tattoo on the left side of his neck. He said something in Turkish and Shepherd grinned. "English," he said.

"Private party," said the doorman.

"I'm here to see Metin," said Shepherd.

"He know you?"

"We've got a mutual friend," he said, but he could see from the deep frown lines that he was having trouble with the word "mutual". Shepherd tapped his trouser pocket. "He knows my friend. And I want to do some business with him."

The man motioned for Shepherd to take out his wallet. When he did, the man grabbed it off him. He looked at the wad of notes inside, mainly euros. The man grinned and pulled out a hundred-euro note. "Entrance fee," he growled.

"I'm not here for the music or the booze," said Shepherd.

The man's grin widened and he took out two more notes. Shepherd grabbed the wallet from the man's left hand. The money was still in the bouncer's right hand so he couldn't throw a punch and Shepherd had all the time in the world to slap him across the throat. The bouncer staggered back, gasping for breath, and Shepherd took the notes from him and put them back in his wallet.

The second bouncer, who had a thick moustache and slicked-back black hair, muttered something in Turkish and pulled a small leather cosh from his jacket pocket. He raised it high to strike but Shepherd blocked his arm and punched him on the chin with so much force that his head snapped back and he slumped back against the railings before sliding down to the ground.

The bigger bouncer was still having trouble breathing, holding his injured throat with his left hand while his right had hold of the railings for balance. Shepherd tucked one of the hundred-euro notes in the man's jacket pocket and patted him on the shoulder. "That should cover it," he said. He straightened up and gingerly touched his left arm. The cut felt as if it had opened slightly from the exertion, but he was sure that the stitches had held.

He went down a flight of metal stairs and passed a booth where a pretty blonde girl was looking after coats and a third bouncer was standing guard, his arms folded across a barrel-like chest. He was wearing Oakley sunglasses, which seemed unnecessary considering how gloomy the venue was. "Is Metin around?" asked Shepherd.

The bouncer nodded at a guitarist on a podium at the far end of the room. "That's him playing."

Shepherd thanked him and walked over to the bar that ran the length of the club. A dark-haired girl in a low-cut black t-shirt said something to him in Turkish and he figured she had asked him what he wanted to drink. "What's the best Turkish beer?" he asked.

"Efes," she said.

"A bottle of Efes," he said. She gave him a bottle and he paid her with Turkish lira that he'd picked up at Gatwick. He turned to look at the podium where a tall man with steel-grey hair and black-framed glasses was

318

playing an Ed Sheeran song on an acoustic guitar, and doing a good job of it. There were a dozen tables in the club, half of them occupied by couples where the men were at least twice the age of the girls. At the far end of the bar were four young men in sharp suits and narrow ties, with a bottle of Cristal champagne in an ice bucket on the bar within easy reach. Shepherd had seen the look — the suits and the champagne — in bars from London to Marbella to Moscow, and it almost always spelled gangster. The four men looked over at Shepherd then went back to their conversation.

Shepherd sipped his beer as he looked around. The bouncer had moved so that he could get a better view of him. Shepherd smiled and raised his bottle in salute, but the bouncer's face remained impassive, his eyes hidden behind the sunglasses.

Metin came to the end of the song to scattered applause. He took off the acoustic guitar and swapped it for an electric one, then started playing "Hotel California". He was good, and clearly enjoying himself.

Shepherd turned and waved the bartender over. He handed her a hundred-lira note. "Do me a favour can you? Tell Metin I'd like a word with him when he's finished. You can tell him I'm a friend of Andy Dunham."

The woman nodded and took his money. Shepherd went over to an empty table and sat with his back to the panelled wall. He nursed his beer through another two songs, then Metin finished his set. The bartender went over and whispered into the man's ear and they both looked over at Shepherd. Metin patted her on the shoulder and headed over to Shepherd's table. He was wearing a plaid shirt and Versace jeans, and black boots with pointed toes. "Andy sent you?" said the man, with only a slight accent.

Shepherd nodded and held out his hand. "My name's Paul. Andy said you'd be able to help me."

"I'm a very helpful person," said Metin. He pulled out a chair, sat down, and mimed at the bartender for her to bring him a drink.

The two bouncers from outside appeared in the entrance to the bar. They spoke to the bouncer wearing sunglasses and the three of them started walking towards Shepherd. Metin looked over at them, and then back at Shepherd. "Have you been giving my staff a hard time?"

"Is this your bar?"

"For my sins."

"I thought you were the entertainment."

"I play for fun. But yes, the bar is mine."

The three men stopped at the table and glared at Shepherd. The big one opened his mouth to speak but Metin stopped him with a wave of his hand. He said something in Turkish, and the big man pointed at Shepherd and replied. Metin grinned and the two men spoke for a minute or so before Metin waved them all away. They headed out, casting Shepherd baleful stares as they left.

"What did you say to them?" asked Shepherd.

Metin smiled. "Omer said you'd beaten them up on the street and I asked him if he thought it would go any differently now that there were three of them." The bartender came over with a large glass of red wine. He took it from her and smiled his thanks.

"Omer was trying to take my money, and there'd be no point in talking to you if I didn't have the cash, right?" said Shepherd.

Metin laughed. "That is true," he said. "So, you're a friend of Andy's?"

Shepherd nodded. "He said you'd be able to supply me with a gun."

"So you're not a policeman."

"Why would you say that?"

"Because if you were a cop, you'd have your own gun. Unless you wanted to kill your wife, that is."

Shepherd frowned. "My wife?"

"You want to kill your wife so you need a gun that can't be traced."

Shepherd's frown deepened. "I'm not married."

Metin pulled a face. "You look married."

Shepherd grinned. "Yeah? Well looks can be deceiving."

"Now that is the absolute truth," said Metin. "You don't look like a man who could beat up two big bouncers, but the proof of that is in the pudding."

Shepherd raised his drink in salute. "Metin, why is your English so good?"

Metin puffed up his chest. "You think so?"

"I think so."

"I lived in London for a while. Wood Green. You know it?"

"Yes, I know it."

"I like London. It's a great city. But it became a little — how shall I put it? Uncomfortable. So I came back to Ankara. And you, my friend? What brings you to Ankara?"

"Business," said Shepherd. He leaned closer to the Turk. "So, can you sell me a couple of guns? Nothing too big. Something reliable and, as you said, untraceable is what I'm looking for, so ideally guns that haven't been used before."

"Automatics or revolvers?"

"Automatics will be fine."

"Glocks?"

"Can't go wrong with Glocks," said Shepherd.

Metin laughed and slapped a hand down on the table. "That is so true," he said. "And how much is your budget?"

"If they're in good condition, five hundred euros each. A thousand all in. Plus a bit more for rounds."

Metin pursed his lips and exhaled. "I could sell you a piece of Russian shit for that, but a Glock . . ." He shrugged.

"Two Glocks, I said."

"Yes, for two Glocks I would need two thousand Euros."

"Can we split the difference? Fifteen hundred?"

Metin smiled. "I get the feeling that you are in urgent need of guns, my friend, which makes it a seller's market. Two thousand euros."

"And you'll throw in the rounds?"

"Two clips for each gun."

Shepherd nodded. "Then we're good."

322

Metin leaned forward. "You have the money?"

"You have the guns?"

"As I said, it's a seller's market."

Shepherd took out his wallet and opened it so that the Turk could see he had several five-hundred euro notes with him. Metin reached for the cash but Shepherd closed the wallet and put it back in his pocket. The Turk laughed and got to his feet. "Come with me," he said.

Shepherd followed him through a door with a sign that said "ÖZEL" into a room with a metal desk, two filing cabinets and a low sofa. Leaning against the wall were three black guitar cases. Metin picked up the middle one, swung it onto the sofa and unclicked two locks. He opened the case. Inside were four hand-guns and several magazines.

He took out one of the guns and handed it to Shepherd. It was a Glock 17. Shepherd ejected the magazine. It was empty. He pulled back the receiver and checked the barrel, then pulled back the slide and dry-fired it. "Has it been used?"

"Not in anger," said Metin with a smile. He took out another Glock, this one a Glock 19. It was similar to the 17, but more compact. The Glock 19 held fifteen rounds, two less than the Glock 17. The Glock 19 was the better model for concealed carry, but the Glock 17's extra two rounds could come in handy and the slightly longer slide gave it an edge when it came to accuracy. It was horses for courses. "I'll take them," said Shepherd.

"Pleasure doing business with you," said Metin. He held out his hand. Shepherd put the guns into the pockets of his coat, then took out his wallet again and counted out four of the high-denomination notes. Metin slid the money into his back pocket. Shepherd took four magazines and put them into his inside pockets.

Metin took him out of the office and into the bar. "Do you want a drink?" he asked. "To celebrate our deal."

"I'm on a tight schedule," said Shepherd. He patted his pockets. "Thank you." Metin grinned and gave him a thumbs up, and Shepherd headed out. The bouncer with the sunglasses was back at his post and he turned to watch Shepherd walk by, stony-faced.

As Shepherd went up the metal stairs he saw the other two bouncers waiting for him at the top.

"You think you're fucking clever, don't you?" said Omer.

"I just needed to do business with Metin," said Shepherd amiably.

The other bouncer had his cosh out again. Shepherd nodded at it. "Seriously?" The bouncer grinned and slapped the cosh against his hand.

Omer prodded Shepherd in the chest. "You made me look stupid in front of my boss."

"You didn't need my help for that," said Shepherd. His eyes hardened. "I don't have time to waste on you, so let me just say this. I went to see Metin to buy a couple of guns. One of those guns — a Glock 19 — is in my pocket, loaded, and pointing at your balls. My

324

finger is on the trigger and even if it means ruining a perfectly good jacket I will pull the trigger and smile while I'm doing it."

Omer looked down and gritted his teeth when he saw the bulge in Shepherd's coat pocket.

"Get out of my way, Omer," said Shepherd. "Or you'll be speaking in a very high voice for the rest of your life."

Omer raised his hands and stepped backwards. Shepherd kept the gun pointed at the man's groin as he moved into the road, then he turned and walked away.

"Bastard!" shouted Omer.

"Sticks and stones, mate," muttered Shepherd. "Sticks and stones."

Warren-Madden looked around when he saw Shepherd walk into the restaurant. He stood up and met him by the door. "All good?" he asked. Behind him, Mrs Jaraf, her son, and Nadia were drinking water and nibbling breadsticks. Mrs Jaraf kept her niqab on as she ate, passing the breadstick underneath the veil and holding it over the cup as she drank.

Shepherd patted his coat pocket. "Two Glocks, each with two clips. How are the ladies?"

"All a bit confused. And not happy about going to Bulgaria."

"You told them?"

"I didn't really have a choice. She's persistent, that Mrs Jaraf." He grinned. "To be honest, if I was her husband and I got to the UK, I'd think about picking up a new wife and starting afresh, wouldn't you?" He took his cigarettes and lighter out of his pocket and gestured at the door. They went outside.

"You're not married, are you?" asked Shepherd.

Warren-Madden chuckled. "I could never find a woman who'd put up with me," he said. He lit a cigarette and blew smoke. "Don't get me wrong, I'm as keen on a bit of the old slap and tickle as the next man, but I've never felt the urge to settle down. What about you?"

"I was married. She died."

"Sorry to hear that. What happened?"

"Car crash. One of those stupid, senseless things."

"When was this?"

"A lifetime ago, it feels like."

"Kids?"

"Just one. A boy. He flies helicopters for the Army now."

"And you never remarried?"

"No," said Shepherd. He didn't want to talk about Katra, or about what had happened to her, so he got back to the matter in hand. "What did you tell Mrs Jaraf?"

"I tried to tell them that there are no seats on any flights from Ankara over the next few days but she flat-out called me a liar. I said that was what you told me, so the ball's back in your court."

"I'll talk it through with them," said Shepherd. He took out his wallet and gave Warren-Madden a handful of Turkish lira notes and some euros. "You go and get the car. Something nondescript but with a bit of power.

You can drive us to Sofia and come back tomorrow, so two days should cover it."

Warren-Madden pocketed the cash and nodded. "I'll be back in an hour or so." He turned to go, then hesitated. "You're sure about this? About driving to Sofia?"

"I'm not happy about it, but I don't see we've got any choice."

Warren-Madden nodded. "I just hope this doesn't end up biting me in the arse." He gestured over at the table. "Save me some food, I'm starving."

Shepherd grinned and patted him on the shoulder. As the MI6 officer left, Shepherd went over to the table. He took his coat off and hung it over the back of a chair before sitting down. "What did we order?" he asked.

"Kebabs, kofte and karniyarik," said Nadia.

"Kebabs I know, obviously, and kofte is meatballs, but I've not heard of karniyarik."

"Baked aubergine," said Nadia. "Stuffed with minced meat and parsley and covered in tomato sauce."

"Sounds delicious," said Shepherd.

"Where is Michael going?" asked Mrs Jaraf.

"We need another car," said Shepherd.

"What's wrong with the car we have?"

Shepherd smiled. "We've a long drive ahead of us and something bigger might make the drive more comfortable."

"I don't understand why we're going to Sofia. There are plenty of flights to London from Ankara, aren't there?"

327

"It's complicated," said Shepherd.

Mrs Jaraf shook her head. "I'm not stupid, Mr Easton. You were planning to get on a plane at Ankara Airport but something happened to make you change your mind. It looked to me that you had seen someone, but I don't understand why that would make you change your plans so drastically."

Shepherd took a sip from a glass of water as he considered his options. Mrs Jaraf was indeed not stupid, and the more he lied to her the less she would trust him. Did that matter? She was only a means to an end — by delivering her and her son to her husband, MI5 would receive vital intel. Whether she trusted him, believed him or even liked him, was immaterial. On the other hand, her life, and the life of her son, was on the line, and surely she had the right to know that. He put down his glass. She was staring at him with unblinking eyes, and while she hadn't asked a question she was clearly expecting him to respond to what she'd said.

"I really don't want to worry you, or your boy, or Nadia, but getting you back to the UK isn't as straightforward as I thought it would be," he said. "What happened was that I saw two men who had been on my flight out from London. They were some distance away and I'm pretty sure they were watching us."

"I didn't see anyone," said Mrs Jaraf.

"They were there," said Shepherd.

"It could have been a coincidence," she said. "Maybe they were businessmen who fly back and forth."

"They were watching us."

328

She frowned. "Why would anyone be watching us?"

Shepherd took a deep breath as he gathered his thoughts. "You understand that your husband has offered to help us, Mrs Jaraf? That's why I've come to take you and your son to join him in England."

"Of course I understand."

"Right, well the problem is that there are people who don't want your husband to help us. They'd like to stop him."

Mrs Jaraf's hand flew up to her mouth. "Did something happen to Salam?"

"No, I told you, he's fine and he's being well looked after. But when he first arrived in London, someone tried to hurt him."

She frowned at him, her eyes wary. "You say hurt, but you mean kill, don't you? Someone tried to kill Salam?"

Shepherd looked over at her son, but the teenager seemed to be taking the news about his father in his stride.

"As I said, he's fine," said Shepherd. "But it appears that someone wants to hurt him and that someone might also want to hurt his family." He put up his hands to calm her down. "Or they might want to follow you to see where we have your husband. I don't know. But either way, I want to make sure that no one follows us."

"And you think that by driving to Bulgaria, we won't be seen? Is that it?"

"That's my plan, yes. We're going to switch cars and we'll be extra careful to check that we're not being followed. Assuming no one follows us into Bulgaria, we'll fly from Sofia to London."

"Do you know who wants to kill Salam?"

"I'm not sure. ISIS maybe. The information that he has could make life very difficult for them."

Mrs Jaraf sat back in her chair and folded her arms. "Then perhaps it would be better if we stayed here."

"Your husband wants you in England, Mrs Jaraf. He wants you and your son with him."

"But it could cost him his life."

"Not if we're careful. And trust me, we will be careful."

She nodded slowly but didn't seem convinced. She continued to stare at him, but then her concentration was broken by the arrival of the waiter with their food. Shepherd realised he hadn't eaten since that morning and he helped himself to some of the stuffed aubergine and a large dollop of rice.

The boy was piling meatballs and rice onto his plate and once he'd finished, Mrs Jaraf and Nadia helped themselves. They ate in silence but Shepherd could sense that Mrs Jaraf was still unhappy with what he'd told her.

"When do we go?" Mrs Jaraf asked eventually.

"To Sofia? As soon as Michael has fixed us up another car."

"And how far is Sofia from here?"

"Eleven hours maybe."

"So we drive through the night?"

"That's the plan," said Shepherd. "I know it's a long drive and I know you're all tired, but you can sleep in the car."

"And we are already booked on a plane?"

"No. Once we've arrived I'll buy tickets on the next available flight to London."

Mrs Jaraf picked at her food, clearly unhappy, but her son wolfed down his meatballs and rice. They had finished their food and Shepherd was drinking a cup of bitter Turkish coffee when Warren-Madden returned. He came over to the table, twirling a set of Mercedes car keys. "All done," he said, pulling up a chair and sitting down. There were still several kebabs on the serving plate and he put three on his plate with mounds of rice and vegetables. Shepherd picked up the keys. "It's a 2010 C-Class," said Warren-Madden.

"Insurance is okay to take it into Bulgaria?"

"All good," said Warren-Madden. He held up a kebab. "I'm starving," he said, and bit into it with relish.

Gil Stern's phone rang. It was Dinah Klein. "Please give me some good news," he said.

"They've switched cars, they're in a Mercedes now. I'll text you the number plate."

"Do you have eyes on them?"

"We're ahead of them now. Adam is behind them. They're driving towards Bulgaria."

"So Sofia, do you think?"

"I can't see them driving all the way back to London," she said.

"Right, you need to hang right back," said Stern. "This guy Easton clearly has a knack for spotting surveillance so let's not give him any reason to get jumpy. Tell Adam to go straight to the airport and wait there. I'm going to book you all onto every flight leaving Sofia for London starting tomorrow morning. I'll text you the details as and when I get them arranged. Then I'll fly back to London and wait for you there."

"There'll be no problem crossing the border between Turkey and Bulgaria?"

"No, the cars are fine and your passports are good. Just remember what I said, put plenty of distance between you and their car. They need to think they're free and clear."

It was a five-hour drive to Istanbul and another three hours to the Bulgarian border. When they reached the border crossing they all had to show their passports, and the guards on both sides insisted that Mrs Jaraf remove her veil. It was a woman on the Turkish side but it was an obese bald man on the Bulgarian side, and Mrs Jaraf said she wouldn't remove her veil. That annoyed the man and he started asking more questions, wanting to know why Shepherd and Warren-Madden were driving two Muslim women across the border. The cover story they'd agreed — that Nadia and Mrs Jaraf were family friends of Shepherd and that Warren-Madden had agreed to give them a tour of Turkey and Bulgaria before they flew to London — just about held up, but the man was clearly unhappy at Mrs

Jaraf's refusal to remove her veil. "She needs to understand that this is Bulgaria, we are not a Muslim country, and she needs to respect that," he said to Warren-Madden.

Warren-Madden apologised and then said something to the man in Bulgarian. The border guard was clearly surprised to hear his own language and the two men chatted back and forth for a while before the guard moved away from the car.

"He's going to get a woman to check Mrs Jaraf's face," said the MI6 officer.

"Sounded like you were having quite a chat there," said Shepherd.

"It's not a difficult language," said Warren-Madden.

"I got the impression you were talking about our passengers."

Warren-Madden grinned. "Let's just say that the Bulgarians have a more robust approach to multiculturalism than we do in England."

The guard returned with a female colleague. She motioned for Mrs Jaraf to get out of the car. Shepherd wound down the window and handed the guy Mrs Jaraf's passport. Mrs Jaraf turned so that her back was to the Mercedes and then removed her veil. The guard looked at her face, back at the passport, then nodded and gave the passport to the male guard. The male guard gave it back to Shepherd and said something to Warren-Madden. Both men laughed, and from the contemptuous way the guard stared at Mrs Jaraf, Shepherd got the impression that what he'd said wasn't complimentary. Warren-Madden saw the look of concern on Shepherd's face and he grinned. "It loses something in the translation," he said. "But we're okay, they're letting us through."

Shepherd nodded but didn't say anything. Mrs Jaraf got back into the car. Shepherd turned and smiled. "Everything okay, Mrs Jaraf?"

"Everything is fine," she said coldly.

She stayed silent for the remainder of the drive. She and her son napped for most of the time, but Nadia stayed awake and was constantly turning to look at buildings and landmarks that attracted her attention. By the time the Mercedes pulled up in front of the departures area at Sofia Airport, in the centre of the Bulgarian capital, it was just before ten o'clock in the morning. "What do you want to do?" asked Warren-Madden.

"In what way?" said Shepherd.

"Do you want me to stay here until you're sure you're not being watched?"

"That's not a bad idea," said Shepherd. He slid his Glock out of his coat pocket and into the glove compartment.

"Though if you are, what then? Do we keep driving across Europe?"

"Hopefully it won't come to that." He closed the glove compartment and patted Warren-Madden on the shoulder. "But yeah, stay close and keep your phone on."

Shepherd got out of the car. Warren-Madden opened the rear door and Shepherd took out the bags while Mrs Jaraf and her son brought over a trolley. As they loaded the bags on the trolley, Warren-Madden waved at Shepherd, flashed him a mock salute, and drove off.

Shepherd pushed the trolley inside, followed by Nadia and Mrs Jaraf's son. Mrs Jaraf brought up the rear.

There were three flights for London leaving around noon: one by Wizz Air, one by Ryanair and one by EasyJet. Wizz Air flew to Luton, Ryanair to Stansted and EasyJet to Gatwick. Shepherd wasn't a fan of Luton Airport, but it was the closest to Hereford, less than a three-hour drive, so he went to the Wizz Air desk and used his Paul Easton credit card to buy four tickets seated together.

They checked in and then Shepherd took Mrs Jaraf, her son and Nadia over to a coffee shop and bought them drinks and sandwiches. He wanted to phone Pritchard and the Major before passing through security, plus he wanted a last look around to convince himself that they weren't being followed. "I've got to make a couple of calls," he said, taking out his phone. "Please don't go wandering about."

He walked to a quiet area and called Pritchard, all the time scanning faces around him. Pritchard answered and Shepherd told him where they were and what flight they would be on.

"We've got a problem," said Pritchard. "Mei-feng Chan, aka Jasmine, has been trying to get in touch with you. She's called several times and sent two text messages."

"Does she say what she wants?"

"No, just that she wants to see you and is asking that you book her. The worry is that she turns up at the flat and finds Harry Fletcher living your life. Basically we need you in the flat to meet her."

"I'll be landing in just over five hours, but I have to get Mrs Jaraf and the boy to Hereford."

"Why don't you have the Major's people drive them to Hereford and you can bring Nadia to Thames House? Then once we've got Nadia under wraps, you can contact Jasmine and arrange a meet. Find out what she wants and if it's just social, find some way of putting her off. Telling her you have the clap will probably do it."

"I dare say it will," said Shepherd. "Okay, I'll talk to the Major and see you at Thames House at about three or four o'clock, depending on traffic."

Shepherd ended the call and rang Major Gannon. He explained the change in plans and the Major agreed to have two of his men waiting at Luton Airport to drive Mrs Jaraf and her son to Hereford. "I'm at the barracks today," said Gannon. "But there's two men with Jaraf twenty-four-seven and the two who are collecting Mrs Jaraf can stay at the house for as long as you need them."

"Thanks, boss," said Shepherd. "Tell the guys meeting us that I'm wearing a black reefer jacket and will be with two Asian women and an Asian kid, and we'll have four big bags."

"No need, Spider," said the Major. "You know them both. Mike Travis and Chris Wheeler. They're both on leave this month and were keen to earn a bit of extra cash."

"Excellent," said Shepherd. He knew both men from visits to the SAS's Stirling Lines camp, though Travis and Wheeler had joined the Regiment after Shepherd left.

Shepherd thanked the Major and put his phone away. He headed for the exit, walking quickly, then at the last minute turned around, watching to see if anyone behind him was wrong-footed. But nobody was paying him any attention, so he walked back to the coffee shop, bought a coffee and a croissant, and joined the others.

He sat with them at the table, drinking his coffee, eating his croissant and scanning the departures area for familiar faces. By the time he was finished he was satisfied that no one had followed them. He stood up, brushing crumbs from his coat. "Let's go," he said.

They passed through security with no problems, though the Jaraf boy had a full bottle of water in his backpack that he had to give up. Immigration was just as smooth. The immigration officer was a young woman who smiled at them all as she checked their passports. Mrs Jaraf and her son went through together, followed by Nadia, with Shepherd bringing up the rear. The woman wished them all a safe trip.

They settled into another coffee shop, airside. Nadia kept looking at Shepherd and grinning, clearly happy to be on her way home. Mrs Jaraf still seemed to resent the fact that they were flying out of Sofia and not Ankara but she kept quiet. Her son had asked for a toasted sandwich and muffin. He had already eaten the sandwich and he unwrapped the muffin. Shepherd sipped his coffee and kept checking the faces of anyone in the vicinity but he didn't see anyone he recognised.

"I'm just going to use the toilet," he said. He stood up. In fact he didn't need the bathroom, he just wanted to check if anyone was watching him. He walked slowly towards the bathrooms, then did a detour to a shop selling magazines. He flicked through a newspaper as he looked around, bought a comic for the kid, then went to the bathroom. He went inside, stopping just to wash his hands, then went back outside. By then he was sure he wasn't being followed, and he didn't see anyone off in the distance watching him.

He went back to the coffee shop and gave the comic to the boy, who mumbled his thanks.

"We should head for the gate," said Shepherd. "They'll be boarding soon."

Half an hour later, they were on the plane. They were close to the front, sitting either side of the aisle. Shepherd sat next to Nadia, who was still grinning. "I can't believe it," she said. "I'm going home." She reached over and grabbed hold of his arm. It was the arm with the stitches in and he winced, but she didn't notice his discomfort. "Thank you, Mr Easton," she said. "Thank you so much."

"No need to thank me," said Shepherd. He looked over at Mrs Jaraf. She was sitting stiffly, her arms folded, her face emotionless. He wanted to give her a reassuring smile but she was studiously ignoring him. A stewardess started the safety demonstration and Mrs Jaraf ignored her too, lost in her own angry thoughts.

When they stepped off the plane there was a woman in a Border Force uniform holding up a sign with "PAUL EASTON" on it. She was in her forties, her hair cut short, and she was wearing red-framed spectacles. Shepherd smiled at her but didn't get a smile in return, as if she resented the task she'd been given. "I'm to escort you through just to make sure that there are no issues," she said curtly once he had identified himself.

There was an electric golf cart behind her and she motioned for them to get in. She sat behind the wheel while they climbed in with their hand luggage.

She drove them to immigration, parked, and took them to the far side of the hall, away from the main lines. There was a grey-haired officer with half-moon spectacles standing behind a podium and he smiled when the woman walked over. "Hello, Amy, you're looking full of the joys of spring."

"It's Christmas, Alfie," she said, but she was blushing. "These are the Home Office cases I told you about." She waved a hand at the group.

Alfie peered over the top of his glasses at Shepherd. "Shot in the dark, but I'm guessing you're the one who's with the Home Office?"

"Paul Easton," he said, handing over the Easton passport. Alfie flicked through it, swiped it through his scanner, and nodded. Shepherd gave him the passports for Nadia, Mrs Jaraf and her son. Alfie looked at

Nadia's passport photograph and smiled at her. She smiled back. He didn't run it through his scanner.

He looked at Mrs Jaraf. "I'm sorry, madam, but I need to see your face."

She shook her head. "No," she said.

"I'm afraid I can't allow you into the country without seeing your face." He looked at Shepherd. "She understands what I'm saying, right?"

"I understand," she said.

Shepherd looked over at the female Border Force officer. "Amy, could you help us, please?"

Amy sighed and stepped forward. She took Mrs Jaraf's passport from Alfie and moved to the side so that Mrs Jaraf could turn her back on him. Mrs Jaraf then removed her veil and Amy compared her face to the picture in the passport. She spent several seconds staring at Mrs Jaraf as if trying to prove a point, then nodded curtly and gave the passport back to Alfie. Mrs Jaraf replaced her veil.

"Does the Home Office want me to stamp the Palestinian passports?" Alfie asked Shepherd.

"If you would, please."

"Six months?"

"Perfect," said Shepherd.

Alfie stamped both passports and scribbled in them, then handed all three back to Shepherd, who put them in his coat pocket.

"Do you need help collecting your bags?" asked Amy, in a tone that suggested she really didn't want to offer him any assistance.

340

"No, we're good," said Shepherd. "Thank you for your help."

"All part of the service," she said, and he couldn't tell if she was being sarcastic or not. She walked back to the golf cart.

"That's it, we can go?" asked Nadia.

"Welcome to England," said Shepherd. They walked by Alfie who acknowledged them with a nod and a smile, and out into the baggage area. The luggage from their flight was due at carousel number two and they headed over to it. Shepherd grabbed a trolley while Mrs Jaraf and her son went to sit on a bench. Nadia waited with Shepherd, clearly thrilled to be back in England.

Their bags were among the first off. Shepherd loaded them onto the trolley along with their hand luggage, then he took them through the "Nothing To Declare" section of customs. It didn't appear to be manned, though the area was well covered with CCTV so he was fairly sure they were being watched.

Shepherd spotted Travis and Wheeler as soon as he pushed the trolley into the arrivals area. Travis was taller than the average SAS trooper, and spindly thin with arms that appeared to be a couple of inches too long for the sleeves of his jacket. He was in his late thirties but still had the nickname he'd earned on Selection more than ten years earlier, when an instructor had allegedly called him Thrombo because he was a slow-moving clot.

Wheeler was shorter and stockier and had grown a beard since Shepherd had last seen him. His skin was tanned; that and the beard suggested he'd been out in the Middle East on operations. Wheeler had acquired the innocuous nickname of Three during his years as a paratrooper prior to joining the SAS.

Both men were wearing leather jackets over thick pullovers against the chilly December weather. Shepherd left the trolley and went over to greet the two men, feeling their hidden guns pressing against his chest as they hugged.

Shepherd took them over to his travelling companions and introduced them. "Mike and Chris will take you to your husband," Shepherd said to Mrs Jaraf.

"Where is he?" she asked.

"Not far," said Shepherd. "A few hours' drive. Don't worry, you'll be with him soon."

Wheeler and Travis took Mrs Jaraf's bags and escorted her and her son to the car park. Shepherd smiled at Nadia. "Right, let's get a cab."

"Where are we going?"

"To an office where you can look at some photographs. We need to talk to you about how you can help us."

She forced a smile. "Quid pro quo? I help you and you help me?"

He picked up one of her suitcases. "It's a good deal for you, Nadia. There are plenty of girls in the camp back in Turkey who'd love to be in your position."

"What about my parents?" she asked. "Can I call them?"

"To be honest, I'd rather you didn't," said Shepherd. "I'd prefer it if as few people as possible were aware that you are back in the country."

342

"They'll be worried about me."

"Nadia, they think you're in a refugee camp in Turkey, they know you're alive and well. When they do hear that you've been allowed back into the UK, they're going to be pleased and relieved. But the intelligence you have is only of value while no one knows what you've told us. Once the bad guys know that you're talking to us, they'll disappear, like cockroaches when you turn on the light. We need to keep your presence here a secret, for a while at least."

"For how long?"

It was a good question, and the honest answer was: as long as possible. If Nadia truly was able to identify home-grown jihadists who had returned to the UK to carry out terrorist acts, MI5 needed to put them under observation to see who they were in contact with and who was helping them. A fully fledged surveillance operation could take months. But that wasn't what Nadia wanted to hear. "Sooner rather than later," he said. "A few weeks maybe."

"A few weeks!"

"These things take time, Nadia. But I can promise you, if it looks as if it's going to drag on we'll get your parents in. They can meet with you and we can explain why there has to be a level of secrecy. Okay?"

"I suppose so," she said, but she didn't sound convinced.

They walked to the taxi rank and climbed into a black cab. "Millbank, near Lambeth Bridge," Shepherd said to the driver. Almost every taxi driver knew that MI5 was based in Thames House, so telling them to drive to Millbank avoided any spy jokes. They'd usually make some sort of quip about James Bond, even though James Bond was actually employed by MI6. Mind you, Shepherd had met plenty of MI6 officers over the years and had never come across any that resembled Sean Connery, Roger Moore, Pierce Brosnan or Daniel Craig. Many of them were like Michael Warren-Madden: dishevelled, out of condition and generally looking for the easiest way to get any task done. And unlike the fictional versions, most real MI6 officers didn't know one end of a gun from the other. When they needed guys with guns, they tended to call in the SAS or SBS.

Shepherd settled back in his seat. He couldn't see the rear-view mirrors so the only way to get a view out of the back was to turn around. When he did, Nadia tensed. "Do you still think we're being followed?" she whispered. "I thought we'd be safe in London."

Shepherd scanned the vehicles behind them. "It's a habit with me," he said. "I always like to know who's behind me, wherever I am."

"So you can never relax?"

Shepherd chuckled. "I relax when I'm sure I'm not being followed."

"And how do you feel now?"

He sat back in his seat and smiled. "Relaxed," he said. Dinah Klein walked into the arrivals area with Nathan Segal. They both had wheeled hand luggage. Adam Sharon was a few metres behind them, carrying a black North Face backpack. Klein stopped and looked around, then smiled when Gil Stern stepped out from behind a pillar. He was wearing a brown leather jacket, blue jeans and Timberland boots. He hugged Klein and shook hands with Segal and Sharon. Klein was looking around. "Don't worry, they've gone," he said.

"Yeah, they were at the front of the plane and we were at the back," said Klein. "We kept well clear of them and made sure we were last off the plane. We didn't have any bags and they did, so we stayed airside and came through with passengers off a later flight."

"They came out as a group but they split up immediately," said Stern. "Easton and the other girl caught a black cab, I don't know to where. The others went with two men who looked like military, I'm guessing special forces."

"If they're SAS or SBS, that's not good news," said Adam.

"We've got the element of surprise," said Stern. "At the end of the day, a man's a man." He looked at his watch. "We need to get going," he said. "They went to a white Honda CRV and we've got it under surveillance. It's heading north-west to Milton Keynes." He started walking and the three of them fell into step with him. "Micha and Ben are on bikes and will alternate eyeball. Leah is in a car with one of our London people and we have two more cars, each with two more operatives. We obviously don't know where they're taking them, but wherever it is we'll be prepared."

He took them outside where two cars were waiting, both Peugeot SUVs. "Dinah, you come with me in the front vehicle, Adam and Nathan, you get in the second."

The driver of the lead SUV popped the rear door and Klein put her suitcase in the back and closed it before climbing into the rear of the vehicle with Stern. The driver and the front seat passenger twisted around in their seats. Stern introduced them. The driver was Yosef and the front passenger was David. "*Shalom aleichem*," they said, almost in unison.

"*Aleichem shalom*," replied Dinah.

"Sitrep?" asked Stern, fastening his seat belt.

David had a tablet in his lap and looked at it. "They're about two miles outside Milton Keynes," he said. "Adam's on the M1 ahead of them."

Yosef put the car in gear and they pulled away from the curb. Daniel reached between his legs and pulled out a black nylon holdall which he passed back to Stern. Stern unzipped it. He took out two black ski masks and two pairs of latex gloves. "You'll need these at some point," he said to Klein. He opened the bag wider and showed her what else it contained. Two Glocks. "And one of these."

The black cab took just over ninety minutes to reach Millbank. Shepherd had the driver drop them fifty metres down the road from Thames House, then paid him in cash and asked for a receipt. He made the mistake of reaching for Nadia's bag with his left hand and winced as he felt his arm wound open. He used his right hand to pull the suitcase along the pavement, while Nadia followed with her other suitcase. As they

346

walked into the entrance, heads turned to look at them, and he was sure that security staff were paying just as much attention to the CCTV monitors covering the area. Nadia was wearing a hijab, and while quite a few of the women who worked in Thames House also wore one, they didn't turn up with bags that could in theory contain enough explosives to bring the building down. Shepherd moved slowly and kept his face up so that he could be recognised. He motioned for Nadia to wait on a sofa while he went over to the reception desk to show his ID and sign her in.

There were rooms in Thames House with beds and showers, but the facilities were basic to say the least. Shepherd knew that Pritchard would want her kept in the building at least until they were sure that she had useful intel, but there was no way Shepherd could be spared for babysitting duties.

He went back to Nadia and gave her a visitor's badge. She frowned as she looked at it. "MI5?" she said. She looked around. "This is MI5? You said we were going to the Home Office."

"I said an office. And the office is here." She bit down on her lower lip and shook her head. "This is where the databases are, Nadia. A lot of the information they have is confidential and isn't allowed out of the building. We won't be here long."

"How long?"

"Just until we've looked at the files." He nodded at the badge. "Clip that to your clothing, it needs to be visible at all times." He gestured at the reception desk. "I have to make a quick call."

Shepherd went back to the desk and called Pritchard on an inside line. Pritchard said that he was to wait with Nadia until he had assigned an officer to start her initial debriefing. Shepherd put the phone down and joined Nadia on the sofa. She was sitting with her arms folded and her legs crossed, clearly uncomfortable with her surroundings. "It's just an office, Nadia," he said, trying to put her at ease.

"It's where they hunt people like me," she said quietly.

"You're not a terrorist, Nadia."

She shook her head fiercely. "Not terrorists. Muslims. They hunt Muslims."

"No, they hunt jihadists. They hunt the ones who are planning acts of terrorism, who want to damage our way of life."

"You say that, but I can see the way they looked at me when I walked in. Like I was the enemy."

Shepherd laughed and shook his head. "They were looking at you because you arrived with luggage as if you were checking into a hotel, that's all," he said. "You're not the enemy, Nadia." He was about to say more when they were interrupted by the arrival of a young Asian girl wearing a beige hijab that matched her suit. She offered her hand to Shepherd. "I'm Zarah, Mr Pritchard sent me down to take care of Nadia," she said. "He'd like to see you in his office right away."

Shepherd stood up and Nadia looked at him anxiously. "You're leaving me?"

Zarah smiled down at her. "I'll be looking after you while you're here," she said. "I'll show you to a room where you can leave your things, and then I thought we could pop along to the canteen. You must be famished. You've come such a long way, haven't you?"

Nadia ignored Zarah and continued to look anxiously at Shepherd.

"It'll be okay," Shepherd said to her. "Zarah will take good care of you and when I've finished my business we can sit down and start looking at some photographs. Don't worry, everything will be fine."

"And you'll let me talk to my parents?"

"Once you're settled in we'll review it," he said. "As I said before, at the moment it's best that no one knows you're back in the country."

Zarah pointed at the bigger of the two cases. "Shall I take this one?" she asked.

Nadia stood up. "Yes, please, if you don't mind."

"I'm here to help," said Zarah.

They all went over to the metal detector arch. A uniformed security guard examined the contents of Nadia's two suitcases, finding only clothes and personal items, then waved them through the arch.

They went up in a lift together, and Zarah and Nadia got out on the second floor. Nadia was clearly still anxious, but she seemed happier now that Zarah was with her. She flashed Shepherd a tight smile as the lift doors closed.

Amy Miller was at her desk and she told Shepherd to go straight in. Pritchard was behind his desk, peering at a computer monitor. He smiled when he saw Shepherd and waved him to one of the two chairs facing his desk. "So I gather you got Nadia Shah here safely."

"Yes, and two SAS guys are driving Mrs Jaraf and her son to her husband in Hereford as we speak."

"So job well done," said Pritchard, leaning back in his chair.

"So far so good," said Shepherd. "What matters is how good the intel is from Jaraf and Nadia. I just hope they come through."

"On that score, I have some good news about Ali Karim. The surveillance team followed him on the train to London. He had a meeting with a so-far-unidentified Asian male who gave him a bag. Karim took the bag back to his storage unit and we've been in to check it." He slid a file over the desk and Shepherd opened it. There were surveillance pictures of Karim meeting with an Asian man on a park bench, and leaving with a Nike backpack. There were also pictures of the backpack in the storage locker, zipped and then unzipped with the contents spread across the floor.

Shepherd recognised the plastic-wrapped packages immediately. "Semtex?" he said.

"The good stuff," said Pritchard.

"How the hell did ISIS jihadists get Semtex into the UK?" There were detonators lined up next to the packs of explosives. Shepherd peered at them. They looked like commercial rather than military detonators.

"It was part of the consignment Gaddafi sent to the IRA in the eighties."

"So ISIS has linked up with the IRA?"

Pritchard shook his head. "A few days ago an IRA activist by the name of Brendan O'Carroll was shot to death in Stoke Newington. And a small-time Russian

350

arms dealer was stabbed. Bystanders saw three Asian men driving away in a hatchback. O'Carroll was old-school IRA, very much around and active in the eighties."

"So the Asians bought — or stole — part of an old IRA arms cache?"

"That's how we're reading it, yes."

"How does that tie in with the ricin?"

"Maybe it doesn't. Maybe there's been a change of plan."

Shepherd closed the file. "Are you going to bring him in?"

"We'll let it run a while longer. But clearly the intel Jaraf has given us so far is spot on. Hopefully we'll now get more. What about Nadia?"

"She's definitely more of a gamble, but she seems eager to help and she saw a lot of people pass through the ISIS camp."

"Any problems at all?" Pritchard took off his spectacles and began polishing them with a dark blue handkerchief.

"Just the run-in with the bastards who attacked Nadia that I told you about."

"Is she okay?"

"She's fine, but she was a bit shocked at the time." He rubbed his left shoulder. "I took a slash to my arm but I got stitches put in and I'm as right as rain."

"Do you need to see a medic here?"

"I think I'm okay, it seems to be healing. If there's any sign of infection I'll get it checked, but at the moment it's looking good."

"Okay. And you met Zarah downstairs?"

Shepherd nodded. "She seems on the ball."

"Double first from Oxford, we're lucky to have her," said Pritchard. He tapped his fingers on his desk. "Right, Mei-feng Chan, the lovely Jasmine. She called your phone three times but didn't leave a message and then sent you two texts saying that she misses you and wants you to book her."

"I wonder why her bosses are so eager for her to see me?"

"It might be connected with the fact that we had Harry talking to a girl from the China desk in the canteen, and she mentioned the situation in Hong Kong. Nothing major, just a teaser."

"So you think they want to get Jasmine closer to me? A honey trap?"

"It's possible. I mean, it might just be that she's drumming up business, but then these agencies aren't about making money. The plan might be to see if Jasmine can get you talking about Hong Kong. Or maybe see if you're suitable for a spot of blackmail."

"I told her I was divorced."

"True, but sleeping with hookers would probably get you dismissed."

"Really?"

"If it became a security risk. And if they had photographs and threatened to go to the papers. Not that they would, but if they thought you were genuine, they might feel safe making the threat." He shrugged. "I don't know, obviously. It's all guesswork at this stage. But what we can't do is to ignore her message. We don't

352

want her or the agency suspecting that there's something wrong. And worst possible scenario, we don't want her turning up at the flat and seeing Harry there."

"So how do you want me to play it?"

"You'll take Harry's place tonight. Go and catch up with him first so he can fill you in, then make a booking with the phone to see Jasmine at eight. You'll then go back to the flat with the phone this evening. I'll make sure that Amar is geared up to record anything that happens. You need to see what she wants and do whatever is necessary to make her stop bothering you."

"Tell her I've got the clap, you said."

Pritchard grinned. "That was just off the top of my head."

"And what about Nadia?"

"Let's see how it goes with Jasmine. If it's straightforward, you can start debriefing Nadia first thing tomorrow. But if not, Zarah should be able to handle the initial chat." He looked over at his computer monitor, letting Shepherd know that the meeting was over.

Mrs Jaraf reached over and took hold of her son's wrist so that she could see the time on his watch. She leaned forward. Mike Travis was driving and Chris Wheeler was in the front passenger seat of the white Honda CRV. She could see that both men were worried about being followed — they were constantly checking their side mirrors and they had fitted a second rear-view mirror so that Wheeler could get a good look at what was going on behind them. "I need to use the bathroom," she said.

Wheeler looked at his watch, a Rolex Submariner with a black bezel. "We'll be there in an hour," he said, twisting around in his seat. "Can you wait?"

Mrs Jaraf shook her head. "It's my period," she whispered. "I don't think I can wait." She shrugged. "I'm sorry."

"No, no, it's okay," said Wheeler hurriedly. "I'm sorry."

"There's a service station coming up," said Travis. "And we could do with fuel."

Both men checked their mirrors as they approached the exit. Travis kept in the right-hand lane and didn't indicate until the last moment, before swerving across to the exit. A van driver pounded angrily on his horn but no one copied the manoeuvre. They drove to the service station and parked. Wheeler twisted around in his seat again. "Right, stay close to us," he said. "If you need to buy anything, let me know."

"I just need the bathroom," said Mrs Jaraf.

"Can I have a burger?" asked the boy.

"No problem," said Travis. "I could go a burger myself. But we'll buy them and eat them in the car on the road, okay?"

The boy nodded.

They all climbed out of the vehicle, with Travis and Wheeler looking around for possible threats. They escorted Mrs Jaraf to the ladies toilet and watched her go in. Wheeler waited outside while Travis took the boy to buy burgers.

There were four cubicles and all were vacant. A young woman in tight jeans and a puffer jacket was standing in front of the washbasins, applying mascara. The woman glared at Mrs Jaraf, her lip curling back in a sneer. Mrs Jaraf looked away, not wanting a confrontation. She went into a cubicle, locked the door and sat down. The woman at the mirror muttered "Fucking Muslims" loud enough for her to hear. Mrs Jaraf stared at the door, breathing slowly and evenly. She heard someone else come into the bathroom and go into one of the cubicles, and then a few minutes later the woman in the puffer jacket went out. The cistern flushed and whoever was in the other cubicle went to the washbasins, washed their hands, and left. Mrs Jaraf continued to stare at the door and to breathe slowly, hoping that she hadn't made a mistake.

The door to the bathroom opened and someone came in. Whoever it was went into the cubicle next to hers, closed the door and sat down. Mrs Jaraf heard a rustling sound and she looked down to see two small plastic-wrapped packages being held under the side wall of the cubicle. She took them and slowly unwrapped the first one. It was an iPhone 11, already switched on. She knew that the phone had been adapted to work as a bug and a tracking device. They had been able to track her through the GPS in the watch the boy was wearing, but the phone would be more accurate. She put it into her bag and opened the second package. It was a Beretta BU9 Nano, a micro compact pistol just over five inches long and weighing just under twenty ounces. She ejected the magazine. It contained six 9mm cartridges. She slotted the magazine back in place. The Nano had no external safety or slide lock, which reduced the likelihood of the gun snagging when it was pulled from a bag or clothing. It was the perfect concealed weapon, and even with the super-short barrel it could be fired accurately up to twenty metres. She slipped it into her bag, stood up, and then flushed the toilet before leaving.

She went out of the bathroom where Wheeler was waiting for her. They joined Travis in Burger King, where the boy was placing his order.

"Do you want anything, Mrs Jaraf?" asked Wheeler.

She smiled and shook her head. "No thank you." Her stomach was churning and she doubted she could eat anything.

The boy finished giving his order, the two men said what they wanted, and Travis paid.

"I'm going to get coffees — Mrs Jaraf, do you want one?" asked Wheeler.

"Yes, thank you," she said. "Can you get me a latte?"

"No problem." He walked away. He had a confident walk. He certainly had a military background, almost certainly special forces. That made sense, as they were heading for Hereford, where the Special Air Service was based. He seemed like a genuinely nice guy. His partner, too. She just hoped that she wouldn't have to kill them.

Harry Fletcher was sitting by the window of the canteen nursing a cup of tea and staring unenthusiastically at a bowl of fruit salad. Shepherd stopped about ten feet away and mouthed "Are we okay?" just in case the man had his phone with him.

Fletcher nodded. "We're good," he said.

Shepherd went over to the counter and ordered sausage and chips and a coffee. He carried his food over to the table and sat down opposite Fletcher. "Is the phone in your office?" he asked as he poured ketchup over his meal.

"In the desk drawer."

He looked at the chips longingly and Shepherd grinned. "I thought you might want one," he said, nodding at his plate.

"I shouldn't," said Fletcher.

"One won't hurt."

Fletcher smiled ruefully. "Get thee behind me, Satan."

Shepherd chuckled and pushed the plate towards him. Fletcher sighed, grabbed a chip and devoured it. He licked his lips, shook his head sadly, and took three more chips.

"So how's it been going?" asked Shepherd.

"It's fine," said Fletcher. "They don't want to push too much stuff through the phone too quickly so just a few innocuous conversations a day. They've given me an office and we keep a do-not-disturb sign on it most of the time. I just sit and do other work so they can hear the keyboard activity, and I make general calls on the landline. Every now and again we have a staged conversation about something or other. Just scene-setting at the moment."

"And the messages from Jasmine?" He tucked into his sausage and chips.

"She called three times, but I didn't answer, obviously. Then yesterday I got two text messages asking you if you'd book her. Again I didn't reply."

"I'm going to need to see the phone," said Shepherd. "And I'll need the flat tonight."

"You're going to meet her?"

Shepherd nodded. "We need to know what's going on."

Fletcher nodded at the plate and Shepherd held up his knife and fork. "Help yourself," he said. Fletcher grabbed another couple of chips.

"So we'll go to your office and I'll call the agency. Then I'll see her tonight."

"You'll take the phone with you?"

"Best it stays in your office. I'll come back and collect it at five."

Fletcher reached into his pocket and took out the flat keys. "It'll be good to sleep in my own bed again."

Shepherd finished his sausage and chips — with help from Fletcher — and then the two men took the elevator back to Fletcher's office. Fletcher unlocked the door and led Shepherd inside. The office was windowless and tiny, with just enough space for a desk and a filing cabinet. There was only one chair, behind the desk, and Fletcher sat in it while he pulled open the drawer. He took out the phone and gave it to Shepherd. Shepherd tapped in the four-digit code to unlock it, and checked the text messages. The first SMS from Jasmine was short and to the point: "*Charlie, I miss*

358

you. Can you book me again? Jasmine xxx". So was the second: "*Pleeeeease!*"

The text messages hadn't come from the mobile number that the agency used. There was a pen on the desk and Shepherd picked it up and scribbled a note on a sheet of paper. "DID YOU GET THE NUMBER CHECKED?"

He showed the note to Fletcher. Fletcher nodded, took the pen from him, and wrote underneath it: "BURNER".

Shepherd nodded. That was to be expected. He pointed at the phone to let Fletcher know that he was going to make a call, then pressed the number for the agency. It was answered within a few seconds by a woman. "Asian Angels," she said.

"Hi, can I arrange to see Jasmine for two hours tonight?"

"What time?"

"Eight would be good?"

"Incall or outcall?"

"She can come to my place."

"Two hours outcall, three hundred and fifty pounds."

"That's fine."

"Address please."

"She's been before."

"I still need the address."

Shepherd gave her the address of the Pimlico flat and the line went dead. Shepherd frowned. It would probably reassure most clients that the agency didn't keep their addresses on file, but now he was worried they might send him a different girl. He put the phone down but it beeped to let him know that he'd received an SMS. He checked it. "JASMINE. TWO HOURS OUTCALL. 8PM."

He put the phone down and nodded at Fletcher. He pointed to himself, then held up five fingers, then pointed at the floor. Fletcher nodded. "See you at five," he mouthed.

"How much further?" asked Mrs Jaraf, peering out of the window. She saw a road sign that said Hereford was six miles away.

"We're nearly there," said Wheeler.

"Hereford, is that where we're going?"

"Yes," said Wheeler.

"And that's where my husband is?"

"Don't worry, you'll be with him soon," said Wheeler. He checked the side mirror, but there were no vehicles behind them. There hadn't been for more than ten minutes.

"Why aren't we in London?" asked the boy.

"Hereford is safer," said Travis.

"Does it have a McDonald's?"

Travis laughed. "It's got everything," he said. "McDonald's, Burger King, Nando's . . ."

"What's Nando's?" asked the boy.

"Chicken," said Wheeler. "Spicy chicken."

"Is he in a house, or an apartment?" asked Mrs Jaraf. "Or in a prison?"

"Why would he be in prison?" asked Wheeler, twisting around in his seat.

"Mr Easton, he said that my husband was in danger."

"Easton?" repeated Wheeler.

"She means Spider," said Travis. "Secret squirrel. Your husband is being well looked after, Mrs Jaraf, don't worry."

"He is well protected?"

"Two of the best guys in the Regiment are looking after him," said Travis. "He's in good hands."

"Just two? That is not a lot."

Wheeler laughed. "Trust me, Mrs Jaraf, it's more than enough."

Mrs Jaraf stared out of the window. Wheeler turned back. He patted the Glock in its underarm holster as if to reassure himself that it was still there.

Giles Pritchard knocked on the door and opened it without waiting for a response. There were five officers inside sitting in individual pods, each with three large screens and half a dozen small screens in front of them. CCTV monitoring was a boring but necessary part of MI5's remit, but it was time and labour intensive. It was all well and good setting up CCTV, but every minute had to be watched by a human being, and generally it had to be done in real time.

All five officers looked up to see who had opened the door, but then went back to studying their screens. Diane Daily was sitting at the pod closest to the window. She was in her late twenties and she had joined MI5 after five years in the Royal Corps of Signals. One of her instructors during her MI5 training had given her the nickname Scaley Daily, which unfortunately had stuck with her when she moved to Thames House. Royal Signals soldiers were referred to as Scaleys, or Scaley Backs, because back in the old days they had to use primitive transmitters with massive batteries, which would often leak acid over the operator's back.

Pritchard made a point of never using nicknames, no matter how well he knew the person. "Thanks for the call, Diane," he said. "What time did they go in?" He walked around her pod to get a better look at the screens.

"Twenty minutes ago," she said. "I called you straight away."

She had two surveillance pictures of Ali Karim taped to the side of one of her monitors. He looked at them, then at the screen, where four Asian men were unpacking drones in Ali Karim's storage locker and laying them on the floor.

"So Karim isn't there?"

"He's working at the Post Office," said Daily. "Surveillance has eyes on him."

"And what about there at the storage locker? Do we have a team there?"

"No, there's no team there yet. Should I have ordered one?"

"No, that's okay, I'll get that up and running," said Pritchard. "We need photographs and details of any vehicles they're using. Who was the first one in? The one who had the keys?"

Daily leaned forward and pointed at one of the men on the screen. He was in his thirties with a white skullcap and a thick beard. He had square-lensed glasses and was wearing a parka with the fur-lined hood down. "This guy."

Pritchard watched as the men unpacked the drones and placed them on the floor. The fact that they were preparing the drones meant that whatever they were planning wasn't far off. Pritchard could call in armed support and have the men arrested, but he needed to know who else was involved. Karim and his people were in Birmingham, but the Semtex had come from London. Pritchard had watched video of Karim taking delivery of the explosive outside Euston station and all the body language suggested that it was the other man who was running the show. They needed to know if the man had given Semtex to any other jihadists, and what their intended targets were. The man's face hadn't come up in any database searches. They were checking every mobile phone that had connected to phone masts in the Euston area, but looking for a needle in a haystack didn't even come close, and even if they came up with a number it would in all likelihood be a burner phone.

"Get me the best stills you can from the feed and let's see if we can identify anyone in there," he said. He pushed his glasses further up his nose and stared at the screen. "It doesn't look as if they're planning to move the drones, right? They didn't bring any bags with them?"

"They could put them back in the boxes for transportation."

Pritchard nodded. "Sure. But I'm guessing they'd want to be surreptitious about it once they've attached IEDs. This looks to me like purely preparation. If you see anything to the contrary, call me immediately. I'll have ARVs on standby but I don't think they're going to be a threat tonight. What time are you due off?"

"I'll be here as long as I'm needed," she said. "I've already told my husband to get his own dinner."

Sean Hook's phone rang and he answered it. He was sitting in the kitchen drinking coffee and reading the sports pages of the *Daily Mail*. It was "Three" Wheeler. "We're almost there," said Wheeler. "ETA three minutes."

"All good here," said Hook. "Jaraf was asleep last time we checked."

"See you soon."

The line went dead. Hook stood up, finished his coffee and put the mug in the sink. His gun was on the kitchen table next to the newspaper. He picked it up and slid it into its holster, then went along the hallway to the living room, where Reynolds was lying on the sofa. His eyes were closed but they opened as soon as Hook stepped into the room. "What's up?"

"They'll be here soon."

Reynolds swung his legs off the sofa. "What's the plan then?" he asked.

"The boss says we can work it however we want, providing that there are always two of us with the

364

principal. We can take it in turns to kip upstairs or we can leave, so long as we stay in phone contact."

Hook stood up and stretched. They heard an engine outside and Hook went over to the curtains and peered through a gap. "It's them," he said. A white Honda CRV had turned into the road and was driving towards their house.

Hook had left their Range Rover in the street so that Travis and Wheeler could park in the driveway. Reynolds went to the front door while Hook kept an eye on the street to make sure that no one was following the CRV.

The Honda pulled into the driveway. The lights went off and the engine died.

"All good!" Hook called out, and Reynolds opened the front door. Travis and Wheeler climbed out of the SUV. Travis went to the rear of the vehicle and took out a wheeled suitcase and a large holdall. Wheeler opened the rear passenger door and a woman in a black burqa climbed out. Reynolds had served in Afghanistan, Iraq and Syria, where women were almost always covered, but it still annoyed him to see it in England. He'd read the Koran, believing that to understand the enemy you had to understand what motivated them, and nowhere in the Koran did it say that women were forced to cover their faces. All the Koran said was that women should dress modestly. The burqa and the niqab and the rest of it wasn't about following the religion, it was a way of men dominating women, and while he could understand why women had no choice in Muslim countries he knew that they did have a choice in the UK.

A teenage boy got out of the car, his head down. He was holding a backpack. Wheeler closed the door and went to help Travis with the bags. The woman was looking around as if she wasn't sure which way to go. Reynolds waved at her but she seemed to ignore him. Travis and Wheeler brought the bags towards the front door. Reynolds stepped inside and motioned at the woman. "This way," he said.

Hook came up behind him in the hallway. "What's wrong?"

"The woman's jittery," said Reynolds.

"She shouldn't be hanging around outside," said Hook. He pushed past Reynolds and walked towards her, his arms outstretched. "Mrs Jaraf, please, come inside," he said. "Your husband is upstairs."

The woman nodded. Her eyes looked fearful as if she was scared that Hook was going to hurt her, so he broadened his smile. "Everything is okay," he said.

Hook noticed two high-powered motorcycles parked further along the road. They hadn't been there the last time he'd looked, and the house they were parked outside belonged to a retired couple. "Burt, did you see those bikes arrive?" he asked.

"What bikes?" said Reynolds.

Hook pointed at them. "Over there." He turned back to the woman. "Please, Mrs Jaraf, you and the lad need to go inside."

"I'm coming, I'm coming," she said. She put an arm around the boy and guided him towards the front door.

A man was walking down the street, talking into his phone. Then a car appeared at the far end of the road. It was a Peugeot SUV. "Burt," said Hook.

"I see it," said Reynolds.

As they watched, the SUV pulled into the side of the road, six houses along.

"Inside, Mrs Jaraf," said Hook.

Mrs Jaraf and the boy stepped into the hallway. Hook and Reynolds stood either side of the door, looking out. The doors to the Peugeot stayed closed. "All good?" asked Travis as he pulled a wheeled suitcase inside.

"Some activity in the street, a car's just pulled in and there are two bikes that weren't there earlier."

They all flinched as they heard a loud bang from the kitchen. "What the fuck?" said Hook.

Travis and Wheeler dropped their suitcases and headed down the hallway towards the kitchen. Hook put his arm around Mrs Jaraf to protect her, while Reynolds wrapped his arms around the teenager.

Two men appeared in the kitchen doorway, both of them wearing full-face helmets. The first one had a shotgun, the one behind was cradling an Uzi.

"Gun!" shouted Travis.

The man with the shotgun pointed it at Travis's chest and pulled the trigger. There was a loud bang and Travis fell to the ground, his body twitching violently.

Hook reached for his gun but Mrs Jaraf twisted from his grasp. From under her burqa she produced a gun and thrust it up against his neck. "Pull out your weapon and I'll blow your fucking head off!" she shouted.

The teenage boy dropped down and slammed his elbow into Reynolds's groin. The unexpected blow caught him by surprise and he doubled over with a grunt.

Wheeler pulled his gun from his holster but the man with the shotgun was too quick, pumping a second round into the chamber and pulling the trigger. There was another loud bang and Wheeler slumped to the ground without a sound.

Hook twisted around to see what was happening but Mrs Jaraf pressed the gun harder against his neck. "Stay exactly where you are or your brains will be all over the ceiling," she said.

Reynolds straightened up and reached for his gun, but a man and a woman wearing ski masks ran down the drive and into the house. The man raised his pistol and brought it crashing down on the side of Reynolds's head. It was a glancing blow and didn't quite knock him out, but the man hit him again and Reynolds staggered back against the wall and slid down it, his eyes closed.

The man and the woman walked into the hallway and said something in a language that Hook didn't recognise. The man with the shotgun answered, and chambered another round. Two more men in ski masks came down the driveway, holding Glocks close to their legs as they walked.

"Who the fuck are you?" shouted Hook.

"Hush," said the woman in the ski mask. She pulled a Taser from her pocket, thrust it against Hook's neck and pulled the trigger. He went into spasm and fell to the ground.

They all looked up at the sound of a door opening, and then Salam Jaraf appeared at the top of the stairs. "What is happening?" he said, his voice trembling.

"Nothing to worry about," said Mrs Jaraf. "Just come down the stairs."

"Who are you?" asked Jaraf.

The woman removed the veil from her face. She was grinning. "What, you don't recognise your own wife?" she said, and then she laughed.

Jaraf frowned in confusion. Then the man with the shotgun raised his weapon, aimed at Jaraf's chest and pulled the trigger. Jaraf's whole body trembled, his legs buckled and he fell head first down the stairs.

Shepherd was watching Sky Sports with his feet up on the coffee table when his doorbell rang. He went over to the console by his door and saw Jasmine standing outside. She was wearing a black coat and had a Louis Vuitton handbag over her shoulder. He pressed the button on the console and watched her disappear into the building.

His Charlie Warner phone was on the coffee table, next to the coffee he'd been drinking. He took a quick look around to make sure that everything was as it should be, put his work phone in the bedside cupboard and then went back to the door just as Jasmine knocked on it. He opened it and she rushed at him and gave him a hug.

"Thank you for booking me," she said. "It's like a Christmas present. Thank you."

"A late Christmas present," he said. "But better late than never."

She was still hugging him as he closed the door, then she broke away, took off her coat and dropped it on the floor. She stood back so that he could get a better look. He couldn't help but smile. All she was wearing was a scarlet bra and suspender set, with black fishnet stockings. Her hair hung behind her like a black satin sheet, framing her olive skin. She put her hands on her hips and thrust her breasts higher. He loved the curve of her hips, and the way she tilted her head up to look him in the eyes. "I was going to take you out for dinner," he said. Her face fell, then she grinned as she realised that he was joking. She threw herself at him again and this time she wrapped her legs around his hips and kissed him full on the mouth.

"Do you want a drink?" he asked when he managed to tear his lips from hers.

"I want to drink you," she said. She looked into his eyes. They were a brown so dark that they were almost black. "Carry me to the bedroom."

"Jasmine, baby, I'll do my back in."

"I weigh thirty-eight kilos," she said. "A big strong man like you can manage that."

Shepherd laughed. "If you were in a bergen, maybe."

"A bergen?"

"A rucksack," he said. "A backpack."

"I'm not a backpack but I could ride you like a horse," she said.

370

"You are crazy."

"Take me to the bedroom," she said, and kissed his neck.

Her urgency wasn't sexy, it was worrying. She had been keen the last time she came to the flat, but not this keen.

"What about your money?"

"Later," she said. "Where's your phone?"

"Coffee table. Why?"

"Just leave it where it is. I want your undivided attention."

He laughed. "How come your English is so good?"

"Do you want to ask me questions or fuck me?"

"Baby, we've been through this. Just a massage, okay?"

"Bedroom," she said. "Now."

He laughed and she squeezed him with her thighs. "You've convinced me," he said. He carried her to the bedroom and put her down on the bed. She pulled him on top of her. She took off her bra and tossed it away, then took his hands and placed them on her breasts. She arched her back and ground herself against him. She laughed when she felt him grow hard. "I was starting to think you didn't like me," she said.

"Oh, I like you," he said.

She unbuttoned his shirt, then while he sat up and took it off, she pulled off her pants and then undid his jeans before kissing him again, her soft hair around them like a curtain. She noticed the dressing on his left arm and frowned. "What happened?" she asked.

"I cut myself shaving," said Shepherd.

371

Her frown deepened. "You shave your arms?"

He laughed at how serious she was. "I'm joking," he said.

She gently touched the dressing. "So what happened? Seriously?"

"It was at work. I caught myself on a door. It's nothing."

"You worked over Christmas?"

He laughed. "I'm like you, I work every day."

"I'll try not to hurt you too much," she said as she worked his jeans down his legs.

"That's good to know," he said. "But just a massage is fine. Okay?"

"We'll see," she said. She pulled off his jeans and threw them onto the floor. There was something frantic about the way she was behaving, and he wondered if she'd taken cocaine or amphetamines. There was a jerkiness to her movements and her pupils seemed dilated, though the darkness of her irises made that a tough call. She pulled off his Calvin Klein underpants and waved them in front of his face. "Good brand," she said.

"Thank you."

She tossed them behind her and fell forward onto him, then fastened her lips onto his mouth and kissed him hard. She put her hands either side of his head as she kissed him and ground her lithe body against his. He managed to break away, gasping for breath. "Massage," he said. He rolled onto his front.

"Really?" she said, her voice loaded with disappointment.

372

"Really," he said.

She sighed, then slipped on top of him, her thighs either side of his hips, and began to massage his shoulders. She worked on his shoulders and arms, putting a lot of effort into it. "Good?" she asked.

"Really good," he said, and meant it. She moved down his back and made a couple of attempts to slip her fingers between his thighs but both times he laughed and told her to behave herself.

Eventually she stopped and kneeled beside him. "Can I ask you a question, Charlie?"

"Sure."

"You work for MI5, don't you? The Security Service."

Shepherd's mind started to race. This wasn't a question an escort girl asked of her client. This was a question one spy asked of another, and he would have to answer as Charlie Warner not Dan Shepherd. He forced a laugh. "Why would you say something like that?"

"You can be honest with me, Charlie."

"I'm a civil servant with a very boring job."

She laughed softly. "You need to be a better liar than that if you work for MI5," she said. She stroked his back gently.

"But I don't. I compile economic forecasts. I have the world's most boring job."

"You work in Thames House, and that's where MI5 is."

"You're crazy." He rolled over to look at her. She kissed him gently on the lips. "Can I tell you a secret, Charlie?"

"Of course."

She kissed him again. "I'm like you. I'm a spy, too."

Shepherd laughed, but his mind was racing even more now. Why was she telling him this? Was she toying with him before she did something bad to him? He hadn't eaten or drunk anything since she'd entered the flat, and she was completely naked in the bed next to him so there was no way she could have a weapon, but he still felt the hairs on the back of his neck stand to attention and his heart was pounding as his adrenaline levels went into overdrive. "Don't be silly, Jasmine," he said.

"I work for China's Ministry of State Security."

Shepherd laughed. "No you don't. What is this, some sort of sex game? You're Mata Hari and I'm James Bond. Is that what's going on?"

She frowned. "Who is Mata Hari?"

He smiled at her confusion. "A famous female spy. Long before your time. My time too."

"This isn't a game, Charlie. I'm serious." She sat up. "I need a drink. Do you have wine in the fridge?"

"I'll get it," said Shepherd. He didn't want her going into the kitchen and returning with something sharp. He slid off the bed, expecting her to argue, but she just rolled onto her back and smiled up at him.

He grabbed a towelling robe and went into the sitting room, wondering if he should let the surveillance team know there was a problem. But then what? They couldn't arrest her, it would blow the whole operation. He opened the fridge and took out a bottle of prosecco.

374

He closed the door and jumped, almost dropping the bottle, when he saw that she was standing behind him.

"Sorry, I didn't mean to surprise you," she said.

"You didn't," said Shepherd, taking two glasses out of a cupboard.

"I just wondered if you had anything to eat?"

He laughed. "Frozen stuff, mainly."

"Fruit?"

"Sure, there's some grapes and oranges in the bottom of the fridge."

She opened the fridge door and took out a bunch of green grapes, and then went back with him to the bedroom. She lay on the bed while he opened the bottle. She popped a grape between her lips and put one in his mouth. He bit and swallowed. The sudden thought hit him that she might have poisoned the grape, but he realised his imagination was running away with him. She sat with her back to the headboard, her legs out in front of her.

He poured prosecco into a glass for her and gave it to her. Then he poured a glass for himself and put the bottle on the bedside table. He sat down next to her and stretched out his legs. He clinked his glass against hers. "Cheers," said.

She smiled. "*Ganbei*," she said.

"*Ganbei*?"

"It means empty cup. It's what we Chinese say instead of cheers."

He clinked his glass against hers. "*Ganbei*," he said. They both drank, then she popped another grape into her mouth. "Are you really a spy?" he asked.

She nodded seriously.

"So what are you doing working for an escort agency?"

"That's my mission. There are twenty-one of us girls here in London."

Shepherd laughed and shook his head. "You have a vivid imagination."

"How else would I know you work at Thames House?"

"Who says I do?"

"I do, Charlie." She looked at him. "I'm serious."

"I can see that. So why are you telling me?"

"Because I need your help. I need MI5's help."

"But why me?"

"Because you seem like a nice guy, the sort of guy I can trust. I've been looking for someone who can help me, and I think that's you."

"Help you how, exactly?"

She sighed. "I never wanted to do this job. I was a student, studying fashion. But one day I was called to the principal's office and told that I was being offered a job with the Ministry of State Security. It wasn't the sort of job offer that you can turn down." Her face hardened. "They wanted me because I was pretty, because I had a good body. They wanted me to fuck for them . . ." She shook her head and then forced a smile. "Look, Charlie, I'm part of a Ministry of State Security honey trap. We fuck men and if they have useful information we bug their phones. That's what we did to you and that's how I know you work at Thames House."

376

"So what do you want?"

"I want to live in England. I want asylum. Maybe even work for you. For MI5. In return, I'll tell you everything I know."

"And why now. Jasmine? Why are you telling me this?"

"Because you work for MI5. The others I've come across work for different government departments or businesses, they can't help me. But I think you can help me, Charlie."

He sipped his prosecco. "So tell me, is Jasmine your real name?"

She smiled and raised her glass. "Is Charlie your real name?"

"I'm not the one asking for help," he said.

"True," she replied. "My name is Chan Mei-feng," she said eventually. "It means beautiful wind."

Shepherd nodded. So she was telling the truth. About her name, at least. "That's a pretty name," he said.

"And is Charlie Warner your real name?"

"I never used my family name with the agency."

"That's right. My bosses have been looking at you, Charlie. That's what they do. And that's how I know your name and who you work for."

"Mei-feng, why are you telling me this now? Why've you changed your mind about working for them?"

"They forced me, Charlie. I was never given a choice. Don't get me wrong, they pay me well and there are all sorts of perks that come with the job." She smiled. "I've lived in Dubai, in Hong Kong, in Los

Angeles, in New York. If my clients give me presents — and a lot of them do — then I get to keep them. But I hate what I do. I hate the job."

"How long have you been doing it?"

"Seven years."

"So why are you looking for a way out now?"

She sighed and took a sip of her prosecco. "I was always worried about my parents. And my sister. They never threatened my family but I knew if I left that nothing good would happen. But my mother and father died a few months ago."

"I'm sorry."

"They were in a car crash. Hit by a drunk driver."

"I'm sorry. Really sorry."

She forced a smile. "Thank you."

"And your sister?"

"She married an American. He got her a spouse visa and she's in the States now."

"Your bosses didn't realise that they were losing their hold over you?"

She smiled. "They're not as smart as they think they are. They were too busy watching what we were doing here to worry about what was happening at home. But now that my sister is in San Diego, they have no hold on me." She sipped her prosecco and licked her lips. "So, Charlie, will MI5 help me?"

"You still think I work for them?"

She sighed. "Charlie, when I was here last time I put a program in your phone that means my bosses can hear everything you say, and see every message you send and photograph you take. It tracks you everywhere you go."

"That's why you didn't want the phone in my bedroom?"

She nodded. "And it's how I know you work in Thames House. I can help MI5, Charlie. I can tell them everything my bosses have been doing here."

Shepherd sipped his prosecco, not because he was thirsty but because he needed time to think. MI5 already knew what her bosses were doing — the plan was to use them to plant disinformation back in Beijing. If Mei-feng sought political asylum then the whole operation would come tumbling down. So any decision on what happened next would have to be taken at a higher level. "Let me talk to my boss," he said.

"Thank you," she said. She leaned over and kissed him on the lips. "Can I stay here tonight?"

"What will your bosses say?"

"I'll call them and tell them you want to book me overnight. It's an extra eight hundred pounds."

"I think that's a bit above my budget."

She laughed and stroked his groin. "I'll pay," she said.

"Seriously?"

"I don't want to go home," she said. "I want to stay with you. Okay?"

Shepherd raised his glass. "Sure," he said.

"I'll call them," she said. She put down her glass, rolled off the bed and padded into the next room. He heard her make a call and speak in Chinese, and then she reappeared at the door, hands on hips, tossing her hair. "Do you want another massage?" she asked.

Shepherd laughed. "Why the hell not?"

Shepherd's phone woke him from a dreamless sleep. He looked around and couldn't see the phone, then he remembered he'd put it in the bedside cupboard. He pulled open the drawer and took it out, sitting up and peering at the screen. It was Pritchard. And it was three o'clock in the morning, which meant it could only be bad news. He took the call. "What's wrong?" he asked, instantly wide awake. Mei-feng was curled up on the other side of the bed, her hair spread out across the pillow.

"They've taken Jaraf," said Pritchard. "I need you here now."

Pritchard ended the call and Shepherd rolled out of bed. He went around to Mei-feng's side of the bed and gently touched her shoulder. "Wake up," he said.

She opened her eyes. "What's wrong, baby?" she asked sleepily.

"You have to go," he said.

"What time is it?" She closed her eyes again.

"Three o'clock." He shook her gently. "You need to go."

"I paid for the night, Charlie. Don't worry." She curled into a ball. Shepherd looked at his watch again, even though he knew what time it was. He wasn't happy at the prospect of leaving her alone in the flat, but he didn't want to waste time getting her to leave. The flat was fully sanitised — everything in it was in accordance with the Charlie Warner legend and there was nothing there that would connect to Dan Shepherd.

He ordered an Uber and by the time he had dressed and grabbed his coat, a white Prius was waiting for him outside. There was little traffic and less than ten minutes after Pritchard had called, Shepherd was walking into his office. The man himself was sitting behind his desk, jacket off and White's club tie at half mast. He was talking on the phone and he waved for Shepherd to sit. Shepherd chose the sofa and took off his coat before sitting down.

Pritchard finished his call and stood up. "Well the shit has well and truly hit the fan," he said. He began pacing slowly up and down but kept his eyes on Shepherd. "Gannon's men delivered Mrs Jaraf and her son to your house in Hereford, exactly as planned. Except Mrs Jaraf had a gun and then half a dozen guys burst in, armed to the teeth. Well, five guys and a woman, they say."

"Are Gannon's people okay?" asked Shepherd.

"They were Tasered, hog-tied and gagged, but the only thing hurt was their egos. I don't think you SAS types take defeat well." He reached his office door, turned and started pacing back to his desk. "Whoever it was that attacked them took Jaraf. And the so-called Mrs Jaraf and the boy went with them."

"So it's a kidnapping?"

"Either that or they want to kill him somewhere else," said Pritchard.

"And our guys were Tasered?"

Pritchard nodded. "They used a Taser shotgun. It fires Taser missiles up to something like a hundred feet. There aren't many around — Taser dropped development after American law enforcement had their budgets cut. The Home Office was looking at it with a view to ordering it for British cops but they scrapped the tests when Taser pulled the plug."

"This can't be ISIS, it's not their sort of thing," said Shepherd. "This is too well organised, too methodical."

"Agreed," said Pritchard.

"And Mrs Jaraf had a gun?"

"A Beretta Nano, according to Gannon's boys."

"How the hell could she have gotten a gun?" asked Shepherd.

"I was hoping you might have been able to tell me that."

"I was with her all the way to the UK," said Shepherd. "She went through security at Sofia Airport, there's no way she could have got a gun onto the plane. And I was with her every step of the way until I delivered her to Wheeler and Travis."

"Wheeler and Travis?"

"They're SAS. They're smart guys, I don't see that they would have left her alone."

"So it'll remain a mystery how she got a gun, but a gun she most definitely had when she went into your house. And as I said, another six heavies piled in, all masked, with heavy firepower and Tasers. It was all over in seconds. They Tasered our guys, ziptied and gagged them, and took Jaraf with them. Major Gannon went

382

around when they didn't answer his calls and he phoned me. He's obviously fairly embarrassed about what happened, but the guys who carried out the job were clearly professionals."

Shepherd ran his hands through his hair, unable to understand what he was being told. "What the hell was Mrs Jaraf doing?"

"It wasn't his wife. She was a ringer."

"I saw her passport. And her son's."

"Presumably fakes. Did she talk to Salam while you were with her?"

Shepherd shook his head. "She didn't make a big thing about it and the times I spoke to Major Gannon he wasn't at the house. Jaraf didn't have a phone." He rubbed the back of his neck. "Jaraf knew where his wife was, he knew she was at the camp. Presumably he must have spoken to her?"

"Not necessarily. A letter, maybe. A phone call from someone working at the camp. Maybe he never actually spoke to her."

"So the whole thing was a set-up? We were sent to bring her to Jaraf so that he could be kidnapped? And how did those other guys get to the house so quickly? Wheeler and Travis are professionals, they would have spotted a tail."

"You said you spotted surveillance at Ankara Airport?"

Shepherd nodded. "Yes, two guys who were on the same flight as me on the way out."

"But no tail to the airport? And no tail from the camp to the embassy?"

"None that I saw."

Pritchard stopped pacing. "She was carrying some sort of tracking device. Her or the boy. They didn't need mobile surveillance, at least not close up, because they had GPS."

Shepherd scowled as he realised that Pritchard was right. He'd wasted his time driving them to Bulgaria and flying out of Sofia. They had always known exactly where Shepherd was going, every step of the way. It didn't matter what airport they flew from or what plane they were on, or how careful they were when they got her into the car at Luton. But who were they?

"We need to know who this so-called Mrs Jaraf is."

"I can help you there," said Shepherd, reaching into his coat pocket. "I've still got her passport. And her son's."

"Finally, some good news," said Pritchard.

Shepherd handed Pritchard the two Palestinian passports and he scrutinised them. "They look real enough, but I'm no expert." He looked at his watch. "I need to run these photographs through facial recognition. Let me check if there's anyone here."

Pritchard left the office and Shepherd took out his phone. He called Major Gannon, who answered almost immediately. "Spider, you've heard what happened?"

"That's why I'm calling, boss. Everyone's okay?"

"No one got shot, which is the good news. But they took Jaraf. It makes us look like bloody amateurs."

"She had a gun, I'm told."

"Yeah, and some very heavy back-up. But even so, our guys were tasked with protecting Jaraf and they dropped the ball."

384

"Do you mind if I talk to Wheeler or Travis?"

"Sure, they're both here. I'll put Three on."

The line went quiet and after a few seconds, Wheeler was on the line. "Spider, mate, so sorry about this."

"Sounds like you were outgunned, and they were well organised," said Shepherd. "And to be honest, I was the one who brought the bitch to you. I don't know how the hell I got fooled, but fooled I was. Did you get a look at them?"

"Four of them were wearing ski masks and two had motorbike helmets on. Six in all. One had an Uzi and four of them had Glocks. And one of them had a Taser shotgun thing."

"And Mrs Jaraf — or whoever she is — had a gun?"

"Tiny little thing. Beretta Nano. You know the one, six in the clip. It's only 9mm and me and Travis had the same thought, we charge her and take our chances, but before we could do anything her pals arrived and it was game over."

"How the fuck did she get a gun?" asked Shepherd. "We went through full airport security so she must have been clean when she arrived at Luton."

"We stopped, once, on the way. She needed the bathroom."

"That's it then. She must have got the gun then."

"That doesn't make sense, Spider. No one was following, I can guarantee that. We had eyes on every vehicle anywhere near us and we weren't tailed."

"They must have had a plan in place, that's why she wanted the bathroom."

"But they had no way of knowing where we were headed. How could they have arranged a pick-up at the service station?"

"She must have had a tracker on her," said Shepherd. "GPS. They knew exactly where she was so they could have been ahead of you rather than behind you."

"Yeah, but how did she know to stop off at the service station?"

"They must have had some way of communicating with her," said Shepherd. "The kid had a chunky digital watch, they could have used that to get messages to her."

"Bastards," said Wheeler. "She got very talkative when she was back in the car. Where were we going, house or apartment, wouldn't shut up."

"Maybe when she was in the service station they give her a bug as well so they could pick up on the conversation. Or even a phone. They could have been listening to every word you said so when you arrived they were all ready to go."

"Who are these fuckers, Spider? Who would go to all this trouble over a single raghead?"

"We're working on it, Three," said Shepherd. "Let me talk to the boss."

Wheeler gave the phone back to the Major. "The house is secure now and we're back at Stirling Lines," said Gannon. "Do you need me to do anything?"

"Nah, we're good, boss," said Shepherd. "The important thing now is to track down this team and find out what they've done with Jaraf."

386

"I'm here if you need me," said the Major, and he ended the call.

Pritchard walked back in and went back behind his desk. "There's an analyst in working overtime on the photo recognition desk, so I've put her on Mrs Jaraf." He grimaced. "Though I suppose we need to start calling her something else now." He sighed and sat back in his chair. "All that time, all that effort, and all we did was lose the one bloody intel source we had. You know, if it wasn't for the two attacks on his life, I might wonder if this was some elaborate scheme for Jaraf to get into the country."

Shepherd rubbed his chin. "He was already here. And we'd have let him stay so long as his intel was good."

"I was half joking," said Pritchard. He swore out loud and banged his hand down on the desk. "The best laid plans, huh?"

Shepherd shrugged, not sure what to say. Not every operation went according to plan. All you could do when something went wrong was to try to put it right and to learn from any mistakes you made. Shepherd should have made more of an effort to check that Mrs Jaraf was who she claimed to be. At the very least he should have arranged for her to speak to Jaraf on the phone. And he should have told Travis and Wheeler to not let her out of their sight, toilet or no toilet. But hindsight was always twenty-twenty; all they could do now was to move forward. "What about Nadia?" asked Shepherd.

"She's still settling in," said Pritchard. "Zarah's going to start looking at pictures with her tomorrow." He smiled. "Today."

"Why don't I do that? I've more experience in that area, obviously."

"Obviously." Pritchard's forehead creased into a frown as he considered his options, then he nodded. "Why not?" He looked at his watch. "She'll still be on Turkish time so she'll probably be up early. Why don't you get a few hours' sleep and start at eight?"

"That works for me."

"Just so you know, I'm not expecting great things from her. We're still drawing a blank on the mysterious Hasan Mahmoud. What's especially worrying is that no passport has been issued in that name for anyone in his age range."

Shepherd frowned. "That's not good."

"No it's not, is it? It begs the question of how he managed to get to Syria without a passport."

"Unless he gave Nadia the wrong name," said Shepherd.

"In which case maybe everything else he told her was a lie," said Pritchard. "Anyway, we'll know soon enough once she starts looking at our most-wanted pictures."

"What about facial recognition on the Jaraf woman? How long will that take?"

"How long is a piece of string?" asked Pritchard. "A PNC check won't take long, ditto a check with the UK passport office. But there's little likelihood she'll be on either. We can run the picture through Interpol and Europol, but again there's no obvious European

388

connection. Turkey isn't in the EU of course, and getting information from them is like pulling teeth."

"They are in Interpol though."

"Sure, but for the Turks it's a one-way street most of the time. The Turkish Government uses Interpol to issue arrest warrants for people who disagree with the regime, and to get intel on Turkish citizens who live in the EU, but they drag their feet when anything is asked of them."

"She and the boy both had Palestinian passports," said Shepherd. "Israeli intelligence is second to none, and they're in Interpol."

"We're sending the photograph to Mossad as we speak. I mean photographs, plural. We're looking for the boy, too, obviously. All we can do now is to wait for the technology to do its work."

Shepherd stood up and stretched. He was dog tired and could do with some sleep, albeit just a few hours. "Are you going home?" asked Pritchard.

"I wish," said Shepherd. "No, Mei-feng is still at the Pimlico flat. I have to go back to see her. There have been some interesting developments." He quickly explained what had happened.

"That puts us in a very difficult position, obviously," said Pritchard once Shepherd had finished. "If she claims asylum, they'll shut down the agencies. And we'll lose the pipeline to Beijing."

"On the plus side, we get a Chinese intelligence officer telling us everything she knows."

"She's a honey trap. How much do you think she can give us?"

Shepherd shrugged. "I take your point."

Pritchard thought for a moment. "But if you could persuade her to be a double agent, at least for a while, she'd presumably be able to give us the details of all the girls working at the agency. And of the people running the agencies. That would be helpful. It'd be useful to have someone on the inside."

Shepherd nodded. "I'll talk to her. And in principle we can offer her asylum."

"In principle, yes."

Shepherd left the office and headed out of Thames House. He walked back to the Pimlico flat, and when he arrived he let himself in and went upstairs. Mei-feng was still asleep, curled up on the side of the bed. He set his phone alarm for seven-fifteen, stripped off his clothes and climbed into bed. She didn't wake up but pushed herself back against him. He put his arms around her and rested his chin on the top of her head. She really was tiny. She was warm, too, and soft. It had been a long time since he had slept next to anyone but it felt natural with her, and he fell asleep almost immediately.

Anwar Rafiq sipped his orange juice as he studied his laptop screen. Dawn was breaking and he could hear the muffled chatter of worshippers in the street outside heading to the mosque. Rafiq lived in a terraced house a hundred metres from the Baitul Futuh Mosque in Morden, south London, next door to Morden South railway station. The mosque was one of the biggest in Europe, allowing up to thirteen thousand men and women to worship together. Rafiq would be joining the worshippers at morning prayers, but first he had to check the draft email folder that he used to correspond with his ISIS paymaster in Syria.

Rafiq's jihadist cell was made up of just four of those worshippers, four men who like Rafiq had spent months in Syria being trained for their mission. That mission was heading for completion, but the ultimate decision to go ahead wasn't Rafiq's.

He opened the folder. There was a new message. It had been created three hours earlier. "*Is all proceeding as planned? Did you deliver the consignments?*" The man who sent it used the name Al-Muntaqim — "The Avenger". By "consignments" he meant Semtex. Rafiq's paymaster had been pleased with him for getting the Semtex. Rafiq's plan had been to buy it, but his paymaster had insisted that there be no loose ends and that the Russian and the Irishman should be killed. Once they had the explosives and detonators, Rafiq was tasked with distributing them to other cells in Leeds, Birmingham and London. So far he had done everything that had been asked of him.

He began to compose a new email. "*The consignment has been delivered. The packages are being prepared. Alhamdulillah. Are we authorised to proceed?*" He closed the email and saved it as a draft. Then he closed Gmail and turned off the laptop.

He stood up, finished his orange juice, and headed out to join the throngs of Muslims in the street. He felt safe and loved, surrounded by his own kind. Everywhere he looked there were Muslims. Good, respectful people

391

who worshipped Allah and followed the teachings of his prophet. He took a set of prayer beads from his pocket and ran them through his fingers. Hopefully the day would come when the whole country bowed down to Allah. That was what Rafiq yearned for more than anything, to make the United Kingdom a truly Islamic country that Muslims from around the world could call home. It would happen one day, he was sure of that. People would have to die — a *lot* of people would have to die — but eventually the day would come.

Shepherd's phone alarm went off and he rolled out of bed and switched it off. He padded through to the kitchen, made two cups of coffee and took them back to the bedroom. Mei-feng was still fast asleep. He put her coffee down on the bedside cupboard and shook her gently. "Wake up, sleepyhead."

She moaned softly and rolled over onto her back, blinking. She smiled when she saw him looking down at her. "Good morning," she said.

"Good morning." He sat down on the bed next to her and sipped his coffee.

"Did you go out last night?" she asked sleepily. "Or did I dream it?"

"There was a problem at work," he said. He looked at his watch. "You're going to have to go, I've got to get back to work."

"Can I wait for you here?"

Shepherd shook his head. "No, you need to go. The agency is going to think there's something wrong if you stay with me."

She sat up, her hair falling around her shoulders. "I don't want to talk to them again."

"I know, I understand," said Shepherd. "I spoke to my boss about what you said, and in principle there's a deal to be done."

She frowned. "A deal?"

"They can offer you asylum but they don't want the agency to know that you've come to us, not yet anyway. They want details of everyone working for the agency. For all three agencies. And details of everybody working at the office in Knightsbridge."

"I can do that for you."

"And what would be great is if you could get a list of all the phones that have been bugged."

She frowned. "That would be harder but yes, maybe. And if I do that, they will let me live in England?"

Shepherd nodded. "That's what my boss said."

"And I can trust him?"

"He's a good guy. He won't let you down."

She took her coffee and sipped it, then wrinkled her nose.

"What's wrong?" asked Shepherd.

"It's not sweet enough," she said.

"I put one sugar in."

She grinned. "I usually have three."

Shepherd laughed. He took her mug into the kitchen and added two more sugars. As he turned to head back to the bedroom, he noticed she'd moved into the sitting room and was sprawled naked on the sofa. "I always get horny in the morning," she said.

"I have to get to work," he said, handing her the mug.

"Can I see you tonight?"

"I don't know, the job I'm working on is going to take a lot of my time."

"What if I have something for you?"

Shepherd glared at her and pointed at the Charlie Warner phone on the coffee table. He pointed at his ear, reminding her that the phone was being monitored.

Her mouth opened in surprise as she realised what she'd done.

"You are insatiable," he said. "I think you've given me more than enough, I need time to rest."

"Well if you want to book me again, just call the agency," she said. She grimaced. "I'm sorry," she mouthed.

"It's okay," he mouthed back.

"I will," he said. "Once I've got my strength back." He pointed at the bedroom door. She nodded, stood up, and took her coffee into the bedroom. Shepherd followed her. He closed the door and flashed her a reassuring smile. "It'll be okay, don't worry."

"I'm such an idiot."

"We covered ourselves. It's all good." He gestured at the bathroom. "You can shower first."

She smiled mischievously. "Why don't we shower together?"

"Because it'll take ten times as long and I've got to get to work."

"I could make you come really quickly if I wanted."

Shepherd laughed. "I bet you could."

394

She pouted prettily and carried her mug into the bathroom. After a few seconds he heard the shower kick into life.

Shepherd picked up his work phone. There were no messages or missed calls. He drank his coffee while Mei-feng showered, then when she was done he showered too, taking care not to get his dressing wet. He changed into a dark blue suit, a white shirt and a blue tie.

When he went back into the sitting room, Mei-feng was sitting on the sofa, dressed and ready to go. "So book me again soon, okay?" she said.

"Definitely," he said. She stood up and kissed him on the cheek. "Thank you," she whispered. He let her out and used the Charlie Warner phone to order an Uber while he watched her leave the building on the monitor.

The Uber was downstairs within ten minutes and he was at Thames House just after eight o'clock. He took the lift to Harry Fletcher's office, let himself in and placed the Charlie Warner mobile phone on his desk.

Nadia was staying on the fourth floor and when he got there, Zarah was sitting outside the room checking her smartphone.

"They've got you on guard duty?" asked Shepherd.

Zarah looked up and smiled. "I offered to stay in the room with her but she said she wanted to be alone."

"So you sat here all night?"

"A colleague has been rotating with me," she said. "I wouldn't want to lock her in even if the doors were lockable, and we wouldn't want her wandering around obviously." She grinned and held up her phone. "It's no biggie, I've got Netflix."

"Well the good news is that I'll take it from here," he said. "Giles Pritchard has asked me to run Nadia through our databases so you can stand down for a while." He nodded at the door. "Before you go can you do me a favour and pop in and let her know I'm ready when she is."

Zarah stood up and tucked her phone into her jacket pocket. She looked remarkably fresh considering that she'd spent most of the night sitting on a chair in a corridor. "Will do," she said. She knocked on the door, opened it, and slipped inside. After a few minutes she reappeared. "She'll be a couple of minutes." She forced a smile. "She's a bit overawed by everything that's happening."

"Understandable. She's been through a lot."

"She's desperate to stay in the UK. She's terrified she'll be sent back."

"I don't see that happening, Zarah," said Shepherd.

"She seems to think that if she doesn't give you what you want, you'll take her passport away."

"The passport she has is just a travel document. The government has already taken away her citizenship. But yes, if she comes through on this, her citizenship can be reinstated. It's up to her."

"That's a lot of pressure for a young girl to be under," said Zarah. She folded her arms and leaned against the wall. "She reminds me of my sister."

"In what way?"

"I'm the oldest, right. So you get the undivided attention of your parents. You're special. Okay, when you get a sibling you're not the sole focus of the family any more and that can cause resentment, but it's always harder for the second one. They're always having to compete for attention, they're always aware that they weren't first."

"So they try harder?"

Zarah smiled. "Sometimes. But more often they tend to play up. Push the limits."

"You think that's what Nadia was doing when she went to Syria? Playing up?"

"Not so much that, but the fact she was a second child probably made her more vulnerable. If someone treated her as if she was special, she might try to fit in with what they expected from her."

"I didn't know she had an older sister."

"We've spent a lot of time talking about her family. She misses them, obviously."

"The sister wasn't involved?"

"No, not at all. Nadia says she didn't say a word to her sister."

"So you think Nadia was groomed, is that what you're saying?"

"Of course," she said. "I don't think for one moment she spontaneously decided to move to Syria to shack up with jihadists, do you? Someone had to put the idea in her head." She bit down on her lower lip as she considered her words. "If they'd tried it with me when I was a teenager, I'd have told them where to get off, you know. Maybe even reported them. But someone like Nadia, she'd be flattered. She'd feel special. And the more they worked on her, the more special she'd feel. So, yes, I'd say she was groomed."

Shepherd nodded. "And what about your sister?"

"She's fine now. She's at university and that gave her more confidence. She might be working here one day."

"She's got a good role model in you, that's for sure. Are you okay helping me debrief Nadia? I think she'd welcome a friendly face around."

"Mr Pritchard said I'm to be available as and when you need me."

"Excellent," he said. "Can you fix us up with a private office? Ideally with a window, I don't want her to feel trapped. We'll need at least two terminals and several whiteboards. Every time she comes up with a name I want the face up because that'll help her remember more."

"Will do," she said. "And I have to collect some photographs from Diane Daily. Apparently they've started assembling IEDs in the storage locker you went to in Birmingham. She has some photographs they've been working on."

The door opened and Nadia appeared. She was wearing a dark blue hijab that matched her sweatshirt, and blue jeans. She looked apprehensive so Shepherd flashed her his most encouraging smile. "I thought we'd get some breakfast in the canteen and start our chat there," he said.

"Okay," she said. She stepped forward and hugged Zarah. "Thank you," she said.

"I'll arrange the office while you have breakfast," said Zarah. "And I have to shower and change." She put her hands on Nadia's shoulder. "Don't worry, everything's going to be all right." She hugged Nadia, patted her on the back, and then walked down the corridor, heading for the lifts.

"She's nice," said Nadia, watching her go.

"Yes, she is," said Shepherd. He wasn't sure just how much Zarah had been faking the niceness, but she had certainly done a tremendous job to bond with Nadia in such a short space of time.

He took her along the corridor and up the stairs to the canteen. He nodded for her to sit at one of the tables by the window. "What can I get you?"

"Orange juice, please. And do they have toast?"

"They have toast and croissants and muffins, plus you can have eggs and . . ." He stopped short of saying "bacon". He smiled. "Anything else you want. The omelettes are good."

She smiled. "An omelette and toast would be great."

She sat down at the table and Shepherd went over to the counter and ordered two omelettes, toast, Nadia's orange juice and a mug of coffee for himself. When he carried the tray over to the table, Nadia was looking out of the window, close to tears. He put the food down and placed the tray on the adjoining table. "It's going to be okay, Nadia," he said. "I know this is a stressful time, but there's light at the end of the tunnel."

She turned to look at him, then wiped her eyes with the back of her hand.

"Here," he said, giving her a napkin.

She thanked him and dabbed at her eyes.

Shepherd picked up a fork and began to eat, hoping that she would follow his example. She did, first nibbling at a slice of toast and then sipping her orange. Before long she had her knife and fork in her hands and was devouring her omelette. The two of them ate in silence. He waited until she had finished before putting the plates on the next table. "So, tell me more about this Hasan," he said. "The man who saved you."

"What do you mean?"

"You met him in Birmingham, you said. He was the brother of a friend of yours and you went to the same mosque."

She nodded.

"Then one day he just disappeared and then he turned up at the camp in Syria?"

"That's right."

"But when he went, you must have tried to contact him."

She shrugged. "His phone was off. I guess he'd thrown the SIM card away when he left the country. Or they'd taken his phone off him, like they did with me."

"What about social media?"

"He had Facebook but he stopped posting."

"Twitter? Instagram?"

"He hated Twitter but he had Instagram. But that stopped too."

Shepherd took out his phone. He had the Facebook app on it, though he never used it. "You're on Facebook, right?" he said.

"Sure, but I haven't posted since I went to Syria."

400

"Okay, I need you to show me Hasan's page." She reached for the phone but he held it away from her. "Nadia, you mustn't post anything or like anything or let anyone know that you've been online."

"I won't."

He looked at her intently. "I'm serious."

She nodded. "So am I."

"Just log on and then show me Hasan's page."

"Okay," she said.

He gave her the phone and then got up and walked around the table so that he could see what she was doing.

"You really don't trust me," she said.

"I do, I just want to see what there is," he said.

She frowned as she stared at the screen. "It's gone."

"You're sure?"

She nodded. "It's not there any more."

"What about his sister? Is her page still there?"

Nadia tapped on the screen and then handed the phone to him. "There she is. Deena."

Shepherd looked at the page. Deena Mahmoud was a pretty girl with laughing eyes. In her profile picture she was wearing a white hijab. Most of her posts were about music and movies and make-up. Her list of friends was visible to anyone. She had more than a thousand. Hasan Mahmoud wasn't among them. Shepherd gave her back the phone. "Do me a favour and scroll through her friends, and see if there's anyone there that Hasan mentioned or that you saw in Syria."

"Sure," she said. She sat back and scrolled through the profile pictures and names. From time to time she stopped scrolling and frowned at a picture, but she didn't say anything. Eventually she stopped and nodded. "This guy," she said. "He went to our mosque and Hasan said he was at the camp. I never saw him. Latif Shaikh. Everyone called him Milky."

"Milky?"

"Milk Shaikh. Milky." She shrugged. "We thought it was funny when we were kids."

Shepherd looked at the profile picture. A young Asian man in an Aston Villa football shirt. He clicked through to the profile. Shaikh's last post had been two years previously, him with a group of fans at Villa Park. He scrolled through the posts but there was nothing that suggested that Shaikh was a fundamentalist or involved with jihadists in any way.

"You're sure?" he said.

"Oh, Hasan definitely talked about him. He said Milky had gone back to Birmingham about the same time as I arrived in Syria."

"Which was what? A year ago?"

Nadia nodded.

Shepherd frowned as he looked at Shaikh's Facebook page. The fact that Shaikh had returned to the UK but not been active on social media suggested that he had been well trained and had gone dark. That was a bad sign.

He gave the phone back to Nadia. "Have a look at the rest of her contacts, will you?"

He sipped his coffee as she scrolled through the profiles. Eventually she shook her head. "No, just

402

Milky," she said. She looked wistfully at the phone. "I really want to call my mum."

"I know you do, Nadia. But they can't know that you're here. Not just now. You've spoken to them already, right? When you were in the camp in Turkey?"

"A couple of times, when Margie let me use her phone. But they'll be so worried about me."

"Let's get started on looking at the pictures we have, and if that works out I'll talk to my boss."

"Promise?"

"Cross my heart."

"Do it then," she said.

Shepherd solemnly made the sign of the cross over his heart.

"If you lie, you die," said Nadia.

Shepherd looked at her solemnly. "I won't lie," he said.

She smiled coldly. "Everybody lies," she said.

"I try not to." He put the phone away. "Think back to when Hasan was talking to you, in the camp," he said. "Can you remember any names?"

"I'm not sure," she said.

"Try to remember."

"I thought you were going to show me photographs."

"I will," he said. "But there's an element of randomness to that. You might have to look at thousands of photographs to spot one face you recognise. But if you can give me a name, I can look it up. It might save time."

She sipped her orange juice and her forehead creased into a frown. Then her face brightened and she put her glass down. "There were two guys he spoke about a few times. He thought they were idiots." She laughed. "He was always saying they were too stupid to tie their own shoelaces which is why they always wore sandals. They were from Iraq and Hasan said they were on a mission to kill Tony Blair."

Shepherd didn't interrupt her, but he already knew who she was talking about. Jaraf had mentioned the two Iraqis, Tariq Al-Majid and Naseer Salim, but they had both died in the back of a refrigerated lorry in Portsmouth. The information was useless, but the fact that she had it was a good sign and added veracity to her story.

"I think one was called Tariq." She nodded. "Yes, Tariq. And the other one was Naseer Saleem. Or Salim."

Shepherd nodded. "Brilliant. Well done."

"Aren't you going to write it down?"

Shepherd tapped the side of his head. "I've got a good memory." He sipped his coffee and watched her over the top of his mug. Her eyes widened and she wagged her hand excitedly. "Oh, yes, wait, I remember. He said the brother of one of my besties was out there. He had been at the camp for about three months and he left the day that Hasan arrived. Hasan said it was a pity because he could have brought him to see me."

Shepherd gave her his phone and she logged onto her Facebook account again. She scrolled through her list of friends and then selected a profile. "That's her," she said. "Gazza we call her, but her name's Gazala. Gazala Noor. Her brother's called Gulzar."

Gazala hadn't made her friends private so Shepherd was able to look through them. There was no Gulzar. "Is he not on Facebook?" asked Shepherd.

"He was," said Nadia.

"Did Hasan tell you anything about Gulzar?"

"Just that he'd gone to another camp for specialist training."

"Did he say what sort of training?"

Nadia shook her head. "It was just after we got together at the camp," she said. "He was more careful about what he said, back then."

"Okay, no problem," said Shepherd. "Any other names spring to mind?"

She thought for a while, then frowned and shook her head. "It's like the harder I try to remember, the vaguer everything feels. Do you know what I mean?"

The idea of struggling to remember something wasn't one Shepherd could comprehend, but he smiled and nodded. "I understand," he said. "Just relax and it'll come back to you. We've plenty of time."

"I really want to help," she said.

"I know you do," he said.

She bent her head towards him and lowered her voice as if she feared being overheard. "Please don't send me back," she whispered.

Giles Pritchard woke with a start as his office door opened. It was his secretary, Amy Miller. She was wearing a Burberry raincoat and carrying a Marks and Spencer bag. "Rise and shine," she said. She pulled the string to open the blinds.

He sat up, blinking, and looked at his watch. It was eight-thirty.

"Have you been here all night?" she asked.

"Something came up in the early hours so I figured I might as well stay," he said. He ran his hands through his hair. "Though the way I feel now, that probably wasn't the brightest of ideas."

"You know you have a finance and strategy meeting at nine? And a JTAC briefing at ten-thirty."

Pritchard groaned. He'd forgotten about both. He could at a push send someone else to the finance and strategy meeting, but there was no way he could avoid the JTAC briefing. He went over to his desk, pulled open the bottom drawer and took out a British Airways amenity kit. "I'll shower and shave in the gym," he said.

Amy opened one of his cupboards and took out a towel and a white shirt on a hanger. "You'll be needing these," she said.

"You read my mind," he said, taking the towel and shirt from her.

He went down to the gym, shaved and showered, and changed into the fresh shirt. He made the first meeting with a couple of minutes to spare. As always budgets were under threat, so Pritchard had to fight his corner, though it was the Northern Ireland Counter Terrorism Section that was under the most pressure. The Irish had gone quiet and would hopefully stay that way for the foreseeable future, but with the American president assassinating Muslim leaders around the world, the UK was bracing itself for retaliation.

406

When he got back to his office, Amy had a mug of coffee and a croissant ready for him. "I'm guessing you didn't have time for breakfast," she said.

"You're a life-saver," said Pritchard. He sat down and took a bite of his croissant. It was almond, his favourite, though obviously Amy knew that.

"And you had a call from Jennifer Clare. She said she needed to see you urgently."

"Can you ask her to come now?" asked Pritchard. He sipped his coffee. Clare was the analyst he'd given the Mrs Jaraf passport photograph to. He took another bite of his croissant. There was no way he could miss the Joint Terrorism Analysis Centre briefing. New Year's Eve was fast approaching and while the country's national threat level was currently set to "substantial", there were rumours that it was going to be raised to "severe" or perhaps even set to its highest level: "critical".

Substantial meant that a terrorist attack was considered likely, severe meant highly likely, and critical meant that an attack was highly likely in the near future. Today would be the first time that Pritchard would raise Jaraf's intelligence with JTAC and he wasn't looking forward to it.

For almost a decade, MI5 and the police's anti-terrorist units had been using a triage system for assessing risk, in the same way that doctors decided on priorities for medical treatment. If intelligence was received that impacted on an ongoing operation, it was passed on to the relevant department. But if the intelligence was new, it had to be given a priority level before the actions to be taken could be determined.

The lowest level was Priority 4. This level involved individuals who had previously been regarded as a threat to national security who were now supposedly in the clear, but had a risk of re-engagement.

Priority 3 was uncorroborated intelligence, where there were rumours or suggestions that there might be a threat, but where more work was needed to establish whether the threat was real or not.

Priority 2 meant there was evidence of medium or high-risk extremist activity, such as jihadists planning to travel overseas to join a terrorist army or getting involved in large-scale fundraising.

And if there was credible and actionable evidence of attack planning, then it was Priority 1.

After the initial search of Karim's storage locker, it was clear that he had the ingredients for ricin production but hadn't actually made any of the poison. That meant an attack was not imminent, which made it a Priority 2. But the fact that jihadists now had access to Semtex and were adapting drones to carry IEDs meant there was credible and actionable evidence, so Pritchard had no choice other than to give the intelligence that had come from Jaraf a Priority 1 rating.

The snag was that the director general had to be informed of all Priority 1 investigations. But Pritchard knew that as soon as the DG saw the intel he'd want to know where it came from, and that meant he'd have to be told about Jaraf and what had happened to him. He frowned and sipped his coffee. The DG wouldn't be pleased, obviously, but hopefully Nadia Shah would go some way to redressing the balance. Swings and roundabouts.

Pritchard didn't see that he had any choice other than to recommend that the threat level be raised to critical. He would be one of a dozen people at the meeting so the decision wouldn't be his alone, but once he gave details of the Ali Karim surveillance operation he doubted that he would be overruled.

Jennifer Clare appeared in the doorway. She was in her early twenties, a recent recruit from Durham University who was a talented Photoshop artist with a good eye for spotting faked photographs and videos. "I've had a hit on the passport photograph, the woman." She placed four surveillance photographs on Pritchard's desk. "Leah Levy, almost certainly Mossad."

Pritchard raised his eyebrows. Mossad was one of Israel's three intelligence agencies, tasked with foreign intelligence gathering and analysis, and covert operations. It worked alongside Aman — military intelligence — and Shin Bet, internal security. Mossad was the most secretive of the three; hardly surprising as it was the agency that carried out assassinations of the country's enemies. Its full name was Mossad Merkazi Le Modiin Uletafkidim Meyuhadim, Hebrew for "Central Institute for Intelligence and Special Operations".

Pritchard looked down at the photographs. Three of them showed a dark haired woman entering and leaving a building. In each of the photographs she was on her own, but in the fourth she was in a restaurant with a portly bald man that Pritchard recognised instantly. Seth Kaplan. Up until five years ago he was Mossad's main man in London, but he'd returned to Israel when he developed pancreatic cancer. Pritchard had dealt with Kaplan on several occasions, and it was Kaplan who had introduced him to his successor, Joel Schwartz. They had met at The Delaunay, a restaurant in Covent Garden, and it appeared to Pritchard that that was where the surveillance picture with Levy had been taken. Kaplan had picked at his food and was much thinner than he appeared in the surveillance photograph, which had obviously been taken before the illness had started to take its toll. There was a date on the photograph: July 18, 2014.

"She was never based here," said Clare. "Or at least she never appeared on any embassy staff lists and was never granted diplomatic privilege. But her name has cropped up on several MI6 reports. There was chatter that she was attached to Kidon, but nothing concrete." She flashed him a tight smile. "But then there's rarely anything concrete where Kidon are concerned."

Pritchard nodded. Kidon was Hebrew for "tip of the spear", the department within Mossad that was tasked with the assassination of Israel's enemies. In the last two years alone Kidon had been responsible for targeted killings in Kuala Lumpur, Syria and the Lebanon. The most famous Mossad assassination operation was codenamed Wrath of God, and followed the 1972 Munich massacre where the PLO and Black September terrorists murdered eleven members of the Israeli Olympic team. In retaliation, Mossad tracked

410

down and killed dozens of terrorists over the following twenty years.

Pritchard thanked her and she left, leaving the photographs on his desk. He had Joel Schwartz's mobile number, so he called it. Schwartz answered almost immediately and didn't seem surprised by Pritchard's request for an urgent meeting. "Official or off the books?" growled Schwartz. Official meant that anything the two men said was just that, and such meetings would be at the embassy, Thames House, or on neutral ground such as White's, the exclusive members-only club that still refused to admit women. Any conversations had on that basis could be recorded and relayed back to their bosses.

"Let's make it social," said Pritchard. "Are you up for a game of squash?"

"Today?"

"The sooner the better."

"Paddington Sports Club?" The sports club was about four miles north of the Israeli Embassy, which was in South Kensington, close to Kensington High Street. The club was actually tucked away in a quiet area of Maida Vale, far enough from the government offices and embassies that Pritchard had never bumped into anyone he knew professionally. There were squash courts in Thames House, but that obviously wasn't an option for an off-the-books get-together.

"You read my mind," said Pritchard.

"Five-thirty? Six?"

"Six works."

"See you there." Schwartz ended the call. He hadn't asked why Pritchard had wanted a meeting so urgently, which almost certainly meant that he knew what was on the agenda. Schwartz was on the embassy staff list as a public affairs manager, but in reality he was Mossad's representative in London. That's not to say he ever got involved in active operations — he had been deskbound for more than a decade — but he was the only man permitted to talk about the organisation's activities, on or off the record.

Even having been told that the talk would be off the books, Schwartz would still be concerned about the possibility of being recorded, which is why Pritchard had suggested squash. Stripping down to their underwear in the changing room would prove that no one was carrying recording devices, and the featureless walls of a squash court were as difficult a place to bug as you could get.

Pritchard sat back on his chair and steepled his fingers under his chin, deep in thought. Mossad were a law unto themselves, and cared little for the laws of other countries. If an action served the interests of Israel and its people they would carry it out, regardless of what laws they broke. But why had they targeted an ISIS instructor? It made no sense, which meant that Pritchard wasn't privy to the full story. And if there was one thing Pritchard hated with a vengeance, it was being left out of a loop.

Shepherd opened an envelope and took out copies of the surveillance photographs of Ali Karim picking up

412

the explosives from the bearded man outside Euston station. He passed the photographs to Nadia. "Do you recognise either of these two men?" he asked.

They were sitting in a small office on the second floor of Thames House with a single window overlooking the river and Lambeth Bridge to the left. There were three desks, each with two monitors and a keyboard, and there were two large whiteboards leaning against the wall. There were two photographs of Latif Shaikh on one of the whiteboards and two pictures of Gulzar Noor on another. The two pictures of Noor were from Facebook, as was one of the pictures of Shaikh. The other picture of Shaikh was a blown-up passport photograph. Shepherd had written their names and dates of birth underneath the photographs, along with "BIRMINGHAM".

Nadia picked up one of the photographs, examined it carefully, then put it down and picked up a second. "I don't think so," she said. There were four photographs and she studied them all. "I'm sorry," she said eventually, shaking her head.

"That's okay, don't worry about it," said Shepherd, gathering up the photographs and putting them back in the envelope.

There was a knock on the door and it opened. It was Zarah. She was wearing the same clothes and hijab that she'd had on earlier, but she looked fresher and had applied new make-up. She was holding an envelope similar to the one that Shepherd had and she gave it to him. "These are from Diane Daily," she said. "From the storage locker in Birmingham."

Shepherd opened the envelopes. There were more than a dozen printouts of computer-enhanced photographs from the camera that Amar Singh had placed in the locker. "Have they been run through the various databases?" he asked.

"It's being done as we speak," said Zarah. "If she gets any hits Diane will let me know ASAP." She pulled a chair away from one of the desks and sat down as Shepherd began handing the photographs to Nadia, one at a time.

Nadia's eyes widened as she looked at the first photograph. "Oh my goodness," she said. She looked up, wide-eyed. "That's Milky," she said.

"Milky Shaikh? Latif Shaikh?"

She nodded and pointed to the pictures on the whiteboard. "Milky. The guy I told you about." She handed the photograph to Shepherd. It showed a man holding up a drone and grinning. It was the man wearing an Aston Villa football shirt on the whiteboard. The beard was longer in the surveillance picture and he was wearing an Aston Villa hoodie and baggy tracksuit bottoms.

"Well done," said Shepherd. He took the photograph from her and stuck it under the two that were already on the whiteboard.

Nadia continued to look through the pictures. She held out one to him. "I saw this guy out in Syria but I never knew his name."

"Did you talk to him?"

She shook her head. "I just saw him in the camp. He had an AK-47 with the handle bit folded up. He always had it with him, hanging on his back."

414

Shepherd stuck the photograph on the whiteboard underneath the pictures of Gulzar Noor and drew three question marks underneath it. "Did Hasan ever mention someone called Ali Karim?" he asked her.

Nadia frowned and she wrinkled her nose. "I think so. Maybe. I don't know." She sighed in frustration then stood up and went over to the window. She turned to face him. "I'm sorry," she said.

"Sorry for what?" asked Shepherd.

"Sorry I'm not more help," she said. "It's just hard to remember. It was so horrible there in Syria that I tried hard to forget everything. I sort of blotted it all out and now when I try to remember it's all foggy."

"I understand, but don't worry. Everyone's memory is different. Things will come back to you when you least expect it."

"Hasan did mention someone called Ali. A few times." She smiled. "He was from Birmingham, that's why. He always got excited when he met someone from Birmingham. I remember now. Yes, Ali Karim. From Saltley."

"Did you ever meet him?"

"I don't think so," she said. "Or at least Hasan never pointed him out. I suppose I might have seen him without knowing who he was. Do you have a picture?"

"He was one of the guys in the first pictures I showed you."

"Then for sure I never saw him in Syria," said Nadia.

Nadia carried on going through the photographs, then she smiled at one. "Gulzar," she said. She gave the

415

photograph to Shepherd. "Those are drones they're holding, right?"

Shepherd nodded. "We think they're planning to use the drones to cause problems."

"At airports, you mean?"

"We're not sure," said Shepherd. In the photograph, a bearded man in a bomber jacket and jeans was kneeling by one of the boxes and looking up, and the camera in the fluorescent light fitting had caught him perfectly. There was no doubt that it was the man in the pictures on the whiteboard. Gulzar Noor. He took the photograph over to the whiteboard and stuck it under the two that were already there.

Nadia continued going through the pictures and stopped when she got to the last one. "I don't believe it," she said. She held the photograph up so that Shepherd could see it. "This guy is the son of one of the imams at our mosque. Mohammed Joinda. MoJo we call him. Butter wouldn't melt in his mouth, he's a complete softy."

"Was he in Syria?"

"No, he wouldn't say boo to a goose." She looked at the picture again and shook her head sadly. "Me and my friends always thought he was gay, you know?"

"Is Joinda his family name?"

"No. It's El-Sayed. Mohammed Joinda El-Sayed."

Shepherd took the picture from her. El-Sayed was clean-shaven but wearing Islamic clothing — a long thawb and a white skullcap. He stuck the picture under the photographs of Gulzar Noor and wrote the man's name along with "BIRMINGHAM". He took a step

416

back and looked at the whiteboards. "We're making progress, Nadia. Well done."

Nadia beamed, and Zarah also nodded her approval.

"Can I call my parents and tell them I'm here?" asked Nadia.

"Soon," said Shepherd. "Let's just work on this a bit longer and then I'll arrange for you to meet them."

Tears welled up in Nadia's eyes and Zarah hurried over and gave her a hug. "Don't worry," said Zarah. "Everything's going to be fine."

The JTAC meeting was actually more of a pre-meeting, a non-minuted discussion as to the events, ongoing and predicted, that should influence the next threat rating. Thrashing out any disagreements in advance of the actual meeting meant that the rating itself could be announced with everyone already on board. JTAC was a standalone agency, composed of counter terrorist experts from sixteen government agencies and police departments, but it worked closely with MI5's International Counter Terrorism Branch and reported directly to the Director General of MI5. The director general, in turn, reported to the government's Joint Intelligence Committee.

The head of Northern Ireland Counter Terrorism, Mary Garner, was outlining possible threats across the Irish Sea, and the news was good. Pritchard listened with half an ear as he ran through what he planned to say. Eventually Garner came to the end of her summary and everyone looked expectantly at Pritchard. He took off his glasses and began polishing them as he spoke.

"It's good to know that things are quiet on the Northern Irish front, but I'm afraid my news is less encouraging." He ran through what they had discovered about Ali Karim and how the drones in the Birmingham storage locker were being converted to carry IEDs.

"What about potential targets?" asked one of the police representatives, Commander Gary Burgess. Burgess was the Head of SO15, the Met's Counter Terrorism Command.

"Unfortunately we've drawn a blank there. We have access to Ali Karim's computer and are monitoring his communications, but no specific targets have been mentioned. As you all know, we have anti-drone measures in place at all major airports, which allow us to deny them entry into airport air space and to track their operators. Those measures are classified and not widely known, so it is possible that airports are the targets. But drone-carried IEDs could be used to attack individual and mass targets anywhere in the country."

"The government needs to do something about these drones," said Burgess. "As things stand, the laws are far too lax."

"I couldn't agree more, Gary, but we have to go with the hands we've been dealt. And in view of the very real threat these drones pose, I don't think I have any choice other than to recommend critical." He put his glasses back on. "There is another issue. The explosive currently being incorporated into the drones in Birmingham was obtained from a source in London. We still haven't identified that source but the worry is

418

that it might have been distributed to other terror cells too."

"What is the explosive?" asked Garner.

"Semtex," said Pritchard. "We think it came from an IRA cache on the mainland."

Garner frowned. "Why is this the first I'm hearing of this?"

"We literally only saw the explosives yesterday. The serial number matches the numbers in the consignment sent by Gaddafi way back when. We think this might be connected to the recent murder of Brendan O'Carroll and Ivan Sokolov in Stoke Newington."

Garner sighed in frustration. "Giles, really, I would have appreciated a heads-up on this."

"I'm sorry, but this is all happening pretty much in real time. My priority at the moment is looking ahead to see where the threat lies rather than trying to work out how we got to this point. Where the explosive originated isn't a major issue; what we need to know is who the guy is who supplied it to Ali Karim and who else he has given it to."

"You said a Russian was also killed, is that significant do you think?" asked Commander Burgess.

"Ivan Sokolov sold drugs and arms around north London," said Pritchard. "The thinking is that he was acting as a middle man between Brendan O'Carroll and the jihadists." He turned towards Garner, who was clearly unhappy. "Mary, I do apologise for not telling you about the Semtex sooner. As you can imagine I've had a lot on my plate. I'll get someone to pop along to bring you up to speed this afternoon."

Garner smiled and nodded, somewhat mollified.

"I haven't had a chance to talk to GCHQ. Do we know what's happening chatter-wise?" Pritchard asked.

"I had a briefing with them yesterday," said Caroline Connolly, Head of Digital Intelligence Operations. "It echoed what we've been hearing, that there's a lot of chatter at the moment. But then there usually is at this time of year. Nothing specific, but just a general sense that something big is being planned for the holiday season. The chatter is very general and there's every chance it's wishful thinking."

"Are they talking about particular venues?" asked Pritchard.

Connolly shook her head. "London has been mentioned, but so have cities across the UK. There's also chatter about Germany, Sweden, France and even Australia. As I said, nothing specific, just an anticipation that something is brewing."

The meeting went on for another fifteen minutes. No vote was taken but there was a clear consensus that at the meeting proper the threat level in the UK would be raised to critical. Northern Ireland had its own threat level and the feeling was that it should remain at substantial.

On the way to the lifts, Pritchard found himself next to Commander Burgess. "Any plans for New Year's Eve?" asked the Commander.

"A chicken tikka masala, bottle of lager and the TV," said Pritchard.

"Seriously?"

Pritchard shrugged. "I'm not a big one for crowds," he said. "Unless I'm monitoring them on CCTV. And there's always the worry that something might happen on New Year's Eve."

"We've been lucky so far," said the Commander.

"Yeah, it's the old IRA thing, isn't it? We have to be lucky all the time, the bad guys only have to be lucky once."

"Well the Irish have gone quiet. I get the feeling they're wanting to see how Brexit works out."

"You mean a united Ireland might fall into their laps?"

Burgess shrugged. "It's a possibility, so they don't want to spoil what chance there is by setting off bombs. But that drone thing is a worry, isn't it?"

"Just one of many," said Pritchard. "We've got just under seven hundred active investigations, mainly British-born jihadists, but it all seems to be under control." He smiled ruefully and reached over to tap a door frame. "Touch wood."

"Why not take a night off, then?" said the Commander. "Come along to New Scotland Yard. We've got this huge terrace over-looking the river, we get a great view of the fireworks." He grinned. "And there's champagne and canapés."

"How does that get budgeted for?" he asked.

The commander chuckled. "You'd have to ask the commissioner about that," he said. "But seriously, you should come. Shall I put your name down?"

Pritchard paused. "Why not? Yes, okay, thanks."

"Significant other?"

"Sorry, what?"

"Do you want to bring anyone?"

Pritchard shook his head and smiled. "No, just me."

"You'll be on the list," said the commander. "People start coming from about ten onwards."

Nadia shook her head. "No, I don't recognise anybody. Sorry." She was sitting at one of the desks with Shepherd and Zarah either side of her. They were showing her surveillance pictures of a group of Asian men training at an outdoor gym in a park in west London.

"Don't worry, you're doing fine," said Shepherd.

"But I'm not, am I? You're showing me hundreds of photographs and I'm not recognising anybody."

"It's a slow process, we understand that," said Shepherd. "Most of the pictures we're showing you weren't taken in Birmingham, and only a very small percentage of the people we have files on left the country for training. And of those that did, only a few went for training in Syria."

"It's like looking for a needle in a haystack," said Zarah. "It's a very big haystack with only a few needles."

"It just feels like I'm wasting your time," said Nadia.

There was a knock on the door. Giles Pritchard opened it and nodded at Shepherd. "Can I have a quick word?" he said. He flashed Zarah a smile as Shepherd stood up and headed out into the corridor. Pritchard pulled the door closed. "Just so you know, the threat level is being raised to critical on the back of this investigation." He was carrying a sports bag with a compartment for a racket.

"It makes sense, they're clearly getting ready for whatever it is they have planned."

"How is Nadia coming along?"

Shepherd grimaced. "Not great, it has to be said. I mean, she's very willing and is doing her best, but she's nowhere near as effective as Jaraf would have been. Jaraf could have given us names and would know for sure which of the men he had trained had returned to the UK." He saw the look of annoyance flash across Pritchard's face and he raised a hand. "I'm not crying over spilled milk, I'm just saying that it's going to take time."

"I'm not sure that we have time," said Pritchard. "There's chatter that something big is planned, and that chatter isn't confined to the UK."

"That's the other worry, isn't it? Jaraf said that guys he'd trained had gone back to Germany and to Sweden. Nadia's going to be no help there."

"That's true, but as I've already said once today, we have to play the cards we're dealt. Is she any use at all?"

"Oh yes, no question. She's identified two of the guys who were photographed in Ali Karim's storage locker. And she does remember Hasan Mahmoud talking about a guy called Ali Karim. But we already had him in our sights."

"And the guy who gave Karim the Semtex?"

Shepherd shook his head. "No, she didn't recognise him. What's happening with Mahmoud?"

"He's not on any of our databases, and he's most definitely not been an agent. I've also received confirmation from the top of Six that he has never worked for them. They have had officers using the name Roger many times, but never for operations in Syria or Turkey. The last time it was used as an alias in the Middle East was Iraq at the time of Desert Storm."

"So what now?"

"I'm running the name and details through Europol and our allies in the Five Eyes, but nothing has come back so far." The Five Eyes was an intelligence-sharing alliance between the United Kingdom, the United States, Canada, Australia and New Zealand. He looked at his watch. "I've got to go."

"Tennis?" said Shepherd, nodding at the sports bag.

"Squash," said Pritchard. "Do you play?"

"I'm not a great one for knocking a ball around," said Shepherd.

Anwar Rafiq unwrapped the lamb kebab and took a bite, then sat down and switched on his computer. The sky was darkening outside but he had left his curtains open. He had a glass of water on the table next to him and he took a sip, before entering his password and opening Gmail. There was a new message in the draft email folder. It was headed with the phrase "Slow Burn" in Arabic. "*Yes, you are to proceed as planned. Alhamdulillah.*"

May Allah be with you. Rafiq smiled to himself. He had absolutely no doubt that Allah was with him, because everything he did was for the glory of Allah.

424

Every infidel he killed brought joy to Allah, the Giver of Life and the Bringer of Death.

He took another bite of his kebab and then opened a new draft email, this one for Muktar Kamel in Leeds. He knew that Muktar would be equally pleased that after all the months of planning and training, the time had finally come to act.

Pritchard had started playing squash at university, mainly to get close to a girl he fancied. He soon tired of the girl but he had grown to love squash, partly as a means of keeping fit, but mainly because of the complexity of the game. It was as much about strategy as it was about stamina and technique, and a wily old player could often beat a young enthusiastic opponent by out-thinking rather than out-running them. Joel Schwartz was a wily player, and some, and generally he would win three or four out of the five games in a match with Pritchard. Pritchard generally won the first game, but Schwartz almost always won the second and third by outplaying him. What happened after that usually depended on what the purpose of the meeting was. If Schwartz wanted something from Pritchard, he'd usually let him win the last two games. Not by much, but Pritchard would win. If it was Pritchard who was asking for a favour, Schwartz would play hard and usually win. His nickname was the Black Fox, and there was definitely something foxlike about the man. He was small with pointed features and a laugh that was more akin to a bark than a human sound. He had thinning black hair that he combed back to cover a growing bald patch, and his nails were bitten to the quick. Schwartz didn't drink or smoke and nail-biting was his only stress-relieving habit. Joel Schwartz was under a lot of stress, Pritchard was sure of that.

They got to the sports club at about the same time, though Pritchard was sure that the Israeli had been waiting close by, just to check that Pritchard had arrived alone. The two men checked each other out as they changed, and Pritchard made a point of doing a full three-sixty. They both had Head rackets, though Schwartz's was much older and had been re-strung dozens of times. Pritchard tended to just buy a new racket every few years and the present one had a fluorescent green frame, green strings and a black grip. Schwartz's clothing was also old — a grey sweatshirt with loose threads around the collar, and baggy black shorts, with Nike trainers that must have been ten years old or more. Pritchard's shirt and shorts were almost new, as were his Reeboks.

They spent five minutes warming up, then they got down to the game. Pritchard could tell that Schwartz was taking it easy, though he made Pritchard run for every victory. Pritchard won the first game 11-6 and his shirt was damp with sweat by the end. They went straight into the second game. Pritchard was fit enough that he could reach any spot on the court from the T in two steps, so his game plan was to dominate the T and return every shot until his opponent made a mistake.

Schwartz played a different game, more like a chess player looking ahead two or more moves. He rarely went to the T; he favoured being further back, closer to the wall. He kept his shots high and to the side, meaning that Pritchard was forever running back to get the ball, and Schwartz would place it so that Pritchard struggled to hit it hard. Schwartz rarely took more than one step to a shot — if any more were needed, he would just let the ball go. By conserving his energy, he stayed relatively fresh while the sweat stains on Pritchard's shirt continued to spread. Schwartz won the second game 11-8 and the two men sat down on the floor to get their breath back.

"So how can I help you, my friend?" said Schwartz. "Other than by offering you advice on your backhand volley."

Pritchard chuckled. "Time's on my side, Joel," he said. "The older you get, the slower you get."

"And the smarter I get," said Schwartz. "I'll be retired and back in Jerusalem by the time you start beating me."

"Are you thinking about retirement?" asked Pritchard.

"Who said anything about retirement? I'm only fifteen years older than you, Giles." He shook his head. "No, I want to be back home. London is too stressful for me, especially when there was a chance that Britain would have an anti-Semite leading the country." He shuddered. "That man and his hateful party. You know if Corbyn had won, almost half the Jews in the UK were going to pack up and leave. And with good reason."

"Water under the bridge," said Pritchard. "Anyway, we have a problem. A big problem, and all the signs are that your people are involved. We had one of our informers abducted from a house in Hereford yesterday. And we have a positive identification of one of the people involved: Leah Levy."

"That's a common name," said Schwartz.

"Yes, it is. But this Leah Levy is twenty-nine years old, born in Tel Aviv, and she was a frequent visitor to the Israeli Embassy in London two years ago."

"So MI5 spies on Israel's embassy? That's no way to treat a friend, is it?"

"We monitor comings and goings at all embassies," said Pritchard. "As I'm sure you do in your own country. We haven't managed to find a Leah Levy on your embassy staff lists and she doesn't have diplomatic privilege, but we are reasonably sure that she works for Mossad."

Schwartz smiled. "Reasonably sure wouldn't get you a conviction in court."

"No it wouldn't. But we both know what went down in Hereford, Joel. A Mossad team kidnapped a Palestinian man who was offering to supply MI5 with information on home-grown jihadists active in the United Kingdom. And it looks to us that Leah Levy identified the location of said intelligence source by pretending to be his wife."

Schwartz shrugged but didn't say anything.

"We took Miss Levy to the house where the informer was staying, along with a boy we believed to be his son, only to have her produce a gun at the same time as a number of armed men burst in. We believe those men also worked for Mossad."

428

"Again, I doubt that you have enough evidence to get a court conviction."

"This isn't a criminal case, Joel. And I doubt that either of us will benefit from the details appearing in open court."

"So what do you want me to say, Giles?"

"I'm hoping that you'll tell me that Jaraf is alive and that you're interrogating him. And if that's the case then I'm hoping you'll say that you're prepared to share any pertinent intelligence with me."

Schwartz grimaced. "I'm sorry, my friend. Jaraf was dead within an hour of being taken from the house. Dead and buried."

Pritchard frowned. "So why didn't you kill him at the house?"

"They were doing you a favour. Saving you any embarrassment. He was in the country unofficially — with no body, who's to say it ever happened?"

"You didn't seem to be worried about that when your people tried to poison him at the airport."

"We weren't sure that our plan B would work at that point," he said. "Poisoning seemed to be the best option." He smiled apologetically. "And yes, the guy with an Uzi on the back of a motorbike wasn't our proudest moment. But things were moving quickly at that point."

"But when you knew that Jaraf was trying to bring his wife and son over, you knew you could take your time? Is that what happened?"

"We had them in the camp for at least a month before he knew they were there. He knew if he stayed in

Syria we would get him there, so once he knew his family was safe he ran to London. We followed him and when you put him in the airport hotel we saw there was a chance to end it then and we took it. Once you were aware that someone wanted him dead, we had to throttle back and wait for plan B."

"And all this effort, all this manpower, was just to kill a single ISIS instructor?"

Schwartz flashed him a tight smile. "My friend, you have no idea."

"So educate me. Explain why you would go to all this trouble for one man."

Schwartz nodded slowly. "You know Jaraf as an ISIS instructor, a terrorist who has probably trained dozens of your own people to wreak havoc in the UK. But what you probably don't know is that before ISIS he was with Hezbollah. He started as a teenager throwing rocks and petrol bombs at Israeli troops, then graduated to IEDs and then to drones. He cut his teeth on drones in the West Bank, killing our people. The guy was a genius, he embraced drone technology in a way that no one else had. He killed four Israeli soldiers in separate attacks, and then started to go for high-value targets. Two years ago he killed one of our generals, along with his wife and family. Like all our high-value targets, the general travelled in a bulletproof and bombproof vehicle. Jaraf flew a drone with an IED over the car as it stopped outside their house after they had visited their local synagogue. It killed the general, his wife and their two young daughters. Jaraf fled back to the West Bank. The decision was then taken at the

430

highest level for Kidon to assassinate Jaraf by whatever means necessary."

"So why didn't you get him in the West Bank?"

"We tried. And failed. He was being protected by a Hezbollah security team and they died protecting him. Jaraf ran, and he took his wife and son with him. He ended up in Syria and figured that we'd never be able to get him if he was protected by ISIS. So he offered them his services, in exchange for protection." Schwartz smiled thinly. "He was wrong. It wasn't easy, and it took time, but we tracked him to the camp in Syria. We couldn't send in a team, obviously, but we passed on the intel to the Americans at the highest level and they sent in a Reaper. It was daytime and we were damn sure it was him that was targeted, but there was a cock-up and Jaraf escaped. He ran, leaving his wife and son behind." He chuckled. "They always leave their women and children behind, do you notice that? They run like dogs and care only for themselves." He shook his head. "Real men stay to protect their wives and children, but men like Jaraf . . . what are they? Even animals defend their own. Anyway, he fled and moved from camp to camp. We continued to track him and there were two more drone strikes, but again he was lucky. He realised that we would get him eventually so he kept moving west and ended up in the Emirates. We tracked him there and we were about to move on him when he boarded a plane to London."

"And by then you had your own people posing as his wife and son?"

Schwartz nodded. "It was easy enough to do. The original idea was that he would go to the camp to get them, but once he ran to the UK we realised that he would almost certainly ask for the British to bring them over as part of any deal he was able to arrange."

"And his real wife and son?"

Schwartz shrugged carelessly. "Dead. After the initial strike, the Reaper destroyed the camp and they died then. You've seen the damage a Hellfire missile can do. There isn't much left to identify."

"So you faked Palestinian passports for Leah Levy and the boy and got them into the camp?"

"It wasn't difficult."

"And the boy? Is he Leah's son?"

Schwartz grinned. "Of course not. He's older than he looks. Nineteen going on twenty, but he can pass for fourteen or fifteen. Not for much longer, though. He's the son of one of Kidon's stalwarts and destined for great things."

"So that's it? It's over?"

"We wanted Jaraf dead and he is dead. Leah and the rest of the team flew out of the country last night and are already back in Tel Aviv being congratulated on a job well done. And the world has one less terrorist to worry about." He shrugged. "All's well that ends well." He got to his feet and began swinging his racket around.

"Except all's not well," said Pritchard. "Jaraf was going to tell us the names of home-grown jihadists who are now back in the UK."

Schwartz stopped swinging his racket and turned to face Pritchard. "You see that's what I don't understand, my friend," he said. "Why you British allow these scumbags back into your country? You know they are terrorists, you know they wish you harm, but time and time again you welcome them back."

"It's not as simple as that," said Pritchard.

"Oh but it is," said Schwartz. "It's not as if you are averse to killing your enemies. You send SAS and SBS hit squads out to Syria and Afghanistan and Iraq with instructions to kill your own citizens. You accept the fact that they are enemy combatants and treat them accordingly. And yet when they come back to the UK . . ." He shrugged. "Were you in London when that bastard went berserk near London Bridge?"

Pritchard nodded. "Usman Khan."

"Yes, exactly. Usman Khan. In 2012 you put him in prison for terrorist offences. So you tell me, my friend, how does someone you put away for terrorism offences end up going on a killing spree wearing a fake suicide vest? And what about Sudesh Amman? You put him away because you know he's planning a terrorist attack. You let him out after just thirteen months and he puts on a fake suicide vest and starts stabbing people in Streatham High Road. He then gets shot dead by armed police who were following him because they were warned that his extremist views hadn't changed. Why would anyone think he wasn't a danger, Giles? People like that need to be locked away forever. Or put to death like the animals they are."

"I get the point you're making, Joel."

433

"Do you?" said Schwartz, his eyes narrowing. "Do you really? You had these people, you had them behind bars, you know exactly who they are and what they are capable of, and still they're allowed to murder civilians in cold blood. I don't know much about Salam Jaraf but I know one thing for sure."

"That he won't be committing any more acts of terrorism?"

Schwartz grinned. "Exactly." He patted Pritchard on the shoulder. "The world is a better place without Salam Jaraf in it," he said. "So far as the other jihadists are concerned, you need to be dealing with them as soon as they appear on your radar and not depend on some child-killing Arab to do your job for you." He tightened his grip on Pritchard's shoulder.

"I hear what you're saying," said Pritchard. "But by killing Jaraf, you've made my life a lot harder, and put a lot of British lives at risk."

Schwartz kept his hand on Pritchard's shoulder as he looked him in the eyes. "And for that I apologise, my friend. Which is not something that Mossad does lightly. So I owe you one. I owe you a favour. A big favour. Yours to call in when you need it."

Pritchard forced a smile. "Thank you."

"Meanwhile, can I offer you some advice?"

"Sure."

Schwartz let go of Pritchard's shoulder. "When you're going for a backhand shot and the ball is below your knee, turn your shoulder more. Think of it as a golf swing rather than a cricket stroke."

Pritchard grinned and nodded. "Got you. Thanks."

434

"Always a pleasure, my friend," said Schwartz. "Now let's continue with the game."

Harry Fletcher was sitting on the sofa with his feet on the coffee table, munching on celery and carrot sticks as he watched a Netflix movie. It wasn't great and part of him wanted to find something else to watch, but he was tired and couldn't be bothered picking up the remote. He was wearing boxer shorts and a dressing gown and hadn't got around to taking off his socks.

There was a knock on the door and he frowned. Visitors had to press a button at the entrance and be buzzed in. He put his plate of vegetables on the coffee table and walked over to the front door. He peered through the security viewer and his frown deepened. There were two Asian girls outside, one with short black hair, the other with long hair, dyed blonde.

He opened the door. "Charlie!" said the blonde. She barely reached up to Fletcher's shoulders, even with her three-inch heels. She was wearing a bright red coat with black buttons and had a Chanel bag with a gold chain over her shoulder.

"Yes?" So they wanted Charlie Warner, which meant they had come from the agency. But he hadn't booked them and he couldn't think why they had turned up on his doorstep.

"Jasmine sent us," said the other girl. She was wearing a coat that was almost as black and glossy as her hair. She was also carrying a designer bag, Prada.

"There's some mistake," he said. "I didn't make a booking."

The two girls moved towards him and he took an involuntary step backwards, then another. Before he realised what had happened they had stepped inside and the blonde had back-heeled the door closed. "I'm Candy," she said, taking off her coat and tossing it onto a chair. She was wearing a low-cut black dress with a zipper that ran from her cleavage down to the hem. She began to slowly pull down the zip, releasing her full breasts.

"And I'm Sandy," said the other one.

"We're sisters," said Candy. The zipper reached her navel.

Fletcher didn't believe that for one minute, but they did look similar. High cheekbones, tiny white teeth, perfect unblemished skin that he knew would be soft to the touch.

"Ladies, you really have been misinformed," he said. "I didn't . . ."

Candy squatted, pulled down his boxer shorts and took him in her mouth in one smooth movement.

"Oh my God . . ." said Fletcher.

Sandy ran her hand along his stomach and then up his chest. She gently stroked his right nipple as she smiled up at him. "Jasmine said we were to make you happy," she said.

"I . . . I . . . it's . . ." He tried to speak but what Candy was doing with her mouth made it almost impossible for him to gather his thoughts.

Sandy took off her coat and threw it on top of Candy's. She was wearing a tiny white top and an equally tiny white miniskirt. There was a tattoo of a dragon winding around her left leg, breathing fire from its mouth. She moved so that he could get a better view. "You like?" she asked.

Fletcher tried to speak but the words caught in his throat, so he just nodded.

Candy stood up, licking her lips. "You taste good," she said.

She held him between the legs and pulled him towards the sofa. "Why did Jasmine send you?" he said, his voice a hoarse whisper. He had grown so hard that he had trouble walking, coupled with the fact that his boxers were now halfway down his thighs.

"She wants us to make you happy," said Sandy.

They pushed him down onto the sofa. Sandy knelt down between his legs and took him in her mouth, continuing from where Candy had left off.

"Are we making you happy?" asked Candy, unzipping her dress all the way down to the hem, and then shrugging it off. It fell onto the floor. Fletcher gasped. Her skin was faultless and she was completely shaved, totally hairless.

"Oh my God," he said.

She laughed and as Sandy moved away, Candy straddled him and kissed him on the lips. "Do you want me to fuck you?" she whispered in his ear.

"Oh my God, yes."

"Are you sure?"

He slipped his hands around her back and pulled her against him. "Yes," he said.

"Beg me," she said. "Beg me to put you inside me."

He felt a sharp pain in his leg, just above his knee. "Ow!" he said. "What was that?"

Candy said something to Sandy in Chinese, and Sandy replied. Candy smiled down at Fletcher. "All done," she said. She bent down and kissed him on the forehead.

"What do you mean all done?" asked Fletcher. He was feeling suddenly tired and his hands were numb as he reached up for Candy's breasts.

"I mean *you're* done, you fat fuck," said Candy.

She slid off Fletcher and started putting her dress back on. Sandy was grinning at him. In her right hand was a hypodermic syringe. It was empty. "What?" he said. He tried to say more but he was losing the feeling in his lips.

Sandy put a cap on the needle and then dropped it into her Prada bag.

Fletcher tried to get to his feet and he almost made it, then the strength faded from his legs and he fell back. The two girls stood together and looked down at him, smiling as he passed out.

Shepherd arrived at Thames House just after eight o'clock in the morning. He'd walked from his Battersea apartment, figuring he needed all the exercise he could get. The office was empty so he went to the canteen where Nadia and Zarah were sitting by the window eating breakfast. "We made an early start," said Zarah. She was wearing a black shawl over a long blue denim dress and had on a dark blue hijab.

438

"I couldn't sleep," said Nadia, who was eating a fruit yoghurt. "So I asked Zarah if we could start at five."

"We're working through as much of the Birmingham surveillance videos as we can," said Zarah. "Nadia has recognised several faces from her mosque, but no one else from Syria yet."

"It'll take time," said Shepherd. "But we'll get there." He gestured at the counter. "I'll get some food and join you," he said.

"Actually, I was wondering if I could pop home and change," said Zarah. "I don't live far away."

"Of course, no problem," said Shepherd.

"Will you be okay on your own?" Zarah asked Nadia.

"It's okay." She looked earnestly at Shepherd. "You'll be with me, right?"

He smiled reassuringly. "I'm not going anywhere," he said. He laughed. "Actually, that's not true, I'll leave you to get some breakfast and then I'll be right back."

He went over to the counter and ordered scrambled eggs on toast and a mug of coffee. When he got back to the table, Zarah finished her coffee and headed out, promising to be back as quickly as possible.

Nadia laughed as Shepherd started eating his eggs. "What's funny?" he asked.

"I was just thinking about a guy Hasan used to tell me about. His name was Nazam. Nazam was always complaining about the food at the camp. I mean, always. He'd been there for something like three months before I arrived and Hasan said he moaned at every meal. He really hated the eggs they had in the camp. Hasan said he always claimed they weren't from chickens, he said he thought they were goat eggs and nobody knew if he was serious or not. I mean, he had a point, the food was really bad. I didn't meet Nazam but I did meet one of his friends once. Mo, his name was. There were so many Mohammeds there that they called him Mo-D. Mohammed Desai." She frowned. "Where was he from? He had a London accent, I remember that. He always said he had trouble with the Brummie accent but in my mind he was the one who talked funny. Tower Hamlets, that's where he was from, I think. Is that a place in London? Tower Hamlets?"

"It sure is," said Shepherd. The borough of Tower Hamlets was on the north of the River Thames, to the east of the City of London, and included much of the redeveloped Docklands areas. The Canary Wharf financial district was in Tower Hamlets, along with some of the country's highest paid bankers. But the near three hundred thousand population was on average the poorest in London and had the highest unemployment rate in the city. Muslims accounted for almost forty per cent of the population of Tower Hamlets compared with a national figure of five per cent, and there were over forty mosques in the borough. Local schools were often at the centre of allegations of extremism and it wasn't unusual to see ISIS flags and banners openly displayed on council estates. The Bethnal Green Academy in Tower Hamlets became notorious when Shamima Begum and two other girls from the school flew to Syria to join ISIS, but the borough had long been a source of fighters and jihadist brides.

"I'm pretty sure that Hasan said he went back to Tower Hamlets."

"Who? Mo-D or Nazam?"

"I think they went back together. They were both from Tower Hamlets but they didn't have the same accent. I think Nazam was born in Pakistan and moved to England when he was a kid."

She finished her yoghurt and spread strawberry jam on a piece of toast as Shepherd tucked into his scrambled eggs.

"The early birds," said a voice and they looked up to see Giles Pritchard holding two packs of sandwiches and an orange.

"Nadia was here at five," said Shepherd.

"I'm impressed," said Pritchard. He held up his purchases. "Breakfast at my desk."

"Nadia has just come up with two more names," said Shepherd, and he explained about Nazam and Mohammed Desai.

"I'll get them checked out," said Pritchard. He smiled at Nadia. "Well done."

"Have you managed to find Hasan?" asked Nadia.

"I'm afraid not," said Pritchard. "But believe me, we're looking." He gestured with his chin at Shepherd. "Can I have a quick word?"

"Sure," said Shepherd. "Excuse me, Nadia." The two men walked away from the table.

"I had a very interesting chat with Mossad's man in London last night," said Pritchard. "They were behind Jaraf's abduction and, I'm afraid to say, his murder."

441

"What?" The news hit Shepherd like a punch to the solar plexus. It was the last thing he'd expected to hear.

"They tried to kill him at the hotel, but they had a plan B lined up. The woman and teenager we thought were his family were actually Mossad agents. We took them straight to Jaraf."

"But what did Mossad have against Jaraf?"

"Before he was at the ISIS training camp, he was active on the West Bank, organising drone attacks against Israel. In one of those attacks he killed an Israeli general and his family. Including two young girls. The Israelis wanted revenge, and as you know, they don't fuck around."

"Is that why Jaraf was so keen to get asylum in the UK? He wanted to hide from Mossad?"

"That's what the timeline suggests. He fled the West Bank and sought sanctuary with ISIS. He probably thought that he'd be safe from Mossad there, but then the camp was attacked and he realised he was still in danger. He makes his way to Dubai and decides that his best bet is the UK. Mossad had their plan B in place and Jaraf learns that his wife and kid are in the camp in Turkey."

"So what's happened to the real Mrs Jaraf and the boy?"

"I was told they died in the drone attack on the camp."

"Or they reached the camp and Mossad . . ." Shepherd left the sentence unfinished.

442

"I like to think it was the former," said Pritchard. "Anyway, all the principals are out of the country now. It's over."

"And we can't extradite from Israel?"

"They generally don't extradite their citizens. But in this case, I don't think we'll be requesting her extradition."

"So she gets away with murder? It's bad enough they killed Jaraf, but the Border Force officer was a total innocent in all this."

"It was an accident."

Shepherd shook his head. "Poisoning a burger isn't an accident."

"I'm afraid in this case we have to look at the bigger picture," said Pritchard. "The Israelis are our allies."

"They used Tasers on my friends."

"They could have used guns."

"That's your answer?" Shepherd sighed and shook his head in frustration.

"I understand how you feel. But a court case would open up a whole can of worms; about Jaraf, about our policy on asylum for former terrorists, and about foreign intelligence services operating on British soil. Some stones are best left unturned."

He turned and headed for the door. Shepherd went back to the table and sat down opposite Nadia, who was staring after Pritchard. "I don't understand why they're having such trouble finding Hasan," she said thoughtfully. She turned to look at Shepherd. "He was working for MI5, so why don't they know where he is?"

"It's a big organisation, with a lot of separate departments," said Shepherd. "Sometimes the right hand doesn't know what the left hand is doing. Also, if he's still in Syria, he might not be contactable."

"I'm worried about him," said Nadia.

Shepherd flashed her a smile but couldn't think of anything to say that would make her feel better. Going missing in a war zone usually ended badly.

He finished his eggs and washed them down with what was left of his coffee. "Okay," he said. "Back to work?"

Yusuf Butt opened his holdall and took out the drone. Mohammed Desai and Nazam Miah followed his example, placing their drones on the long metal table. They were in a plumbing supplies warehouse owned by Miah's father. All the employees had been given two weeks off over Christmas and New Year, so the warehouse was empty.

Desai connected a soldering iron to an electrical socket. He would be doing all the electrical work — he had the steadiest hands. But they were all able to prepare the IEDs, following the training they had been given in Syria.

Butt picked up the holdall containing the Semtex and put it onto the table. He took out the blocks of explosive and the detonators, and three second-hand Apple Watches. "Right, brothers, you know what we have to do," he said. "Exactly as Jaraf taught us."

The Semtex had to be sliced and gently formed into a flat disc about two inches thick. Screws, nails and washers were then pressed into the explosive until it was completely covered by metal. It wasn't the explosive itself that did the damage, it was the deadly shrapnel that ripped through bone and flesh. The three men worked slowly and carefully as they prepared the explosives and wrapped them in grey duct tape.

Next they worked on the Apple Watches. Each watch had a virtual SIM card that allowed it to make and receive calls. Butt had purchased three pay-as-you-go SIM cards and transferred the details to the watches. Butt and Miah stood and watched as Desai prepared the circuits, wiring a detonator and a nine-volt battery into the watch's interior. It was fiddly and he had to use a magnifying glass on a stand to see what he was doing, but eventually all three were done. Once the watch was called, it would close the circuit and the detonator would explode.

The next stage was to use duct tape to strap the watch and battery to the explosive, and then use more tape to fix the package to the underside of the drone. The three men worked slowly and methodically, Jaraf had drummed it into them that it was not a job to be rushed. When they had all finished. Butt inspected the drones prepared by Miah and Desai. He studied them carefully and nodded his approval. "Nice work, brothers," he said. The detonators on all three IEDs were lying next to the drones, each connected by two wires. They wouldn't be inserted into the explosive until the last moment. Butt patted Miah on the shoulder. "What do you think, bruv? Can we leave them here? Or is anybody likely to come in?"

"The staff are away until Wednesday, the only reason anyone would come in would be if the alarms went off."

"We don't have to turn the alarms on, do we?"

"Fuck me, bruv, my dad'll hit the roof if we get robbed."

Butt chuckled. "Bruv, burglars don't work over New Year, don't you know that?" He waved at the drones. "Is there somewhere out of the way we can leave these?"

Miah nodded. "There's a cupboard in the toilet for cleaning supplies. The cleaner definitely won't be coming in."

"Perfect," said Butt. They carefully put the drones in the hold-alls, and Butt packed away the soldering iron, the spare wire and what was left of the Semtex.

Miah showed them where the bathroom was and they stored the holdalls in a walk-in cupboard containing buckets, mops and cleaning fluid.

"That's us done, brothers," said Butt, closing the cupboard door. "In two days we'll change this country forever. No one's ever going to forget what we're going to do."

The three men grinned and hugged.

Giles Pritchard was sitting at his desk organising surveillance on two of the names that Nadia had provided: Nazam and Mohammed Desai. Both men were known to MI5, but only because of tip-offs received. MI5 ran an anti-terrorist hotline where members of the public could phone in information, anonymously if necessary.

Pritchard searched the MI5 database for "Nazam" and "Tower Hamlets" and immediately found a Nazam Miah. A worshipper at Miah's local mosque phoned in to say that Miah had been boasting about going to Syria for jihad training. The worshipper didn't want to leave his name but said that Miah was often seen in the company of two men who had gone on to be killed in Syria. On checking, Pritchard found that the two other men he had named had actually been killed by an SAS hit team, sent out to Syria with a list of home-grown jihadists that the government would rather didn't return to the UK. MI5 had taken a look at Miah but decided there was nothing to merit putting him under surveillance. Just because a man associated with terrorists didn't automatically make them a terrorist, too — if that were the case, half the population of Belfast would be behind bars.

The information on Mohammed Desai was equally nebulous, a phoned-in allegation that he and his father had been raising funds to send to ISIS fighters in Syria. The father owned several corner shops. MI5's financial intelligence unit had checked out the family's business and personal accounts but had found no evidence of irregularities. No evidence didn't necessarily mean an absence of guilt. The problem was that many Muslims used the hawala system to transfer money around the world, using a network of middlemen who functioned as hawala brokers or *hawaladars*. Everything was based on trust and no records were kept — it was the perfect system for terrorist groups. The allegation had been left on file but no further action had been taken.

The full details of both Mohammed Desai and Nazam Miah were on the system, so Pritchard made them a priority for surveillance. He was having less luck with the two other names that Nadia had come up with: Latif Shaikh and Gulzar Noor. Neither was on MI5's databases, or the Police National Computer, and despite what Nadia had said about them going to Syria, neither man had applied for a British passport. They could well have applied under different names, but tracking them down was going to be difficult. He was leaning back in his chair, considering his options, when his phone rang.

"He looks familiar," said Nadia. She was leaning forward and pointing at a man on a surveillance video that Zarah was showing her. It had been taken in a park and five Asian men in hoodies and tracksuit bottoms were standing by a bench. One was doing leg stretches, another was touching his toes and the three others were talking. The man Nadia was pointing at was in his thirties with a neatly-trimmed beard. He was laughing at something one of the other men had said.

Zarah clicked on the mouse to freeze the video and give Nadia a better look. "What do you think?" she asked.

448

Shepherd was standing at the window looking out over the Thames. He turned and went over to the desk.

"It's from a surveillance operation in south London two weeks ago," said Zarah. "Morden Park."

Nadia wrinkled her nose. "I think I remember him. It's hard to say with the hood up."

"Did you talk to him?" asked Shepherd. "Did Hasan mention him?"

"No. But I'm pretty sure I saw him in the camp, not long after I arrived. Remember I told you we were taken to a tent and then men came and dragged the girls out? He was one of the first in the tent. He tried to grab me but I told him to fuck off and I think he was so shocked that I spoke English that he took another girl instead."

"Do we know him?" Shepherd asked Zarah.

"No, unfortunately not. The guy touching his toes is in Belmarsh for planning terrorist acts and the guy stretching is a poppy-burner and has been fined for vandalising a church." She pointed at the man standing next to the one Nadia had recognised. "This guy is the one who sparked off the surveillance. He spent six months in Syria fighting with ISIS."

"Training, you mean?"

Zarah shook her head. "No, he was already trained. He did four years with the Duke of Lancaster's Regiment. He apparently underwent a conversion at some point, became a Muslim and enlisted with ISIS in Syria."

Shepherd frowned. "So why wasn't he arrested and thrown in prison?"

449

"I think the feeling is that by watching him we'll be able to identify other jihadists. His phone and computer are being monitored, but so far he hasn't put a foot wrong."

Shepherd's mobile rang. It was Pritchard. "Are you in the building?" he asked.

"Sure," said Shepherd.

"Pop along to my office, will you," said Pritchard. "We need to talk."

Pritchard's secretary was at her desk and she waved for Shepherd to go straight in. Pritchard was standing at the window, looking out. "Sit down, Daniel," he said, waving at the sofa without turning around.

Shepherd sat down and Pritchard joined him. From the look on the man's face it was clear that something was wrong. Very wrong.

"Harry Fletcher is dead," said Pritchard, crossing his legs and smoothing out the creases of his trousers.

Shepherd's jaw dropped. "What happened?"

"It's been made to look like suicide. He's naked on his sofa with a plastic bag on his head and child porn playing on his laptop."

"What?"

"It was the Chinese obviously. The three escort agency websites have all shut down and the Knightsbridge flat is empty. They've bolted."

"And Mei-feng?"

"We're expecting the worst, obviously. They'll either have killed her or spirited her out of the country."

"They can't get away with this," said Shepherd.

"That's a nice sound bite, but this is the real world," said Pritchard. "Somehow they found out that Mei-feng was going to betray them, so they've taken her out and killed Charlie Warner as a warning to us."

"How the hell did they get into the flat?"

"We don't know. But there are no signs of a struggle."

"What about the video surveillance?"

"They used some sort of a jammer. There's a possibility we might get footage from the entrance to the building, but these guys are professional so I won't be holding my breath."

Shepherd sat back and looked up at the ceiling. "What do we do?"

"I'm sorry, I don't think there's anything we can do. Mei-feng must have slipped up, and she and Harry have paid the price."

"We can't let them get away with killing an MI5 officer."

"I'm as angry and frustrated as you are, but the people responsible will already be out of the country. We've lost this battle, but there'll be others. What we need to do now is to concentrate on these jihadists."

Shepherd nodded, but he was still thinking about Harry Fletcher. And Mei-feng.

"Okay?" asked Pritchard.

Shepherd snapped back to reality. Pritchard was right. The job in hand had to be his priority. The Chinese could wait. "I'm okay," he said.

* * *

Abdullah Rahman kept the black Honda hatchback at a steady seventy miles an hour. The last thing he wanted was to be caught speeding. A photograph on a speed camera would be bad enough, but it would be a nightmare if an unmarked police car flagged them down. Three young Asian men on their way to London with three explosive-packed drones in the back — they'd throw away the key.

"So where are we are staying tonight?" asked Waheed Choudary, who as always was sitting in the back.

"I've booked us into the Premier Inn by the river," said Muktar Kamel. "It's the building that used to be County Hall apparently. I got us a good deal."

"Three rooms, right?" said Choudary.

"We ain't fucking royalty, bruv," said Kamel. "We've got a room with three beds."

"Fuck," said Choudary, folding his arms and staring at the traffic that was passing them by.

"Bruv, if you'd ever slept in an ISIS camp like me and Noodles, you wouldn't be moaning about a hotel room. Remember what we had to put up with, Noodles?"

"Yeah, it was rough," said Rahman. "Bloody cold at night, too."

"I thought you was in the desert," said Choudary.

"The desert gets fucking cold at night," said Rahman. "Cold enough to freeze your balls off." He looked across at Kamel. "What's the plan for tonight?"

"No plans, we can just eat and see the sights. We'll do a recce during the day tomorrow and then we'll see what it looks like at night."

452

"Do we get to do a practice run?" asked Choudary.

Kamel twisted around in his seat. "Are you fucking retarded, bruv?" he said. "How the fuck can we fly drones with explosives in London for practice? Do you not think that someone might see what we're doing and wonder what the fuck's going on?"

"I was just asking," said Choudary.

"Yeah, well don't ask stupid questions. We're only two days away from showing these infidels what true Muslims can do. Then when we've got their attention, they can be told to pull their troops out of all Muslim lands."

Choudary said nothing as he stared out of the side window.

"You hear me, bruv?" asked Kamel.

"Yeah, bruv, loud and clear."

"You're going to be a true hero, we all are," said Kamel, sitting back in his seat. "People will remember us forever."

Nadia kept yawning and was clearly having trouble keeping her eyes open. Shepherd looked at the clock on the wall. She'd spent more than twelve hours studying photographs, and Shepherd knew that they'd reached the point where continuing would be counterproductive. She was so tired she probably wouldn't even recognise a photograph of her own mother. "We should call it a day, Nadia," he said. "You've done really well."

"I'm okay, I can keep going."

"No, you need to rest." He looked over at Zarah. "Will you get someone to stay with Nadia tonight?" he asked.

"I'll do it," she said.

"You've been at it all day, and last night."

"And so has Nadia. If she can do it, so can I." She put her hand on Nadia's. "Shall we go and get something to eat and then you can shower and get some sleep?"

"Thank you," said Nadia. She looked tearfully at Shepherd. "I'll start again first thing," she said. "I won't let you down."

Zarah took Nadia by the hand and led her out of the office. Shepherd leaned back in his chair and ran his hands through his hair. He was dog-tired too. There was nothing physically demanding about sitting at a desk all day, but it was mentally exhausting doing nothing but looking at surveillance photographs. He stood up and stretched, went over to the window and looked out over the Thames. He could see Lambeth Palace directly ahead of him, picked out with floodlights, and the London Eye further down the river.

He thought about going to the canteen to eat, but realised that what he really wanted was to get some fresh air, so he decided to walk home. He took the lift down to the ground floor, went through reception and turned right along Millbank. He reached Chelsea Bridge and walked across it, the four towering white chimneys of what used to be Battersea Power Station to his left.

454

Shepherd reached the end of the bridge and turned right into Battersea Park. He was deep in thought but counter surveillance was something he did on auto-pilot, so he spotted the man in the trench coat loitering behind a tree the moment he stepped into the park. Not that the man was hiding; he was staring out over the Thames and smoking a small cigar. Shepherd walked towards the man, knowing that it couldn't have been a coincidence that Richard Yokely was in the park. Yokely was in his fifties and had spent half his life working for US Government departments known by their initials, though Shepherd knew that his prime role was with Grey Fox, a group that carried out missions for the president that were too sensitive to be handled officially.

Yokely didn't look around as Shepherd walked down the path, though Shepherd was sure that the American was aware of his presence. "Richard?" he said as he came up behind the man.

Yokely turned and feigned surprise. "Dan," he exclaimed. "What a surprise. Of all the parks in all the world, you had to walk into mine."

"To be fair now, this is my park." He gestured at his apartment block. "That's where I live, but I'm sure you know that."

Yokely grinned but didn't reply. He took a long pull on his cigar. Under the trench coat he was wearing a dark blue blazer, a crisp white shirt and a dark blue tie. As ever his black leather tasselled shoes were gleaming as if they had been freshly polished.

"So how can I help you, Richard?" Shepherd asked. "I'm assuming you want something."

"Do you mind if we walk?" asked Yokely. "I need to stretch my legs. I seem to spend half my life on planes these days."

"Sure. I've been at a desk most of today. I was thinking of going for a run."

"Do you still do that thing where you run with a rucksack of bricks on your back?"

Shepherd laughed. "Not so much."

"You look fit though," said Yokely. He patted his own stomach. "I need to exercise more but you know how it is these days."

"No rest for the wicked?"

Yokely laughed. "You never said a truer word." He started walking along the path that ran parallel to the river, towards a children's zoo. The American blew smoke at the river but the wind whipped it away immediately. "You've been lifting a lot of stones looking for Hasan Mahmoud, I gather," he said.

"We'd like to have a chat with him, yes," said Shepherd.

"I'm afraid that's not going to be possible," said Yokely. "It goes without saying that anything I tell you is off the record and totally deniable," he said.

"And yet still you say it," said Shepherd.

"Just laying down the ground rules," said Yokely. "This is very sensitive."

"If not awkward."

"Mahmoud's life is on the line here," said Yokely.

"So you've been running him?"

456

"Not me personally, no. But he's been a CIA asset for going on three years."

"I'm assuming this wasn't cleared with my bosses," said Shepherd.

Yokely blew smoke again. "You have to understand that the UK's political climate has been in a state of flux for some time, at least until the last election," he said. "There was every possibility that you might have had an anti-Semitic Trotskyist as prime minister, a man who seemed set on befriending every terrorist group on the planet, and that greatly concerned our president. Our intelligence agencies were tasked with making our own arrangements so that if the worst came to the worst we'd still have dependable intel."

"You were planning to stop cooperating with our agencies?"

Yokely took another pull on his cigar. "Orders from the White House," said Shepherd. "And to be honest, it was a fair point. Could we ever trust a man who was so clearly anti-Israel and pro-IRA? His views on disarmament alone meant we could never trust him. We needed our own intelligence sources in place."

"And so you recruited Hasan Mahmoud?"

"He was recruited, yes. At his mosque. He's smart, he's committed to British values and the British way of life, he's one of the good guys."

"Which begs the question, what's he doing working for Americans?"

Yokely flashed him a tight smile. "It's complicated," he said quietly.

Realisation dawned and Shepherd's eyes widened. "He doesn't know?"

Yokely flashed him another smile. "So long as he is working for the greater good, does it matter?"

"Actually, yes, it does," said Shepherd. He stopped walking. "So he was recruited under false pretences?"

Yokely turned to face him. "He wasn't told that his intel was being used by the CIA, that's true."

"And whoever approached him claimed that they were working for MI5?"

"That impression might well have been given," said Yokely.

Shepherd shook his head. "You duplicitous bastard," he said.

"Not me personally," said Yokely. "I'm just the middle man here. Reaching out to a friend to make sure that something bad doesn't happen to a valuable intel source."

"How valuable?" asked Shepherd.

"Mahmoud has been one of our greatest successes," said Yokely. "He helped us locate Abu Bakr al-Baghdadi, or at least gave us enough of a location that we were able to track him to the compound at Barisha."

"That whole operation to kill al-Baghdadi was down to Mahmoud?"

"He played a big part. He'd visited the compound with some high-ranking ISIS officers and managed to get word back to us."

"And he gave you intel on British jihadists he'd trained with?"

Yokely nodded but didn't say anything.

"And none of that intel was passed on to MI5?"

Yokely looked pained at the accusation. "Some was, if there was a way of passing it on without revealing our source."

The American started walking and Shepherd kept pace with him. "You realise what you're saying? The CIA has been withholding intel regarding possible terrorist attacks in the UK simply to protect a source?"

Yokely shrugged. "A source who led us to the most wanted ISIS terrorist on the planet."

"The ends justify the means? We all know where that leads."

Yokely drew on his cigar, then blew smoke up at the dark sky. "I'm just here making sure that our man isn't compromised."

"Your man? A man you recruited under false pretences? Are you ever going to tell him that he's been working for the CIA?"

"He's working for the West, that's all that matters."

"You've been lying to him from day one."

"And you've never lied to an agent?"

Shepherd gritted his teeth but didn't reply. Lying went with the turf and yes, he had often played fast and loose with the truth to achieve an objective. But that didn't make what Yokely was telling him any less unpalatable.

"There you go then," said Yokely. "Look, I'm not here to fight with you. You just need to know that if you continue rattling all sorts of cages looking for Mahmoud, you're going to put his life in danger."

"Where is he?"

"He's still in Syria. That's all I can tell you."

Shepherd stopped walking again. He looked into Yokely's eyes, trying to get a read on the man. Did he know that Shepherd had brought Mahmoud's girlfriend back to the UK? Did he know that she was sharing some of Mahmoud's intel with MI5? Yokely looked back at him, a slight smile on his face. Shepherd would hate to play poker with the man, he never gave anything away. If Yokely did know that Shepherd had brought back Nadia from Turkey, he must have known who else he brought, and that would mean he knew about Jaraf. And if he knew about Jaraf, had he also known about the Israeli operation? Shepherd smiled and averted his eyes. The only way to find out how much Yokely knew would be to ask him point blank, but that would mean showing his own hand. "So what do I tell my boss?" Shepherd asked.

"You can tell him what I've told you, but off the record. A word to the wise."

"A nod and a wink? He won't be happy."

"We're not in this business to make friends," said Yokely. "Though sometimes it does happen." He turned left and started walking towards the boating lake. "Do you know much about the history of this park?" asked Yokely.

Shepherd shook his head. "I'm not a history buff."

"It played a vital role in defending London during World War Two," said Yokely. "There were anti-aircraft guns and barrage balloons all over the park and there were bomb shelters here. They're probably still there, under the ground. There was a pig farm here, and a lot of the land was given over to allotments so that the locals could grow vegetables." He grinned. "Wars were different back then."

"That definitely is true," said Shepherd. "Barrage balloons and allotments are no good against terrorists."

They headed south towards the all-weather sports ground.

"What about Mahmoud?" asked Shepherd. "How's he going to react when he realises he's been lied to from the start?"

"Well in the words of the late Ted Kennedy, we'll cross that bridge when we come to it."

"With all this reading you do, I guess you must know the difference between coincidence and serendipity."

"I'm ready to be enlightened."

"Well, the way I see it is, a coincidence is an occurrence of events that happen at the same time by total accident. And serendipity is the occurrence of an unplanned fortunate discovery."

"Well, you live and learn."

"The thing is, Richard, you being here today is neither serendipity nor a coincidence, is it?"

Yokely shrugged. "I did have a message to deliver, that's true."

"But the timing is what interests me. The day after my boss reaches out to Mossad, you reach out to me. So I guess my question is, what does Mossad have to do with Hasan Mahmoud?"

461

Yokely exhaled. "Now that is a question, isn't it?"

Shepherd smiled. "Always a good sign when you answer a question with a question. It shows that I'm on the right track. You see now, I know what Mossad have been up to in the UK. What I don't understand is why you're involved."

"Coincidence?"

Shepherd shook his head. "Hardly. Look, we had an ISIS source all revved up and ready to give us intel on home-grown jihadists who had returned to the UK. But he's now out of the picture thanks to Mossad. Coincidently, we've got access to Mahmoud's girlfriend, who seems to know some of the jihadists that were trained by our ISIS source. She's working through pictures, but it's taking forever."

Yokely frowned. "Girlfriend? You're saying Mahmoud has a girlfriend?"

"Had. A girl called Nadia. From when he was in Birmingham. He cut off all contact when he went to Syria but they got together in a training camp. Just one of those things. She was taken there as a jihadi bride and he linked up with her."

Shepherd could see from the look on Yokely's face that this was news to the American.

"You've got to remember that they had history, so he trusted her," said Shepherd. "Anyway, he told her what he was doing." Shepherd smiled. "At least he told her what he thought he was doing — spying for MI5. And he told her the jihadists he'd met, and what they planned to do."

"And she's here in London now?"

462

"In Thames House."

"He shouldn't have done that."

"I think he needed a friend. It can be brutally lonely when you're undercover. It was pillow talk."

"It was stupid and unprofessional."

"Yes, but Mahmoud isn't a professional, is he? He's an enthusiastic amateur. And he's putting his life on the line for people who are lying to him."

Yokely chuckled. "Do you tell all your agents the truth?" He grinned. "It's a rhetorical question." He took a long pull on his cigar.

"So Mossad kills our ISIS informer, we then use Mahmoud's former girlfriend as a plan B, and then you pop up and tell me that Mahmoud is working for you and would we please back off."

"That's a fair summation of the situation."

"So you knew that Mossad killed our intel source?"

Yokely nodded. "Salam Jaraf. Yes. Mossad had been after him for some time. He killed an Israeli general and his family. An eye for an eye."

"So you must have known that Jaraf left Syria because the Americans attacked the camp he was in. I thought that maybe he was just unlucky, but in light of recent events it's become clear that Mossad wanted Jaraf dead because of what he did in Israel. And when he found out he was on Mossad's hit list, he fled to Syria."

Yokely smoked his cigar but didn't say anything.

"So putting two and two together, it feels to me that Israel asked its American friends for help, in tracking down Jaraf and taking him out. Is that what happened,

Richard? Did your guys send a drone to the camp to take out Jaraf?"

Yokely smiled but still didn't say anything.

"And was it Mahmoud who found Jaraf and gave you the location? That would explain why Mahmoud left Nadia behind. You sent him to look for Jaraf. He found him and you sent the drone."

Yokely wrinkled his nose. "It was a mess," he said. "I'm still not sure what went wrong, but Mahmoud was there when the drone launched its missiles. They missed Jaraf and Mahmoud came this close to being killed."

"Did you know that Mossad tracked Jaraf to the UK?"

"Not until after the event. Last night, in fact. They just wanted help to get him in Syria. We thought we'd killed him but then it turned out he was still alive and he'd fled to the Emirates. Mossad said they'd handle it from there."

"And you didn't know what they were doing in the UK?"

"Absolutely not. Not until it was all done and dusted. I had absolutely nothing to do with what happened in the UK." He had a thoughtful look on his face as he smoked his cigar.

"So I'm right, Mossad told you yesterday that Jaraf was dead?"

"I received a call, yes. At the same time that your people were trawling for information about Mahmoud. To be honest, I thought I was ahead of the game but this is the first I've heard that Mahmoud had a girlfriend."

"How much longer will you be using Mahmoud?" asked Shepherd.

"I can't tell you. Sorry."

"Need to know?"

Yokely nodded. "I'm afraid so."

Shepherd sighed. "What do you want from me, Richard? You're the one who crept up on me."

"I want you to stop looking for him. You're going to draw attention to him and that could be fatal."

"The easiest way to stop MI5 looking for him is for you to tell my boss officially that Mahmoud is working for the CIA."

Yokely looked pained. "That's not something I'd be happy with."

"So this is completely off the record? Just a chat between friends."

"Exactly. And I'm letting you know — off the record — that if you continue looking for Mahmoud, you could get him killed. And even if you find him . . ." He shrugged. "He's our man now. You can tell your boss that, but there's no way you'll ever hear it officially."

Shepherd looked out over the park and sighed. He hated being outplayed, but it seemed that Richard Yokely was always several steps ahead of him. "How about a little off-the-record quid pro quo?"

"I'm listening."

Shepherd sighed again. He knew that he had no bargaining power. He either backed off as Yokely wanted, or he put Hasan Mahmoud's life in danger. It was a classic no-win situation so far as Shepherd was concerned. All he could do was ask for a favour, crumbs from the man's table. "How about you pass on to me any intel pertinent to the UK?"

Yokely frowned. "I'm not sure how we do that without blowing Mahmoud's cover."

"You feed me the intel. Names and details of home-grown jihadists who are back in the UK. I run the names and pictures by Nadia. If she recognises them then we're good to go."

"So it will look as if the intel has come from Nadia?"

Shepherd nodded. "And the more we get from her, the less we need to look for Mahmoud. In fact, if we get some good hits, everyone will lose interest in Mahmoud."

Yokely nodded slowly. "Okay," he said. "That might work."

"How soon can you get the intel to me?"

"I'll look through the file. You have to understand we're not in direct contact with him. We have other agents in play and when they can meet up with him, there's a debrief — we haven't given him any comms. When the Israelis wanted Jaraf, it took us almost a month to get Jaraf in play."

"So you don't even have GPS on him?"

Yokely smiled thinly. "I didn't say we didn't know where he is. But we can't ring him up for a chat. But sure, he's given us names of individuals at the camps who have since returned to the UK. I can pass those names on to you."

"I'm especially interested in any names of guys who were at the camp being trained by Jaraf."

"I understand that."

"So when?"

Yokely flicked ash onto the ground. "You're being a bit pushy, I have to say."

"Yeah, well it's a bit disconcerting knowing that these people are out there but not knowing who or where they are."

"Maybe you should try keeping a closer eye on your own people — especially Muslims who fly over to the Middle East and Asia for extended stays." Yokely shrugged. "But I understand, you have to play the hand you've been dealt." He took a final drag on his cigar and flicked the remains onto the grass. "Okay, how about this? Later tonight I'll send you a text from a burner phone, names and whatever details I have. You do with those names what you want. But you didn't get them from me."

"Understood," said Shepherd. "And thanks. I owe you one."

Yokely grinned. "We can add it to the list." He turned up the collar of his trench coat and walked back towards Albert Bridge.

Shepherd was asleep when Yokely sent the message, but the beep woke him. He sat up and peered at the screen. There were four names — Abdullah Rahman, Yusuf Butt, Latif Shaikh and Anwar Rafiq. Next to Rahman's name was "*Bradford*" and a date, "*July 11*", presumably the man's birthday. And two words:

467

"nickname Noodles". Yusuf Butt's name had "*London*" next to it, plus "*studied at Westminster College*". Anwar Rafiq also had "*London*" next to his name, as well as "*mother's name is Huda, nurse at Hammersmith Hospital*". There was an address in Birmingham after Latif Shaikh's name.

Shepherd put the phone back on the bedside table. After a few seconds it beeped again and he groped for it. The message read: "*Butt had a friend who was a cop with the Met. Deep cover*".

Shepherd knew there was no point in calling Yokely for any more information. He was sure that if the American had anything else he would have sent it, and by now he would have destroyed the SIM card and the phone. The fact that one of the jihadists had a friend who was working as a police officer was a worry. A big one.

He lay down and closed his eyes but sleep was a long time coming. He eventually drifted off an hour or so after Yokely had sent the texts, but he slept fitfully, tossing and turning. He woke up at seven. Part of him wanted to exercise, either with a run or a spell in the Thames House gym, but the pull of the three names that Yokely had given him was too strong. He shaved and showered, dressed in the same suit as the day before but with a dark blue shirt this time, and called an Uber.

The office was empty which suited him just fine. He sat down at one of the terminals and logged on. He typed in the first of the names that Yokely had sent him. There were two Abdullah Rahmans, though one of them also had the name Mohammed. The one with Mohammed was seventy-two years old and ten years previously had been convicted of sending money to his son while he was in Pakistan undergoing training at a camp on the Afghanistan border. The first Rahman's address wasn't Bradford, it was Leeds, but the date of birth matched. He was known to MI5 because he had attended anti-war demonstrations in the city and had been photographed burning poppies. He made a mental note of the investigation number.

There was no Yusuf Butt in MI5's database, but he was on the Police National Computer for minor drugs offences, all of which had been dealt with by a caution. There had also been a rape allegation made against him three years earlier, and as part of that he had been fingerprinted and had his DNA taken, but the allegation was later dropped. Shepherd sat back as he studied Yusuf's file. He had been photographed in the custody suite of West End Central police station. Yokely's text had said Butt had studied at Westminster College, but it was actually City of Westminster College, where he had been studying construction and engineering. There was nothing in the PNC file about Butt travelling overseas, but that was to be expected. Border Force didn't check the passports of anyone leaving the country, be they citizens or foreigners — and if he had gone overseas he wouldn't have been questioned on his return. There were no surveillance pictures of Butt — just the police photographs, front and side views.

There was no point in typing in the third name that Yokely had given him — Latif Shaikh — so Shepherd went straight to the last name. He typed in Anwar Rafiq. There were no Anwar Rafiqs in MI5's database but there were two on the Police National Computer. One was a sixty-seven-year-old man in Leicester who had been fined seven times for shoplifting, and the other was a forty-five-year-old sales rep in Glasgow who had been banned from driving after his sixth speeding conviction in as many years.

He went through to the DVLA database and this time there were six Anwar Rafiq's, including the sales rep. Shepherd went through them one by one. When he got to the fourth one he stopped and sat back in his chair. "Bingo," he said to himself. It was the man who'd given Ali Karim the bag full of Semtex outside Euston station. The man was thirty years old and lived in Morden, south London. Shepherd logged into the Passport Office database. Rafiq's latest passport had been issued six years previously.

The door opened. It was Nadia and Zarah. "Oh, you're here early," said Zarah.

"I couldn't sleep," said Shepherd. "Do you want to pop off and shower and change and I'll take Nadia for breakfast?"

"You don't mind?"

"It'll be a pleasure," said Shepherd. "I feel bad because of all the hours you have to put in."

Zarah grinned. "It's no hardship hanging out with Nadia, it really isn't."

470

"She's been so helpful and supportive," said Nadia. "She was saying that maybe one day I could work here."

"I'm sure that's a possibility," said Shepherd.

"I'll catch up with you guys later," said Zarah, and she left, closing the door behind her.

"Nadia, before we go and eat, can you just have a look at these guys for me."

"Sure," she said, and moved to stand behind him. He showed her the passport photograph of Anwar Rafiq. She looked at it for several seconds and then shook her head. "No, I don't think I've seen him before," she said.

"Did Hasan ever mention an Anwar Rafiq? From south London."

She frowned. "If he did, I don't remember," she said.

"What about this guy? His name's Yusuf Butt." He showed her the police photographs. She shook her head again. "I'm sorry," she said.

"There's no need to apologise," Shepherd said. "What about this guy? Abdullah Rahman. They call him Noodles."

Nadia grinned. "From Leeds, right?"

Shepherd nodded. "You saw him over in Syria?"

"No, but Hasan spoke about him. There were two guys out from Leeds and one of them was called Noodles. Hasan said they were really enthusiastic, but they were always complaining about how cold it was at night." She frowned. "What was the other guy's name? It was an animal. Some sort of animal." She laughed. "Kamel. Hasan said that you'd have thought a camel would have been used to the desert."

471

"What about his first name?"

Nadia frowned and she shook her head. "I don't remember. Just Noodles and Kamel. And I never actually saw them. Hasan just spoke about them."

"Excellent," said Shepherd. He logged off the terminal and stood up. "Right, let's eat."

He took her to the canteen and ordered breakfast for them both while she sat at a table by the window. She wanted toast and orange juice. Shepherd ordered scrambled eggs, toast and coffee again. He carried his tray over to the table and sat down opposite her.

"How long do you think this will take?" she asked, after she'd sipped her orange juice.

"To go through all the photographs we have?" He shrugged. "Yesterday we went through the surveillance photographs from about forty operations. At the moment, MI5 has more than seven hundred active investigations."

She frowned as she did the calculation. "So it could take a couple of weeks?"

"There's no quicker way of doing it, unfortunately," he said. "We can't confine it to particular areas of the country because all you saw were faces. The men in the camp could have come from anywhere. And it's not as if one investigation is more likely than another. We just have to go through them all." He saw the look of disappointment flash across her face. "I'm sorry, there are no short cuts. You have to look through all the pictures to see if you saw any of the players out in Syria."

"Players?"

"It's what we call people who are under surveillance."

"You make it sound like a game."

"I'm sorry, you're right. It isn't a game, it's just the jargon that people use."

They finished their food, then Shepherd got himself another coffee and Nadia a bottle of water to take back to the office.

Once she was sitting down in front of her monitor, he logged on and called up the next investigation. It was a surveillance operation based around a mosque in Ealing, where one of the younger imams had been sending young men over to Jordan. He was allegedly doing it for religious training, but MI5 had received information from the Jordanian General Intelligence Directorate that suggested that the teenagers he sent were ending up in training camps in Syria. MI5 had tried and failed to recruit agents from the mosque, and had failed to get its own people close to the imam, but there were hundreds of photographs of the imam talking with young worshippers.

Shepherd opened the file and Nadia began clicking on the individual photographs.

After two hours, Zarah returned. She brought with her a coffee for Shepherd and a fruit juice for Nadia. "Can you hold the fort while I check in with Giles Pritchard?" asked Shepherd.

"Sure," said Zarah. "Anything I need to be aware of?"

"No, we're good. Nadia's confirmed two names in what appears to be a Leeds cell, so we're off to a good

473

start." Zarah turned to look at the whiteboards. "I'll put them up when I get back," said Shepherd.

Shepherd had to wait for ten minutes before Pritchard was free. The man was at his desk, his shirt sleeves rolled up and his club tie at half mast. "Daniel, please tell me you've got some good news for me?" He waved Shepherd to one of the wooden chairs.

Shepherd sat down. "We're getting there," he said. "First of all, we've got an ID for the guy who had the Semtex in London. His name's Anwar Rafiq. He's clean and not known to us. He has a driving licence and a passport so we have his photograph and address."

"That's great news. Excellent. Sounds as if Nadia is earning her trip back to the UK."

Shepherd forced a smile. He didn't want to lie, but he also didn't want to volunteer the information had come from Richard Yokely. "Absolutely," said Shepherd. By agreeing with Pritchard he wasn't exactly lying. And truth be told, it didn't really matter where the intel came from so long as they had the right man in their sights. "I'm just about to put the details in the computer."

"Email me when it's done and I'll arrange surveillance. And while you're at it, could you copy in Mary Garner? Her nose is out of joint because I didn't tell her about the Semtex coming from an IRA cache."

"Not a problem," said Shepherd. "Also we have two more names of what appears to be a cell in Leeds. Both names that Nadia remembers Hasan talking about. Abdullah Rahman and an associate of his called Kamel. That's the family name. I have Rahman's details, but

474

it'll take some digging to pin down Kamel. And we have a Yusuf Butt, he's in London and on the PNC but not known to us."

"So we need surveillance on all three?"

"That would be my recommendation, yes."

"Send me the details and I'll arrange it," said Pritchard. He sighed and looked at his watch. "Okay, I have to move. Harry's death has caused all sorts of problems." He realised what he'd said and grimaced. "I mean, I know it's a tragic loss and I'll miss him and all that, but admin-wise it's a nightmare. Thankfully he doesn't have much in the way of family to inform, but it's still a mess."

"Let me know when and where the funeral is," said Shepherd. He nodded at the door. "I'll get back to Nadia."

"Citizenship-wise, she's done enough, would you say?"

"Definitely."

"Okay, I'll set the wheels in motion. But we need to hold off having her talk to her parents. We need the element of surprise on this."

"Of course," said Shepherd, as Pritchard turned back to his screen.

Ali Karim knocked on the shutter of the storage locker. "It's me, brothers," he said. After a few seconds the shutter rattled up. There were five men inside and one by one they embraced Karim. Latif Shaikh, Mohammed Joinda, Gulzar Noor, Umar Begum and Faisal Amin.

"Are we ready to go?" asked Karim as Noor pulled the shutters down.

"We're all done," said Shaikh, pointing at the six drones lined up on the floor. All now had explosive packages and Apple Watches wired into detonators.

"Faisal, your car's ready?"

Amin worked as an Uber driver and had a white Prius. "Yes, brother."

"Tank's full?"

"Of course."

"Right, so MoJo and Gulzar can ride with Amin. Milky and Umar can come with me."

"Where are we staying tonight?" asked Begum.

"Faisal's got a cousin in Newham, in east London, who's got a boarding house. He's got three rooms ready for us. Now, the cousin's a good Muslim and all but when we're there, we don't tell anyone what we're doing. The drones stay in the cars. Then tomorrow afternoon we'll take a walk down by the river before the crowds start to gather. Okay?"

The men nodded.

"And if anyone asks, we're in London for a wedding. You don't tell family the real reason, you don't tell friends. You don't tell no one."

"We got you, bruv," said Joinda.

Pritchard looked up from his terminal when Amy gently knocked on it. "Donna Walsh needs a word, urgent," she said.

"Send her right in," said Pritchard.

476

Donna Walsh headed up MI5's London surveillance operations, a job that meant juggling a multitude of officers and vehicles to cover literally hundreds of targets. It was a logistical nightmare, but Walsh never seemed fazed by her ever-increasing workload. Her husband ran a golf tour company and she was a scratch golfer herself, though Pritchard didn't know how she found the time to play — she was usually one of the first in and almost always one of the last to leave. "Giles, the bad news keeps on piling up, I'm afraid," she said as she walked into his office. She wore dark-framed glasses and her chestnut hair was pinned back from her face. "Abdullah Rahman, the name you gave us in Leeds, and his associate, Kamel. We found a Muktar Kamel who goes to the same mosque as Rahman and their phone records show that they've been in frequent contact with each other. And number plate recognition shows a black Honda owned by Rahman heading south to London. At the moment we've lost them but we're hopeful the car will surface again. They don't appear to be hiding."

"That's not so bad."

She nodded. "But it does get worse, I'm afraid. Half an hour ago the six targets we've been watching in Birmingham went to the storage locker rented by Ali Karim. They were seen loading boxes, which we believe contain the IED-carrying drones, into two vehicles, and said vehicles are now heading towards London. Fortunately the GPS trackers that were placed in the drones are all working so we're having no problem

477

following them — but obviously the worry is that they're getting ready to strike."

"And what about the other names I gave you? Yusuf Butt and Anwar Rafiq?"

"We had no trouble locating them. Butt lives in Tower Hamlets but isn't at home at the moment. We have a van outside his building. Rafiq is at home, in Morden, and we have him under surveillance as we speak."

"What about contacts for them both?"

"We're trying to get their phone records but there's a backlog of requests. The assumption is that Butt and Rafiq are part of other cells, but so far we have no names in the frame. I really do think we're running out of time on this. The fact that we have a cell from Leeds and a cell from Birmingham on their way to London suggests that the capital is the target and that the attacks are going to be sooner rather than later."

"What are you suggesting?"

"At the very least we should think about taking the guys we're following into custody."

"The problem is that if we do that, the other cells, if there are any, will just go dark."

"It's a tough call," she said. "It's just that tomorrow evening there'll be more than a hundred thousand people lining the banks of the Thames to watch the fireworks."

"I hear you, Donna. Let me give it some thought. And send me everything you have on this Anwar Rafiq."

"I will do. Not that there's much to send."

478

Pritchard thanked her and went back to looking at his screen. He clicked on the file containing the surveillance photographs of Ali Karim collecting the Semtex and worked his way through them again.

The message arrived within five minutes. There was a photograph of a thirty-year-old bearded Asian man that had been used to apply for a passport, and another that was on his driving licence. No criminal record and nothing on MI5's database, but Donna had used the address on the driving licence to track down Rafiq's Vodafone contract.

Pritchard stood up and began to pace up and down. It always helped him to think, and he had a lot to think about.

That Anwar Rafiq was planning terrorist attacks was beyond doubt. He had supplied Semtex and detonators to at least one terrorist cell and probably others. The cell he had given the Semtex to was now heading towards London. So was another cell. Maybe they had explosive-laden drones or maybe they didn't, but the ones from Birmingham most definitely did.

So what to do? Rafiq probably wasn't working alone in London. If he had stolen the Semtex from Brendan O'Carroll then he must have had help. That meant another cell. So even if they had the Birmingham cell and the Leeds cell arrested, there was still a strong possibility of another cell being ready and waiting.

If he organised surveillance of Rafiq, they might get lucky. Or they might not. Rafiq might be an organiser, a facilitator, and he might not meet up with the London cell.

He went over to the window and looked out over the river. Come New Year's Eve there would be thousands upon thousands of men, women and children thronging both sides of the river to watch the fireworks. A single drone could kill dozens, but hundreds could die in the panic that ensued. It didn't bear thinking about but Pritchard had no choice — that was his job, to think the unthinkable.

He turned and began pacing again as he considered his options, which seemed few and far between.

Rafiq was bad, there was no doubt about that. He'd supplied Semtex to Ali Karim and that Semtex had been incorporated into IEDs in the Birmingham storage locker. The surveillance video alone could send Rafiq to prison for many years. And if those drones did actually kill people, Rafiq might go down for life. Not that that would be any consolation to the relatives of the dead. And there was always the chance that a good lawyer might be able to argue that Rafiq didn't know what was in the bag.

The more that Pritchard thought about it, the more he realised that if he played by the rules, people were going to die. There wasn't time to play a waiting game, he had to do something now. Something decisive.

He caught sight of his squash bag leaning against the side of his desk and stopped pacing. It was a long shot, but sometimes long shots paid off. He needed to talk to Joel Schwartz, but he needed to do it without leaving a trail. He went over to his desk, sat down and pulled open the bottom drawer. There were four burner phones there, all cheap Samsung models with pay-as-you-go SIM cards. Two had labels on them showing who they were used to contact, but two were unused. He took out one of the unused ones, then checked Schwartz's number on his work phone. He called him on the burner phone, hoping that Schwartz would answer even though he wouldn't recognise the number that was calling.

Schwartz answered with an aggressive "Who is this?"

"It's me Joel. I need an urgent conversation. On a safe line."

"This line is safe."

"It's a mobile, so it isn't," said Pritchard. At least Schwartz had recognised his voice.

"But you're on a mobile."

"Mine's a burner. Is yours?"

Schwartz sighed. "I'll call you back."

"I'd appreciate that."

Pritchard stood up and continued to pace until his phone rang. It was a landline so he assumed Schwartz had found a phonebox. "What's the problem?" growled the Israeli.

"You remember how you owe me a favour?"

"Vaguely."

"I need to call it in. Now. As a matter of urgency."

To the Israeli's credit there was no hesitation or reluctance. "What do you need?"

"I'm pretty sure that one of the names that Jaraf was about to give us was a home-grown jihadist by the name of Anwar Rafiq. It looks to me that Rafiq is organising several cells across the UK and they are planning to strike tomorrow, with explosive drones.

Two of the cells are already on the move. And tomorrow being New Year's Eve . . ." He hesitated, wondering how best to phrase what his fears were.

"So bring in this Anwar Rafiq and question him."

"We've nothing concrete. I mean, yes, of course, we can bring him in for questioning, but that won't get us anywhere. All we have is surveillance footage of him handing a bag to a member of a cell in Birmingham. Okay, we have photographs later showing that the bag contained Semtex and detonators, but it's all circumstantial. He'll lawyer up and that might be the end of it. We can get his computer and go through that, but that'll take time. And even with incriminating evidence on his hard drive, we might only be looking at conspiracy." He looked at his watch. "New Year's Eve is just a day away. And they're definitely up to something. We've got nine jihadists who are all on the move at the same time, and all of them have been trained in the use of drones as weapons of terror. And while we know that they're heading to London, we don't know for sure where they're going to attack. They could be getting ready to strike anywhere in the country — any airport, any city, any venue. We don't know where, but Anwar Rafiq does know. And he'll know who else is involved."

"So what are you asking?"

"I'm asking you to get the intel I need. By whatever means necessary."

"So a hard interrogation? And then what?"

Pritchard swallowed. He knew exactly what Schwartz was asking, and that Rafiq's life was in his hands. But if the jihadist survived what Schwartz described as a hard interrogation, and if he went to the police, it could lead to all sorts of problems. "It would probably be best if the case was closed permanently."

"You are asking a very big favour, my friend."

"I understand that. But it's only necessary because we no longer have access to Salam Jaraf."

The Israeli said nothing for several seconds. "You have an address?"

"I do. Yes."

"Then give it to me."

Donna Walsh worked in an open-plan office with more than a dozen officers wearing headsets sitting in pods, each with three screens. Walsh also had a headset and she was deep in conversation when Pritchard walked in. She waved to acknowledge his presence and continued to talk, making hand gestures as she spoke. Pritchard looked around the room. The blinds were down and the overhead fluorescent lights were all on. It was the nerve centre of MI5 surveillance operations, where Walsh and her team could monitor all live feeds and communicate with the watchers on the ground directly or through their team leaders. On one of the screens in each pod was a satellite map with flashing red and green lights showing the location of various surveillance teams and their vehicles. It was similar in layout to Diane Daily's CCTV monitoring room, but whereas CCTV monitoring was mainly a passive operation, Walsh and her group were constantly assisting the surveillance teams on the ground with communications, intelligence and logistics.

Walsh ended her call and moved her mouthpiece away from her lips. "Good news on the Leeds cell, they're off the motorway and we have eyes on. They're heading south, towards the river."

"Excellent," said Pritchard. "Some more good news: we can pull the surveillance off Anwar Rafiq and use those resources elsewhere."

"Did something happen?"

"I got word from a confidential informant that he's laid up with flu and won't be going anywhere," said Pritchard.

"I could keep one man outside, just in case," said Walsh.

"No need. I'm told he's in bed and won't be going anywhere for a few days."

"Okay, no problem," said Walsh. "I'll pull the team off and get them ready for the arrival of the Birmingham cell." She held up her hand to let him know she had another call on her headset, and as Pritchard left she was already talking animatedly as she paced up and down.

There was a knock on Anwar Rafiq's door and he frowned. He wasn't expecting anyone. He never had visitors. Ever. Almost no one knew where he lived. It wasn't something he talked about. If he met friends he would go to the mosque or to a restaurant.

He tiptoed across the room and peered through the security viewer. It was a woman, wearing a full burqa with her face completely covered. Did he know her?

Surely no sister would be knocking on the door of a man she did not know.

He opened the door. "Yes?" he said.

"*As-salamu alaykum*," she said.

"*Wa alaykumu s-salam*," he said. "How can I help you, sister?"

"I am sorry to bother you, but I have moved into the flat above you and a pipe has burst in my bathroom. I have got a plumber there now but he thinks a lot of water has gone through the floor. Do you have a leak?"

"I don't think so, no."

"Do you mind checking? The plumber wants to know if he should lift the floorboards."

"Okay, yes, I will check for you," he said. He left the door ajar and turned to go to the bathroom. He heard the rustle of her burqa, and then something pressed against his neck and everything went black.

Anwar Rafiq heard voices muttering in a language he couldn't understand. He tried to swallow but his mouth was bone dry and he almost gagged. He started to cough, then he threw up in his mouth. He spat and heard a man curse. He opened his eyes but everything was a blur. He blinked furiously, trying to clear his vision.

A man said something, and a woman replied. It wasn't English. Or Urdu. Or Arabic.

Rafiq opened his eyes again. The taste of vomit in his mouth made him want to throw up again. He tried to use his hand to wipe his lips but he couldn't move his arm. He looked down, still blinking. His arm was tied to a chair with rope. He looked over at his left arm. That too was tied. He blinked again and then saw his feet out in front of him. He was naked, he realised. His legs were resting on something, he could feel the pressure on his calves. He blinked again and peered at his feet. His ankles were tied with rope, binding them to an oil barrel that had been turned on its side.

"Wakey, wakey," said a man to his left. Rafiq turned and tried to focus on his face. He was in his twenties, darkish skin and jet-black, curly hair. He was wearing a Taylor Swift t-shirt and Levi's jeans, and what appeared to be washing up gloves. Yellow ones. Rafiq remembered his mother had always worn gloves like that when she did the washing up. Marigolds, she called them. She was allergic to washing up liquid and so always wore gloves.

Rafiq tried to speak but his mouth was just too dry. He tried to ask for water but even that was too much of an effort. The man knew what he wanted and he moved out of Rafiq's vision, returning with a bottle of water. He held it to Rafiq's lips and he drank greedily. The man let him drink his fill before taking the bottle away.

"Who are you?" Rafiq gasped. "What's this about?"

The man placed the bottle on a metal table. Rafiq looked around as best as he could. There were metal beams overhead, under a sloping roof, and in the distance was a metal shutter. There were no windows; the only light came from fluorescent tubes hanging from the roof. He could smell engine oil and petrol. It was a garage, maybe, or some sort of workshop.

The man grinned down at Rafiq. "That's not how it works, Anwar," he said. "We ask the questions. You answer them."

A second figure appeared. It was a woman. Late twenties maybe. She was wearing one of the paper overall suits that forensic investigators wore, and a hairnet. Like the man, she also had on yellow washing up gloves. She was holding a pair of bolt cutters in her right hand. She was pretty, and as Rafiq looked at her eyes he realised she was the woman who had appeared on his doorstep, wearing the burqa. "Sister, please, what is happening here?" he asked.

"I'm not your sister, Anwar," she said.

Rafiq struggled against his bonds but they had been expertly tied. He heard a noise behind him, the sound of a shoe brushing concrete. So there were at least three of them, he realised. Not that the number mattered.

"Please, I don't know what this is about, just tell me."

"It's about what you and your friends are planning," said the woman. "You and Abdullah Rahman and Yusuf Butt, and Ali Karim."

Rafiq's eyes widened as she said the names, but he fought to keep a straight face. "I don't know any of those guys," he said. He shook his head. "May Allah be my judge, I've never heard of them."

The woman looked pained and she shook her head sadly. "You really shouldn't be lying like that, not to Allah," she said.

"We don't have time to listen to your lies, Anwar. And we don't have time to waste playing games. You need to tell us what you and your friends are planning."

"I told you, I don't know them!" shouted Rafiq. He tried to pull his arms free. He realised there was a plastic tube leading to his wrist where it disappeared under a strip of plaster. He frowned at the tube, then turned to see where it went. His jaw dropped when he saw a liquid-filled plastic bag hanging from a metal stand. "What the fuck?" he shouted. He turned to stare at the woman. "What the fuck is that?"

"Epinephrine, and a few other things just to make sure you don't pass out," said the woman. "And an anticoagulant so you won't bleed to death."

"What?"

"This is going to hurt, Anwar," said the woman. "It's going to hurt a lot. And if we keep having to revive you, it'll take forever." She waved the bolt cutters at him. "I'll be starting with your toes, then working on your fingers, then your ears . . ." She pointed at his crotch with the cutters. "And we'll finish up with your dick." She looked over at the man. "Dick last, right? Or dick first? Which is best?"

"Dick last, definitely," said the man.

The woman smiled at Rafiq. "Dick last it is."

"No, wait! Stop! Please."

"Stop what? I haven't started yet," she said. "And if you tell us what we want to know, you won't get hurt. So just tell us. What are you and your friends planning to do?"

488

Rafiq shook his head fearfully. "Nothing. I don't even know who you're talking about."

"It's bad enough you lying to Allah, but lying to me just means you're going to be losing a lot of digits and be in a lot of pain," said the woman. "Abdullah Rahman, Yusuf Butt, Ali Karim. You were all in Syria. You all trained with Salam Jaraf. He showed you how to use drones to kill people. That much we know, so it's pointless you lying." She tapped his left foot with the bolt cutters and he flinched. "Start talking, Anwar."

"Sister, please."

"I'm not your sister," said the woman again. "Fine. It's your call." She opened the bolt cutters. Rafiq tried to pull back his feet but they were tied too tightly. She put the blades either side of the little toe on his left foot and started to apply pressure. Blood trickled around the blades.

"I'll talk, I'll talk!" screamed Rafiq at the top of his voice. "Please, stop, I'll tell you anything you want! Anything!"

The woman removed the bolt cutter, held it in front of Rafiq's face and clicked the blades together. "You'd better not be fucking with me, because if you are I'm going straight for your dick."

Tears ran down Rafiq's face. "What do you want to know?"

Anwar Rafiq spoke for the best part of twenty minutes. He told the Mossad team everything they wanted to know and answered every question that was asked of him. He gave the names of another eight jihadists who had trained with him in Syria and explained what they had been ordered to do.

No more threats were needed; once Rafiq had started to speak the words kept tumbling out. Several times he had to stop as he was gasping for breath, and once he asked for more water, which they gave him.

Eventually he was finished. Drained. Exhausted.

The girl looked at the man and he nodded. Then they both looked at the man standing behind Rafiq, the one he still hadn't seen. He said something to them in the same language they'd been speaking earlier. The woman walked over to a bench and put down the bolt cutters. "Is that it?" asked Rafiq. "Can I go now?"

The woman smiled. "Yes, we're done."

"You'll untie me?"

She picked up a small plastic box and took out a hypodermic syringe. "Yes. Don't worry."

"What's that?" he asked, his voice trembling fearfully.

"It's what we used to drug you so that we could bring you here," she said. "We'll knock you out and take you back to your room. When you wake up, it'll be as if you had a bad dream." She smiled. "Don't worry, you won't feel a thing." She walked towards him, pressed the needle into his neck and pushed the plunger. Rafiq shuddered and went still. "Well that was easier than I thought it would be," she said.

"He was a coward," said the man standing behind Rafiq. He was holding a plastic bag and had a roll of duct tape under his arm, holding it against his side. "This whole business of them wanting to die carrying out jihad so that they can be in heaven with Allah is just

490

bullshit. The only ones prepared to die are the mentally retarded or the brainwashed. The rest of them will do whatever they have to in order to save their miserable lives." He placed the bag over Rafiq's head and used the duct tape to seal it around his neck. The bag gradually misted over. His chest started rising and falling rapidly but the rest of his body remained perfectly still. After two minutes the chest stopped moving.

"What do we do with the body?" asked the woman.

"I'm tempted to put him in his bed with gay porn showing on his phone, but I gather MI5 have his room wired up so it's not an option." The man took off the latex gloves he was wearing and dropped them into a black rubbish bag. "Just bury the body somewhere it won't be found. The New Forest is always good."

"I've got friends going out in London tonight for the New Year's Eve celebrations," said the woman. "Can I warn them?"

"Tell them they'd be better off staying in and watching it on the TV," said the man. "No specifics, obviously."

Pritchard was at his desk sipping his morning coffee when his mobile rang. He didn't know the number but he recognised the gruff growl of the caller. Joel Schwartz. "I need to see you, now."

"Where are you?"

"Victoria Tower Gardens."

Victoria Tower Gardens was one of the smallest of the Royal Parks, a tiny parcel of green space between

Millbank and the Thames. It was only three minutes' walk away. Pritchard went over to his window and looked to the left. He could just see the edge of the park, beyond Lambeth Bridge. "I'm coming now," he said.

"Do not bring your phone," said Schwartz, and he ended the call.

Pritchard grabbed his coat and caught the lift to the ground floor. He hurried along the pavement to the park, his heart pounding. Schwartz was standing by the Buxton Memorial Fountain, which commemorated the ending of slavery in the British Empire. He had his hands in his pockets. He nodded when he saw Pritchard, but didn't offer to shake hands.

"You've got problems, my friend," said Schwartz.

"Tell me about it," said Pritchard. He looked around. There was no one else in the park. In the distance, looking down on them, was Victoria Tower, the square tower at the corner of the Houses of Parliament.

"I will, but first . . ." Schwartz's right hand emerged from his coat pocket, holding something metallic. Pritchard flinched, expecting a gun. Schwartz chuckled. "Do not worry my friend, I'm not here to kill you."

Pritchard laughed. "That's good to know."

Schwartz held out his hand. It was a small plastic box with three lights on it: red, orange and green. "I just need to reassure myself that you're not recording this conversation."

"I'm not," said Pritchard. "But go ahead."

Schwartz ran the box up and down Pritchard's chest and groin area, then walked around and did his back. "Now I am reassured," he said, slipping the box back into his pocket. He began walking and Pritchard kept pace with him. "As I said, you have problems. Rafiq headed a terrorist cell in London. Him and four others, all British-born jihadists." He put his hand inside his coat and took out an envelope, which he gave to Pritchard. "All the names and what details I have are here," he said. "Basically they are planning to fly drones laden with explosives above the crowds prior to the New Year's Eve fireworks — here, along the Embankment. Several of the men received training from Salam Jaraf in Syria. The original plan was to use the drones to drop ricin, but then Rafiq was told to use explosives. He was put in touch with a Russian middleman who arranged for a delivery of Semtex."

Pritchard nodded. "We're aware of that."

"The really bad news is that Rafiq went on to distribute the Semtex to three more terror cells: one in Birmingham, one in Leeds and another one in London. In each case Rafiq knew the name of the leader of each cell, but not the individual members." He nodded at the envelope. "The names he was aware of are in there. Plus he has his own cell of four men. They have prepared their drones and plan on using them tonight. Just before midnight. Their names and addresses are also in there. Along with the lock-up where the drones are currently being stored."

"And are they all planning attacks in London?"

"That's the problem, he doesn't know. He was tasked with sending funds to the cells, and supplying them with the explosives, but the individual cells were controlled by ISIS, he thinks out of Syria. His main ISIS contact uses a pseudonym — Al-Muntaqim — which means 'The Avenger'. Rafiq was told before he left Syria that Al-Muntaqim was actually al-Baghdadi's defence chief, Iyad al-Obaidi, the man they think is now running ISIS. From what Rafiq said, this Avenger is in contact with the individual cells. And all communication is through email."

"And there's no way that Rafiq could be lying about any of this?"

Schwartz shook his head. "He wasn't lying. By the time we got to the end, he was telling us everything."

"I'm sure he was," said Pritchard. He held up the envelope. "Thank you for this."

"And we are all square now?" asked Schwartz.

"I guess we are."

"Then I'll wish you good luck," said Schwartz. "*Lehitra'ot.*"

"*Lehitra'ot,* goodbye," said Pritchard as Schwartz walked away.

Shepherd's mobile rang. It was Amy, Pritchard's secretary. "Could you pop in for a chat with Mr Pritchard, please?" she asked.

"On my way," said Shepherd. He stood and Zarah and Nadia looked at him expectantly. "I won't be long," he said. He looked at his watch. It was just before midday. "Do you two want to go and have lunch?" They

494

had been watching surveillance videos for four hours without a break and were looking tired.

"I'm okay, what about you, Nadia?" asked Zarah.

Nadia rubbed her eyes and nodded. "I could do with a break," she said. "My eyes hurt."

"I'll take her to the canteen," said Zarah.

"What about tonight?" asked Shepherd. "What are your plans?"

"I was planning on being here with Nadia."

"You don't want to go out with friends?"

Zarah patted Nadia's hand. "Nadia is my friend," she said.

Nadia grinned. "Thank you," she said.

"Nothing to thank me for," said Zarah. "I thought we could watch the fireworks from here, we should get a great view. And I'll bring in some Lebanese food from my favourite restaurant."

"Sounds like a plan," said Shepherd. He left the room and headed for Pritchard's office. Amy waved for him to go straight in. Donna Walsh was sitting on the sofa with Frank Russell, one of MI5's Metropolitan Police liaison officers. Russell had moved to MI5 after a distinguished thirty-year career with the Met, retiring as a chief superintendent. He had superb contacts across the force and was used to fast-track requests for assistance from the police. He stood up as Shepherd walked in and shook hands with him. It had been almost a year since their paths had last crossed. He was in his mid-fifties but still had a head of jet-black hair that was thicker than most men half his age. "Good to see you again, Spider," he said.

"Spider?" asked Walsh.

"You've never heard that?" said Russell as he sat back on the sofa. "He ate a spider once. A big one."

Walsh pulled a face. "What did that taste like?" she asked.

"Like a big spider," said Shepherd. "What can I say? I was young and stupid."

"Grab a chair and I'll bring you up to speed," said Pritchard, who was in his high-backed chair behind his desk. Shepherd took one of the wooden chairs, positioned it so that he could see Walsh and Russell, and sat down.

"Thing are moving quickly and we need to stay ahead of the game," said Pritchard. "Donna's people have done an amazing job tracking the two cells who have come to London from Leeds and Birmingham," he said. "The Leeds cell, consisting of Abdullah Rahman, Muktar Kamel and another so-far-unidentified Asian male, have booked into one room at the County Hall Premier Inn."

"They are presently walking along the South Bank," said Walsh. "We have eyes on them."

Pritchard nodded. "Donna's people have checked out the vehicle the men are using. They've had sight of three drones, which have been adapted to carry phone-detonated IEDs, along the lines of the ones we've seen being assembled in the Birmingham storage locker. The director general is off today but I've run the situation by him and he agrees with my assessment that we should move in and arrest them now. With the drones ready to go, they could be in the air within a

496

matter of minutes." He looked over at Shepherd. "Because they're in a busy tourist area, and in view of the fact that crowds are already starting to gather along the river in anticipation of tonight's fireworks display, I want to use the Increment, namely armed plainclothes SAS troopers. I'll reach out to Major Gannon, and I was thinking you could organise the team and perhaps lead them?"

Shepherd nodded. "No problem."

"Ideally they can be taken at the hotel with little or no fuss. Frank can arrange for the police to take them into custody and to get a bomb disposal team to take care of the drones."

Russell nodded and scribbled in a small notepad.

"Donna's people have tracked the Birmingham cell to a guest house in Newham. They drove there in two vehicles and are currently parked up behind the building. One of the vehicles is a white Prius owned by one Faisal Amin. The other is a blue Honda Civic owned by Ali Karim, who we have been looking at for some days now. We have video of Karim and his friends assembling IED-carrying drones and those drones were transferred to the vehicles." He looked over at Shepherd. "There are six men in all, four of whom are on your list: Ali Karim, Latif Shaikh, Mohammed Joinda and Gulzar Noor. We're running checks on the other two — Umar Begum and Faisal Amin — as we speak. My feeling, and again the DG agrees with me, is that we should take them into custody immediately. We don't want to risk even one of their drones being launched. There aren't many tourists in Newham, and there's plenty of police activity dealing with the drugs problem in the area, so I'm proposing we go in with CTSFOs in covert vehicles, make arrests and then deal with the devices out of public sight. There'll be a media blackout, but if we have a few drugs squad vehicles out, the public should get the message." The Counter Terrorist Specialist Firearms Officers were the most highly trained of the Met's armed officers. Unlike the regular armed police, they didn't ride around in ARVs looking for trouble — they were only used on assigned missions that required their abilities. They did a lot of their training with the SAS in their Stirling Lines barracks.

"When do we need this done by?" asked Russell.

Pritchard looked over at Walsh. "Where are they now, Donna?"

"Last I heard, inside the house. Their two vehicles are parked behind the house and the drones are in boxes in the vehicles."

"Then we should strike while the iron is hot, as they say. And let's put tents around the vehicles before we open them up. And make sure the bomb squad people aren't identifiable as such. No labels or vehicles. Softly, softly. That goes for the Premier Inn, too."

"Understood," said Russell.

"We also have a third cell, operating out of Tower Hamlets. We have three names — Yusuf Butt, Mohammed Desai and Nazam Miah."

"All three men have been in regular phone contact over the last few days, but that's now ceased, which suggests they are together," said Walsh. "We're not sure where they are right now, but we have teams outside all their addresses. The only one with a vehicle is Mohammed Desai, who has a Ford Fiesta, which is currently parked outside his house. A tracker has been installed."

"As soon as any of them surface, let me know," said Pritchard. He picked up a sheet of paper off his desk and took it over to Russell. "There are four more names here that we need bringing in. And there's an address of a lock-up where they're storing drones and explosives. Again, this can be a pure police operation, just bring them in for questioning." He went back to his desk. "Once they've been arrested they need to be taken to different custody suites," he said.

"That might be hard to juggle," said Russell.

"That's the way it has to be," he said. "We need each cell to be held separately, and we don't want them to know that other cells have been picked up."

Russell nodded. "I'll make sure the Met understand what needs to be done."

Shepherd looked over at the sheet of paper that Russell was holding, and wondered where the intel had come from. He also wondered why Pritchard hadn't been more forthcoming about the source. It was clearly on a need-to-know basis, and for some reason Pritchard had decided that Shepherd didn't need to know.

"Fuck me, you can see right into Buckingham Palace," said Waheed Choudary. "Do you think the Queen's at home?"

"You can tell by the flag on the roof," said Muktar Kamel. "They only fly the flag when she's at home."

"What's that building there?" asked Abdullah Rahman, pointing at a huge stone building overlooking the river.

Kamel was holding a map that showed all the buildings visible from the London Eye, and he checked it against the view. "That's the Savoy Hotel," he said.

"I bet their rooms are bigger than ours," said Choudary.

"We're not here on holiday," said Kamel, switching to Urdu. They were in one of the thirty-two capsules on the London Eye, and were halfway through the thirty-minute circuit. There were twenty-five people in the capsule — the rest were Europeans, Japanese and Chinese, most of them taking selfies against the scenic backdrop. Kamel pointed down to the left. "See that park, there? That's called Archbishop's Park. We can walk there from the hotel." Then he pointed at the Houses of Parliament, on the other side of the river. "See the terrace over there? That'll be full of MPs and other rich bastards. That's our target. It'll be easy to see at night because the whole thing will be lit up. We launch the drones at half-eleven."

"There'll be cops around though, right?" asked Rahman.

"There won't be anyone around," said Kamel. "The park closes at sunset and any cops will be monitoring the crowds and won't be looking at the park. Once the drones are up, there's no way of telling where they're

500

controlled from. We fly them straight across the river to the Houses of Parliament and that's it, job done."

A Japanese man tapped on Kamel's shoulder. He mimed taking a photograph, and then pointed at his family, a wife and two small boys, all wearing round-lensed glasses. "Sure, man," said Kamel. He took the man's iPhone and took several pictures as the family posed at various places around the pod. Eventually the man thanked him profusely in Japanese with a lot of bowing, and Kamel gave him the phone back. "No problem," said Kamel. "You have a great holiday."

"These are two of the three targets," said Shepherd, putting two photographs on the table. "Muktar Kamel and Abdullah Rahman," he said. "They're staying at the County Hall Premier Inn with another Asian male who hasn't yet been identified. MI5 have them under surveillance, all we need to do is pick them up. We'll escort them to a police van where they'll be cuffed and taken away. We're not expecting any armed resistance, though they do have IEDs in their vehicle."

The three men standing with him studied the pictures and nodded. They were in a ground floor room at Wellington Barracks, just three hundred metres from Buckingham Palace. The barracks were used by the Queen's Household Division, who guarded the royal palaces, but they were also used by the SAS as their London base. Shepherd hadn't met any of the three men before, but they were all part of the Regiment. Ricky "Mustard" Coleman had joined eighteen months earlier, though he had been a paratrooper for ten years; Terry Ireland had been in for five years; Dean Spicer had been in for twelve. Spicer was known as "Spicelord", for reasons no one could recall, and Terry had been given the nickname Paddy, which always caused confusion because he was from Norfolk. All three were recently back from Syria and were bearded and suntanned. They had been working undercover in Westfield Shopping Mall in Shepherd's Bush, but the Major had agreed that they could be used to pick up the London cell.

Coleman, Ireland and Spicer arrived with Glocks in underarm holsters. Shepherd had requested a Glock but a stone-faced corporal in the armoury had flat-out refused without written authorisation, which was going to be next to impossible to get on New Year's Eve.

"Two of these guys have had ISIS training in Syria," he said, tapping the pictures of Kamel and Rahman. "We don't know about the other guy. We're going to pick them up with the minimum of fuss, ideally no one will even notice it."

"They're jihadists, right?" said Spicer. He had a strong east London accent.

"No question," said Shepherd. "And they're planning to launch the drones tonight. If they succeed they'll kill dozens. Hundreds maybe."

"Here's what I don't understand," said Ireland. "When we were in Syria we had hit lists of these guys. Kill on sight, no questions asked. But now they're back in the UK we're supposed to handle them with kid gloves. It makes no sense."

502

"Back here they have rights, Terry. In Syria, they don't."

Ireland shrugged. "It would have been much cleaner to have dealt with them in Syria, that's all I'm saying."

"You're preaching to the converted," said Shepherd. "But the rules of engagement today are that we pick them up and hand them over to the cops, and no one gets hurt. Unless they get violent, in which case we do the necessary."

The three men nodded. They were all professionals and Shepherd had no doubt they would follow his instructions to the letter.

The four unmarked armed response vehicles parked a mile from the target house and the CTSFOs checked their weapons. They were wearing grey uniforms and they all had Glock pistols on their hips. There were three SIG MCX carbines in the gun safe, which was set into the back seat. The officers had been briefed at Leman Street police station, close to Tower Bridge, where they had been shown photographs of the six men they were to take into custody.

Weapons checked, they climbed back into the ARVs. There were three armed officers in each vehicle; two in the front and one in the back. The officer in the front passenger seat was responsible for navigation, but they all knew where they were going.

The sergeant in the lead vehicle made a final radio call to the leader of the surveillance team, who had the target building under observation. He confirmed that all six targets were in the house and that the main entrance was unlocked.

They had studied maps of the detached Victorian house and its location, and they had been given a floor plan of the building, which would make their life a lot easier. Three of the cops would be going through the rear door into the kitchen. The rest of the team — six men and three women — would be going in through the front door. According to the floor plan there was a reception area to the left and two large rooms to the right — a sitting room and a dining room. Next to the kitchen was a laundry room and a storage area. There were five bedrooms on the first floor and another three rooms in the attic. They didn't know for sure how many people were in the house in addition to the six targets.

The ARVs pulled away from the kerb and headed for the house. There were two Mercedes Sprinter vans and an ambulance parked down a side street a quarter of a mile from the target, along with an unmarked windowless Ford Transit van, which contained three members of the Met Counter Terrorism Command's Explosive Ordnance Disposal Unit, better known as the bomb squad. There was also an unmarked black Vauxhall Vectra containing two detectives from Counter Terrorism Command.

The ARVs pulled up outside the house and the twelve armed police officers piled out. One stood back from the house just in case anyone inside decided to jump through a window. Three ran around to the rear of the house, their boots crunching on the gravel drive. The other eight headed single file towards the main entrance, a sergeant leading the way. They weren't expecting armed resistance so they weren't using bulletproof shields, and would rely on their Kevlar helmets and ballistic vests for protection.

There was an Asian woman in a black headscarf standing at the reception desk. She opened her mouth to scream but no sound came out, and she staggered back against the wall. "Keep your hands where we can see them!" shouted the sergeant. He went into the sitting room. "Clear!" he shouted as soon as he saw that room was empty.

The man second in line went through the door into the dining room followed by the third man. Meanwhile the back five headed up the stairs.

"Armed police, down on the ground!" shouted one of the officers at the three Asian men sitting at a large dining table looking at what appeared to be a map of London.

"Now!" shouted the officer behind him. "Do it now!"

The two officers kept their carbines trained on the men as they stood up and one by one went down onto their knees, before lying down on the carpet. The sergeant entered the room and used plastic zipties to bind the wrists of the three men, then he rolled them onto their backs and took a computer printout from one of the pockets of his ballistic vest. He grinned. "Ali Karim, Mohammed Joinda and Faisal Amin. Welcome to London, lads. Looks like you should have stayed in Birmingham."

Two CTSFOs emerged from the kitchen. "All clear in the back, Sarge."

There were more shouts from upstairs and the sound of thudding boots, and then it all went quiet. One of the officers from upstairs came thundering down and gave the sergeant a thumbs up. "All good sarge," he said. "Nine bodies upstairs, including Umar Begum, Gulzar Noor and Latif Shaikh."

"That's a full house, then," said the sergeant. "Right, I'll call the vans. As soon as they're here, get our six out and away."

"What about the rest of them, sarge?"

"The anti-terrorist boys will want a word with all of them before releasing them," said the sergeant. He reached for his radio.

As Shepherd climbed out of the black cab, his phone beeped to let him know he'd received a text message. He held the door open for Coleman, Ireland and Spicer and paid the cabbie before checking his phone. It was from Donna Walsh. "*3T Archbishop's Park*". 3T. Three targets.

"Right guys, this way," said Shepherd, turning his back on the London Eye and walking towards the park. The River Thames was off to their right, and beyond it the Houses of Parliament and its clocktower covered in scaffolding. He called Walsh as they walked. "Hi Donna, we're en route," he said.

"We have two watchers with eyeball," said Walsh. "They're by the children's play area, heading west. Kamel is wearing a grey puffer jacket, Rahman has a parka with a fur-lined hood, and the third tango is wearing a black North Face windbreaker."

"What about the cops?"

"We have a Sprinter van on standby at St Thomas's Hospital, two minutes away. The bomb squad are already at the hotel taking care of the IEDs."

"Roger that," said Shepherd. "I'll call you back once we have them."

The four men walked into the park. It was busy, with tourists taking selfies, families walking with children and lots of dog walkers. Shepherd spotted the three targets almost immediately, but it took him a little longer to identify the MI5 watchers. One was a blonde girl in an Adidas tracksuit limbering up on the grass, the other was a man in his fifties with a walking stick, sitting on a bench pretending to read a copy of the *Financial Times*.

"Okay," said Shepherd. "Spicelord takes Puffer Jacket, Paddy takes Parka and Mustard takes North Face."

The three men nodded.

"They need patting down, then we escort them off the park and head west to Lambeth Palace Road, opposite the hospital. As low profile as we can."

They nodded again. Shepherd held back as the three men moved towards their quarry. Spicer started to tell a joke and there was teasing back and forth — just three guys out for a walk, probably heading out for a drink.

The three targets were looking west to where the river was, and Kamel was pointing, presumably showing them where the drones would be flown. They all turned to look as Spicer, Coleman and Ireland approached.

Shepherd had a quick look around. The man with the *FT* was talking into his phone. There were no police around and no one was looking over at the targets. Ireland had opened his jacket, presumably to let them see his gun.

Kamel began to wave his fist at Spicer and shouted something, but Spicer acted quickly, punching him under the chin and snapping his head back. Spicer caught him before he fell and tossed him over his shoulder. Spicer wasn't a big man but he had no problem carrying Kamel. The other two targets gave themselves up without a fuss, walking meekly alongside Ireland and Coleman. Shepherd followed. Nobody, other than the two MI5 watchers, had noticed anything.

Pritchard walked into the surveillance ops room. Donna Walsh was on her feet as usual, talking into her headset. She had placed a whiteboard on an easel and written on it the names of all the targets that were being picked up, next to any photographs they had available. There were ticks next to the six members of the Birmingham cell, and ticks next to the three men that were being picked up by Shepherd and his SAS team. There were no ticks by the names of the three members of the Tower Hamlets cell — Yusuf Butt, Mohammed Desai and Nazam Miah.

508

The remaining four names on the board were the names that Schwartz had given him, the ones in Rafiq's London cell. None had ticks by them.

Walsh was still talking in the headset as she walked over to the whiteboard, flashed Pritchard a grin, and ticked off two of the names at the bottom. Then she swung the mouthpiece away from her lips. "So far so good," she said. "The three men that Spider took into custody will be taken to Charing Cross police station. The three drones in their vehicle have been made safe and are being taken away as we speak. The six members of the Birmingham cell are on the way to the custody suite at Bethnal Green, but they're packed at the moment so two will be diverted to Stoke Newington. The bomb squad have made the IEDs there safe, and they'll be taken away within the hour. Interestingly, the anti-terrorist team found two of their most wanted at the guest house, totally separate from our operation. They'll handle that themselves." She tapped the three names at the top of the list. "No sign yet of Butt, Desai or Miah. Desai's car is still parked outside his house. There are no drones or explosives on board and we have eyes on it."

Pritchard grimaced. "They might not be using that vehicle, obviously. And if they have drones, they could be stored anywhere. What about their phones?"

"They all have phones on contracts but they're all switched off. They were all last used in Tower Hamlets yesterday."

"Well that can't be a coincidence."

Walsh nodded. "And if they've any sense at all they'll be using burners."

"And we've two of the men from the other London cell, right?" he said, pointing at the bottom of the board.

"Yes. One of them, Qadri, was on his laptop when the cops went in and there's all sorts of ISIS stuff on it. There was also a selection of machetes, knives and manuals for drones in his flat, plus a copy of the ubiquitous *Anarchist's Cookbook*. The bomb squad went into the lock-up and they struck gold, too: five drones, all fitted up with IEDs, and packs of explosive that are a match to the Semtex that was used by the Leeds and Birmingham cells."

Pritchard said a silent prayer of thanks. So long as there was plenty of evidence to convict the men, no one would care where the original tip-off had come from.

"They'll be held at Sutton police station. So it's looking good so far."

"Nice work," said Pritchard. "How are you fixed time-wise? Are you okay to stay with this, New Year's Eve and all?"

"I'm happy enough here," said Walsh. "My husband's taking care of the kids and to be honest I wouldn't want to be out tonight, what with all this going on."

"I'll be here until ten or so, then I'm heading for New Scotland Yard. But I'll be on my mobile all night."

Shepherd and the three SAS troopers watched the police load Kamel, Rahman and the third man into the back of a Sprinter van. All were protesting their innocence and demanding to talk to lawyers, much braver now that they were dealing with regular cops and not hard-faced men with guns.

"They whine a lot, don't they?" said Spicer.

"Fucking snowflakes," said Coleman. He looked across at Shepherd. "Drink, Spider?"

"I'd love to lads, but I have to stay with this until it's over."

"It's New Year's Eve," said Ireland.

"Yeah, exactly. Are you guys not working tonight?"

"We're on days at Westfield," said Spicer. "New Year sales, they'll be as busy as fuck. But I'm planning on watching the fireworks tonight. More than two million quid they cost."

"Knock yourselves out, guys," said Shepherd. "But keep your eyes open. There's still more of these nutters out there."

"Next time, take care of them in the sandpit," said Ireland. "It's so much simpler."

"Like I said, you're preaching to the converted," said Shepherd. The men hugged and said their goodbyes.

"If you're done by midnight, give us a call," said Spicer.

"Will do," promised Shepherd.

As the men walked off in search of a pub, Shepherd took out his mobile and called Pritchard. "We're all done here," he said. "All three of them are in custody."

"So I gather," said Pritchard. "And we have the Birmingham cell as well. No joy with the Tower

Hamlets cell, though. No sign of any of them, we're just hoping they haven't gone dark."

"Can I help?"

"I don't see why not. Your pal Matty Clayton is running the surveillance there, I'll text you the location."

"What about the lock-up you talked about? The one in south London."

"Came up trumps there. Drones all ready to go. We've got two of the men in custody and hopefully we'll have the other two before long."

"You never did say where the intel for those four came from," said Shepherd. "It wasn't from Nadia."

"I've got to go, Daniel, we'll talk later," said Pritchard and the line went dead. Shepherd stared at the phone, wondering why Pritchard was so reluctant to say how he'd come up with the names, especially as the intel was clearly bang on. His phone beeped. It was an address in Tower Hamlets. Shepherd called for an Uber.

The Openreach van was parked in a road of semi-detached houses, most of them looking the worse for wear. Shepherd figured they were mainly buy-to-lets, owned by landlords who were more concerned with collecting rents than maintaining their properties.

The rear door opened as Shepherd walked up. Janet Rayner grinned out at him. "We can't keep you away, can we?" she said.

Shepherd held up a tray of three Starbucks coffees. "I come bearing gifts," he said.

512

"Then get thee inside," said Rayner.

Matty Clayton looked up from his computer keyboard. "Welcome back." He kicked a small plastic stool over to Shepherd.

Shepherd handed out the coffees and sat down. Rayner sniffed hers. "Two sugars?"

"Of course."

"How do you remember that?" she asked.

"I remember everything, Janet," he said. He waved his coffee at the monitors. "How long have you been here?"

"Six hours?" said Rayner, looking over at Clayton.

"Nearer seven," said Clayton. "We're lucky, there's a pub down the road so we've been able to use their toilets and buy sandwiches."

"Ruined your New Year?"

"Not really," said Clayton. "I'm not a big one for celebrating the start of a new year," he said. "And I'm not a big one for crowds."

"Most people in our line of work aren't," said Shepherd. "Crowds are unpredictable and difficult to control. We like things ordered and planned."

"Bloody hell, listen to you two," said Rayner. "Right couple of doom and gloom merchants. I saw the fireworks at the Thames last year, it was amazing. Took the kids and had a whale of a time. Bit annoyed at having to buy a ticket to watch them, seeing as how it was my council tax that had paid for them, but even so . . ."

"What about this year?"

"Tonight? I told my hubbie to keep the kids inside." She shrugged. "I know that nine times out of ten these things come to nothing, but I'm getting a bad feeling about this evening."

Shepherd sipped his coffee. "Yeah, you and me both."

Pritchard looked at his watch. It was ten-thirty. He remembered his invitation to watch the New Year's Eve fireworks at New Scotland Yard. It was a fifteen-minute walk from Thames House, so if he set off now he wouldn't be too late.

He walked through the crowds that were making their way to the Embankment. Sweethearts walking hand in hand, parents with children, tourists with their cameras at the ready.

A police helicopter flew overhead. There would be several flying around during the night, though they would be well away from the fireworks when they went off at midnight.

There were plenty of uniformed police walking around, though Pritchard didn't see any carrying weapons. There would be an increased police presence on the river, too, though they were there as much to rescue any drunken revellers who fell in as they were to keep the peace.

He reached the entrance to New Scotland Yard and showed his credentials before passing through the metal detector and taking the lift up to the top floor. A uniformed sergeant checked that his name was on the list before allowing him onto the terrace. The top brass

514

were already out in force, all in uniform, medals on show, accompanied by wives, husbands and significant others. A bar had been set up at the far end of the terrace and two men in white jackets were pouring champagne while two white-jacketed waitresses handed out canapés. Pritchard couldn't help but smile to himself. The Met was always claiming to be under-funded but there never seemed to be a problem supplying champagne and snacks for the powers that be.

"You've had a busy night," said a voice behind him. He turned to see Commander Gary Burgess holding a glass of champagne in one hand and a small piece of toast with something brown on it in the other. "I wasn't sure if you'd make it."

"We're mopping things up as we speak," said Pritchard.

A blonde waitress appeared with a tray of canapés. She smiled brightly. "Wasabi shrimp with avocado on rice crackers, mascarpone sprout canapés with pickled onion, smoked sesame seeds and wine salt, and smoked salmon on mustard, chive and dill butter toasts," she said.

"That's a mouthful," said Pritchard. He took one of the smoked salmon things and thanked her.

"That Newham guest house business worked out very well," said Burgess. "You got your six jihadists without a shot being fired and we picked up two guys we've had on our most wanted list for a month." He raised his glass. "So thanks for that."

"Pleasure," said Pritchard.

"Let's get you some bubbly."

"To be honest, I'd prefer a beer."

The commander grinned. "I'm sure we can manage that," he said.

"Here we go," said Clayton, looking at one of the screens. A bearded Asian man in a long coat was walking purposefully along the road towards the Ford Fiesta. There was a photograph of Mohammed Desai stuck to the side of the van — along with photographs of Butt and Miah — but Shepherd didn't need it to recognise the man.

"Yes, that's Desai," said Shepherd. "But it looks like he's on his own. He's probably going to pick up the others. Who else is out here?"

"It's just us," said Clayton. "But there's a tracker on the car so we won't lose them."

Desai opened the driver's door and climbed in. He pulled the door closed but the lights stayed off. "He's waiting for someone," said Rayner, echoing Shepherd's thoughts. They sipped their coffees and watched the screens. Ten minutes later a second figure appeared. Shepherd recognised him immediately. It was Yusuf Butt, wearing a black puffer jacket. He got into the front passenger seat and this time the lights came on.

"We're off," said Clayton.

The Ford Fiesta moved away from the kerb. The driver of the Openreach van waited until the Fiesta was at the end of the road before following. Shepherd was able to follow the car's progress on one of the monitors, where a green flashing light showed its position on a Google Earth map.

The Fiesta headed west through Tower Hamlets then turned north to Bethnal Green. It slowed as it reached the entrance to a small industrial park, and then it turned in and parked in front of a metal-sided warehouse belonging to a plumbing supplies company. A man emerged from the shadows, also wearing a puffer jacket. The hood was up but Shepherd could still recognise him. Nazam Miah. Miah went over to the shutter and unlocked it. He raised it up and the Fiesta drove in. Miah followed the car inside and pulled down the shutter.

"That's unfortunate," said Rayner.

"At least we know where they are," said Clayton. "But we don't know what they're doing."

Shepherd rubbed the back of his neck. Presumably the men were picking up the drones, but that was an assumption and he preferred to deal with facts rather than guesses. There were no windows in the warehouse, and even if there had been it would be too much of a risk to go over. All they could do now was wait.

The men stayed inside the warehouse for almost an hour, then the shutter rattled up and the Fiesta drove out. Miah relocked the shutter, got back into the car, and it drove slowly back to the road.

"Let's follow them for a while and see which way they're heading," said Shepherd.

Clayton nodded and gave instructions to the driver. The Openreach van followed the Fiesta at a safe distance.

The Fiesta drove back through Tower Hamlets and then turned right into Whitechapel, heading west.

"Yeah, they're going to Westminster for the fireworks," said Rayner.

"Let's not count our chickens," said Shepherd.

They drove past the Tower of London on their left, still heading west.

"Looks like you're right," said Shepherd. "Let's call in an ARV. None of the other guys who were arrested today have been armed, but better safe than sorry."

Rayner put on her headset and started talking into her mouthpiece. The Fiesta drove along Lower Thames Street, with the river to the left, and past the approach to London Bridge. It passed through an underpass, before turning north, away from the river.

Shepherd looked at the map. They were on the wrong road if they were heading west.

"This doesn't make any sense," said Clayton. "There are no crowds here, they're all down near the Houses of Parliament, right?"

"They're going to circle back round to Blackfriars Pier," said Shepherd.

"ARV is on its way," said Rayner.

The Fiesta stopped near the pier and the lights went off. The van parked some distance away, on the road, but they had a good view from one of the cameras hidden in the roof. They watched as the three men climbed out of the Fiesta and began unloading drones and controllers from the rear.

"I need to get out," said Shepherd. "The ARV isn't going to get here in time."

"Are you armed?" asked Rayner.

Shepherd shook his head. "No."

"He's former SAS," said Clayton. "He doesn't need a gun, he can kill them with a steely glance."

"Good to see you're maintaining your sense of humour, Matty," said Shepherd. He shuffled off his stool and opened the door. "I don't suppose you want to come with me?"

"I'm good," said Clayton.

"Be careful, Spider," said Rayner.

"Always," he said, slamming the door shut. He began jogging towards the pier.

The three men were standing by the pier with their backs to him. They were about ten feet apart and had placed the drones on the ground. They were holding their controllers, heads bent over the screens. Ahead of them was the river, inky black, dotted with the lights of passing boats, and far beyond them the ninety-six-storey Shard tower, piercing the night sky like a massive blade.

One of the drones rose into the air and Shepherd started to run. The men were so busy concentrating on their screens that they weren't aware of him until he was right behind them. It was Butt who had his drone in the air and Shepherd punched him on the side of the head with such force that the man collapsed without a sound. The control unit crashed to the ground, but the drone continued to rise into the air.

The man next to Butt — Miah — turned to see what was happening. His thumbs were still working the controls and the propellers of his drone began to whirr.

It rose to head height and then continued upwards. Miah backed away from Shepherd. Shepherd rushed at him and Miah kicked out, catching Shepherd on the knee, then Shepherd chopped his hand across Miah's throat. Miah gasped and dropped the control unit. Shepherd stamped on it, smashing it into pieces, but he stamped twice more to make sure that it was completely destroyed. Miah clawed at Shepherd's face but Shepherd punched him twice and he went down.

The third man — Desai — launched his drone and it rose quickly to join the other two. "Drop it, now!" shouted Shepherd, but Desai swore at him and continued to operate the controls. Shepherd lashed out, his punch connecting with Desai's chin, then he grabbed for the control unit and pulled it from Desai's grasp. He ripped off the tablet, dropped it onto the ground and stamped on it. "You're too fucking late!" shouted Desai triumphantly. Shepherd stamped on the tablet again, then when Desai continued to laugh Shepherd punched him twice in the solar plexus. When the man bent double, Shepherd hit him on the back of the neck. Desai slumped to the ground, unconscious.

All three drones were now about eighty metres in the air and heading west. Butt had regained consciousness and was reaching for his controller. Shepherd stamped on it, then on Butt's hand, but the drones continued to fly. Then realisation dawned. They were flying on a pre-programmed course. Or at least they were heading to the first waypoint on that course.

Behind him, a BMW X5 roared up and screeched to a halt. Three armed officers piled out with their carbines at the ready. "Armed police, on the ground!" they shouted in unison. The team leader was a female sergeant. Strands of red hair had slipped around her Kevlar helmet and there was a sprinkling of freckles across her nose.

Shepherd raised his hands. "I'm with MI5," he said. "These guys have just launched three drones carrying IEDs."

The three cops frowned in confusion. Shepherd pointed up at the drones in the distance. "There. Three drones. They've been fitted with explosives."

"Hands in the air!" shouted the sergeant.

"Look, we need to stop those drones or people are going to die," said Shepherd. The sergeant continued to glare at him and her finger was on the trigger of her carbine, so Shepherd slowly raised his hands.

The sergeant's eyes flicked to the three Asian men lying on the ground in various stages of unconsciousness, and then flicked back to him. "Who the hell are you?" she asked.

"Can I make a call? I think you should talk to my boss."

"What?"

"My boss. You need to talk to my boss. I'm not armed. I'm going to take out my phone now." Shepherd took out his phone slowly, showed it to the woman, and then called Pritchard. He quickly explained the situation, aware that time was fast running out.

"Believe it or not I'm on the terrace at New Scotland Yard, standing next to the commissioner," said Pritchard. "Put the officer on."

Shepherd held out the phone. "The commissioner wants to speak to you," he said.

She frowned, took the phone from him, listened, said "Yes, ma'am" twice, and then gave him the phone back. "What do you need?" she asked.

"Get me a police launch now, and a weapon," said Shepherd.

"What?" said the sergeant.

"A police launch. Now. At the pier. We have to go after those drones."

The sergeant finally realised what was being asked for and she reached for her radio.

As the sergeant called for a launch, Shepherd turned to the officer who had been driving the ARV. "I need your carbine," he said.

"I can't give my gun to a civilian," he said, in a Liverpool accent.

"I'm not a civilian." He sighed. "Your ARV is issued with three SIG MCX carbines, gas operated, short-stroke piston system with a rotating bolt. It fires the standard 5.56mm Nato round, with thirty rounds in an AR-15 type aluminium magazine. The barrel length is eleven and a half inches and it has flip-up iron sights. It's a good reliable hundred-yard rifle. At that range you'll get good wound capacity and in most cases the round will go through personal armour. I probably wouldn't recommend taking a shot at over two hundred metres, but then I guess you guys never do. Last time I fired one on the range I was getting one-inch grouping at fifty metres and not much worse at a hundred. Trust me, I can handle it."

522

The sergeant had finished her call and caught the end of the conversation. The officer looked at her expectantly. "Sarge?" he said.

"Give him your gun," she said.

The cop handed the weapon to Shepherd, who quickly checked it over. "Thank you," he said.

"The launch is on its way," said the sergeant. She gestured at the three drones, now in the middle of the river, about eighty metres above the water. "I don't get this. How are they still flying if you smashed the controllers?"

"They've been pre-programmed," said Shepherd. "They have an onboard GPS and they can be programmed with waypoints, specific locations and altitudes. They're on the way to the first waypoint now. Then they'll follow the programmed route."

"And they've got IEDs on board?"

"Probably half a kilo of Semtex and plenty of shrapnel. Enough to kill a lot of people."

"And the drones are heading for the Embankment?"

"We've got time," said Shepherd. "The drones fly at between two and three metres a second. That's five or six miles an hour. A regular police launch can manage, what? Twelve knots or more. An RIB can do treble that."

"An RIB?"

"A rigid inflatable boat." He grinned and pointed at the pier. "One of those."

A police RIB made a graceful turn and pulled up at the pier. "I'm coming with you," said the sergeant.

"The more the merrier," said Shepherd. "It might be easier if you explain to the boat guys what's what."

The sergeant jogged onto the pier and over to the RIB. Shepherd followed her. She had a quick conversation with the driver, pointed at Shepherd, and then pointed at the drones, which by now were just white dots in the night sky. She climbed in and Shepherd jogged over and joined her.

There were three officers in the boat, one driving and two at the back, all dressed in waterproof gear and wearing life jackets. One of them held out a life jacket but Shepherd shook his head. "I need to be able to move freely to shoot," he said.

"Health and safety, mate," said the driver.

"I can swim."

"I can't take you out unless you're wearing a life jacket. End of."

Shepherd growled in frustration, then handed the gun to the sergeant as he put on the life jacket. Then he held her weapon as she put one on. Only then did the boat's twin engines roar. It pulled away from the pier. Shepherd pointed at the drones in the distance, now almost a quarter of a mile away. "There they are."

"I see them," said the driver. He pushed the throttle forward and the bow raised as it sped across the water.

"What's your name?" Shepherd asked the sergeant, shouting over the roar of the engines.

"Karen. Karen Campbell."

"Okay Karen Campbell, each of those drones is carrying up to a kilo of high explosive. They require a detonator to explode and a bullet passing through won't set them off. We'll get as close as we can and then we need to shoot them down."

"You're not asking much," she said.

"I know, it's not something you've trained for, but it's doable. You want to be leading a metre or so ahead. I'd recommend single shots or you'll burn through your ammo too quickly. How many magazines do you have?"

"Three."

"Let me have one."

She pulled an aluminium magazine out of one of the pockets on her vest and gave it to him. Shepherd shoved it in his pocket.

The drones were about two hundred metres ahead of them.

"They're not following the river," she said. "They're going to fly over land. By Waterloo."

Shepherd peered at the drones. She was right. In a minute or so they would be over land. "They're flying to the first waypoint," he said. "That'll be by the river but it will fly in a straight line to get there." He frowned, picturing a map of the city and the river. He nodded. "It'll reach the river again at Jubilee Gardens. We're going much faster so if we miss them here, we can go along the river and catch them when they reach the park."

The drones were about a hundred metres away now. The boat was bucking along the water and the stock of the carbine kept jumping against his shoulder. "Can you slow the boat a bit?" he shouted to the driver.

The driver eased back on the throttle. Shepherd sighted on the closest drone, then aimed about a metre ahead of it. He pulled the trigger and the gun fired, but the bullet missed. There was no way of knowing if he'd gone to the right or left, whether he'd missed it by metres or almost clipped it. The round was lost in the night sky. "Tracers would be nice," he muttered.

"Sorry, what?" said the sergeant.

"Tracer rounds, so we can see where our shots are going."

She smiled. "No need for them in our line of business," she said.

Shepherd put the stock to his shoulder and fired again, three rounds in quick succession. The drones continued on.

Campbell raised her gun. She fired three times and cursed when nothing happened. Then she fired a fourth shot and the nearest drone disintegrated. Bits flew apart and then fell into the river.

"You star!" shouted Shepherd.

She looked at him in amazement. "I did it! I bloody well did it."

"Yes, you bloody did!" said Shepherd, clapping her on the back.

The boat veered to the right. The bank was close now and the remaining drones were flying over the land. Shepherd tapped the driver on the shoulder and pointed down the river, west. "Head for Jubilee Gardens!" he shouted. "We should be able to intercept them."

He and the sergeant sat down heavily as the driver pushed the throttles forward and the boat leaped through the water.

526

There was plenty of traffic on the river, mainly tour groups and dinner cruises, but the RIB was highly manoeuvrable and it was able to power at almost full speed.

They passed the OXO Tower on the left, then the National Theatre, then they roared under Waterloo Bridge. They went by the Royal Festival Hall and under the Hungerford Bridge and the Golden Jubilee Bridges. Then Jubilee Gardens was ahead of them. Shepherd scanned the night sky.

"I don't see anything," said Campbell.

"There!" shouted the driver, pointing.

Shepherd moved his head from side to side, knowing that peripheral vision was better at spotting movement, and within seconds he had spotted the two white dots moving towards the river.

"See if you can get us under them," said Shepherd.

"Will do," said the driver, moving the boat closer to the South Bank.

The two drones were still eighty metres above the ground. Shepherd figured that wouldn't change until they reached the first waypoint.

As the drones began to cross the river, Shepherd and Campbell shouldered their carbines and began firing single shots. The fact that they couldn't see their rounds made it difficult — no one shot was more likely to hit the target than any other. All they could do was to keep shooting and hope for the best.

Campbell was firing faster than him and she finished her magazine, replacing the empty cartridge with a new one.

The drones were about halfway across the river now.

Shepherd sighted on the lead drone and fired three shots in quick succession. He smiled when the third hit home, the drone shattered into small pieces.

"Yes!" said Campbell.

She started shooting again. Shepherd lowered his weapon. As Campbell continued to fire, he realised where the drone was heading. New Scotland Yard. He took out his phone and called Pritchard. "There's one drone left and it's heading for New Scotland Yard!" he shouted above the noise of the engines. "You need to get everyone inside!"

Campbell fired at the drone, and missed. Then she fired a short burst until her ammunition was gone. She ripped out the magazine and slotted in a new one.

Shepherd put his phone away. He knew he had only four rounds left. He took aim, sighted a metre in front of the drone and squeezed the trigger four times. The boat was still moving and his aim was off. He growled in frustration as he ejected the empty magazine and slapped in a full one.

Campbell was firing again, back to single shots. The drone was getting near the embankment now and Shepherd knew that the closer it got to land, the more danger there was that they would hit one of the buildings, or that rounds would fall into the crowds.

He shouldered his weapon again and started to fire continuously; single shots, but so close together that they sounded like a burst. He emptied the magazine but the drone was still moving inexorably towards the building.

Then the drone stopped. It was level with the terrace, and just a few metres away from it. There was a flash of light and a loud bang that he felt as much as heard, and then dozens of windows smashed inwards and broken glass fell to the ground, tinkling on the pavements like a wind chime.

The boat crew and Campbell stared at the damage, open-mouthed.

Shepherd pulled out his phone and called Pritchard. It rang out, and the silence between the rings seemed to stretch for eternity. Campbell looked at him anxiously.

The driver put the engines on idle.

The phone continued to ring out. Shepherd closed his eyes and said a silent prayer. Then the ringing stopped. Pritchard was on the line. "We're okay," said Pritchard. "Everyone's okay."

"Sorry it got so close," said Shepherd. "Looks like there's quite a bit of damage."

"It's worse than you think," said Pritchard. "The commissioner spilled her champagne all down her uniform. She's not happy."

Shepherd laughed. "Tell her I'll pay her dry cleaning bill."

"You should come here and tell her yourself. The fireworks start in a few minutes."

"Nah we're good," said Shepherd. "I've got some mates who promised me a beer."

Pritchard laughed. "Tell me where you end up. I think I've seen enough fireworks for one night."

Shepherd ended the call and patted the driver on the back. "Drop me on dry land, will you?" he said. "I need a drink."

Other titles published by Ulverscroft:

SHORT RANGE

Stephen Leather

Dan "Spider" Shepherd's career path — soldier, cop, MI5 officer — has always put a strain on his family. So he is far from happy to learn that MI5 is using teenagers as informants. Parents are being kept in the dark, and Shepherd fears that the children are being exploited. As an undercover specialist, Shepherd is tasked with protecting a fifteen-year-old schoolboy who is being used to gather evidence against violent drug dealers and a right-wing terrorist group. But when the boy's life is threatened, Shepherd has no choice but to step in and take the heat. And while Shepherd's problems mount up on the job front, he has even greater problems closer to home. His son Liam has fallen foul of the Serbian Mafia, and if Shepherd doesn't intervene, Liam will die . . .

TALL ORDER

Stephen Leather

He is one of the world's most ruthless terrorists, codenamed Saladin. He plans and executes devastating attacks and then, ghost-like, he disappears. Ten years ago he blew a plane out of the sky above New York — and now he's struck again, killing dozens in London. But one of the latest victims is the goddaughter of the acting head of MI5, who knows exactly who she wants on the case: Spider Shepherd. Dean Martin, a psychologically damaged former Navy SEAL, was the only person in the world who can identify Saladin. But Martin was killed ten years ago — wasn't he? Shepherd must find Martin and take him back to the killing fields on the Afghanistan-Pakistan border. Revenge on the world's most wanted terrorist is long overdue, and Shepherd is determined to deliver it . . .

LIGHT TOUCH

Stephen Leather

Working undercover is all about trust — getting the target to trust you and then betraying them in order to bring them to justice. But what do you do when you believe an undercover cop has crossed the line and aligned herself with the international drugs smuggler she was supposed to be targeting? When Lisa Wilson stops passing on intelligence about her target, MI5 sends in Dan "Spider" Shepherd to check that she's on the straight and narrow. Now two lives are on the line — and Shepherd discovers that the real danger is closer to home than he realised. As Spider finds his loyalties being tested to the limit, an SAS killer is on a revenge mission in London, and only Spider can stop him . . .

DARK FORCES

Stephen Leather

A violent South London gang will be destroyed if Dan "Spider" Shepherd can gather enough evidence against them while posing as a ruthless hitman. What he doesn't know is that his work as an undercover agent for MI5 is about to intersect with the biggest terrorist operation ever carried out on British soil. Only weeks before, Shepherd witnessed a highly skilled IS sniper escape from a targeted missile strike in Syria. But never in his wildest dreams did he expect to next come across the shooter in a grimy East London flat. Spider's going to have to proceed with extreme caution if he is to prevent the death of hundreds of people — but at the same time, when the crucial moment comes, he will have to act decisively. The clock is ticking . . .